Truth be Told

Truth be Told

Cathy Criss Adams

Portico/Open Gate Media, Inc.

This is a work of fiction. The events described are imaginary, and in the case of reference to actual historical events, liberties have sometimes been taken in regard to the specific years in which such events took place. The characters and dialogue, with the exception of reference to publicly known, published and/or historical figures, are fictitious and not intended to represent specific individuals.

ISBN 0-9762189-0-9

Published by Open Gate Media, Inc. Portico Book Division

Birmingham, Alabama

www.porticomag.com

Printed in the United States of America by EBSCO Media 2004

First Edition

Book design Claire Cormany
Jacket and author photographs Karim Shamsi-Basha
Styling Shannon Chambliss

For Tommy,

with love

Sometimes a man hits upon a place to which he mysteriously feels that he belongs. Here is the home he sought, and he will settle amid scenes that he has never seen before, among men he has never known, as though they were familiar to him from his birth. Here at last he finds rest.

W. Somerset Maugham
The Moon and Sixpence

I feel very strongly that I am under the influence of things or questions which were left incomplete and unanswered by my parents and grandparents and more distant ancestors. It has always seemed to me that I had to answer questions which fate had posed to my forefathers, and which had not yet been answered, or as if I had to complete, or perhaps continue, things which previous ages had left unfinished.

C. G. Jung
Memories, Dreams, Reflections

Chapter One

Society's dictates, ingrained from childhood, tell Violet that it is past the hour when nice people have drawn the drapes.

She contemplates mud brown velvet panels, hanging like limp arms from the shoulders of the wide molding framing the window. On the horizon, a hellish globe of setting sun competes with spires of flame in a mad competition of pyrotechnics.

Birmingham is a small town as the fading nineteenth century prepares to meet the brash comeuppance of the twentieth. People talk. Word has spread. Horses' hooves clip clop slow rhythm from the street below. Violet twists the scrap of rag in her hands and imagines a lengthy line of carriages, conveying the curious, who steal glances at the window, reassuring themselves that unfolding tragedy is happening to others.

Violet scowls at the dowager humped back of the tiny woman in black silk stubbornly staring out the offending window. Minerva Maude Buford Hatton has defied the good manners her superior breeding should have granted her since the day she was born, has no more cared than swatting a gnat about setting tongues to wagging.

Violet's daddy taught her that we all have a place in the scheme of things and best when we know that place and stay in it. No use arguing with hard headed Miss Minnie about drawing drapes or anything else.

What is taking place in this room is out of the natural order of things, as if their politely structured universe is spinning as crazily out of control as it did on the night all of those years ago when Miss Minnie's doomed brother Alexander was born, the night in the 1830s when the stars fell on Alabama. That star shower was a foretelling that evil would eventually claim its just reward on all who were burdened with the name of Buford.

A child is not supposed to die before its mama. In the just completed cycle of rising and setting suns it has already happened once in this house, and now it's happening again. Miss Minnie can stare out the window at that hotel down the street busily burning itself to the ground until she's blue in the face, but milk that has soured cannot return to sweetness.

The men who built that hotel proclaimed it fireproof, painted that word right on the bricks as if tempting fate to torch it. Miss Minnie, especially since the war with the Yankees took her brother, barks like a rabid dog that she doesn't have spare breath to waste begging favors from a god who doesn't choose to listen. She mutters instead to those deities from a darker age, from the myth stories her daddy told her, those spiteful gods who take pleasure in plotting perversity.

"Violet...have to dress...peach or green," whimpers a voice that has lost a once familiar music. "Have to go...can't be late."

"Shush, baby, shush baby," Violet croons, as she dips the rag into a porcelain basin of lukewarm water, impotently wishing for the cooler balm of ice to fight the fever mottling Kitty's face.

The ice delivery is not due until tomorrow. By then it will be too late.

All that remains in the oak ice box on the service porch is a puddled residue, of no more benefit than wasted memories of better days.

The runoff from the ice box trickles through a hole in the floor and waters the tangled carpet of mint growing by the back steps. Be needing mint tomorrow, when this sorry day is done. June's turned as hot as if the dog days of August are baying at the door. All those weather wilted ladies, coming corseted in their finest silks and satins to have a final look at Kitty, will be expecting and demanding cold sweet tea to reward their effort.

Kitty's husband Sam can afford an extra block of ice. They have not been hungry in so many years that you would think they'd forgotten what it was like to go to bed with a rumbling stomach.

Rare for her race, Violet can read. Cloaked in a servant's invisibility, she peered over Sam's shoulder as he wrote out the message for the boy to take to the telegraph office. "Your finest caskets, one adult, one child sized. Ship south on the next express train." Had to send all the way to Cincinnati for burial boxes good enough for Kitty and the little one.

They have at least and at last won brief reprieve from Bess's hysterical hollering. On a good day, Minnie's older spinster daughter is prone to fits of nervous palpitations, and on a day like this one Violet has to wonder if they don't all of them need a healthy slug of that cocaine tonic Bess is so fond of swigging.

Miss Minnie earlier took offense at Bess's shearing that dead baby in the parlor nearly bald before his little heart was commenced cooling. Bess and her mama engaged in an altercation so cater-wauling that it brought their battleaxe nosy neighbor Adelaide Ashcraft over to investigate.

Violet has been for once glad of Adelaide's intervention. As Mrs. Ashcraft points out, a woman of Bess's too pleasingly plump physical size and mental limitations has to take pride in something, and weaving hair from the dead into complicated mementos mori of samplers and jewelry is an every evening industry and one of the few occupations at which Bess is successful.

Violet very much doubts that Sam will appreciate the watch fob Bess plans to knit for him from his dead son's wispy curls, but there is no more use arguing with the daughter than there is with her mama.

At Adelaide's urging, Bess has been dispatched to rob the neighborhood of every blooming gardenia. Violet's sinuses ache in anticipation of the cloying scent that will permeate the parlor, soak into the velvet and horsehair to sneak out and taunt like a spiteful souvenir in the months to come.

Death is at his meanest in a sultry southern summer.

Sam sent his and Kitty's girls, Isabel and Lydia, to stay with neighbors. He wants their last memory of their mama made when this crisis is passed, when Kitty is lying quiet and comfortable in that finest of coffins, shipped from Cincinnati.

The sinking sun acknowledges a cause lost. Violet touches a match to the gas in a wall sconce. Shadows play a game of tag against the flowers on the wallpaper.

"Silver bracelet . . . engraved with Shakespeare," Kitty mumbles, thrashing against the sodden sheets as if frantically riffling through her quilted satin case of baubles. "New hair ribbons . . . Bess says . . . match my eyes."

The hair ribbons were purchased just two days ago, in the hours before Death scratched his name on Kitty's dance card. The silver bracelet is a sentimental favorite, a party memento from the ball held on the night when Kitty, fresh from the country, in defiance of poverty a belle by anyone's reckoning, met Sam.

From the hall below, the old grandfather clock prematurely chimes twelve stokes. Brought from Scotland with Minnie's mother's people, it is an arrogant heirloom that has a mind of its own about keeping time.

Kitty struggles against the pillows, her last words called out with surprising clarity. "Violet, must go. Midnight . . . lead the dance . . . ballroom . . . Caldwell Hotel."

A shower of tears sprinkles Kitty's face as Violet seals with a kiss the eyes just kinder days ago so blue that Bess compared them to the bachelor buttons growing in her garden.

From across the room, she hears Minnie mutter wasted words to the ghost of her dead brother, complaining to his spirit that if he had shared the location of the gold buried on White Gardenias Plantation Kitty would not be dying here in the foul fumed foundry town of Birmingham.

That dead big brother Miss Minnie so worshiped has said all that he plans on saying, and anyone with any sense would have long ago given up straining to hear him.

Though Alexander Buford's death preceded Violet's birth, Miss Minnie has shared with her, so many times that she has them memorized, her brother's last words, his foretelling that the curse on the family must be broken by the one destined to be called last in the line of Buford.

As Minnie stubbornly stares on at the inevitable, fingering a gold locket holding a likeness of her brother like a talisman, the brick walls of the Caldwell Hotel shudder and buckle inward. The roof collapses, and the inferno of flames, freed, streaks toward heaven.

***

Carrie Lancaster woke from deep sleep as abruptly as if splashed with cold water.

In a waking from a bad dream gesture automatic after years of marriage, she reached across the bed for her husband Nick. She touched only the loneliness of cold sheets. It did not surprise her.

Going to sleep and awaking alone were becoming patterns. She refused to allow herself a mental picture of another woman's head snuggled securely on his shoulder.

As an easier alternative, she struggled to retain, to decipher, details of the dream, played out on a stage setting as unfamiliar as its cast of characters.

From what stretch of her imagination could Violet have sprung, as completely comprehended as if Carrie had unfettered access to the woman's innermost feelings?

Carrie surveyed the not yet familiar room in which the last few weeks had found her waking. Roses wilted on faded wallpaper. The matched ivory bedroom suite had turned over passing time the sallow yellow of an old blonde aging badly. It was a room in a house in which time hung suspended.

Crossing the room to a skirted dressing table, she picked up a tarnished silver hand mirror. The crazed glass reflected the face of a woman of twice her age, cross hatched with the battle scars of years of sorrows. The Carrie she was becoming?

In such a short span of time, life had become so confusing. She felt like a shell, an outer wall emptied of life force and flung by the sea onto a foreign shore, abandoned.

Carrie slammed the mirror down, stared at the silver shards of broken glass on the dressing table. Out of the back of her mind, out of the past, from a place double locked, a voice recited a snatch of poetry, "Sea shell, sea shell, sing of the things you know so well."

Feeling panic rise from the pit of her stomach as her mind opened the locked door a crack wider, let escape an image to merge with the voice, just a pair of hands, holding a book, Amy Lowell's *Verses for Children.* She gritted her teeth and slammed shut the memory rising, so long forgotten, too often lately threatening returning.

She had reached a place of fearing mornings with the same intensity with which she had once met each new day with enthusiasm.

He was coming back to her, bit by bit, and she wasn't sure that she had the strength left to fight him.

Sleep had become her sanctuary.

The last thing she needed in a life turned topsy turvy was the intrusion of troubling dreams.

Less than six months after she had lost a baby and almost died herself in the process, maybe it was not so odd to dream of death demanding that a mother abandon her children.

A detail from the dream broke free. The children, Isabel and Lydia, had been sent away.

Isabel. Through a fluke of fate, Carrie found herself living in a house built by a woman named Isabel McShan Preston, a woman more than two decades dead and buried. As if proof that you can't take it with you, all of Isabel's belongings remained in place, all the material facets of her life still exactly where she had left them.

It was becoming a source of constant conflict. If Nick had his way, it would all be tossed in the trash, down to the last pearl handled fish fork, a good riddance to rubbish.

The cardboard boxes containing their own personal possessions were beginning to gather dust. Carrie didn't have the energy to sort through Isabel's belongings or her own.

Pulling on the same wrinkled clothes she had discarded on the floor the previous evening, leaving the room, she cast a longing look at the bed from which Isabel Preston had departed this world.

Retreating back to the safety of sleep was not an option.

She had to go downstairs, to face the inevitable.

Her mother was going to expect some answers.

* * *

His dog at his side like a comforting shadow, Nick Lancaster inhaled the crisp early morning air, feeling irrationally grateful to be out of the house.

He was working too hard and worrying himself into exhaustion over Carrie. The house had come into their lives as a surprise development to both of them.

He wondered if he were a coward, should have prevented them moving in or was delaying getting them out of the house until he had the plain spoken allied support of Carrie's mother on his side.

Nick paused at the edge of the woods separating the house from its nearest neighbor and studied the pitched gables interrupting the roof line above the cut limestone facade of the Tudor monstrosity he could not bring himself to call home. The exterior walls, massive blocks of a cold pewter gray, were almost a foot thick, as if the builder had constructed not a home but a fortress. Broken panes in an attic dormer window caught his attention like an invitation to investigate precincts of the house that he had not had the interest, or maybe the nerve, to enter.

The house had too long sheltered others' secrets. His family had no business being there.

A rustle and crunch of leaves in the woods disrupted his reverie. His dog abandoned his fascination with a treed squirrel and growled, the hairs on his back bristling alert.

Late for work, Nick whistled for the yellow Labrador retriever. As man and dog crossed the yard, a figure, watching, waiting, moved deeper into the concealing shelter of ancient oak and elm trees.

Nick hesitated, a hand on the door of his car, trying to shake off the uncomfortable sensation that he should not leave Carrie by herself, sleeping and unprotected, from exactly what he could not have named.

A doctor who did not believe in stockpiling patients in the waiting room, the sight of a gun metal gray car cruising smoothly up the steep driveway told him that this morning that was about to happen.

"Despite my jet lag I just had to come right over and investigate this extraordinary turn of events." Mallory Hudson offered her cheek for a kiss, a firm grip on Nick's arm making it clear that she intended to claim whatever amount of his time she wanted.

"Welcome home, Mallory. How was Scotland? Any luck nailing down that mysterious missing ancestor?"

"Scotland remains, as it was when my forebears sailed from it, as cold and damp as a mausoleum. I had the good luck of finding the church where my five generations back great-grandfather preached such inspiring sermons, but unfortunately it has been deemed redundant, deconsecrated and turned into a pornographic video store. I wandered the graveyard, but over the centuries that harsh Scottish climate has worn the stones illegible."

Nick politely tried to look sympathetic. Genealogy, and specifically the search for one elusive ancestor who could provide the missing link joining ancient and more recent branches of the family tree, was a hobby his mother-in-law pursued as an almost full time avocation. Carrie termed it an obsession.

"Nothing as boring as another's travelogue," she said by way of changing the subject. Nick was as good a guinea pig as any for testing the arguments she would put forth when others asked about Carrie's recent irrational actions.

"There was all the logic in the world in moving from that tiny little shoe box house the four of you have been living in all these years," she began like a defense attorney making an opening statement. "I still find it hard to believe that you, an orthopedic surgeon with a prosperous practice, would have let your children graduate from high school still obliged to share a bedroom."

"But, Nick, who would have ever guessed in their wildest dreams that your father would turn out to be a long lost relation of the Prestons? I can understand that your mother has no interest in investigating her, shall we charitably say humble, beginnings, but imagine your daddy having such prominent ancestors and not even knowing it! The Prestons, and Mrs. Preston's family the McShans, were among the finest of the founding families of this city, originally from solid old Selma Confederate stock. Hatton Preston in his day was a best selling author. This house was a splendid statement of their wealth and social standing. After a bit of renovation, just imagine the fabulous parties and charity galas you and Carrie will be able to host."

Respect for the concern he knew Mallory felt for Carrie kept Nick from making the cynical retort that her daughter and his wife, a woman who had difficulty getting out of bed most mornings, was hardly likely to suddenly pop her self-spun cocoon and emerge a social hostess butterfly.

"I should remind my daughter that some good comes even from bad experience," Mallory continued. "As much as we all hated what happened, she really emerged with a much trimmer figure."

Nick tried to suppress a painful mental image of the woman he had left sleeping. Carrie, her father's daughter in personality and appearance, only five feet tall and always a few pounds too round to suit her weight conscious mother, now resembled one of the stick figures their daughters drew in preschool. She was too busy sleeping to eat, existing by opening cans and nibbling at tuna fish, while he was not enjoying most of his meals in the hospital cafeteria.

"Nick, your mind is a million miles away."

"Sorry, Mallory, running late for work. Why don't you try to catch Carrie before she goes back to bed before breakfast? That seems to be her routine most mornings."

Mallory frowned down at a wisp of wrist watch, the face circled with diamonds. Inherited from her mother, it still kept perfect time. She could not imagine wearing a time piece that told the hour digitally, as if the wearer lacked education enough to translate the Roman numerals. "Surely you're not telling me that she's still in bed at nearly nine o'clock in the morning? Carrie used to be such a bundle of energy."

Nick winced. "Carrie used to . . ." was sounding a refrain in their lives, as if she existed in the past tense.

He took a deep breath before replying. "Mallory, I don't know how much longer we can go on ignoring Carrie's mental condition."

"Nicky, Nicky, Nicky! There is not one thing wrong with Carrie's mind! Poor darling went through a devastating trauma. You don't get over something like that overnight. I know."

For more than twenty years her son-in-law, he knew better than to suggest that she amplify her final statement. Pleading a full schedule, guiltily feeling grateful to let his wife for the moment be her mother's problem, he excused himself.

As Nick drove away, Mallory gathered her shopping bags of gifts for Carrie and entered the house.

In the woods, still watching the house, the man who waited snapped open an old gold pocket watch and scowled in frustration. Time, the most precious commodity in which a man can trade, was running out.

He had no choice. Carrie was the means to his end. He was sure of it. Confronting her when she was alone, with no one else in the house, was essential.

The waiting must continue.

Chapter Two

In the kitchen, Carrie rummaged through a box marked miscellaneous household items, searching for aspirin in anticipation of having to swallow a healthy dose of her mother's good advice.

"Dooley, I'm as crazy as a betsy bug. Obvious to everyone around me," she rehearsed her opening lines to her mother to the dog lying at her feet. "I drove myself right into the state of denial like I had a road map. I could have stopped it. I could have stopped it, just like I could have stopped . . . NO!"

"Carrie, what in the world is wrong with you?" Mallory froze in the kitchen doorway.

"Reprimanding the dog, Mother," Carrie stammered. "He was trying to chew up my slipper."

"Maybe that dog is more intelligent than I have given him credit for being. Probably trying to tell you that any self respecting person would have her hair combed and presentable clothes on by this time of morning."

Mallory assessed the outmoded kitchen, so much in common with the servants' sector of her childhood. A chipped white enamel kitchen table. A row of empty glass milk bottles in a metal rack by the service door like soldiers innocent that the battle was over, the milkman having a double dozen years before ceased to pick up and deliver. Underfoot, cracked linoleum, speckled faded blue of broken bird eggs.

This was not going to do. What would a friend think if she on the spur of the moment stopped in for coffee? Carrie used to have so many friends. Carrie had sealed herself off as if her physical, and of course they were only physical, problems were contagious. After a while, even the best of friends moved on to other things.

Mallory picked back up the conversation on the same train of thought from which her mind had meandered. "It was always one of my mother's cardinal rules. A lady does not descend the stairs in the morning until she is fully dressed and, pearls in place, prepared to meet the public."

"Mother, if your mother had been Emily Post the book on Southern Etiquette would have run to fourteen volumes. It's my house, and if I want to sit around looking like something the cat drug in all day long I have every right to do so."

"We'll get around to discussing this house, but first things first. Carrie, if you don't pull yourself together, and do it in relatively short order, Nick is going to do something drastic."

"Like replace me with someone off of the best dressed list?"

"Don't be silly! Nick would never leave you. He is, however, dropping none too subtle hints that he thinks you should seek some treatment, and you know we can't have that. No one in this family has ever needed psychiatric therapy. Surely things cannot be that out of hand."

"Why ever not, Mother? Because you have our impeccably mentally healthy genes meticulously documented back to a first cousin of Anne Boleyn? Don't forget that all of that complicated genealogy hinges on one tiny but as yet unidentified ancestor. That irritating missing branch on the family tree is probably as heavily laden with nuts as that big pecan tree in your back yard."

"We need to discuss your actions, and what you plan to do to stop people from talking about you. Really, Carrie, I go overseas on a brief working holiday and come back to find that you've pulled a stunt worthy of your mother-in-law."

"Speaking of whom, Ellen loves my house. If it hadn't been for Ellen, we wouldn't be sitting here today."

"I might have known that I would smell the fishy odor of Ellen in this."

"The house just fell into our laps, Mother, like it was fate or something. A lawyer called Nick's dad, explained that the last direct Preston heir had died intestate and that after months of searching they had determined that Jack was a distant cousin and next in line to inherit this house. Jack put his foot down that he was too old to move again and refused to even come look at it. As soon as Ellen got the keys in her hand she practically kidnapped me to come explore it with her. The minute I set foot in this house I felt as if a huge weight had lifted after months of forcing myself just to put one foot in front of the other. I felt like I had a purpose again, Mother, that this house and I needed each other."

"Carrie, you've never had an impulsive bone in your body. Couldn't you have at least discussed it with Nick?"

"I did discuss it with Nick. He said no."

"A sensible man, so unlike his mother. Nick feels no need to reinvent himself every six months as Ellen seems to."

Carrie declined to rise to her whimsical mother-in-law's defense, a decades old argument. "One of Ellen's friends from the days when she sold real estate had out of town clients desperate to buy something immediately. I threw out a ridiculous price for our house, and before I knew it the papers were signed. The house was in my name, so I didn't need Nick's blessing. Ellen said that it would do me good to grab the bull by the horns. I had to do something to get my life back together, Mother. Why can't you and Nick understand that?"

Old fears brushed like feathers across Mallory's heart. She took a deep breath before speaking. "And just who was this last descendant? When Isabel Preston died, I heard that there weren't five people at the funeral and not one member of the family on hand. When my mother passed away, the same year, the procession was so long that the police had to divert traffic around downtown Montgomery."

"All families reach the end of the line at some point, Mother. Perhaps there wasn't anyone left to mourn," Carrie interrupted, as if somehow excusing Isabel Preston the ultimate social faux pas, a poor crowd at her funeral. "When Isabel died more than twenty years ago, her great-granddaughter was an artist living in Paris. Six months ago she also died, in a car accident. In her will Isabel provided a trust fund for the nominal upkeep of the house. The house is far from falling down, Mother. I prefer to consider it like an aging lady who just needs to get out of her housecoat and put the pearls in place."

"I find it unfathomable that a sole surviving descendant could neglect to feel some obligation to remove the family heirlooms," Mallory argued, frowning, thinking of her own house, some day Carrie's to clean out and close down. Where there were family heirlooms in the dining room there were also inevitably corresponding skeletons in the closets.

"Mother, at the risk of your responding with a derogatory comment, Ellen has decided to become a writer. She's fascinated with historical southern fiction and has read everything Hatton Preston ever wrote. Aren't you at least impressed that a famous author once lived here?"

Mallory's words drifted out slowly as her mind filled with shards of dusty gossip. "There were some fairly nasty rumors at the time of Hatton Preston's death. People said that Isabel had built this house as a showcase for her son, that she was obsessed with him. So many people pointed a finger of blame at Isabel when it happened, Hatton dying before even reaching forty, at the height of his fame and fortune. It was rumored at the time of his passing that his mother hadn't even spoken to him in months, that they didn't even get the chance to say a proper goodbye to each other."

Carrie felt a chill run through her that had nothing to do with the November wind rattling old window panes like loose rotten teeth in a skeleton's skull. The conversation threatened to veer off the road into the personal territory of things not spoken.

"I fail to see how the death of someone sixty years ago could have anything to do with me in the here and now," Carrie interrupted. "I could care less whether Hatton Preston was hit by a streetcar or died with his pants down in a compromising position. The people who lived in this house have been dead for a very long time, Mother, and I am sure that they plan to stay that way. Something in this house cried out to me to save it. Can't you feel it, Mother? This house is more than stone and plaster. This house has a soul."

* * *

A block from the house, Mallory pulled her car to the side of the road, buying herself time to stop both her heart and her mind from racing.

Nick was a doctor and approaching Carrie's confused state clinically, as years of schooling had trained him.

Mallory, on a more basic level, was her mother, and she also operated from the position of having experienced Carrie in childhood plunging into an abyss of which Nick had no knowledge.

She had kept what happened to Carrie all of those years ago to herself, and she was not about to break her most steadfast rule and discuss it.

Everyone in town talked about how well she had adjusted to widowhood over the past year, how she had efficiently processed her grief and plunged into projects.

Sitting by the side of the road, she put her head on the steering wheel and swallowed the bubbling bile of tears. Adjusted well? Hardly. She was simply too experienced at going through the motions of living as a survivor.

Carrie was in trouble again, and this time David wasn't around to help her. All those years ago, themselves broken beyond repairing, the two of them had taken their child's hands and walked Carrie, step by step, back from the blackness.

Mallory took a deep breath and put her car in gear, signaled that she was rejoining the traffic.

There was no shame in seeking therapy. Half of the people she knew went regularly. What they could not risk was some psychiatrist probing deeply enough, some medication setting demons free, to send Carrie crashing back to that terrible black pit from her childhood.

She would bring Carrie back this time as she had the last, with something more powerful than any pill the best psychiatrist had to offer.

Mallory Hudson would be her daughter's role model, her protector, in keeping sealed off something too painful to process, in a locked away hiding place where it could not harm her.

***

Jack and Ellen Lancaster were just a few years short of celebrating a fiftieth anniversary. He could not have named a single day in the span of decades when he would have described his wife as predictable. Even though he was not expecting her, it came as no surprise when she burst through the door of his office a few minutes into the hour of the morning when appointments were never scheduled, the time reserved for emergencies.

"Jack, you've got to help me!" Out of breath, she fell into one of the leather chairs facing his desk.

"Obviously, there is some sense of urgency, Ellen. Can you categorize whatever crisis is chasing you as medical, legal, or merely emotional?"

"None of the above. It's professional. I cannot continue any farther with my novel until I have help in figuring out how to insert the little round symbol for degrees on the computer. I am including some of the main character's recipes in my novel, and I need to tell the readers at what temperature to preheat the oven."

"I'm sure that we can solve that predicament fairly easily," he answered, pulling a paperback manual from the credenza behind his desk. "I wish that I had an instruction book for ironing out the problems facing Nick and Carrie. He's almost beside himself with worry over her obsession with that ridiculous house, and I'm sure that he's justifiably blaming us for their landing in it."

"It's just a house, for goodness sake. The way Nick's acting you would think that Carrie had turned their whole lives upside down or something."

"That's exactly what Carrie has been doing for the past six months, Ellen. Nick doesn't know where to turn next."

"Carrie is at a tough time of life. It's scary when you've spent your whole adult life as a mother, and the kids go off to college, and it hits you that the whole looming void of the rest of your life is staring you in the face. Losing the baby just put a punctuation mark on that sentence."

"I seem to remember that when Nick left for college you got heavily involved with amateur theater, decided that your missed calling in life was acting."

"I wish that someone had clued me in at the time that writing was my forte! No telling how many books I would have already published. At my age, I am in a hurry. What if I dropped dead tomorrow, leaving all of my faithful readers not knowing whether Ambrodesia followed her heart with the poor but passionate cowboy or meekly submitted to her father and married for wealth and social prestige rather than love?"

He kindly refrained from pointing out that as an unpublished author she had no faithful reading public and returned to the previous subject. "You've had a full tour of the house, Ellen. How bad is it?"

"Well, considering that it's been sitting empty for more than twenty years, the first word that comes to mind is dusty, but I refuse to think negatively. Architecturally, it is incredible. Crown moldings a foot deep, parquet floors, limestone mantels carved with the family crest, all sorts of details you couldn't even find a craftsman capable of duplicating today. My former boss at the real estate agency says that house is one of the two or three finest homes ever built in this city, designed by the most talented architect who ever practiced here, given an unlimited budget by a nutty lady."

"Nick called in this morning to say that he would be late because Mallory is on the scene. We'll see what Mallory has to say about this."

"Mallory will no doubt say plenty," Ellen said, shaking her head. "It's the things about which Mallory refuses to let anyone speak that are the heart of the problem, if you ask me. I think that some of the loose threads in that family's past have started unraveling in the last year."

Chapter Three

Her mother having taken an abrupt leave, Carrie idly wandered through the house, pausing in the hall to shuffle a dusty stack of bills on a marble topped console.

She frowned down at an age yellowed envelope, a bill from a department store as long ceased doing business as this house's former occupants were at living.

In a house in which where to start was an obvious question, a suffocating sensation of taking on Isabel Preston's left unfinished obligations gripped her. Was she expected to make a final restitution to a downtown department store, driven out of business by suburban shopping malls decades ago?

Back across the years Carrie's mind began to gallop. On the crowded sidewalk outside that same store the day after Thanksgiving, curtains parting, children's eyes widening at the magic of the Christmas displays unveiled in the windows. From the back of her mind the familiar voice she thought she had forgotten, "Dad! That's it! That's the train I want!"

No, no, no! Her childhood was behind her, in the hidden place where she could not, would not go. Stumbling into the living room, she stilled a shaking hand on the back of a sofa upholstered in faded cabbage rose chintz. Isabel must have loved roses. Roses budded and bloomed throughout the house like a theme song.

Just beyond the room's French doors, what was once a formal raised bed rose garden, bordered by a low wall of stones, was now a compost heap of moldering leaves. Only one stubborn rose bush, bearing a solitary egg yolk yellow bud, remained, a single surviving soldier refusing to admit surrender.

Disturbed, more than she wanted to admit and exactly why she couldn't say, by her mother's negative comments about Hatton Preston, she crossed the room to examine a photograph of Hatton standing handsome and arrogant against a background of his mother's profusely blooming roses.

As she lifted the blackened sterling silver frame the rotten grosgrain backing slipped loose, and the image of Hatton in the rose garden fell free. Behind it was another, an obviously older, photograph, mounted on black pasteboard.

She turned the picture in her hand, squinting to decipher a faint inscription on the back. "Darling Kitty, lest you forget us, and your home place White Gardenias. Selma, Alabama, 1879."

In the fading photograph, grouped on the front porch of a paint peeling Greek Revival house were four people. A petite middle aged woman sat in a rocking chair, her feet not quite reaching the floor, standing next to her a younger and decidedly less attractive female companion. Posed in back of them were a black couple, presumably servants. The man was grey and stooped, the girl next to him an imposingly statuesque teenager.

Carrie felt a jolt of recognition. Although photographed at a younger age, the girl was without a doubt the same Violet of the previous night's dream.

She sat down on the piano bench and took a deep breath, trying to reassure herself that in wandering through the house she must have, surely must have, seen another picture that provided life to the face in her dream.

Her grandmother in Montgomery had stacks of old photograph albums, a favorite childhood rainy day activity poring over pictures of her mother and her grandmother as children, almost every photograph featuring some long suffering servant hovering in the background.

Childhood . . . rainy afternoons . . . Grandmother's cool dark house with nooks and crannies for hide and seek . . . "Ready or not, Carrie Beth, here I come!"

"Stay away from me, please stay away," she sobbed as she ran up the stairs and fell across Isabel Preston's unmade bed.

Sleep was the only solace, the safe place where he could not find her.

A cold rain drips through the jagged rents in the buggy's canvas canopy. "Catch our death of cold as if that weren't all we needed," the older of the two women complains, rattling the reins to urge on the bag of bones that is their last remaining horse.

"Hyperion!" she shouts into the rainy night. "See to the animal." She passes the reins to a grizzled old man who emerges from the shadows of the porch, where he has been waiting their return, worrying about two women with no business being out and about by themselves this time of night.

As the last male in their lives, Miss Minnie's daddy, brother and husband so long dead that they are no more than a trio of bad memories, Hyperion feels a sense of responsibility tempered by the knowledge that since Miss Minnie never bothered to listen to any of her family protectors all those years ago she is not about to start listening to the likes of an old leftover slave like him tonight.

Minnie scowls as the old man leads the horse toward the barn, thinking bitterly, look at us, mired here in the mud of broken dreams in the eighteen hundred and eighty ninth year of the Lord who abandoned us. Damn those Yankees.

Gone the days when she traveled the ten miles to Selma in such style, in a fine vermillion carriage, its doors emblazoned with the family coat of arms, the four matched Cleveland Bays that pulled it sacrificed in the service of the Confederacy.

If you asked her, that Confederacy had demanded of her family too many sacrifices. All of it gone, and all for nothing. All but the one thing no Yankee, no matter how damnable, could ever take away from her. She would go to her grave having been born a Buford.

Inside the house, she lights an oil lamp and stares in undisguised disgust at her daughter Bess, thirty four years old and looking twice the mother's age of fifty. She'll be a burden on me till I die, Minnie mutters.

"So, Mama, what thought you of the spirit session?" Bess asks, timidly, sensing Minnie's foul humor. "I heard dear Papa speak quite forcefully to us."

Hocus pocus hooey from the supernatural world! Truth be told, what Mama thought was that it was all a lot of hogwash and a waste of a trip into town. "If your papa operates in hell as he did on earth he was probably just drunker than usual," Minnie snaps in response as she peels off her wet garments.

The house is impossible to heat without a man on the place strong enough to chop a log. Reduced to living in one room, mother and daughter huddle together under a pile of frayed quilts.

Minnie lies wide awake as Bess snores. Perhaps when spring comes, if it ever does again, she will return to sleeping in the great rosewood bed upstairs, the bed in which she and her brother were both conceived and born, from which her brother left her. Perhaps in a dream will appear clues to the location of her papa's hidden trove of gold, an answer for the impoverished predicament in which they find themselves.

She slips from the bed and presses a concealed latch in the paneling, pulls from the cobwebbed recesses of a secret cabinet the last remaining dusty bottle of her father's brandy and takes a swig, grateful for the small warmth that sloshes in the pit of her empty stomach. Supper has ceased to be a regular ritual.

She takes another sip of brandy and ponders the spiritualism session just attended. Ten miles to town in the rain to hear that British fraud and fabricator Madame Julia claiming communication with the dead, rapping and tapping that table until all those widows in weeds and childless mothers were whipped into a frenzy of moaning like coloreds being baptized in the river. Stuff, stuff, stuff and nonsense!

Truth be told, it did briefly cross her mind to ask Madame Julia to contact her own dead male relations to inquire where the gold was hidden. Papa, no doubt as mean in death as he was in life, might refuse to answer, but she and Alex had held no secrets from each other, never a one, now had they?

Stuff and nonsense! Charon the ferryman only sells one way tickets across that stygian River Styx.

Penniless, she and Bess sit slap dab in the middle of thousands of acres of the richest river bottom land. It has taken a Herculean effort to produce a piddling garden patch of corn. Being gentlewomen farmers without a slave in sight is out of the question.

Bess suggests that they take up writing sentimental fiction, all the talk being of Augusta Evans down in Mobile writing her novel St. Elmo and making herself a tidy fortune. Minnie has kept a daily updated journal since the tender age of twelve. She is accomplished at putting a pen to paper, but who would pay to read the pure and bitter truth, with no attempt at sugarcoating whatsoever?

Teaching school is an option for impoverished women of breeding. Minnie possesses a fine classical education from a prestigious Philadelphia finishing school. She doesn't give a tinker's damn about passing the benefits of her education on to others. The only interesting factor in teaching Bess to read was that Violet, watching over her shoulder, absorbed the lessons with greater alacrity. Function of the intellectual difference in the two men who fathered them, Minnie supposes.

Giving birth to Bess was a waste of time and effort. Bess is absolutely worthless in the scheme of things except for the small change she receives selling the memorial jewelry she weaves from the hair she cuts from the heads of the dead. Bess has always had a morbid fascination with corporal remains. It occurs to Minnie that had she been born a man, her useless daughter might have excelled at the mortuary trade.

Into Minnie's furiously racing mind springs the seed of a very ingenious idea, a perfectly simple solution. Is there really any harm in telling a mother that her much missed boy is well and happy and singing in the sunshine in the bosom of the angels instead of rotting beneath the earth of some blood soaked battlefield not even marked on the map? Certainly there is not!

Madame Bess as a medium? It would beat the stew out of spending the rest of her life watching Bess plaiting and tatting hair.

She takes a last swig of brandy, fortifying herself in the resolution that the rest of her own life has but one single minded mission. She will find that cursed hidden gold, or die trying.

***

"It feels so good to be out of that creepy house!" Betsy Lancaster tossed her long red blonde hair in a practiced move not lost on the male patrons of the neighborhood bookstore's coffee corner.

"Oh, come on, Bets, don't you think you're a little old to be threatening to run away from home?" Betsy's sister Abby, a fraternal twin as short and dark haired as her sister was tall and fair, swirled a spoon through the whipped cream topping her coffee.

Abby had pulled her sister, a fashion merchandising major who wasn't much of a reader, into the bookstore on the pretext of a coffee break, after which she planned to search the shelves of southern fiction in hopes of finding anything written by Hatton Preston. Curiously, despite numerous photographs of him scattered around the house, the same home's bookshelves held not a single volume bearing his name on the spine. Hatton Preston was everywhere in that house except where one might most presume to find him.

"That house is not our home and never will be. You heard it too, Abby. Admit it. Something moves around in that attic after the lights are off."

Betsy shivered for dramatic effect, ran her hands up and down the sleeves of the blue cashmere sweater carefully chosen to compliment the color of her eyes. Born to the role of beauty queen, Betsy was more her grandmother Mallory's genetic match than

Carrie could have ever hoped to be. "And how do you explain smells in the middle of the night? I smelled him, night before last, so strongly I swear he was in the room with us."

"Him? What makes you think it was a 'him'?"

"I know a man smell when I smell it."

Before Abby could make a teasing rejoinder about her blatantly beautiful sister's string of boyfriends, both girls jumped to their feet. The horn blaring the football team fight song of the University of Alabama and the sight of the red and white Jaguar convertible pulling into a clearly marked no parking zone announced that their paternal grandmother was on the horizon.

"What a wonderful surprise running into my two favorite grand-daughters! Like being served a double hot fudge sundae!" Ellen Lancaster swept the girls into a bear hug embrace.

"Betsy, that sweater was made for you," Ellen commented as Abby made her way to the counter to order her grandmother's requested double hot chocolate.

"Thanks, Gramma, Mallory got it in Scotland."

Ellen felt the usual twitch of amusement that her counterpart insisted on being addressed by her given name as if being called any derivative of grandmother was an admission of aging.

"That's our Mallory, off chasing elusive ancestors like a knight on a quest," Abby added. "I wonder what she's planning to do with that ancestor if she finds him."

"Give her credit for single minded interest," Ellen responded. "I admire that. Think of all the years I have chased rainbows, denying the truth that I was born to be a romantic novelist. It's hard work, I don't mind telling you, creating all of those characters and making things happen to them. Just thinking up names for them is enough to wear you out! The name of my heroine, Ambrodesia, came to me like a burst of inspiration in the middle of the night."

Abby mentally enumerated her grandmother's previous string of interests. Interior decorating, involving painting her house, inside and out, varying shades of pink. Real estate agent, selling the pink house and buying a red brick one to replace it. Antique dealing, a manic buying trip to London followed by the opening of a shop in the basement selling fire place accessories. "Ellen's Irons in the Fire" would have probably been a great success if the suburban neighbor-hood government had not been so unpleasant about operating a retail business at home and without a license.

"Gramma, have you ever read any of Hatton Preston's books?" Abby asked.

"All of them, multiple times. It seems to me a cosmic coincidence that I was totally immersed in Hatton's *Red Camellias* series when we got the call that Jack had inherited the Preston house. To write historically compelling fiction you have to read ten pages for every one you commit to paper. Hatton Preston possessed enormous talent. His books could have been ranked with the classics if he hadn't been such an unabashed bigot. Naked prejudice trumps lyrical prose in the long haul of literature."

Betsy frowned, thinking of a quick peek she had taken at Hatton's bedroom, a room so still completely filled with the remnants of his life that it was as if one day he walked away and simply forgot to return home, a room much like one she knew existed in another, a more familiar, house. That room she had never entered because, for all the years of her life, and for years before that, Mallory had kept her dead son's door locked.

"Your mother really ought to donate all of those pictures of Hatton to the Archives at the public library," Ellen said.

"I don't see Mom giving away anything out of that house," Betsy sighed. "It's weird, as though she's holding on to things, polishing the silver in case Isabel and Hatton decide to come back home."

Ellen felt a twinge of guilt for encouraging Carrie to take on the house. After months of sinking deeper and deeper into despondency, as if their old loved and loving Carrie were making daily farther progress on a trip away from them, Ellen had felt strongly that it was past time for someone to do something to break the stalemate.

"Gramma, Mom's going to be okay, isn't she?" There was obvious pleading in Abby's voice.

"Sure she is." Ellen, ever the eternal optimist, put a reassuring hand over her granddaughter's. "You know, darling, when life gives lemons the best way to make lemonade is to embark on some interesting new project that will take your mind on a vacation in a totally different direction. I'd say that's just what your mother is doing, wouldn't you?"

The twins exchanged glances without responding.

A disturbing analogy clouded Abby's mind. The house was filled from cellar to rooftop with the left behind luggage of other lives, and from the bits and pieces she'd heard, not particularly happy ones. She was afraid that wherever her mother was purchasing tickets to take herself, it was going to be neither a short nor a simple journey.

Chapter Four

Waiting, by definition, eventually reaches a conclusion.

Having bided his time from his covert position in the woods, the stranger determined to make an intrusion into Carrie's life swallowed the last of the liquor in the silver flask and took a shortcut across the remains of the rose garden. After all, he reminded himself, Isabel Preston was no longer around to scold him.

Hammering his fist against the door and receiving no response, he twisted the knob. The door was unlocked. Uninvited and unexpected, he crossed the threshold.

Familiarity produced a sudden suffocating sense of confusion. Almost fifty years since he last set foot in this house, and yet everything remained as unchanged as if it were yesterday. On the floor beneath his feet ran a moth pocked Aubusson, color dimmed by time like butter left on a table to melt in sunshine. His shoe left a muddy smear, which he found amusing, as if he further taunted the dead but still despised Mrs. Preston.

He called Carrie's name, softly, then slightly louder.

No reply. Could she have slipped out a side entrance and gone for a walk to his further inconvenience?

Need welled and surged within him. He shouted her name, demanding that to which he was entitled.

A flight of stairs above the foyer, Carrie, by nature a heavy sleeper, startled slightly at the sound of her name, rolled over and tumbled more deeply into sleep's sweet seclusion.

Minnie peers out into the cold November rain, praising the gloomy weather as she awaits the arrival of guests whom she hopes will arrive in melancholy moods.

"Hyperion! Violet!"

The summoned servants appear before her.

"Everything is in readiness?" It is a rhetorical question. She has both trained and trusts them well. Anticipation makes her edgy.

"You want me to serve the wine in those pretty purple glasses?" asks Violet.

"My Venetian amethyst flutes? Good heavens, no, girl!" Minnie shrieks. "Common white trash wouldn't know fine crystal when they broke it."

The teenager's face falls. Violet loves what few pretty treasures Miss Minnie rescued from the house in town that the Yankees burned so slap to the ground it might as well have existed only in a dream. The fire breathing Yankees having come and gone before her birth, Violet has had Miss Minnie draw for her a picture of Hatton Hall that she keeps tucked between the pages of her Bible. Oh, Miss Minnie once led a fine life to be certain!

"Hyperion, a final touch occurs to me. Go to my brother's room and fetch the Red Indian skull that he and I found when we were searching the marsh for arrowheads as children. It will make an appropriate centerpiece for the communion table."

Think, think, think, she mutters to herself. How to create the illusion of a will o' the wisp free floating through the room? She remembers her brother chasing the dancing balls of light in the muddy morass of ground they called the Indian graveyard, Alex assuring her that the will o' the wisps were really just swamp gases, not the spirits of the damned breathing hellfire, as common super-stition proclaimed them. Ignis fatuus, the Latin name meaning fool-ish fires, was how her learned brother termed them, those will o' the wisps that legend said led men to buried treasure. Could her Papa's gold be hiding in the swamp? No time to pursue that train of thought at the moment. Minnie was not afraid of the willies, but the white trash would be.

The arriving visitors comprise a motley quartet. Violet takes sodden cloaks and bonnets, wrinkling her nose in disgust as though her own mistress's garments do not have the same unsubtle sheen of poverty.

Guests follow servant down a hall lined with pocket doors as firmly closed as sealed lips over dirty secrets. The female visitors are morbidly curious to observe first hand just how precipitous has been the fall from how the other half once lived.

"Uppity gal, ain't she?" One of the women jerks her head in Violet's direction.

"All the help what the high and mighty Miss Minnie Buford has left is what I hear," replies the other in a voice of smug satisfaction.

"Welcome, welcome to White Gardenias." Minnie extends fin-gertips to the gentlemen, flicking her eyelashes coquettishly. The older man remembers when Miss Minnie Maude Buford was known as the prettiest belle in the county, all that talk and scandal when she bucked her daddy and eloped with Cap Hatton. Imagine! Cap

Hatton, nought but an over privileged scoundrel, making for himself such a fine war record, ending up dead center in the town cemetery with a big memorial over his grave reminding the world that he was the general who almost saved Selma.

"Do you play?" asks the younger man, eyeing a shrouded harp.

"Oh, heavens no," Minnie says, contriving a pretty, girlish giggle. "The muse Euterpe was absent at my conception."

She lowers her eyes, brushes at an imaginary tear. "The harp was my dear late MáMá's. I speak of her in the Gallic manner in deference to her noble French ancestry. Indeed, we number among our most prized possessions a small secrétaire à abbatant once the personal writing desk of the late Queen Marie Antoinette of Paris, a distant ancestress."

Lead them along without driving the carriage off the track she reminds herself as she realizes from blank expressions that they have understood little or nothing just imparted. Her mother's thick as oatmeal Scottish accent rings in her ears. Born in a town near Edinburgh, Charlotte McDonald Buford hadn't had a French bone in her body.

"I know just how memorizing your old ma pains you, Mrs. Hatton," interrupts the older woman. "Mine was a whiz with the fiddle in her day."

Minnie suppresses a shudder of disgust. What has the world come to, entertaining white trash for cash in her mother's music room?

She lowers her head before appearing to hear a sound. "Hark! The spirits loudly moan and clamor for our attention!" She rises and beckons for the group to follow.

In the room they enter, a whisper of a fire simmers in the grate, the only source of light outside of a single flickering taper eerily illuminating a black veiled woman seated at a lace covered table, hands clasping a skull.

"The spirits are strong tonight! Oh, so strong!" she cries.

"Bless you, great Aeolus," Minnie mutters as a sudden gust of west wind buffets the house. Outside a shutter bangs, and, from the dining room, where more than one window is missing more than one pane, the crystal prisms of the chandelier tinkle.

"Queen Marie's secrètaire," Minnie whispers with a nod over her shoulder as she takes the hand of the man beside her. "Note the exquisite craftsmanship."

"Comment vous appelez-vous, monsieur?" Bess moans, swaying backward and forward in her chair.

"Speaking in tongues! Have mercy!" the older woman shrieks.

"Hush, hush, dear lady, we must be quiet and receptive," Minnie chides. "The tongue in which she communes is French. Perhaps it is indeed the sainted and martyred Queen Marie who comes to us this evening. Should she appear, you will know her by the absence of her head from her shoulders."

She frowns in concentration trying to mentally telegraph to Bess that these are cracker women who have no comprehension of French. "Speak English, you stupid ninny!" she hisses in Bess's direction.

"Les Jacobins! Les Jacobins! Les voilà! Les voilà!" Bess screeches with a strangled sob.

"Jacob, is that you? Oh, Jacob, tell me where you done gone to," begs the young woman, turning so pale that Minnie fears the smelling salts will be inevitable.

"Jacobins! Allez-vous-en!" Bess wails.

"Elysian fields," Minnie translates, kicking Bess beneath the table. "Queen Marie reports that your Jacob tills the eternal farm where all crops prosper."

"But his rotting flesh and skeleton? We don't not know where they are buried."

Merciful heavens, wonders Minnie, what battle took him? Shiloh? Corinth? Probably never got as far as Gettysburg. Would this poor simple woman even know? White trash women die as illiterate as they're born. Doubtful she received letters.

"He has no further use for mortal remains," she soothes. Hyperion, just beyond the cracked doors, pinches his nose and pulls from a gunny sack the fetid remains of a dead goat. Minnie, planner of the little charade, has taken the precaution of pressing a scented handkerchief to her face. Bess, swaying and moaning, appears oblivious.

"And my darling daughter, my Becky, passed through the veil too soon, too soon? What news of her?" begs one of the men.

Minnie raises her voice above Bess's frantic, fractured French. "Mistress of the promised mansion with her wings and halo of the latest Parisian fashion."

"Qui, Monsieur! Qui, qui, qui!" Bess squeals before slumping over the table in a dead faint. Minnie pinches out the candle on the *table. One of the women screams.*

"The signal from beyond. The session is ended. Depart in peace," Minnie intones as she slips the pitifully paltry payment into her pocket. Talk with the dead certainly comes cheaply.

"Ooh, Miss Minnie, we are rich!" Violet sings, as she closes the door on the departing guests.

"Hardly the case." Minnie snaps closed the metal money box. Best not to carry things too far. Her older daughter has always suffered from an extravagance of nerves. Surely, Bess, still moaning in French, can't be taking any of this seriously?

"I thought that I had educated you well as to the proper conjugation of verbs," she replies to Violet. "In our case the only applicable tense is the past. We were rich. We are now simply not quite so poor as last year. We will be rich again when we find Papa's hidden gold, and I bless the fact that you are young and strong enough to so ably assist me with the digging. But, even though we've not yet found it, child, I think we find ourselves in a position to consider the purchase of a new dress for you."

"A store bought dress?" Violet's eyes widen.

"We will have Hyperion deliver us to town in the wagon early tomorrow morning."

"Oh, Miss Minnie, I 'fraid that you going to town sooner than tomorrow!" Hyperion interrupts, entering the room wringing his hands in desperation.

"Unhand me at once, you vile Yankee villain! Mama! Mama! Mama! Help me!" screams Bess from the hall.

Saints alive, thinks Minnie, slipping her money box back into the secret compartment in the paneled wall. What new trouble has ridden into town on the evening train?

"Mrs. Minerva Maude Buford Hatton?" The scowling man enters without announcement. Damned Yankee for sure. No manners at all.

"I am Mrs. Major General Henry Capshaw Hatton," she answers, squaring her shoulders and lifting her chin so that she is at her fully extended height of five feet less a pinch.

"I have here, Madam, a warrant for your arrest. You and your daughter Miss Elizabeth are charged with fraud and chicanery and ordered by the county to be jailed until trial."

"Mama!" Bess screams again.

"My daughter is subject to nervous explosions," Minnie says in

a calm voice that belies her racing mind.

"In my experience, Mrs. Hatton, all women are nervous nellies." In a sudden move he twists Minnie's hands behind her back and into iron cuffs.

"Miss Minnie, do something! Do something!" begs Hyperion, eyes darting from the shackled Minnie to the scuffling figures in the hall.

"Hyperion! Get to town at once!" Minnie barks. "As much as it galls me to petition his help, telegraph to Birmingham to beg Kitty's husband Colonel McShan come post haste to our rescue."

"Daddy, were those Yankees?" Violet's voice quivers as the two resisting women are manhandled from the house.

"Reckon so," the old man sighs, running a hand across eyes through which he thought before this night he had seen it all. "Carpetbaggers no better than cur dogs. Ain't the first and won't be the last time our Miss Minnie manages to get herself up the creek without remembering to take the paddle. Come on girl, you heard the mistress. We got to get the word to Birmingham."

Chapter Five

Carrie placed two rose sprigged cups and saucers, old and delicate Minton, on the table. She willed her hands to stop shaking as cup rattled against saucer. The first unexpected glimpse of him, sitting in a fan back wicker chair, puffing on a pipe, as if he owned the place, had shaken her badly.

It struck Carrie that her mother would kick herself for having left too soon. The man sitting across the wicker table had introduced himself, a household name as a multiple Oscar winning Hollywood screen writer and producer of blockbuster movies. For the preceding six months that he had been in reclusive residence in his late grandmother's Birmingham home Mallory Hudson had been almost as unsuccessfully obsessed with having Wyatt Wallace as a guest at one of her charity functions as she was in seeking a missing ancestor.

Wallace's return to his backwater roots in Birmingham had been much a matter of speculation in the national tabloid press. A losing battle with the bottle was the theory most often propounded, but even the most unflattering picture staring up from the grocery store checkout rack depicted him though bloodshot and craggy still undeniably handsome.

Wyatt Wallace was, for whatever personally motivated reason, Carrie Lancaster's nearest neighbor.

"I must admit that for a second there I thought you were the ghost of Hatton Preston," Carrie stammered.

"Ah, the very shade I seek," he answered, putting a match to his pipe. "Being in this house is like being transported back into my childhood. This solarium is completely unchanged from the years when my grandmother and Isabel sat in these same chairs drinking tea from these very cups. I can so easily imagine myself eight years old again."

Carrie owned not even one backward glimpse of herself at eight years old. Misty memories of early childhood were all gone and were not returning. Not if she could help it.

"As a youngster, I often slipped in through those French doors to commit minor acts of malicious mischief," he continued, grinning as if some of the small, bad boy remained within him. "After Hatton died, Isabel Preston locked herself away upstairs like Mr. Rochester's wife, becoming for me a fascinating figure."

"You knew Isabel Preston?" Carrie felt dizzy.

"Of course. She was my grandmother's nemesis as well as nearest neighbor. They spent as many years of their lives giving each other the silent treatment as they did on speaking terms."

"Did you grow up here?"

"Only occasionally. After graduation from Princeton my father remained there as a professor of English literature for the rest of his life. My mother died when I was eight, and my father, whose head was rarely out of a book, didn't have a clue what to do with a wayward child. Having a penchant for getting myself ejected from various military schools, I was periodically sent back here for rehabilitation by my grandmother."

Going off to Princeton and getting into trouble sang a nagging voice in Carrie's head. Ready or not! Here he comes! NO! Well practiced, she willed it away.

"Carrie, I will get right to the point without wasting precious minutes of the borrowed time on which I'm living and ask your help in joining me on a quest for what is increasingly becoming a personal Holy Grail."

Was he saying he had come back to Birmingham to die?

Seeming to read her thoughts, he locked eyes with Carrie. "At an early time of life, when a man cannot envision living an ending chapter, I let myself be seduced by the easy money temptress of Hollywood. For far too many years I wasted both my time and my talent turning out tripe for a not very discerning public. At the end of my life I am consumed by an overwhelming compulsion to produce that one great work that will live on after me, and I must have your help to do it."

"Wyatt, I am no one's idea of an editor. I left college without getting a degree. I have never been anything but a simple wife and mother."

"No one is asking you to edit anything. Let me explain. Hatton Preston's New York publishers still cling, after all of these years, to the first half of a manuscript that would have been, when completed, the definitive statement of his genius."

"I don't understand how that has anything to do with me."

He moved so close that their faces were almost touching. "Carrie, I have to get in touch with Hatton Preston."

She wondered just how much liquor Wallace had consumed as breakfast before responding. "Hatton Preston has been dead for a very long time, Wyatt."

"Don't you understand, Carrie?" he thundered, pounding fist against palm. "In the last conversation between Hatton and his editor, posthumously published as an interview, Hatton was clear that he was polishing the final pages. He completed that book, Carrie. The missing pages of the manuscript are hidden somewhere in this house, just as surely as we sit here."

"You really believe that, don't you? If you've been living next door for the past six months with every opportunity to poke around this house while it was vacant why haven't you done it before now?"

"Call it creative good timing. I had to reach a certain point in my own work, a play about Hatton, before I risked letting Hatton's voice influence my own. Help me find that manuscript, Carrie, before my time, like Hatton's, runs out."

The voice in the back of her mind teased why not? At the end of the day she could tell Nick that she had done something more productive than sleeping her life away.

* * *

It was a nightly routine, brought with them, like a cardboard box of miscellaneous household items, from having been married more than half of their respective lives. Sitting at Isabel's dressing table, Carrie pulled a brush through her hair, counting out one hundred strokes as her mother had trained her while Nick grunted through a series of sit-ups.

"Where are the girls?"

"Spending the night with Mother. Apparently an entire afternoon at the mall just whetted Betsy's appetite of wardrobe cravings. She has convinced Mother to go to Atlanta with her tomorrow. Abby is going to help me explore the closets."

Nick rested his head on arms folded on his knees. "Carrie, can't we please just hire someone to come in here and toss it all in the trash? You need to get out, have lunch with your girl friends, get back into your old routines. Or maybe you need to find some new interests, volunteer for some good cause. Being all by yourself all day, moping around this godforsaken house, isn't good for you."

She slapped the brush down and turned to face him. "I'm not

my mother! I have no interest in doing volunteer work or digging up ancestors."

Carrie bit her lip until it hurt. A missed opportunity to get it out in the open, to add to the list of what didn't interest her, "having a love affair, like you're doing."

"You've got to get out of this house, Carrie. You're becoming a hermit."

The idea had intrigued her all afternoon. There was a void in her life that cried for filling. Wyatt Wallace and the search for a missing manuscript.

"For your information, Nicky, I didn't spend the whole day by myself. In fact, I met the most fascinating neighbor."

"I hope you didn't give her a full house tour," he groaned. Waiting for her to join him in bed before turning out the light, he reluctantly evaluated the room. A mottled brown stain oozed across the ceiling above him. Something in the attic must have leaked. He hated to imagine what piles of junk rested above his head.

He pulled the lamp cord, wondering if the rotted silk fringed shade represented a fire hazard. "At least get that old woman's clothes out of the closets, Carrie. I'm tired of living out of cardboard boxes."

"That old woman has a name," Carrie snapped. "Her name is Isabel. And, as far as the new neighbor goes, she is a he, and, starting tomorrow, he is going to help me take this house apart room by room."

Although it disturbed him, he chose to ignore her reference to Isabel in the present tense. He would not have been surprised if she had claimed to have spent the day playing cards with Isabel.

"Carrie, I cannot imagine what it is going to take to simply get the wiring and plumbing in this place up to functional standards. We are certainly not in a financial position to hire on some decorator."

"Who said anything about a decorator? In case you don't know, the legendary Wyatt Wallace is our nearest neighbor. He's working on a play about Hatton Preston, who just may have bequeathed to us the final pages of a missing manuscript. I'm going to help him with his research."

Off on a wild goose chase worthy of his mother. Carrie, my Carrie, I no longer know you he thought as he resisted the old comforting act of wrapping his arms around her. Sadness stabbed him.

Were they growing too apart to ever again come together?

Turning her back to him, Carrie was asleep as soon as her head touched the pillow.

It is a picture postcard perfect day for a parade. The dusty streets of Birmingham are capacity crowded, storefronts draped in colorful bunting. Vendors hawk sweets and souvenirs. Everyone seems to be whistling "Dixie."

Birmingham has the honor of hosting the Annual Reunion of the United Confederate Veterans. Five hundred delegations are camped in the heart of downtown.

Fourteen year old Isabel McShan, her sister Lydia, mother Kitty, maiden aunt Miss Bess Hatton, and family maid Violet, holding in her arms three year old Theodore, disembark from the streetcar.

The kind spirited mother refrains from admonishing Isabel to attempt a pretty posture. Victim of a spinal curvature, the teenager has spent years of sleepless nights trussed in a wire brace and has endured painful electrical shock treatments in futile efforts to correct the deformity. The self-conscious adolescent feels as much a freak as the star of a circus sideshow. A core of bitterness festers from the resignation that life will cast her, as Bess too frequently reminds her, in a supporting role as maiden aunt to a prettier sister's children.

Isabel turns spiteful eyes on her younger sibling. Lydia has been showered with an unfair advantage of blessings. While Isabel's frizzy mouse brown hair is impossible to keep pinned, Lydia's bright red curls tumble down her back in a happy profusion. From thick lashed eyes, as green as summer grass in Ireland, to a delicate nose with a gold dusting of freckles above a sunny, ever present smile, Lydia is the family's unabashed darling. It is abundantly apparent that Lydia is destined to become a belle to break the hearts of a multitude of men.

Mining and steel making are the arteries that pump the lifeblood of bustling new rich Birmingham. It is the custom to christen mines, furnaces, and foundries namesake of a favored female relation. As one of the city's wealthiest industrialists, Sam McShan calls his most productive blast furnace the Miss Kitty, his most Midean mine the Mary Lydia. Nothing named for Isabel. She has one too many times caught her father's eyes regarding her with a mixture of pity and disgust.

Matriarch Minnie has declined her daughters' invitation, growl-

ing that she can't squander time on lost causes not worth finding.

Fashion conscious Kitty contemplates a smart lilac suit on display in a store window. She suddenly frowns and clutches Bess's sleeve. "Bess, I am feeling faint."

"Simply the emotion of the moment, Little Sister," Bess answers, tapping an eyebrow in salute to a Confederate battle banner snapping in the breeze.

"This baby sick too," Violet says. "Feel his head, Miss Kitty. He's burning up."

"Violet, we must return home on the next available streetcar. Bess, you can mind Isabel and Lydia." Kitty coughs, one hand on her own forehead, the other on her toddler son's.

"Nonsense! You are simply wilting from the sun's intensity," Bess protests. "We will go to Wintergreen's Drugstore and comfort you with a lemon ice." Bess has longed for this day for months. Still to come are the parade, the laying of the cornerstone for the grand Confederate Memorial, and a performance at O'Brien's Opera House of the play "The Lost Cause."

Tomorrow night Lydia will star, as Alabama's representative, in a stirring tableau "The Solid South." A ball following the pageant will be held in the grand salon of the city's most elegant hostelry, the Caldwell Hotel. It is certainly no time for succumbing to sickness!

Bess is afraid of crowds, particularly a congregation so rowdy and predominantly male as this one, and it will be impossible for her to continue participation in the day's activities without the armor of Kitty's self assurance.

A firm believer in patent potions, Bess turns her younger sister in the direction of the drugstore. A dose of Major Morris Elixir, that fine fixative for anything that ails you from childhood colic to constipation to irregular indignities of the female glands, is just what the doctor would order. All will soon be right as rain.

Chapter Six

Slumped in a brown leather wing chair, avoiding the typewriter as if he and the machine were old friends no longer on speaking terms, Wyatt Wallace reflected on Carrie. He must maintain his focus.

The best thing he had written in years was his signature on the last divorce. There was no time or space in his life for a woman, no need for even a platonic friendship.

Too little time remaining. The familiar fear of dwindling hours running rampantly away roiled the pool of whiskey in the pit of his stomach.

He was burned out. Should have taken Thomas Wolfe's warning to heart. In six months he had found little solace in being home again in this house of many memories, of dark rosewood furniture richly redolent of lemon oil, dreary seascapes in old gold frames, the deep bong of the grandfather clock that hourly chimed the Westminster Cadence.

Nearing the same age at which his father had died, he found himself, in his father's boyhood home, too often reflecting on that other life.

His father died a bitter man, a failed poet, in the eyes of the literary world obscure. It was not an epitaph the son wanted repeated.

The final enigmatic words spoken by his dying father, enunciated clearly, as if the man were having a conversation with his long dead boyhood best friend Hatton Preston, reverberated in Wyatt's head. "Tell my boy what, Hatton? Where will he find it? Why did you hide it? Why should Wyatt complete the telling of your story?"

A commission commanded from beyond the grave.

It was impossible. It was irrational. It had become an obsession. He must read the last words written by Hatton Preston.

He crossed the room, ripped the blank sheet of paper from his father's old manual typewriter and balled it up in his fist in frustration. He stubbornly refused to use a computer. A man who wrote on a typewriter worked harder to get it right the first time.

Reams of wadded wordless paper, white dots like golf balls littering a practice tee, surrounded his desk.

He took the last bottle of Scotch from the cardboard case on the floor, uncapped it and took a healthy swig. The demon was chasing him, and time was running out.

* * *

Carrie prepared for her first all night all alone in the house, although Nick was lately working such long hours that she sometimes felt as though she lived in solitary confinement. She suspected that he was purposely avoiding her.

At least, this night, she knew he was not with that other woman.

Nick and his dog Dooley had joined his father on an overnight duck hunting trip on the family's farm, and the girls had returned to college.

It was near to midnight, alone in a lonely house, and Carrie regretted the two cups of coffee with which she had ended a solitary dinner. Caffeine denied her the consolation of sleep.

She spread the bulging black scrapbooks, found in the recesses of a hall closet, around her on the bed.

"Kitty's Comings and Goings" trumpeted the flyleaf of one volume, the title written in white India ink in a penmanship exuberant with flourishes. Gently turning brittle pages, Carrie studied a complete accounting of the life of Isabel Preston's mother, from the first page wedding photo of Kitty and Sam McShan, continuing through three chubby cheeked babies, a gingerbread trimmed house with wicker rockers and potted palms on the porch, clippings detailing fashionable teas and the meetings of various women's groups, ending with the punctuation of a solemnly black bordered newspaper notice of the untimely deaths of Kitty and her three year old son Theodore. A yellowed handkerchief sheltering two locks of blonde hair and neatly tied with black ribbon was tucked in the back cover.

"City Triumphs and Tragedies!" screamed the introduction to another volume. The darker side of the "gay 90's" in the small southern city of Birmingham included an inordinate number of lynchings, court sanctioned hangings, shootings, and stabbings.

The pages devoted to the early years in the life of Carrie's house mate, Isabel McShan Preston, were disappointingly scant. A short paragraph's newspaper notice of her marriage, a honeymoon souvenir postcard from Lookout Mountain, a fading photograph of the bridal couple, Isabel leaning on her seated new husband's shoulder in a futile attempt to disguise her deformity.

"Our Lovely Lydia" merited a half dozen crammed to bursting volumes. Lydia taking top honors at her high school commencement, Lydia in ermine trimmed cape reigning as Mardi Gras Queen, Lydia's debutante ball, pronounced in the press "the society event of the turning century." Dance cards, crumbling pressed corsages, an age cracked elbow length ivory leather glove, a postcard addressed to Miss Elizabeth Hatton, depicting the Wellesley College campus.

Closing the final album in the stack, Carrie had the sense of having almost completed reading a family saga lacking an ending chapter. Where was the memory book displaying a radiant, white wedding gowned Lydia beaming on the arm of some prince charming as impossibly handsome as she was beautiful? The last half dozen pages of the last book examined were as blank as though Lydia had one day simply fallen out of her family.

She thought in frustration of the attic stairs, rotted risers too dangerous to attempt climbing. Until she could convince Nick to spend the money to have them repaired, the attic was off limits. It had taken all the strength Wyatt could summon just to get the attic access door, as stubbornly stuck as if nailed shut, open earlier that day, after which it just as mulishly refused to be closed back again tightly.

She turned off the light, shivering, at the same time wishing for the warmth of Nick and oddly relieved that he was not there and grumbling about the stream of cold air sliding down from the attic above.

Or the scuttling sounds heard late in the night from the floor above them. She tried to reassure herself that it was only squirrels, accessing territory forbidden to humans through the broken windows in the gable.

The bedroom door nudged open, and Carrie stifled a scream as something fur covered thudded against her face.

Jumping out of bed and turning on the light, she met the stare of a bedraggled yellow cat. He purred what sounded like a plea for acceptance.

She sat down and stroked him, bone structure too palpable beneath the matted fur. He looked like an animal denied the luxury of a decent meal in years. Living off mice, she supposed.

Feeling both a wave of sympathy for the stray and comfort in his company, Carrie carried him to the kitchen, opened a can of tuna and fed him. Licking his whiskers as if savoring dessert, he followed her back upstairs to bed.

All of her life she had wanted a cat. Neither her mother nor Nick had ever been agreeable to that idea. She would deal with Nick's aversion to cats another day.

What a very nice surprise. The cat cuddled close, Carrie dismissed missing manuscripts and misplaced scrapbooks from her mind, and drifted off to sleep.

"Izzy, why do you suppose the mortician hitches white horses to his death wagon? Don't you suppose that black ones would be more fitting?" Lydia strokes a buttercup colored kitten and stares out the bedroom window at the somber vehicle on the curb.

The twelve year old struggles to contain her grief by absorbing the complicated rituals accompanying death. The silver calling card tray in the hall brims to overflowing with black banded notes of condolence that Aunt Bess will paste onto the last pages of her Kitty memory book.

The stairway landing holds a niche, architecturally termed a coffin corner. Despite all the carefully choreographed preparations, someone neglected to remove a decorative urn, and, in transferring her mother from deathbed to downstairs display, the vase was shattered. Lydia heard the curses as the men struggled under the burden of lead lined mahogany, the beautiful burial box from Cincinnati. Caring little for the keeping of scrapbooks, she has pocketed instead a sliver of painted porcelain as keepsake of her mother.

From the Sunday parlor below the two sisters rises the drone of voices as friends file past the double biers in solemn procession. In the conspicuous absence of Kitty's mother Minnie, the neighbor Adelaide Ashcraft presides over the observation of the requisite customs and conventions. Occasionally Mrs. Ashcraft directs an ominous glare upwards to the second floor where Minnie, far from being taken prone to the bed with weeping, is all a hustle and a bustle carrying out her own agenda.

Bess runs itchy fingers over the sharp scissors in her pocket. Sam has threatened her within an inch of her life if she snips one hair from her sister's head before the last mourner takes his leaving. Just before the undertaker bolts fast the lid, she plans to shear Kitty near to scalped. Kitty won't mind. It will grow back.

Everyone knows that after death the hair and nails sprout with a manic abandon.

She looks forward to coming months of after supper evenings artfully weaving exquisite keepsake jewelry for Kitty's many friends and admirers. She takes pride in her work, the greatest accomplishment of her life having been the completion of a sampler depicting the entire Buford family tree woven from tresses of late lamented family members. Appropriately, it depicts a plantation scene, complete with weeping willows.

In the kitchen, Minnie, grunting with effort, drops a load of dresses onto the table next to the neighborly outpouring of pies and pastries, pickled peaches and potato salads.

Violet puts her hands on her hips and glares from Minnie to the collection of garments, apparently representing Bess and Minnie's wardrobes in entirety.

"What has gotten into you this morning?" she asks Minnie impatiently.

"I hope marriage is not turning you into a lazy good for nothing. Wasting your time in weeping when there is work to be done!" Minnie snaps back. Having recently been at odds over Violet's choice of a husband, the pair must operate under a strained truce necessitated by the ill mannered intrusion of death.

Violet turns her back on Minnie and reminds herself that she is now Violet Larson. Mrs. Violet Larson. After all of her life being simply Violet, having a surname is a heady new experience.

"Get that wastrel husband of yours to set the large iron vats to simmering," Minnie commands.

"It's too hot to make soup, and besides we got food enough as it is, and hardly room to put it, what with Miss Bess's dresses cluttering up my kitchen where they got no business being," Violet retorts.

"Get yourself to dyeing these dresses. I have spent the majority of my life in mourning. It will simplify things by half if Bess and I simply remain in ebony only for whatever days we have remaining."

Their stalemate is broken by the appearance of Adelaide, who reprimands Minnie to mind her manners and take her place in the carriage for the procession to the graveyard.

Gentlemen on street corners respectfully remove their hats as the McShan cortege winds its way along the short and final journey to Oak Hill Cemetery.

On one of the two rose palled caskets Lydia has added a ribbon bound bouquet of bachelor buttons from Bess's garden. Since death came to visit, the house has been over ripe with the feuding fragrances of roses and gardenias. Roses to remind Lydia for the rest of her life of loss, she will in the future profess a profound distaste for the flower in any form or fashion.

At last arrived face to face with the inevitable, the little family huddles together next to the twin mounds of newly turned earth, Birmingham's blood red clay.

Sam McShan stares into the distance beyond the open graves. Digging graves in the rock riddled soil of Birmingham is hard work. He has done it. His eyes pause on a far corner of the cemetery where lie the remains of the victims of the cholera outbreak of 1873 that almost pronounced a death sentence on the city then but two years founded. More than a hundred dead in a population of only four thousand, almost every household touched.

They said the contagion rode in on a night train from Huntsville, hiding in the body of a young Negro man. Later blame focused on the common city well that when eventually drained yielded a malignant melange from rotted rope to the moldy corpses of a cat and numerous rats.

His eyes dart around the headstones, a marble roll call of the men who years before helped an orphaned boy make a start at manhood. Sam had thought in those early 1870s of making his way west to California to seek his fortune in the gold fields.

Instead he sold his father's moderate land holdings and threw in his lot with a group of investors who were forming a land company and dreaming of riches from mineral resources.

A practical and a patient man, he held onto that stock through the upheavals of cholera and national financial panic until 1886 when a real estate boom exploded in the fledgling city. The stock of the Elyton Land Company that year paid a dividend of 340%, every single original dollar invested multiplied by thirty five. Sam McShan found himself a wealthy man.

He counted his greatest treasure Kitty. She turned the head of every young man in a town where available suitors outnumbered suitable young ladies six to one.

He feels a pauper at her passing, dreads going home to a lonely bed. He wonders how many years of solitary needy nights loom ahead of him.

He forces his thoughts to the living grouped around him. Because Isabel is self-conscious about her deformity and her tendency to stuttering, Kitty has agreed to let Bess home educate her. Sam worries about some of the notions Bess is planting in her feeble female mind along with sums and ciphers. Hysterical old heifer handing about her temperance literature while hyped to the hilt on patent potions laced with enough alcohol and cocaine to inebriate an elephant, lighting candles and summoning spirits and then crying out in her sleep to a phantom French lover in a voice loud enough to literally wake the dead. While recognizing his responsibility to shelter her, Sam has little patience in regard to Bess.

Lydia, who has fussed and fluttered and been far too interested in funeral preparations, at last gives way to unabashed grief. He fears that his spirited, headstrong younger daughter is going prove a handful in years to come.

Minnie. The old woman has a positive penchant for mischief. It has cost him a pretty penny to buy at auction for back taxes her rotting old plantation house and the land surrounding it. Cotton prices appear on the rise however, and the tenant manager predicts a good crop come the autumn.

In one way at least she and Bess are as much blessing as burden. Through them came the inestimable Violet. With unions on the upswing, and strikes so violent that the governor has recently been obliged to rally the forces of the national guard, it has not been an easy year to be in the mining business. Dealing daily with a mongrel work force of dark skinned convicts leased from the state alongside immigrants arguing in a tower of Babel polyglot of voices leaves a man little spare time for the raising of girl children. A maiden aunt on the premises will save him the onus of finding another wife at his age.

About as much chance of any man removing Bess from his household as there is of anyone ever paying court to Isabel. Some women are simply cursed at birth to be spinsters.

Bess adjusts her black veiled bonnet and catches Sam's eyes appraising her. She lowers tear streaked lashes in a gesture of feminine humility. It is not unheard of, actually almost customary, for a bereaved widower, after a suitable period, to take in marriage the hand of a dead wife's maiden sister. In her mind she begins to formulate the speech of graciously unselfish acceptance, to practice in her florid penmanship a signature with Mrs. at its beginning.

To duty she will respond in the affirmative! Surely, at Sam's advanced age no connubial responsibilities will be expected. Bliss without burden! Ahead lies the best of all possible worlds

Chapter Seven

The full winter moon, hanging like a perfect single pearl against the pre-dawn velvet darkness of the December sky, provided adequate illumination for Jack Lancaster to guide the small skiff through the murky channels of the swamp.

He had navigated this marsh since childhood, could have captained the boat blindfolded.

He pulled a forbidden cigar from the pocket of his oilskin jacket. Ellen only grudgingly allowed him to smoke the things when out of her sight. Ellen lumped cigars, and duck hunting, into a category to which she referred disdainfully as "male things." He supposed that it was also a male thing that he would not admit to her that he had not actually lit a cigar in nearly ten years. There was something about having one in his pocket that brought his father back to him.

He cleared his throat, took a sip of the coffee so strong that only the ancient and filthy percolator remaining in the duck camp shack could produce it, before beginning what he knew was going to be a painful conversation with his son. Whiskey had failed to loosen him up enough to initiate the conversation the night before. Maybe coffee would give him courage. He was not comfortable minding another grown man's business.

Ellen had been adamant. If he didn't try to convince Nick to take some kind of positive steps to get Carrie and the marriage back on track, she was going to jump into the situation with both feet. As much as he loved his quixotic wife, he had lived with her long enough to know that Ellen's involvement in anything sometimes resulted in an unexpected resolution. The house into which Carrie and Nick had moved was a perfect example. He wished that he could go back to the morning that the attorney had called to tell him that he had inherited the place and answer the phone "wrong number."

Ellen had made a worrisome point with which he couldn't argue. Nick, who had carried his better than average all American boy look well into manhood, appeared to have aged ten years in six months. The situation was taking a toll on him.

"Nick, I've never wanted to interfere . . . ," Jack began hesitantly.

"I appreciate that, Dad, and to be perfectly honest I can't look back over the last twenty two years and find many times that anyone would have questioned the lives that Carrie and I were leading. We were just two very average people in love with each other, enjoying raising our kids, trying to conduct ourselves as decent people. If anyone had told me a year ago that we would be where we are today, I would have called them crazy. It's like we were just driving down the road, minding our own business and obeying the speed limit, and suddenly we made a wrong turn and ended up in a dangerous neighborhood. What I can't seem to find is a map to show me how to get out of it."

"She's had a tough year, Nick. You know how devoted to each other Carrie and her father were. When a man just drops in his tracks, as David Hudson did, it's hard to process. You don't emotionally reconcile the loss on the drive home from the cemetery. She had not had the time it takes to deal with a parent's death before getting pregnant and then losing the baby too."

"I think that she blames me, Dad, blames me that I wasn't excited when she told me that she was pregnant."

"Buy a ticket back home from that guilt trip, Nick."

"I would have loved that baby, Dad. You and I both know that. I have spent so many sleepless nights trying to analyze what I've done wrong in this whole fouled up scheme of things. I guess that selfishly I didn't want to share Carrie with the demands of a small child. After the girls went off to college I'm sure the house felt like the empty nest to Carrie, but to me it was like having the honeymoon period we never got at the beginning. I look back a year and realize that it was the happiest time in my life, and sometimes in the middle of the night I wonder if I'm being punished for having taken things for granted."

"She's depressed, Nick. There's help available for that, lots of very good medications to supplement counseling on the market today."

"I know that as well as you do, but they aren't available over the counter, and any mention of psychiatric treatment produces a totally irrational over reaction in Mallory. Carrie's too deep in a hole to see that she needs help in clawing her way out of it. Since we've moved in the house, she's just burrowing deeper. Dad, Carrie means more to me than everything else in the world combined. I have never been this afraid in my life."

Tears streaming, Nick buried his face in Dooley's neck.

**

"Josie, did I dream it, or did you once mention that you have a cousin who's a painter?"

Josephine Jones, for forty years Mallory Hudson's majordomo, stood arms akimbo and glared as Mallory unpacked bags of groceries.

"Mallory, I see fat free this and extra lean that coming out of those sacks, along with some chickens that ran so free on the range that they've got breasts no bigger than a six year old boy's, but I fail to see several things that I put on that list appearing."

Since David Hudson's death red meat had become a memory in the household, along with butter and bacon. Josie knew that Mallory attributed the heart attack that killed him to the enjoyment of food that made cooking for him a pleasure. Josie's answer to that was at least he died a happy man.

Who are you trying to fool, you old fool, Josie asked herself. David Hudson was never again a truly happy man after that terrible day in this house that something died in all of us.

"Josie, I do believe that you're getting hard of hearing," Mallory interrupted her thoughts. "I have asked you three times if you have a cousin who's a painter."

"I do, and as soon as you buy some shortening, as I have requested, I will share his name with you. What are you fixing to paint?"

"I want to get a painter over to Carrie's as soon as possible. We're probably going to need a carpenter too. Perhaps I should just call a general contractor."

"Mallory! Carrie has passed forty. Are you ever planning on letting her be a grown up?"

"Josie, I just hate so for people to talk."

"Seems to me we have walked this road before, Mallory, and I'm going to give you the same good advice I did back then. Worry about Carrie, not what folks are saying about her. All that stewing you did twenty years ago, and look at how well things turned out. Carrie could not have asked for a better husband than Nick."

"I can't disagree with that."

As Mallory put the last of the grocery items in the cabinet, Josie took her coat from a peg by the back door with an exaggerated sigh.

"If you'll excuse me, Mallory, I am going to go next door, where they still eat like normal people, and borrow myself some butter, and some corn syrup, and, most importantly of all, some shortening for a pie crust. I overheard you telling Carrie that you would love to come to her house for a small dinner party, and my contribution is going to be one of those chocolate pecan pies that Nick loves so much. I do believe he loves my pies as much as Jamie . . ."

"Don't go there, Josie. Don't do it. You know very well that I won't have that!"

Josie shook her head in consternation at the other woman's retreating back.

"Someday, Mallory, we're going to have to look back and kiss that dead boy good bye," she whispered.

∗∗∗

In the dining room Carrie surveyed the morning's efforts.

The mahogany table was waxed and buffed, topped with candles awaiting lighting. She had also laid a fire on the hearth, beneath the ornate limestone mantel, carved with a family coat of arms, bearing a Latin motto "Fuimus qui sumusque futuri." Wyatt, apparently proficient at just about anything, had translated for her. "Who we were is who we are and are to be."

The room really looked very nice. Isabel would surely approve. By candle and fire light that evening, the threadbare spots moths had chewed in the Oriental rug would not be nearly so visible.

The cat purring in her arms, she gave the room a final inspection. A centerpiece of glossy magnolia leaves and creamy blossoms spilled from a silver repousse epergne, only slightly bent so that it listed to the left. Old family silver. Greenery made a fine substitute for too expensive fresh florist flowers. Nick had been carping about how much repairs to the leaking slate roof were going to cost. Nick would have a fit if he knew that Wyatt Wallace was paying for the attic stair repairs.

Wyatt had money to spare and was convinced of the good possibility that the manuscript was hidden in the attic. What Nick didn't know wouldn't hurt him. Little or no chance of her husband developing a sudden compelling interest in exploring the attic.

She consulted her watch. Hadn't she always been told to follow her mother's good example? Greeting guests fresh from a nap was as much a hostess ritual for Mallory as uncorking the wine to allow it breathing time.

Despite the fact that it was not yet ten in the morning, Carrie climbed the stairs and into bed with only a sliver of guilt at running away to the new friends peopling her more comfortable dream world.

"Violet! Violet! Where are the tea and toast I requested at least a quarter of an hour ago?" Minnie, banging her cane, calls from the porch where she has spent the morning rocking and watching the world go by.

"I already told you I got no time for tea and toast!" Violet appears, holding by the neck a chicken squawking protest. "I got to wring this hen. Company coming for Sunday dinner as if you don't remember."

"Too much fuss and folderol over a young damned Yankee," Minnie grumbles.

"As usual, you missed a most inspiring sermon, Mama," Bess chides as she climbs the porch steps and takes her seat in the companion rocker. "And I don't mind telling you that in allowing Lydia and Isabel to forego the Sunday service you positioned me in the most uncomfortable situation of having to tell a small white lie of explanation to Mrs. Ashcraft. Honestly, Mama! Mrs. Ashcraft has mentioned more than once that under your supervision Kitty's girls are apt to ride right to Hades in a handbasket."

Bess pouts as her mother refuses to rise to the bait. She wanted to revisit her strong feeling that it is scandalous that Sam allows his younger daughter, who appears older than her actual sixteen years, to ride the streetcar to school and back, without benefit of a chaperone. Bess has tried to communicate to her brother-in-law, without being explicit enough for embarrassment, her fears.

She is not so sheltered as Sam might suppose. Anyone who reads the newspaper knows that in every northern city white slavers ply their evil trading, with hidden hypodermics of potent soporifics stealthily stabbing the arms of unsuspecting virgins, who, duly narcotized, are slipped off the streetcars and into lives of utter degradation.

Truth be told, as Mama has pointed out, she has not heard of such incidents happening on the public transports of Birmingham, but it may be that good families are keeping tight lipped about their personal ruination and that bad families care less. After all, if a northern menace like the labor unions causing Sam to miss luncheon today, can come to Alabama, can white slavers be far behind?

Upstairs, Lydia throws down a silver backed brush in frustration. "Oh, Izzy, I have ruined you! How could Violet, who is such a whiz with hair, be too busy cooking to help us?"

The sisters have spent hours poring over popular ladies magazines in search of a suitable coiffure to copy. Lydia has suggested that bangs would be becoming, but she has done a crooked cutting job and further muddied the waters by overheating the curling iron and scorching the leading edge of Isabel's hair into a ragged fringe of frizz. The acrid stench of burned hair hangs heavy. Lydia throws open the window.

"Too late! He's early. I spy him rounding the corner," Lydia cries as Isabel stares wretchedly into the mirror. "You'll just have to wear a hat." She mists an atomizer of lilac toilet water in her sister's direction.

"No perfume!" Isabel protests. "I should not want to give the impression that I am a harlot."

"Well, Izzy, if your intent is to snare Mr. Willard H. Preston in wedded bliss we have to overcome your smelling like Sherman leaving Atlanta."

Isabel blushes. "Lydia, hush such nonsense! Why, none of us, save Father of course, has even made Mr. Preston's acquaintance."

Willard Preston weaves down the sidewalk on his new bicycle. He runs a finger around his sweat saturated celluloid collar as he appraises the facade of the large house. His employer Sam McShan's home, with its twin turrets and latticed porch, steeply gabled roof and scalloped window skirts, plainly proclaims prosperity.

Before he can raise a hand against the front door, he hears a giggle from the dim recesses of the wraparound porch, turns to see the assembled family grouped and gaping.

"Why, do come closer, Mr. Preston, that we may evaluate you face to face," coos a girl who is surely living representation of one of the Pre-Raphaelite angels in Mr. Rossetti's paintings.

His heart catches. Lydia McShan forms an immediately indeli-

ble impression destined to haunt him until his life's closing moments.

Introductions made, they move inside to serve themselves from the sideboard on which Violet has arrayed a prodigious feast. "Do take a larger portion of dumplings, Mr. Preston," Bess urges as she unloads the contents of a spoon the size of a small silver shovel onto her own already well laden plate.

"I am very fastidious about my diet, Miss Hatton," he responds. "I subscribe to the new theories about physical fitness. I find it does my constitution a world of good to chew each bite the recommended thirty times before swallowing."

Bess looks down at her piled to groaning plate in dismay. At the rate of thirty chews a bite, it would be supper time before she completed her dinner.

"I find the boardinghouse food exceedingly heavy," he continues, cutting a tiny, precise wedge of tomato. "Fortunately I avoid the epidemic malady of congested digestion by enjoying regular mechanical colonic cleansings."

No one having the heart to ask for further amplification, Isabel seizes an opportunity. "So t-t-tell us, Mr. Preston, do you l-l-leave a large family at home in Pittsburgh?"

Willard rolls around and around with his tongue the gummy wad of dumpling, reminding Minnie of the cow out back chewing her cud, before responding, "A widowed mother, three older spinster sisters."

A bad set of circumstances, a whole host of female damned Yankee dependents, Minnie thinks to herself.

"And what do you do for recreation?" Lydia asks, sucking in her cheeks ever so slightly around a single grape, the most sensual display Willard has ever witnessed. Face flaming, he drops his fork, bangs heads with Isabel in a mutually clumsy attempt to retrieve the utensil.

"I spend many hours practicing tunes on my ukelele, and I have an intense interest in the playing of the game of checkers. As well I am a most passionate reader of the poetry composed by Mr. Algernon Charles Swinburne."

Lunch completed, on the porch Willard fidgets under Minnie's grilling. "I believe Sam remarked that your father was engaged in the manufacture of footwear?"

"Yes, Ma'am, I come from a long line of cobblers, going back to my forebears in Ireland."

"Cobblers, yes, well, fitting I suppose since you seem intent on pulling yourself up by the boot straps. I have never thought much of the Irish as a race. You're not overfond of imbibing I hope."

"Why, no, Ma'am, indeed not! I am proud to say that I have taken the pledge and sworn to a life of temperance! As I pass the saloon that neighbors my boardinghouse I look in pity on the dissolute and remind myself of the maxim, 'Within any happy man there lives a healthy liver.'"

Bess sweeps onto the porch twirling a black umbrella and carrying a wicker hamper, Isabel in tow. "I have had Violet pack a delicious mid-afternoon repast to thrill your health conscious heart, Mr. Preston. Cucumber sandwiches with sweet cream butter and mayonnaise, Violet's ginger cookies, my famous deviled eggs to which, having noticed a peaked pallor in your complexion, I have added a few salubrious drops of Dr. Darker's Blood Builder, and a jar of pickled pigs' feet."

"Shall we be off, Mr. Preston?" Isabel asks shyly, tugging the straw hat over her forehead.

Willard stares up at Isabel. Her out of kilter posture gives him an unsettling vertigo. A mistake has been made. Surely Mr. McShan could not have assumed any interest on his part in courting the daughter with the deformity.

"I have a lovely picnic spot in mind," Bess prattles on. "Have you had opportunity to visit the Highlands, Mr. Preston?"

"Miss Lydia will shortly be along to join us?"

"Lydia? Oh, no, Lydia has other plans entirely. You see Sunday is traditionally our time to enjoy a spirited communion with sainted sister Kitty and young Theodore. The graveyard is such a lovely site in autumn, and Lydia wouldn't deny sharing that pleasure with Mama for the world."

"Breaking bread with the dead disrupts my digestion," Minnie mutters.

"Give Kitty our best, Mama, and tell her to rest easy, that sister Bess is taking very good care of her girls, very good care indeed."

Chapter Eight

As Carrie realigned a silver fork in the table setting, Nick cleared his throat, no longer sure the safest way to communicate with his wife. The formally set table looked out of place in their current lives and set alarm bells ringing. She had not cooked two meals in the month that they had lived in the house, never mind considered hosting company.

"You've just got time to take a shower before our guests arrive," Carrie said, so brightly that it frightened Nick. "Don't you think the lace tablecloth looks nice? A few stains and ironing burns, but I suppose that's to be expected of heirloom linens." She gave him a smile that just missed reminding him of the familiar welcome home expression that used to greet him every night.

From over Carrie's shoulder, another unfamiliar face gazing down from over the fireplace gave him a start. He stared back at features too perfectly pretty to have been painted from a real life model. The red haired woman in the portrait wore a tiara and a flowing cape.

He gestured in the direction of the painting. "Carrie, who is that, and where did she come from?"

"Lydia McShan, of course, painted in the late 1890s, when she was queen of the Mardi Gras. I didn't know that Birmingham used to have Mardi Gras balls, did you? I'm going to find that last scrapbook, the one that's bound to have Bess's complete blow by blow of Lydia's fairytale wedding, if it kills me. I told Wyatt this afternoon that Isabel probably hid it in the same place that she squirreled away Hatton's manuscript. Living here is like playing a continuous game of hide and seek with Isabel Preston."

Although she had not answered his question about the provenance of the painting, he had heard enough, more than enough. He had to get her out of the house, the sooner the better. His mind wrestled with the question of where, given her state of mind, it would be most appropriate to take her.

"Carrie, I'm not sure whom you've invited for dinner, but I think that we had better ask them to take a rain check."

"I have invited your parents, my mother, and Wyatt Wallace. Josie baked us one of her fabulous chocolate pecan pies. I am serving beef tenderloin. Unlike health nuts like you and my mother, Wyatt still enjoys red meat, just like my daddy did."

"He was over here again today?" Nick was seized with a sudden memory of one of his daughters coming home from grammar school and announcing that she had a new, to last forever, best friend.

"Wyatt is a fascinating man," Carrie, still fiddling with the flatware, answered. "Both your mother and mine are dying to meet him. Mother will consider it a feather in my cap to have snagged him as a guest. Besides that, she trained me well that a good hostess never sets an odd number of places. Wyatt rounds out the table."

It was too late for further discussion. The doorbell rang.

In need of time to think, Nick mumbled excuses to shower and change from his hunting clothes. Seeing his mother toss her black wool coat, as dusted with short white dog hairs as if she'd just come in from a snowstorm, over Mallory's carefully draped ankle length mink, told him the evening was off to an inauspicious beginning in more ways than one. Be thankful for small favors, he told himself. At least Ellen had left Zippy, her overly energetic Jack Russell terrier, rarely other than at her side, at home.

"Tell us to what we owe the honor of having you in Birmingham," Mallory asked, claiming the opposite end of the sofa from the guest of honor after instructing Jack to mix a round of cocktails. Conversationally, she neatly edged Ellen out of opening round advantage in commandeering the center of Wallace's attention.

"The distractions in California made it impossible to totally focus on my work in progress, a return to my first love of writing for the stage rather than the screen. I was fortunate in having the opportunity to reclaim my grandmother's house, to return to my roots both personally and professionally if you will," Wyatt replied.

"Too few people today understand the importance of roots," Mallory agreed. "Has Carrie mentioned to you that my people come from Montgomery, Mr. Wallace?"

"As did my father's family. Perhaps in an earlier era the two groups were acquainted," Wyatt replied, mentally seeing his grandmother pat him on the back for good manners just before not bothering to stifle a yawn, waving his empty highball glass in Jack's direction for a refill.

Ancestors represented a topic of conversation into which Mallory could sink her teeth and a realm in which she had a decided upper hand over Ellen. "Our ancestral family home, an antebellum architectural masterpiece, was, sadly, after my mother's death, sold by my brother to some insensitive Connecticut businessmen who razed it to build a hideous modern office building," Mallory drawled on, southern accent as thick as melted sugar. "My Casswell great grandparents often hosted President Jefferson Davis for lunch in that home."

"Mother tends to romanticize her girlhood, probably typical of someone growing up in a war zone," Carrie interjected as she wondered if Nick intended to make an appearance before dessert. She had become aware in their brief acquaintance that for Wyatt the cocktail hour began when he got up in the morning, and the good hostess responsibility her mother had trained in her warned that it was time to serve food instead of drink.

Nick, at last appearing as Carrie led the group into the dining room, took his place at the head of the table, feeling oddly uncomfortable at being in the direct line of view of the intensely green eyes of the woman staring down from the painting.

Carrie rolled her eyes at her mother. "No one has ever gotten around to telling folks in Montgomery that the Civil War is over. Or that our side lost the conflict."

"*Phoenix Fully Risen* is the working title of my book, a romantic novel set in the new south of the Reconstruction era, a time of putting the past in the perspective where it belongs," Ellen interjected. "My protagonists are the members of an impoverished family who make a killing in the mining speculation that went on in the early days of this city, when people were much more interested in where a family had the potential to go than in where they had been."

"Sounds fascinating." Wyatt, who could not have cared less, responded, turning his attention from left dinner partner to right. He pushed slightly back from the table, lit his pipe and passed his wine glass to Carrie for a third replenishing.

"Oh, Ellen, Reconstruction was such a repugnant chapter in our history! I can't imagine who in the world would want to read about some miner's family," Mallory retorted, carefully blotting her lips without disturbing her lipstick.

"One of my themes is the blurring of class distinctions," Ellen countered. "I think the average reader will respond positively to a time when all of the so called aristocrats found out how the other half lived."

Mallory smoothed an imaginary wrinkle from the skirt of her simple cashmere dress as she studied Ellen's busily patterned Christmas sweater. The sweater was out of place enough at a dinner party without the insult added to injury of a reindeer brooch with a bright red blinking nose. Unable to imagine owning battery operated jewelry, Mallory found Ellen's gaucherie so terribly trying, as if the other woman had gotten, by marrying Jack, no farther socially than the toe of one foot over onto the right side of the tracks.

"Darling, are you not serving your famous dinner rolls tonight?" Mallory asked as Carrie passed a basket of bakery muffins. Mallory knew that the tenderloin and potatoes had been cooked by the country club because Carrie had eagerly accepted her offer to order the main dish and vegetables and to have them delivered, hot and ready to serve.

Carrie's interest in hosting guests encouraged her. Carrie's ability to carry it off in her current strange state of mind unnerved her.

"The oven seems to be out of order," Carrie muttered, afraid that Nick would take the opportunity to enumerate his entire lengthy list of components of the house needing repair or replacement.

"The ladies of Carrie's generation simply amaze me with their culinary skills," Mallory murmured to Wyatt. "I could never have achieved my reputation as a hostess without my good right hand Josie Jones. Josie and I have been a team for more than forty years. Of course, when I was a young bride, securing good help in the kitchen was as paramount as registering both luncheon and dinner sizes in your silver pattern."

"Wyatt is working on a play about Hatton Preston," Carrie, embarrassed by her mother's pomposity, told the table in general.

Wyatt was only too happy for the conversation to turn to any subject more interesting than a suburban woman's unlikely to ever be published first novel or where some aging southern belle's grandparents grew up. He deftly swung the conversation back in the direction of his favorite topic, himself.

"As boys, Hatton and my father were best friends. Dad took a northern education literally and became what Hatton most abhorred, a converted and convicted liberal."

Ellen, born and raised a die hard Democrat, thought quickly before Mallory could launch into a tirade of conservative political views. "Carrie, I notice that you have a beautiful new bracelet."

"As a matter of fact, Ellen, I think this may be one of the few remaining items of the Preston family jewels. It must have been Isabel's. It has an interesting inscription."

"It's Shakespeare. 'Oh call back yesterday . . . Bid time return,'" Ellen read aloud.

"From the Earl of Salisbury's soliloquy in *Richard III*," Wyatt added.

Carrie, turning pale, dropped her fork as the words of the dream echoed in her head, a dying Kitty McShan asking Violet to find her bracelet. A party favor from a previous century? How had she dreamed of the bracelet before she found it, along with a gold locket containing a tiny painted miniature of a red haired man, wrapped in a yellowed handkerchief tied with faded blue ribbons, wedged in the back of the sideboard drawer from which she had taken the tablecloth?

"Carrie!" Nick's voice, firmly repeating her name for the third time, snapped the spell. "I think that we could all use some extremely strong coffee with Josie's dessert."

***

"You were very quiet at dinner," Carrie commented as Nick stabbed a poker at the smoldering logs in the bedroom fireplace. From the basement the old steam boiler clanged metallic hiccoughs. It was no match for the north wind pummeling the house.

"Hard to get a word in edgewise, between our mothers bickering and Wallace babbling Shakespeare. Carrie, I fail to share your fascination with the neighbor. He's an aging drunk who smokes too much and is in love with the sound of his own voice. You don't need to be wasting your time with him."

"Nicky, Wyatt has pulled me out of the doldrums by involving me in his project. I think you should be grateful that thanks to Wyatt and this house I have a whole new sense of purpose."

Years inured to the soft snorts and snores of Dooley and Nick, breathing in tandem, Carrie slipped easily into the safer than reality realm of dreams.

"You! Boy! Come back here and deliver my paper properly, you

damnable little rapscallion!" The child's knees pump like pistons as he hastily pedals away.

"Miss Minnie, hush up that cussing loud enough for the devil hear." Cleotis Larson retrieves the soggy newspaper from the gutter.

Scowling, Minnie pulls a handful of change from her pocket. "I would like for you to replenish my supply of apple brandy. I shall need fortification to get through the afternoon." She trains the lenses of her brother's old opera glasses across the street in the direction of Adelaide Ashcraft's bedroom window.

"You an old woman who ought to be repenting her sins and seeking her salvation stead of swilling liquor and spying on the neighborhood. Where you get all that money anyhow?"

"Stop being such a born again Baptist. I steal it from Sam's dresser top while he sleeps. Now, get along with you before your wife assigns you another chore. I never saw such a stew and a bustle as is going on in this household this morning."

"Ain't every day we got us a solemn ceremony."

"With Isabel and Bess vying to see which can suffer the more virulent attack of the vapors, the ceremony is likely to be about as solemn as a circus."

She snaps open the newspaper and scans the tight columns of type. Bess wrote out the copy and, in a rare burst of bravery, took the streetcar downtown alone and delivered it to the newspaper office herself. "Miss McShan to Pledge Her Troth" leads the headline. "Mr. Samuel Angus McShan rejoices in announcing that his daughter Miss Katherine Isabel will be joined this day in holy matrimony to Mr. Willard Horace Preston in the parlor of the imposing McShan manse on fashionable Fifth Avenue North. Miss Mary Lydia McShan, a supremely popular young belle known throughout this city for her rare beauty and charm will serve as maiden of honor. The Misses McShan occupy a lofty perch at the very apex of our society. Mr. Preston is the attorney for the vast McShan Coal and Iron Enterprises which have made the father of the bride numerous times a millionaire. After a honeymoon journey to Chattanooga where they will gaze in rapture at the majestic splendor of the Lookout Mountain, the newlyweds will return to a life of peace and tranquility, residing in the home of the bride's father."

The last reads like a bad oxymoron, thinks Minnie as a crash shatters the otherwise peaceful June morning, another piece of

Isabel's wedding china broken by Bess in a constant rearranging of nuptial treasure. Neighbors have come in a steady parade, bearing as gifts such necessities as salt cellars and horseradish spoons, berry bowls and silver bonbon dishes, umbrella stands and Oriental urns. Not to be outdone by any other, Adelaide Ashcraft has waited until the eleventh hour of this morning to arrive on the doorstep with a magnificent sterling silver punch bowl from which that great lady herself plans to ladle her private recipe mock mint julep at ceremony's conclusion.

Isabel has chosen, at Willard's direction, a tasteless pattern of inexpensive china, plates painted with yellow buttercups. In Minnie's estimation, Willard, a man of dubious breeding, has been given much too much choice in matters a woman's prerogative.

A crashing chord from the piano disrupts her reverie. Bess has abandoned the wedding gifts to practice for what seems to be the one hundred and first time this morning Mendelssohn's wedding march.

"O' promise me, that someday we shall have all this behind us," sings Lydia as she joins her grandmother.

Minnie laughs and pats Lydia's hand. "If you're a smart girl you'll elope as I did, save yourself the fuss and folderol."

"Much more romantic, too, being swept away by the dashing man of your dreams," Lydia agrees.

"At the time it was considered a sin, a shame, and a scandal, a succumbing to the slavery of passion. Dreams can be the most dangerous things, my darling Lydia. Often they turn into our worst nightmares when they do come true."

***

In bold penmanship, Willard registers Mr. and Mrs. Willard Horace Preston as guests on the hotel ledger as Isabel blushes shyly at his side. She has said little on the long dusty train ride from Birmingham, deferring instead to Willard, who has outlined his plans for their lives together, promising a house in one of the new suburbs springing up on the south side of the city, the conception of five children, comprised of three sons, two daughters, to be delivered in that exact order, at eighteen month intervals. He speaks of the travel which prosperity will provide, of future trips to the falls of Niagara, the wild western wonder of the Grand Teton Mountains.

She has tried to appear attentive while moaning silent prayers. Aunt Bess, from whom Isabel has received all of her education, from the conjugation of verbs to the cultivation of roses, has put off until the last opportunity illuminating her on the decidedly distasteful business of marital consummation, looming ominously close before her. Isabel has prayed for fortitude, strength, and courage, all of which the maiden aunt has assured her she will need in abundance.

Isabel has never, in all of her eighteen sheltered and sequestered years, slept a night away from home. She surveys the bridal chamber, a scarred dresser topped with cracked mirror, stained chamber pot, rusting iron bedstead. The porter has pointed out the communal washroom down the hall, and Isabel, while feeling ragged and dirty from the soot of the train ride, ponders the safety of retreating there to sponge herself. She looks frantically around the room for some shielding screen behind which she can change from travel attire. Willard, discerning her distress, graciously offers to wait in the hall while she dons her nightwear.

She removes her hat and gloves, unpins and brushes her hair the requisite one hundred strokes, a maddeningly slow exercise during which she can hear Willard pacing in the hall outside the door, repeatedly clearing his throat as if to remind her of his increasingly impatient presence.

Her fingers fumble to fasten the myriad of tiny pearl buttons marching down her night dress from high lace trimmed collar to hem. It is a gift from Violet, lovingly hand stitched.

Despite the stifling heat of the room, Isabel pulls to her chin a full complement of patched sheet, thin blanket, and stained chenille bedspread before bidding Willard enter.

Willard has justified reneging on his sworn pledge of sobriety by rationalizing that a man enters only once into marriage. He has spent his time in the hall, anxious in anticipation of a new experience, gulping from a pocket flask. He enters the room and greets Isabel with a belch.

Isabel, face as pale as a ghost's, lying under the mound of covers, arms rigid at her side and eyes squeezed tightly closed, appears to him a corpse laid out for burial.

She and Willard battle briefly with the bedclothes before he flings Isabel's flimsy armor to the floor. She recognizes the reek of liquor, inspiration for his animalistic ardor, on his breath.

"Mrs. Preston, if you will be so good as to remove that night dress," he burps.

"No, sir," she whispers. "Aunt Bess assured me that I would not be required to remove my clothing completely for the consummation." She winds the nightgown as tightly around her as a shroud.

Willard has never viewed a living breathing unclad female. With all the pent up emotion of a chaste and celibate adolescence riding behind him he can stand it no longer.

Pearl buttons fly like bullets as he rips the nightgown open. With fear fueled strength Isabel thrashes violently and rolls over on her belly. The naked hump of her back causes a wave of bile to rise within Willard. In his mind, the sweet scent of Lydia battles with the sour staleness of Isabel's sweat. He retches onto the floor, consumed with the righteous rage of a man who has settled for second best. He retrieves the flask and slugs down the remainder.

The ensuing pain and indignity are greater than Isabel could have expected or Bess could have warned her.

At the pivotal moment of passion, he screams out the name of her sister.

Chapter Nine

Carrie propped herself on an elbow and studied Nick as he slept, the old peace of waking up snug in the simple security that he was hers as lost as an irrevocably burned love letter from a childhood sweetheart with whom she had long ago lost touch. Just as well they had not talked about what still felt to her like an open wound? Asking questions might provide answers too hurtful to hear.

She told herself that she was trying to live her life by the only method in which she'd been trained, by her mother's rules. If something hurt too much to handle, just put it behind you and don't look back.

The words carved on the fireplace mantel came to her. Who we were is who we are and are to be. Past, present, and future.

She could not decide whether she was more afraid of past or of future. Her head on her husband's shoulder no longer represented a present tense place of security.

A shadowing of grey she hadn't noticed had crept into Nick's sandy hair. Seemed like yesterday she and Nick got married, poured the endless cups of coffee it took to get through medical school's all night study sessions and the constant diaper changing of twin babies, the fun of painting and papering their first house. All those shared days and nights blended and blurred into months and years.

She wondered how long she and Nick would just stumble on this way, if they could go on forever wary occupants of opposite sides of the bed.

The house groaned as the winter wind pounded it. Carrie shivered at the thought of getting out of bed and going downstairs to make coffee in a cold and lonely kitchen.

Christmas was just around the corner. The weeks before were collectively called the Christmas season because it was a time of preparation. At this square in the calendar, in the years leading up to today, she would have been up hours ago, baking, filling the house with the scents of cinnamon and cloves, the same rich holiday aromas from Josie's baking that had wafted up the stairs of their mother's house in safely forgotten childhoods . . . NO!

Burrowing under the covers, as far to the edge of her side of the bed as possible, she slammed the door in her mind and scuttled back into sleep.

"Yankees are here! Hide the silver! Hide my brother!"

"Miss Minnie! Miss Minnie, wake up!" Violet emerges from the house with a bang of the screen door and steadies the frantic motion of the rocking chair. "You are making enough ruckus to wake snakes. Haven't been any Yankees around here for almost forty years now. You just having that same bad old dream again."

"Violet, are you done pressing my afternoon tea frock? How ever will I manage all the changes in costume today? I'll need you to do my hair soon," Lydia calls from the recesses of the house.

"Coming, Miss Lydia," Violet sighs. "Just as soon as I get your Granny settled. This is one of those days when I wish there were three or four of me."

"I will attend to Mama, Violet. Today is Lydia's day and you must see to her every whim." Bess, long sleeved black silk dress a stifling choice considering the humidity of the summer morning, fans her reddened face.

"Oh, Mama, what a glorious day! Our little Lydia being presented tonight to society like a belle of yesteryear."

"Hogwash and humbug!" her mother retorts. "Belles of yesteryear required no 'presentation' to anyone. You were either born into society or you had no hope of ever getting there. Life was simpler then."

"Oh, Mama, shush your grumbling. Mark my words, we will soon again sprinkle rose petals on the path to matrimony."

"Marrying's the last thing on Lydia's mind," Minnie shrugs. "Insisting to her papa that she's going north to further her education. The only head I ever encountered that was harder than Lydia's rested on the shoulders of my brother."

"Sam would have been better served allowing me to school her at home as I did Isabel," Bess adds. "It is well known that an excess of education leads to dangerous disruption of the feminine glands. If I do say so myself, I did a fine job in bringing up Isabel."

"Isabel, at twenty, is the stuffiest old bag of wind I have ever known outside of you, Bess," Minnie snaps.

"Wellesley College!" Minnie bangs her cane on the porch floor. "This family tried a northern education once before, and look at where it got my brother. The damn Yankees costing me my brother

had more to do with their educating than it did with their war wag-
ing. I tried to tell Sam that, but did he listen?"

"I should never have let my Kitty come to Birmingham," Minnie
continues. "My Kitty would be alive today if I had been able to find
Papa's gold and keep her in Selma where we all belonged. Society
in Birmingham? Filthy upstart mining camp of a town with no history, no refinement."

"Now, Mama, if you would just get out more, accompany Mrs.
Ashcraft and myself as we attend to our Christian Temperance
Union councils and church circles you would find almost as much
refinement here as exists in Selma, or even in Montgomery. Have
you not read that Birmingham is being dubbed the Magic City
because the population approaches 8,000 in a city not even in existence at the close of the war?"

"Magic! Humbug!" Minnie thunders, waving her cane. "Seven
thousand of the eight are miners, whores, and hooligans. Bars and
brothels on every corner, shootings in the streets. Mines manned
by prisoners rented for a pittance from the state. You tell me
there's any difference between that convict lease system and slavery?"

"Mama, I wish you'd take a measure of my Nervine." Bess
pulls a brown bottle from her pocket and takes a healthy swig.

"Don't bother wasting wishes."

"You know Mrs. Ashcraft's oft quoted expression, 'If wishes
were horses, we all would ride sidesaddle.'"

Minnie glares at the sidewalk. "Speak of the devil, and she's
apt to appear."

Bess heaves her bulk from the rocker and screeches through
the screen door, "Violet! A pitcher of sweet tea and a plate of ginger cookies! Quickly! Mrs. Ashcraft grants us a visit!"

Minnie stifles a giggle. Adelaide Ashcraft's costume of dark
brown dress with bustle of green ruffles topped by an amazing con-
fection of hat of net and pheasant feathers calls to mind a great
sturdy tree in which a large bird roosts.

"Good afternoon to you, Adelaide," she says with a yawn.
"Have you recovered from your latest journey?"

"I enjoy my usual splendid health, although sadly I cannot say
the same for my Colonel's constitution," she replies as she takes
the rocker Bess has vacated in her deference.

"Lemonade would be more to my liking," Adelaide says as Violet *deposits the tea tray. Violet purses her lips, a look not lost on the visiting neighborhood dignitary, and purposely lets the screen door bang behind her, muttering "should have known a sour drink would suit her better."*

"How ever do you tolerate such impudence?" Adelaide complains to Minnie. "Honestly, good help is becoming as scarce as hens' teeth. I don't know what I shall do when dear devoted Libby, handed down to me like a family heirloom, passes on. Libby is a model for the lessons of submission and humility Mama instilled in her in Montgomery."

"Have you gotten around to telling her she's free yet?" Minnie asks.

"Oh, go on with you, Minnie Maude Buford Hatton! You silly old fool! Libby never entertained a thought in her head of wishing for freedom."

"We are simply bursting to hear the details of your journey to the north!" Bess's squeal matches Minnie's rocker's squeak, and Adelaide winces. What she would really prefer to lemonade would be a nice tot of the sweet sherry she keeps on the top shelf of her pantry for medicinal purposes only.

"Please, dear Mrs. Ashcraft, tell us if you were able to dine with Mrs. Astor," Bess pleads.

"Alas, I fear the Yankee food has deleteriously affected my adoring Colonel's gastric harmony. He is a victim of chronic constipation." Continuing her own line of conversation, Adelaide's face lengthens to a mask of concern.

"Young Mr. Preston is a firm believer in the purgative benefits of twice daily colonic irrigation," Bess says. "He relies on Isabel to perform the procedure."

"Where is Isabel?" Mrs. Ashcraft asks.

Pleased to have some news gleaned during Mrs. Ashcraft's recent absence from the city, Bess leans close and whispers, "Isabel has taken to her bed. Enceinte."

"Already heavy as a heifer," Minnie adds.

"Surely not showing!" Adelaide snorts, counting the months since Isabel's marriage on her fingers. "People will talk!"

"We are given to the delivery of large infants in this family," Minnie says with a glance in Bess's ample direction.

"Let us pray that in the long months of her confinement society does not in the process forget poor Isabel, already so much twit-

tered about for having married a Yankee," Adelaide sighs.

*"Society? Here? Hah! This is not Selma nor ever will it be,"
Minnie snorts.*

*"Mama, please! Mind your manners around Mrs. Ashcraft,"
Bess hisses. "You are going to give me an attack of nerves."*

*"I declare, Bess, I do not know where in the world you got this
predisposition to nervous attack. I've always been too busy for
nerves," Minnie grumbles.*

*"Too busy minding other people's businesses," Adelaide har-
rumphs. "Time flies. I must go and administer Colonel Ashcraft's
afternoon lubricant."*

*"But I have not heard the latest news of Mrs. Astor!" Bess wails
as Adelaide marches down the steps, voluminous skirts billowing.*

*Bess pouts. Mama has run off Mrs. Ashcraft before Bess even
got a word in edgewise about a clever notion simmering in her mind.
Adelaide is planning a trip to London, has hinted that she may possibly be invited to take tea with the Queen. Many members of the
English nobility are feeling hard times. Didn't the Vanderbilt girl's
daddy buy her an earl, or was it a duke? Mr. Vanderbilt has more
money than Sam, but Lydia is prettier than the Vanderbilt girl. Mrs.
Ashcraft can arrange it! A titled husband for Lydia! Bess dreamily
pictures herself as the dowager aunt, rocking away her golden years
on the porch of Lydia's castle.*

***

Driven from the shelter of his den by the demons of writer's
block dancing in his brain, Wyatt turned his face to the cold morning air spitting a drizzle of rain and tried to clear the cobwebs befud-
dling his thoughts.

All the years wasted delivering drivel to a public made up of
idiots too willing to pay for it felt like a bag of rocks on his back.
With his life running out, was it too late to reach back to the past
and reclaim his early talent? It didn't bear considering.

A bright red bird paused in futile pecking at the frozen ground
and cocked a curious eye as the large man stumbled through the
woods, muttering under his breath. His head was pounding. He
stopped in his tracks, pulled his grandfather's monogrammed silver
flask from his coat pocket, and took a healthy slug of the hair of the

dog that had bitten him multiple times over the course of a sleepless night.

He hunkered down in the heavy overcoat as the bitter air bruised his bones, well aware that it would not advance his cause to appear on their doorstep with Nick's car still in the driveway.

He did not need at that point in his life the impediment of a jealous husband when he had not the least romantic interest in the wife.

He had left home without answering the telephone stubbornly ringing. Caller ID warned him not to answer. Ellen. Carrie's mother-in-law had casually commented over after dinner coffee that she knew that he would enjoy being the first professional to have a read of her manuscript, twelve hundred pages and growing. He shuddered. Why did half the world have to think that they had something worth saying on paper? Why did all of his own more inspired pages remain so stubbornly blank?

He supposed that Carrie had shared his phone number. Ironic that directory assistance would have informed Ellen, or anyone else who inquired, that he was "unpublished."

He had ripped the cord from the wall and thrown the telephone across the room for good measure. Hatton Preston, the only person with whom he had the slightest desire to converse, was no longer a part of this world and highly unlikely to be placing any phone calls.

As Nick's car turned down the driveway, Wyatt strode off in the direction of the house.

He accepted Carrie's offer of a cup of coffee in hopes of clearing his head enough to think of logical places they had yet to search.

Caffeine would never do the trick. Wyatt made himself at home, going to the dining room and removing from the sideboard a dusty decanter of what he hoped was brandy. The amber liquid had probably been aging there since Hatton died in the 1930s. He added a shot to his coffee cup.

"I have not done one thing relating to Christmas," Carrie mumbled, running a hand through her sleep mussed hair. "The girls will be home from school in just a few days, and I haven't purchased the first present. Since I moved into this house it's like I've lost all track of time. Nick wants to carry on all of our old Christmas traditions, and for some reason I just can't function as if business is usual. I'm not sure that Nick will ever adjust to living here." She bit her lip.

"Perhaps having your children home for the holidays will help," Wyatt offered. He felt antsy, uninterested in making small talk when the attic was now accessible.

"I wish that were true. Sometimes I feel like I live here all alone, with the girls off at school and Nick working night and day. Despite being married for more than half of our lives, I'm not sure that Nicky and I even know each other anymore."

He considered what a boring proposition it must be to have spent more than half of one's life with the same person.

She seemed to read his mind. "Have you ever been married, Wyatt?"

He laughed, put a match to his pipe. "For some years I made rather a bad habit of it. Marriage is the one addiction I've finally successfully broken. Perhaps I finally just ran the gamut."

"Meaning?"

"Ran through all the motivations for marriage." He began ticking off on his fingers. "I married first for money, for the freedom to pursue my art without the burden of having to make a living. Meredith was one of those eastern establishment horse nut types. When I caught her in the hayloft with a female groom, she was only too happy to buy my silence. My good fortune that years ago people still kept that sort of thing in the closet."

"You blackmailed your own wife?"

"You might say so. Number two," he continued. "Shelley, a shallow blonde jogging on the Hollywood fast track. I had made money enough on my own by then to buy a bride based on looks alone. Shelley was most in love with herself, and I was not sorry to see her go. I found fondling silicone breasts a turn off."

"A third time that was not the charm. Alicia, initially enjoyed drinking with me, but, like my first wife, left me for another woman. Betty Ford. During her month in the clinic she found religion and wisely gave up on me, knowing that I had no interest in either a cure or a creed."

"No children?"

"A few abortions, one miscarriage. I was fortunate in that regard."

Carrie tried to tell herself that at least he was honest. "Aren't you ever lonely?"

"Good heavens, no. I have my work to keep me warm."

Carrie was silent for a long, thoughtful minute, trying to picture her life incomplete without Nick or the girls.

"Don't look so stricken, Carrie. Not all of us were meant to be one half of a tidy, mundane, middle class marriage."

So that was how Wyatt, so worldly wise, summed up the Lancasters. She spoke in her own defense. "For some of us, that's more than enough."

It occurred to him that if he were not so preoccupied with finishing his play he might make time to analyze and fictionalize Carrie, a faithful little wife leading a boring life. He'd lay odds that she'd never known intimately any man but one. No nonsense Nick was probably as boring in bed as he was at the dinner table. If she were a character in one of his plays, he would put a man with more of a sense of adventure in her life.

Despite himself, a writer's innate imagination took hold. "I have a mental picture," he responded. "Traditional southern wedding with a guest list of a thousand. Champagne fountain flowing at the country club reception. Your mother adjusting a train as long as a football field, a proud papa wistfully kissing you goodbye at the altar. I'll wager that you and Nick left the church in a horse drawn carriage covered with roses."

Carrie looked down and twisted her wedding band. "That was the way it would have been according to Mother's carefully plotted plan for my life. When Nick and I met, he was rebounding from the breakup of a serious long term relationship, and we had only had a couple of dates when one night we drank too much and got carried away. One step out of line that determined the whole course of the rest of my life. Can you in your wildest dreams imagine what it was like for me to be not yet twenty years old and pregnant with twins by someone I hardly knew, someone who was still in love with someone else? I was a sophomore in college and scared witless. Nick had just started medical school. It must have been so hard for him to have to tell his girlfriend, just after they had gotten back together, that he was going to do the right thing and marry me. I cannot tell you what it was like to have to face my formidable mother and tell her that there was not going to be a big debutante ball, or an even bigger wedding to follow, that her only child had eloped and given all the wagging tongues in this town the juiciest piece of gossip on which they had ever had a chance to chew."

Wyatt slapped his knee and laughed loudly. "Knowing your mother, even as slightly as I can claim to, I don't think I could imagine anything much worse than the beloved only child bringing shame on the family name."

He looked up from adding a second splash of surprisingly potent brandy to his empty cup to see tiny chips of pain glistening like broken glass in her eyes.

"It was absolutely the worst thing that had ever happened in our family, Wyatt. Well, I suppose not the worst. Certainly, not the worst. I'm not allowed to talk about the worst."

"Carrie, I don't think that I'm following your train of thought."

"I wasn't always an only child."

To Wyatt's consternation, she ran from the room and up the stairs.

Following her, he paused for a moment outside of her closed bedroom door, hearing her sobs, resisting the urge to ask their reason by reminding himself that the sand in the hourglass of his life was down to grains.

Whatever was eating Carrie emotionally had nothing to do with him. As soon as he had the manuscript in hand, and words on blank pages, he would change his phone number and erase the Lancasters and their assorted bits of extended family from his life all together. He pushed open the door to the attic stairs and started up to resume the search for Hatton Preston.

Relegated to the porch, Willard Preston paces the floor.

A scream reverberates. Willard wonders that his wife, after an entire day of ceaseless screeching, has the energy remaining to emit a moan. Leave it to Isabel to make complicated something as simple as giving birth.

Minnie stomps out of the house, banging her cane with every step. "Willard! Make yourself useful. This has gone on long enough. Go for the doctor."

"But, Mrs. Hatton, you know how strongly Miss Bess feels about male intervention in female endeavors."

Minnie narrows her eyes and shakes her cane. "My daughter was born an old fool. Do as I say, and be quick about it before Bess's obsession with modesty costs us the both of them."

Willard pedals off down the street on his bicycle, and Minnie takes to her rocker.

Upstairs, Violet sponges Isabel's face. Adelaide Ashcraft, nor-

mally firmly in command of any situation, wrings her pudgy hands.

"Auntie is here," Bess soothes. She is proud of keeping her composure. Isabel is, after all, the closest thing she will ever have to a daughter of her own. She takes Isabel's hand and, unable to share any personal child delivery war stories of her own, as Adelaide has so unselfishly done, decides to try instead the succor of religion. "Remember, Isabel, dear, that the scriptures tell us, 'in pain thou shalt bear children.' You are going about this just as the Good Book intended and would not wish it any other way."

Isabel answers with another ear shattering scream, and Adelaide decides to join Minnie on the porch before her hearing is permanently impaired.

* * *

"Mr. Willard, the doctor is wanting to see you upstairs." Violet, eyes brimming, clamps her hands on the porch rail, struggling with emotions. She faults herself for not overriding Bess and demanding that a doctor be called sooner. Doing the right thing is more the right thing than remaining in your place.

Willard, entering the bedroom, feels a wave of revulsion. His head spinning, he turns away from the sight of his wife and the dead infant on the bed.

One fleeting glance tells him that the child was female. But an hour before envisioning himself proudly holding his son in his arms, he stands empty handed as thoughts foam and froth in his mind. He is forever free of the burden of Isabel, and Lydia will have to be summoned home for her sister's funeral. His spirits soar.

"Willard, your grief is understandable. Shall I summon Violet with the smelling salts?" The doctor grimaces as he pulls tight the last black thread and ties it off.

"I am man enough to face the truth without medication," Willard answers as he stares at the bed in morbid fascination. Isabel lies splayed naked against blood splashed bed sheets. Two large angry slashes held closed by sutures criss cross on the mound of belly.

Willard gasps, grasps the bed post for support. Surely his eyes must be deceiving him. A slight rise and fall of her breasts. She is breathing. "Not dead," he whispers.

"Not yet, thank heaven, though we must worry for some days to come about the danger of infection," the doctor mutters. "I'm truly

sorry, Willard. I know that every couple desires to have children. I wish that the outcome had been otherwise, but, no doubt due to the spinal deformity, the female organs were in a stunted condition. It was a miracle that she carried the child full term."

"There will be other children in the future," Willard sighs, against his will studying the lifeless infant.

"After today, an impossibility. You must believe, dear man, that I had your future well being and happiness, as well as your wife's survival, to consider in performing the surgical removal rendering your wife now irrevocably barren. This child came near enough to killing her. You must take comfort that her future inability to conceive spares you as a husband from what I must otherwise have ordered, a marital life of absolute abstinence."

The full implications of the doctor's words sink like a stone in Willard's heart. Still to be burdened with Isabel. Subject to the snickers and sneers of other men, who will attribute his childless status to some sort of inadequacy of virility. A small bubble escapes Isabel's lips as she hovers on the edge of consciousness. Willard twists his hands in a rage of hopelessness. He would like to strangle her dead.

"Be prepared to summon an abundance of patience during what will be a long and difficult recovery," the doctor cautions, squeezing Willard's shoulder with a bloodstained hand. "While she is now prematurely deprived of the bloom of youth and will likely soon physically appear twice her true age, women who early cease the monthly fits of nervous collapse also on an average live twice as long as women who go through life's processes naturally."

"Absent infection appearing, you have every hope of having Mrs. Preston at your side for a very long life to come."

Chapter Ten

Lying in bed, stroking the cat, determined to wait up until Nick came home, however late the hour, Carrie felt a lately latent physical longing for her husband.

She tried to ignore the sound of Dooley, relegated downstairs in favor of the cat, barking as if he were an abandoned puppy. Nick didn't know about the cat and was not going to be happy to find a purring ball of yellow fur in his bed and his dog in the kitchen.

Thumbing her nose at creating a situation that would make Nick angry was a foreign feeling. Nick was so even tempered. Carrie told herself that she needed to engineer something to cause a confrontation, arouse enough emotion to get the unspoken out in the open.

She tried to shut the image out of her mind, but it remained, as it had for months, a freeze framed view. Just an otherwise ordinary day, on her way to run an errand, glancing in a restaurant window. The Nick she thought she knew so well sitting across the table from the old first love from whom she had stolen him, holding hands across the table, so engrossed in each other that their faces were almost touching.

The idea of Nick being unfaithful had never entered her mind before that moment. It suddenly made perfect sense to her why he had not been excited about the baby. It hit her like a blow. This time an unplanned pregnancy might not hold him.

She had never mentioned it to him. It was just a few days later that her world came crashing down entirely. Looking back, she was convinced that the baby she carried died that same afternoon.

How long could she live with hurt and mistrust consuming her before she went completely crazy? Wandering through the house by day, examining the remnants of someone else's life as an avoidance tactic, was sure to eventually lose its fascination.

She could not deal with the prospect of losing Nick another day, another night. She had to get it out in the open. It was past time to talk about it.

The phone rang. Mumbled apologies. Another emergency. Pileup on the interstate with multiple victims. Working very late again. Maybe all night again. Don't wait up. Catch a nap in the doctor's lounge.

With only the cat for comfort, Carrie turned out the light and cried herself to sleep.

Bundled in furs, the two young women huddle close to each other in conspiratorial conversation in the back seat of the chauffeur driven limousine. From a passing sleigh, gliding over the snow covered streets of Boston, bells tinkle. Christmas is just around the corner, and they are in high spirits.

"Oh, Lydia, he's going to give you a ring for Christmas. I just know it! The entire family will travel south in our private railroad carriage for a splendid summer wedding after which you will be not only my brother's wife but my very own special sister." Candace Cunningham squeezes Lydia McShan's kid gloved hand.

Lydia's laughter rivals the sleigh bells in spontaneity. "Please, Candace, you are overmuch inclined to romantic fantasy! Simply because your brother has requested the favor of my company for three consecutive Sunday evenings does not mean that he desires to marry me."

Lydia knows that she is being overly modest. She has turned down more than a dozen proposals of marriage, all from suitable suitors. She finds amusing her aunt's letters imploring her to save her hand for the attentions of a member of the British aristocracy sure to materialize in the summer upcoming. Lydia and her closest friend Candace plan a postgraduate grand tour of the Continent under the chaperonage of Candace's mother, a Boston Brahmin matron of impeccable social stature, a lady whom Lydia has written Bess is the New England equivalent of Adelaide Ashcraft.

Two years widowed, Mrs. Warren Conrad Cunningham, III has recently turned her prodigious energies from sponsoring society soirees to confronting social ills. She has traveled to Chicago to tour Jane Addams' Hull House and is most recently returned from Georgia, where she inspected the cotton mills. Having had an unpleasantly eye opening experience in the South, she is on the threshold of a crusade for the passage of child labor reform legislation that will earn her a mention in a few of the future's more esoteric history books. While her children find their mother's fascination with the less privileged classes beneath her dignity, if not amusing, Lydia finds the wealthy matron's change of life direction fascinating.

Mrs. Cunningham has enlisted Lydia and Candace as marchers in a parade in support of women's suffrage. Lydia admires Mrs. Cunningham, an intelligent and well educated woman unafraid to think and speak for herself.

She has questioned Lydia regarding the extent of the commitment of southern women to the cause of suffrage. Lydia has written in inquiry to Isabel, who replied that as Willard does not allow her access to the newspaper, she is ignorant entirely of the matter. Isabel adds that should the gentlemen of the Congress grant women the privilege of the ballot, Willard would never countenance her personally casting a vote.

Poor Izzy, sighs Lydia. Faced with spending the rest of her life under that insipid Willard's thumb. At least Isabel, after more than a year of the silence of unanswered letters, is once again in communication with her younger sister. Isabel took the loss of the baby daughter so very hard, for an entire six months afterwards refusing to leave the confines of her bedroom.

Minnie writes that Isabel and Willard have moved, and high time they did so, out of the McShan household and into a home of their own where they are insistent on their privacy, not very sociable. Bess writes too, hinting in modestly circuitous language that she suspects that the pair is about the business of making another baby, but no announcement to the success of that effort has been forthcoming.

Willard and Isabel's attempts at conception are not a topic for polite conversation, even within the bosom of the family.

Lydia blushes, imagining Isabel and Willard in an act of marital union. She finds Willard, prone to both sour breath and an offensive body odor, physically repulsive. Less sheltered that her sister, possessing a northern education, she is aware of the most basic facts of life. She herself could never engage in such an act with less than a handsome man.

Choosing to spend her summer holidays under the sponsorship of the Cunningham clan, she has become in her three and a half years away from her family a thoroughly modern woman. Her Alabama roots seem dull and provincial. She is in no hurry to return to Birmingham.

Lydia ponders consenting to become Mrs. Warren Conrad Cunningham, IV. Rad Cunningham is handsome, wealthy, Harvard educated, world traveled and sophisticated. She imagines herself alighting from a train in Birmingham with her fiance on her arm. It will be the talk of the town. She giggles, thinking of Willard Preston describing himself on the first evening they met him as a man on the upward move, of Father gifting him with a large block of company stock on the day he married Isabel, as if paying him for a favor performed.

Rad Cunningham will come into a fortune ten times that of Sam McShan. Rad Cunningham has no need for upward mobility. He has been from birth a member of society's uppermost echelon. He will father beautiful children.

Candace interrupts her friend's imaginings. "I have instructed the butler to seat you on Rad's right. While you are as beautiful as the Venus de Milo from any angle, I think your left is your more entrancing profile. Oh, dearest, darling Lydia, I just know that Rad is going to ask you if he might petition your father for your hand!"

Lydia is growing bored with choosing who will have the honor of her hand for an evening's entertainment. She has no grand plan for her life after May's graduation and a summer of travel. Despite a more than decent higher education, marriage and motherhood represent her only future options. Perhaps it is time. Rad Cunningham will do as well as any of the others. This evening she will drop a subtle hint that she is ready to make a commitment. A ring for Christmas, an evening wedding in the early summer, a tour of the Greek Isles as honeymoon. Perhaps when next Christmas comes she will be ensconced as mistress of a Beacon Hill mansion, eagerly anticipating the arrival of a child of her own.

Lydia does some mental maneuvering, considering the evening upcoming. "Candace, are others invited for dinner?"

"It's just too foolish for words! Mother is including one of her pet Socialists who came today on the train from New York to hear of her findings in the South." Candace sighs heavily. "Mother and her radical causes! Poor Papa must be turning in his grave. No matter. As your own mother is departed, planning your wedding to Rad will require great involvement by our matriarch. She will have no time for foreign Socialists representing muckraker magazines. Such a bother that he must join us for dinner! Pay him no mind at all and turn instead the full force and power of your southern charm on my brother."

"Perhaps I shall enter into just enough of a flirtatious tête-à-tête with this radical reporter to jealously inflame your handsome sib-

ling," Lydia, plans falling nicely into place, says with a satisfied smile. Her mind is already mulling over names for her children.

"Oh, Lydia, how you prattle! Mother mentioned that this Livinsky, whom she finds fascinating, is not only a Russian born Socialist but a Jew to boot. I hardly think Rad would find himself turning green with jealous emotion were you to flick your eyelashes in the man's direction!"

"Whisper in Rad's ear that I am very partial to emeralds."

Candace throws her arms around her friend. "Oh, Lydia, what a perfect and enviable future lies in store for you! You are poised to embark on life's grandest adventure!"

"I feel the sudden sensation, Candace, that this may be the most momentous evening of my life, indeed the very beginning of the rest and the best of my life."

***

Wyatt Wallace was long accustomed to having minions to handle mundane transactions. His staff of lackeys left behind in California, in Birmingham he was alone and on his own.

He had no desire to mingle with the southern society of the grandchildren of his grandmother's bridge group. The dinner he had eaten at Carrie's was the only meal he had taken in Birmingham other than alone, a situation exactly the way he wanted things. He rarely left his home except to attend to matters of vital importance.

Venturing out to the liquor store, when midmorning found his study as dry as the parlor of a Baptist church, qualified as such an occurrence.

"Wyatt! What a treat to see you again so soon! Be a gentleman and help lighten my load."

He groaned. Seeing no other option, he took two shopping bags bulging with brightly wrapped packages from the arms of Ellen Lancaster. The little brown and white terrier on a leash at her feet snapped his teeth and shot Wyatt a menacing look.

"Zippy! Mind your manners! Mr. Wallace is our friend," Ellen reprimanded the little dog as he lunged in the direction of Wyatt's ankle. On her lapel the red nose of the cheerful reindeer blinked on and off, on and off, causing Wyatt to shake his head in hung over commiseration. Rudolph at least looked as if he still had a buzz on.

Ellen breathed an exaggerated sigh of relief as he slammed the trunk. "Thank goodness! The last name is crossed off the list. I am officially ready. Bring on Christmas! For your help, I insist on buying you a cup of coffee."

Argument with Ellen was useless. Her red mittened hand on his arm felt like a vise grip.

Settled at one of the marble topped tables in the front of the bookstore, Wyatt, thinking longingly of the just purchased bottle of Scotch on the seat of his car, reluctantly touched his cup of cappuccino to Ellen's as she cheered the season.

Occupying the third seat at the table, Zippy furiously attacked a blueberry scone. Ellen cheerfully dismissed the counter help's protests about health department regulations. "Zippy is functioning as my book editor," she explained to Wyatt. "I read every word aloud to him, and he has an uncanny way of barking at the best parts."

"Don't you just love a cold, grey day?" Ellen enthused as Zippy washed down the scone by furiously lapping coffee from a saucer. "The kind of day that makes you want to go home, and settle in, and just write and write. I bought a new state of the art computer as my Christmas present to myself. I am churning out words like nobody's business."

Wyatt mentally debated the most effective means for mercifully ending a conversation he hadn't time for. Ellen apparently had all the time in the world to waste creating a useless over abundance of pages doomed to rest unread on the floor of some disinterested editor's office.

"What sort of computer do you use, Wyatt?"

"Actually, Ellen, I use my father's old manual typewriter. I find it keeps me more, shall we say, economical with words."

Despite the injunction against smoking posted just below the "no pets" sign in the window, he took pipe and pouch of tobacco from his coat pocket and lit up. The kid behind the counter groaned, unsure whether to search for an ashtray or offer a dog a refill on coffee.

"I would be so honored to have you give my book a quick once over," Ellen said.

He neatly sidestepped the issue by modifying the subject. "Speaking of books, Ellen, perhaps you could select a Christmas gift for me to give Carrie, who has been most gracious in helping me with some vital research on Hatton Preston." He gave himself a point for ingenuity in taking a giant step in the direction of escaping her, having had, until that very second, not the first thought of giving anyone anything.

Ellen looked thoughtful. "You know, Wyatt, Jack and I have always considered Carrie more than simply a daughter-in-law. Carrie has been like a blessing in our lives. She's one of those people you just can't help but love."

"An expression right out of my grandmother's mouth," Wyatt mused, making a mental note of it. "Southern colloquialisms will be essential to the dialogue in my play. I hope that New York audiences will be able to process people who always seem to be 'fixin' to go or to do something."

At last an idea! He felt like fleeing.

"Well, having spent my entire life here, I don't suppose I notice distinctly southern speech unless someone really lays it on thick, like Mallory, always babbling on about her good buddy 'the guvna' and how they do things in 'Mungumry.'" Ellen made a face above her coffee cup. Zippy yapped in apparent agreement.

"Ah, the redoubtable Mrs. Hudson, a southern grande dame if ever there was one."

"Now, don't get me wrong, Wyatt, there's more to Mallory than meets the eye. Despite those airs she wears like an extra fur coat, she'd do anything for you. And her husband David, why, David Hudson was just the salt of the earth. In the year since he died, we have surely missed him, especially Carrie. She was a daddy's girl through and through, just like Jamie was always so much his mother's son. Such a tragic accident."

"Ellen, I am very confused. Carrie's father died in an accident? I could have sworn she said he had a heart attack. She acted uncomfortable with the subject, in fact made the oddest comment the other day, that she wasn't 'allowed' to talk about certain things, as if she were a five year old home from kindergarten in possession of a dirty word."

"If you ask me, which Mallory would never do, some good heart to heart talk with Carrie would be of a darn sight more benefit than a gift certificate for a year with a psychiatrist. To answer your question, David Hudson had a sudden massive coronary. The accident to which I referred involved Jamie, Carrie's older brother. He died at nineteen. Mallory has a very firm rule that they do not talk about

Jamie. I've tried to broach the subject with Carrie any number of times, and at the mention of his name she gets a look on her face like Peter Rabbit facing Mr. MacGregor."

"What happened?"

"It was Thanksgiving weekend of his freshman year at Princeton. He and his father had just come in from hunting. The dead deer was still strapped to the top of the car, dripping blood in the driveway. In a scene that repeats itself too often on southern autumn Saturdays, he was cleaning a gun that he thought was empty. One of the reasons, I don't mind telling you, that I am a strong advocate of gun control as well as a regular contributor to animal rights groups. Despite my own husband's and son's passions for murdering ducks, I abhor killing innocent wildlife and calling it recreation."

"Poor little Carrie absolutely adored him. Jamie Hudson was life in capital letters, the best looking kid I've ever seen, a talented athlete, and brilliant to boot."

"Must have been devastating to the Hudsons."

"I'll never forget the way they looked at that funeral. Mallory was absolutely grim in her self-control. Of course, according to her upbringing, it would have been in as poor taste to show grief as it would have been to engage in a public display of affection." Ellen's expression made obvious her lack of understanding of the methods by which Mallory Hudson operated. "David aged ten years overnight. He had always been such a cheerful, warm, outgoing man, and he had on his face that day a look of haunted desperation that he wore until he died. Of course the whole town turned out for the service, everyone but Carrie. Mallory said that her mother didn't approve of children attending funerals. I've often wondered if they didn't deny her the comfort of any sort of closure at all. I think there are a lot of things in that family left hanging, primarily because of Mallory's refusal to discuss them."

"After Jamie died, they bailed out and ran away to Europe for three years. Do you know that when David died last year, and Mallory had him cremated and slapped his ashes as quickly as she could in the church columbarium, Carrie let it slip that she's never even visited Jamie's grave?"

"It's almost as though in some back part of Carrie's mind Jamie is just away on an extended vacation. Maybe that's partly why I was so worried about Carrie last summer. We were all distressed when she lost the baby, but there was something excessive about her grief. I couldn't help but wonder if Carrie's falling completely to pieces wasn't somehow a long delayed reaction to losing Jamie that she's been smothering all these years."

"Carrie lost a baby? Recently?"

"She hasn't told you?" Ellen frowned. Hadn't Carrie claimed to have spent every day of the past few weeks with this man?

"Hasn't said the first word."

"It took all of us by surprise, most of all Nicky, I don't mind telling you, Carrie getting pregnant at her age, just after the girls went off to college. Carrie was so happy she was just beside herself. Mallory and Nicky, on the other hand, tried to outdo each other to see who could throw the worst fit over the situation. Mallory went on and on and on about how 'ladies' don't bear children after forty. You'd have thought that Mallory subscribed to that old wives tale that big babies or twins mean you enjoyed the sex too much."

Wyatt choked on his coffee. Ellen slapped him on the back and went right on talking.

"I'm ashamed to say that my son pouted like a child from the day she told him the good news. She was almost six months pregnant when the baby died. She must have been aware for some time that it was no longer moving. In fact, the night they took the baby, Nick said that she had seemed depressed for several days and that he had been unable to guess the cause of her blue mood. She was deathly ill with infection. We almost lost her." She shuddered.

"Don't go on if it makes you uncomfortable, Ellen." He needed to go, and the conversation was threatening to stretch to the length of the woman's novel.

"Wyatt, Carrie has obviously come to care about you a great deal in a short time. She's spent the months since she lost the baby suffering from a terrible bout with the blues, and I think a new best friend is what she most needs in her life right now."

Just what I least need in mine, he groaned to himself.

"None of us has been able to make Mallory see the forest for the trees that Carrie needed professional help," Ellen continued. "No shame in that after the last year of her life. Mallory Hudson, give me strength! Babbling on about her ancestors and how there has never been a nut in the bunch. Doesn't take a psychologist or a genealogist to tell you that there's no self respecting southern family without at least one fruitcake hidden in the pantry."

Wyatt made an obvious consultation of his father's pocket watch. His own days dwindling, he had neither time for nor interest in Carrie Lancaster's problems, with the past, the present, or the future.

Ellen had provided some excellent fodder for dialogue. He had a play to write.

Chapter Eleven

The car's horn honked the opening notes of "Jolly Old St. Nicholas" from the driveway.

Carrie, sitting in the attic surrounded by the contents of a just emptied trunk, welcomed the intrusion.

The cat dove for cover as Zippy took the attic stairs two at a time and hurled himself at Carrie like a small furry missile.

"My goodness, Carrie, you must be freezing." Ellen rubbed her hands up and down her arms. Zippy raced in circles, barking.

"That steam boiler is so outmoded that we can't even find anyone to work on it. We need a whole new heating system. Nick says this old house is going to land us in the poor house."

"Don't pay him any mind. Nick was born tight with a dollar, a genetic defect inherited from his father. Carrie, you've always had such a flair for decorating. Put your special stamp on this house, and *Southern Accents* will have you on the cover."

Carrie sighed. "I've wasted the whole morning on a trunk which should have been put on the trash heap without opening."

"Let's see what you've found. Calm down, Zippy! Too much coffee I expect. He refuses to settle for decaf."

"It's really odd, Ellen. Though he died before she built this house, you would think that Isabel Preston packed up her husband and brought him with her."

Ellen considered the items ringing Carrie on the floor. Rotted suits and shirts, a chipped shaving mug with a Masonic emblem, a framed diploma from the University of Pennsylvania law school, a set of yellowed dentures. The mundane material leavings of a man dead for three quarters of a century.

She understood Carrie's reluctance to empty the house in one fell swoop. Although she loved poking through the slightly seedy antique shops that bought and sold the entire contents of houses, it always saddened her to see family photograph albums, tarnished trophies, bent silver baby cups, former symbols of family pride for sale for small change.

"Now isn't this interesting," Carrie muttered as she rooted through the trunk. "Cardboard pictures of half naked women."

"They're stereopticon slides." Ellen held the sheets up to the thin light struggling through the dormer windows. "In a special viewer they produced a 3-D image. Some antique dealer would probably buy these."

"Any antique pornography dealers in the Yellow Pages?"

"Not as far fetched as you might think," Ellen responded. "I'm doing hours of research on the Victorian period. They had lots of interesting outlets for their sexual repression."

"And over the counter cures for what they caught when they expressed it?" Carrie passed Ellen a packet of medicinal powder, the label guaranteeing to "alleviate the symptoms of impotency and other abominable afflictions of the masculine glands."

"Pass me those books, Carrie. Used book dealers pay ridiculous amounts for old books in whatever condition."

Carrie chose a book at random. "Get a load of this one, Ellen. *Woman: Her Sex and Love Life*, subtitled 'How to hold the love of a man, how to preserve sexual attraction, how to remain young beyond the allotted age.' Copyrighted 1902."

Tips she could use in her own life?

Only one item, a sheet of stained paper, remained in the trunk, caught in a crack in the lining. Carrie gently worked it free.

"This proves my point, Ellen. I can't just take a trunk load of old unsorted memorabilia down to some antique dealer and risk making some stranger privy to the family secrets."

"I don't think Isabel would want this sort of thing getting out," Carrie, clutching the paper to her chest, continued. "It's Willard Preston's membership certificate in the Ku Klux Klan."

"Unfortunately, many socially acceptable southern men belonged those days, Carrie. It's only fair to judge people in the context of the times in which they lived."

"More and more, every day, I feel that this is my family, Ellen. I think the house trusts me, and the skeletons in the closets are starting to dance."

Ellen felt a knot in her stomach. Distantly related to her husband though the Prestons might be, the people who had lived in this house, and whatever their secrets might have been, held no relevance to the present.

***

The late afternoon shadows lengthened. Wyatt had not

appeared.   Carrie pulled a crocheted afghan around her and stretched out on the living room sofa with the treatise on how to hold the love of a man. People rarely divorced in those days. Happy or not, they stuck it out. Was it just a matter of time until Nick announced that he was packing his bags, going back to the woman who had owned his heart in the first place?

The book was a compilation of essays written in outmoded, obtuse language. Bored and brooding, she dozed off.

"Twenty five thousand on strike in the mills of Fall River! A long and bitter work stoppage is predicted. Cannot these fools comprehend who butters their bread?" Willard mutters aloud to himself from behind the newspaper.

In recognition of the passing of a milestone thirtieth birthday, Sam has rewarded Willard with a generous boost in salary. Willard and Isabel have at last been able to acquire a home of their own, a two story boxy white Craftsman just one block short of the ultra swank, mansion lined Highland Avenue. Willard and Isabel have, in their minds at least, at a relatively early age almost arrived.

Other than being childless, a fact as never discussed by the family as if it is a sad situation affecting strangers, Willard Preston's life plan is proceeding at a tidy pace along the schedule he has set. He has been accepted for membership in the Country Club of Birmingham and has taken up golf. He follows a rigid regimen of exercise and diet, and, thanks to Isabel, prides himself on going to work each morning and to bed each evening at peace in a system purged of digestive impurities. His hair has thinned to dark ribbons laid across an egg pale scalp, but, unlike most of his contemporaries, he wears only the merest hint of a middle aged roll around his waistband.

Isabel flicks a feather duster over Willard's wing tip shoes, wrinkles her nose and comments, "My, doesn't that ham smell divine! Whatever can be Violet's secret ingredient for basting?"

In the kitchen, Violet, confident that what Isabel doesn't know can't hurt her, adds to the ham another little shot of the bourbon whiskey that she keeps tucked away in the far recesses of a kitchen cupboard. Violet is abstemious, but Minnie, finding visits to her granddaughter tiresome, feels the need for a little calming nip on occasion.

"Isabel, your manic dusting is driving me to distraction!" Willard fumes as he turns to a final page of the day's news. "Strikes break-

ing out everywhere like pox on a milkmaid! In my opinion, our current problems would have been prevented if we had simply closed our borders years ago. I read here that northern European steamship companies have cut their steerage rates to $10 per head. Just clearing the way for more immigrant riff raff to flood in and further complicate the labor force."

"I do apologize, Mr. Preston. I just so badly want everything to be perfect. Four long years." Isabel sighs. "I expect she will have become smart and sophisticated. We will seem to her provincial by comparison."

"We have all changed, Isabel, as has the world around us. Why, think of how our city has grown, our industries expanded. She will marvel at our stately palaces of commerce, the elegant new neighborhoods and shopping emporiums. Perhaps she can persuade your father to relocate. That old neighborhood is decaying, so few of the really fine old families remaining on the north side of the city. Your father and his neighbor Mrs. Ashcraft are the only prominent early settlers remaining on that street."

"Yes, Father commented at the lovely funeral with full Confederate honors Mrs. Ashcraft put on at the Colonel's passing that he has more contemporaries lying beneath the sod of Oak Hill Cemetery than he has strolling the streets. My father would never give up the house in which Mother's memory is so firmly present. Father is set in his ways and undesirous of any change in his situation," Isabel replies as she looks around the room with pride, the matched sets of books with their imitation gold stamped spines, fringe shaded reading lamps.

She has artfully arranged a display of current magazines, the Ladies Home Journal, the Saturday Evening Post, and others exemplifying their good taste, on the library table behind the sofa along with a copy of Mrs. Wharton's recently published The House of Mirth, prominently book marked farther along in its pages than Isabel, who is a slow reader, has progressed. She is anxious for Mr. Cunningham's favorable impressions.

"Mr. Preston, I hope you do not mind that I have extended a gracious invitation to Mrs. Ashcraft to join us at the luncheon table. It was Father's idea actually, and her presence will make our number even. I know you sometimes find her company tedious, but she must be lonely now that her brave Colonel has gone to his reward and her daughter Bitsy married."

"She is a mendacious gossip and an unmitigated bore, grown even more so now that she has added women's suffrage to her crusade for temperance, outdone only by your aunt and grandmother in prattling on about Confederate nonsense. Women are no more capable of choosing our elected officials than foreigners and coloreds." He chuckles, and Isabel gives him a questioning look. "Just an amusing thought, my dear. The very idea of you entering a ballot booth! You would get in such a dither that you would forget for whom I told you to vote. The South is indeed rising again but not in any way that those hide bound to the past ladies would intend or comprehend."

Isabel leans on her broom and purses her lips. "Indeed, Mr. Preston, perhaps Lydia and her husband will have a score of sons, at least a few of whom can be persuaded to someday take up your worthy reins in the world of commerce and industry."

"Your barrenness is a fact of which I do not need reminding," he snaps. "In light of your physical deformity, which I could have had, on taking your hand, no inkling of an idea extended to the private parts of your anatomy, you are extremely lucky to be alive and functioning."

"I am an old woman at the age of twenty four," Isabel sobs into the feather duster. "And Lydia just on the brink of life and in love. They will probably have twelve angelic daughters. Why, why, why has life always been so overly kind to her while cursing me?" She slumps to the chair in a spasm of weeping.

I should like to throttle that surgeon, Willard thinks to himself. Promising me that one very pleasant result produced by the procedure would be the alleviation of nervous fits. She is if possible even more than before as jumpy as a June bug.

Images of Lydia swim before his eyes as he attempts to focus on the newspaper. Over the sickly sweet aroma of the drunken ham drifts a bittersweet remembrance of the lilac cologne. He throws the newspaper to the floor in frustration.

Isabel, forbidden to peruse the pages, wipes her eyes, sniffles into a handkerchief, and retrieves the discarded paper, leaving her husband to brood in solitude. The silences between them have begun to grow noisy.

A short skip across town, Bess hums as she rummages through her jewelry collection, settling on a brooch, jet stones interwoven with the flaxen strands that she tenderly snipped from her dear

dead father's head as he lay in somber state in the worn grey uni-
form of Confederate general. How warlike he looked in waxen faced
slumber!

"Bess! Bess! Get to moving. Lydia's train is due."

"We've plenty of time, Mama," Bess calls back, taking a final
admiring glance in the mirror. Surely Lydia's young man will com-
ment on the intricacy of her handiwork, nicely raising opportunity to
regale him with tales of her father's valiancy in the service of the
noble Forrest. Although Lydia's intended hails from northern
climes, perhaps, like Isabel's most estimable Willard, he can be
brought around to see the folly of his fathers. Why, though trans-
planted from the same soil that spawned Gettysburg, Willard has
through osmosis become as southern as a plate of grits and
greens. If only there existed a society for the Sons-in-Laws of
Confederate Veterans!

How masterfully Willard authorizes every aspect of Isabel's life,
not burdening his weaker half with the onus of making any decision
whatsoever!

Bess takes comfort that Lydia, always too headstrong by half,
will soon likewise reside under the aegis of a husband's masculine
direction. Mrs. Ashcraft says that her society sources in the East
assure her that the Cunningham name is ancient and honored in
the city of Boston. Recent communication with Lydia has been
strangely strained. A few brief postings that she is well and happy,
no firm details of her plans until yesterday, when a telegram arrived
announcing her intentions to return on today's noon train accompa-
nied by the fiancé to whom she proposes to be married at the ear-
liest opportunity.

"Bess!"

"Coming, Mama." Mama needs a dose of Nervine tonic!

The baroque Louisville and Nashville Railway Station is noisy
and sooty. With sparks flying, the train roars into the station. Sam,
Bess, and Minnie crane their necks trying to catch through the thick
oily smoke a glimpse of the longed for face behind one of the pas-
senger car windows.

Thanks to Bess, aided by Mrs. Ashcraft, there is not a worthy
matron within the city limits of Birmingham who has not heard of the
northern prize which Lydia McShan has plucked. Bess anticipates
that the mothers of daughters among them will be as green as
Lydia's eyes with envy when the family arrives at the much antici-

pated unveiling of the Confederate Monument in Capitol Park accompanied by the handsome, wealthy future relation later in the afternoon.

Dressed in a severely tailored grey suit, Lydia has matured into the full beauty of adulthood in the years of absence. Heads turn as she passes. Minnie is struck by the close resemblance Lydia bears to her late beloved brother Alexander. She has the regal bearing of a Buford, thinks Minnie to herself with a simultaneous swell of pride and catch of concern in her heart.

"Oh, Father, Granny, Bess, how I have missed you all!" Lydia gathers them in a collective embrace. The long exuberant auburn curls of girlhood are tamed and trimmed into the shorter style of marcelled waves favored by the smart women of New York and Boston. Her voice has also deepened, become richer in its music. The lilac scent, so distinctly Lydia, has been replaced by a musky patchouli, mysteriously Eastern in its emanations.

"My fiancé," she says in a voice husky with emotion as a tall young man with a full beard and dark curly hair steps out of the crowd and extends a hand to Sam. Minnie and Bess exchange perplexed looks. Many references have been made to the golden blonde curls and short stature common to the Cunningham clan.

A changeling has come in substitution. In the soup pot of their lives a cupful of trouble begins to bubble.

***

Isabel has set a lovely table. The cloth of Irish lace and linen, a bridal shower gift from Colonel and Mrs. Ashcraft, has been starched and pressed to crisp perfection, only slightly marred by a yellow triangle where Isabel left the iron unattended. Despite Lydia's avowed aversion to roses, Bess has sent over a bouquet of her finest yellow blossoms, variety Grandiflora Golden Girl, to center the table and compliment the color scheme.

Violet efficiently circles the table, offering a platter of sliced ham. All take heaping helpings, save Willard, complaining that something in the sauce gives him indigestion, and Lydia's love, who politely pleads the strictures of his religion. He likewise declines potato salad, butter beans, fried okra, and turnip greens, claiming to be content with only a scoop of rice without benefit of gravy.

Violet is in a state of consternation. She has cooked since sun-

rise for this man. In desperation she places a wedge of cornbread on his plate. "It all looks quite pleasing, Miss Violet, but I am Orthodox in my religion and can only partake from a Kosher plate."

"Well, sir, I am Orthodox Baptist, and I have never had anyone turn down my food before," Violet replies in a huff.

"I meant no offense," he offers in a voice sincerely apologetic.

"Don't mind Violet. Her manners are atrocious." Mrs. Ashcraft reaches over to tap the young man's hand in a gesture of understanding. "And speaking of minding manners, I must point out, lad, that you are a guest in a Southern home. We do not address the colored help as 'Miss.'" Adelaide is bursting to get luncheon over and done. The telephone is a modern miracle when it comes to the dissemination of gossip. Lydia McShan home with a suspiciously religioned foreigner! Sam will put a stop to this!

"I believe you mentioned that you are of Russian lineage," Bess comments, as she cuts into a second serving of ham. Finding something simply inspiring about the sauce, she ladles it generously on her vegetables as well as her meat.

"My parents and I emigrated from Moscow," Avram answers.

"Moscow! Oh, my, how very romantic!" Bess claps her hands. "Were your people by chance there acquainted with the Grand Duchess Elena? I follow the vicissitudes of her heart with the greatest of interest. Her flirtation with Prince Vladimir of the Romanes has been simply shameless! I can only imagine that the Dowager Empress must be tearing her hair with worry over her granddaughter."

Minnie unconsciously puts a hand to her own head. She is trying to refrain from making a snap judgment. Lydia has confounded them all.

"I am afraid my family's only interaction with royalty was of a more unpleasant nature," he answers thoughtfully, unsure what to make of Bess's flits and flutterings. "My grandparents were killed in one of the old Tsar's most cruel pogroms, my father's only brother taken on the Bloody Sunday of just this January past when the Tsar's Royal Guards shot into a crowd of workingmen who were merely seeking to present the autocrat their grievances. I follow with a keen interest the rising tide of Bolshevism. The trivialities of the Grand Duchess will be swept away on the tide of history when the people rise up and have their day. Though death has silenced

the great Marx, his goals and aspirations yet live on through the bold Vladimir Ilich Lenin."

Lydia fidgets, wishing to nudge her lover from his soapbox. Outside of Bess's preoccupation with the royal high jinx of the Grand Duchess Elena, no member of her family has the least inclination to be illuminated about either the Russian pomp or proletariat. Alone in bed with Avram, she has found his revolutionary fervor thrilling, but around the ignorance and innocence of the family dinner table she fears his passion waxes didactic. In a very short period of acquaintance, Lydia's life has been consumed by Avram Livinsky.

"Tell us of your employment, Mr. Livinsky." Willard, caring not a whit, asks around a mouthful of butter beans. Isabel has chided him about talking with his mouth full, but a man who must chew each bite thirty times can hardly be expected to do otherwise.

"I am an investigative correspondent for Young's Weekly."

"One of those 'muckraking' organs, is it not?" Willard responds, fork poised dripping turnip greens. That currently popular periodical is missing from Isabel's arrangement in the library. Willard pronounces it filth and obscenity. Isabel would be afraid to touch it. "I hope you're not a disciple of that old toad in the White House Ted Roosevelt."

"A veritable son of Lincoln!" Mrs. Ashcraft booms in agreement. "The nerve of the man, asking Booker T. Washington to dine at his table! And to think, his mama was born in Georgia, and two of his uncles fought for our valiant Confederacy. His poor mama must be turning in her grave at such a deplorable misminding of his manners. Negroes breaking bread at the White House. What is next? What is next?"

"The family probably had property in Atlanta, where the resistance was so strong that Sherman was obliged to burn the city to the ground," Minnie mutters in Adelaide's direction. "Like Selma. Unlike Montgomery, which threw up its hands and surrendered without so much as a stubbing of toes."

"Lest you forget, Montgomery was womb to our beloved Confederacy," Adelaide barks with a glare at Minnie.

"Ladies, please! We have beaten like a dead horse the relative fates of Selma and Montgomery," Sam thunders. "Your haranguing at the table hampers my appetite."

Bess bites her tongue in disappointment. The Roosevelts are apparently off limit conversationally, and her next gambit was to be the enlightening of Isabel, always illiterate of the news of the day, of the excitement astir in the nation's capital over the upcoming marriage of the president's headstrong daughter Miss Alice Lee Roosevelt. Bess has been carefully contemplating staging Lydia's matrimonial moment in the sun post-Alice, lest the Washington woman receive more same day press attention.

"Our mission is to expose injustices brutalizing the working classes." Avram finally manages to get a word in edgewise. "It is but a matter of time until the working men's war commences not only in my native Russia but in the factories here as well. Socialism is everywhere on the ascendance."

Lydia shoots him a warning look. However heroic his idealism, she knows her family well.

"My father, a simple tailor, ignorant of the ways and language of this land, has recently proudly joined the ranks of the garment workers union," Avram continues.

It is past time for a change in subject. Sam clears his throat portentously, and all eyes swivel to the head of the table. "I have waited until this occasion, when we are all gathered here together, in the bosom of the family." He shoots a menacing look of exclusion at Avram before continuing. "To make an announcement of some importance. I have made the decision to take a wife in Kitty's replacement."

Bess draws in her breath, clutches her napkin to her lips. She has rehearsed this scene in her mind a thousand times, expected it to be in a more romantic setting, in the moonlight in her rose garden perhaps, but, no matter. The years of patient waiting are finally at ending. "I do," she squeals. "Oh, yes, I do!"

"Do what, Elizabeth?" Sam asks irritably. Unaccustomed to being interrupted, he continues, "It gives me great pleasure to announce that dear Adelaide has agreed to become Mrs. McShan."

Adelaide beams, Minnie chokes, and Bess bursts into tears. Why should Adelaide Ashcraft, with her furs, her jewels, her friendship with Mrs. Astor, which even Bess has begun to doubt, no proof positive ever having been forthcoming, now have Sam as well? The unfairness of life pummels her heart like a hurricane, and she flees from the room in despair.

"Don't mind her. She's having a difficult change of life," Minnie mumbles to no one in particular.

"You have been using that excuse for the past ten years," Adelaide huffs, supremely irritated that Bess has spoiled the moment.

"With large women the process often makes a very extended progress," Minnie says in defense of her daughter.

Adelaide ignores her, looks from one to another up and down the table, gracing each face with the radiance of her smile. "Imagine, at our ages, being stung by Cupid! We are to be wed without delay, to sell Sam's house and reside in mine for the near time being, my heart being set on a fine new mansion on the Highland Avenue. We will begin construction as soon as we have completed a honeymoon tour of the European capitals."

From the adjoining kitchen Bess clutches at her chest as her heart breaks into a million tiny pieces. A home on the pretentious, prestigious Highland Avenue, a honeymoon tour of the European sites that will forever remain seen to her eyes only through stereopticon views ordered from the Messrs. Sears and Roebuck.

"I do not wish to remove to the Highland Avenue, among the hoi polloi," Minnie grumbles. "Why should I, born a Buford, wish to be a neighbor to the nouveau riche?"

"You and Miss Elizabeth will be obliged to move in with Isabel," Sam says. "Isabel will, in recompense, receive Violet full time."

It is Isabel's turn to turn on the tears. Taking on Bess and Granny, who will demand separate sleeping quarters, will mean that she will once again be obliged to share a bed with Willard. A home of her own, and privacy, were such short lived objectives.

In the kitchen, Violet, flabbergasted, considers taking a sip of the cooking bourbon behind Bess's back. Not being required to divide her time between two houses will lighten her load, but something tells her that life with this never easy family is about to become even more complicated.

Violet wonders what the world is coming to. One child marrying a mean spirited Yankee, her baby sister with her stubborn heart set on a man with a mysterious diet, and old man Sam talking taking up residence with Adelaide. The Yankees scorching Selma seems small potatoes in comparison.

***

"There will be no further discussion, daughter. I will not allow it!" Sam thunders loudly enough for Minnie and Violet, rocking on the porch at day's conclusion, to hear every word. Bess has taken to her bed, clutching her Nervine tonic.

"I am in love," Lydia responds in a voice as resolved as her father's. "I will be his wife. I will bear his children and support him in his every endeavor, with or without your blessing. I have no wish to live a life without him at its center."

"Can't say that I failed to warn him about the hazards of a northern education," Minnie whispers to Violet, who cradles her head in her hands in misery.

"And in what faith do you propose to raise such children? Have you thought any further than the nose on your face, Lydia?"

"I intend to convert to the faith of Avram's fathers," she answers. "I am marrying a man I love with all my heart, not a religious dogma."

"He is the son of immigrants," Sam responds.

"As were you, sir," she counters. "He takes pride in the fact that his forebears were serfs on the steppes of Russia."

"What's a serf?" Violet asks Minnie.

"A slave," Minnie answers.

"Oh, heaven have mercy on us!" Violet wails.

"Hush up, Violet!" Minnie hisses. "I do not imply that his people were colored. With one already married to the son of a cobbler, the other's heart set on the son of a tailor, what a shame it is that Kitty did not have a third daughter. We could have found for her the son of a milliner and had ourselves a complete new outfit."

"He can never hope to give you the kind of life which your mother and I envisioned," Sam says, fighting down the tremor in his voice.

"A life like Isabel's? With a pompous fool ordering my every action? Willard will not even let her read the newspaper, instead tossing her scraps of information as if she were a dog begging a treat at the table. I will not marry simply to satisfy convention."

"Leave Willard and Isabel out of this. You know Isabel never had a sensible thought in her head. Too much of Bess's influence. But, you, Lydia, have the opposite problem. You think far too much for a woman."

"The debutante days are behind me, Father. I will not give up

Avram."

"See him off on the morning train, Lydia. Charge the ticket to my account."

"If he is on the morning train then I must go with him."

Sam snaps off the light. "Go to bed, Lydia. I have spoken."

"Miss Minnie, what we going to do?" Violet pleads. "That child is as willful as her Mama ever was."

"She has the green eyes of my brother. The gods are cruel. They claim the best and the brightest of each generation. Give him up or follow him, I do not see a happy ending to this story. If only I could find a way to get back to Selma and find that gold."

Violet has spent every day of her thirty nine years in the company of the woman beside her. Minnie has been to her mother, confidante, and verbal sparring partner. Through abject poverty and relative plenty, she has watched Minnie meet every eventuality like a battering ram.

Never once until tonight has she seen the stubborn old woman brought to tears. She feels a chill of fear as Minnie stares off into the stars with streaming eyes. Dark days lie ahead.

Chapter Twelve

Carrie stretched on the sofa. A short nap had overstayed its welcome. Outside the window an early dark blanketed the ruined rose garden. She consulted her watch. Five thirty. Her daughters were due.

From the depths of the basement a voice called to her.

The basement was a dismal cellar holding nothing but a half century's collection of moldy newspapers and broken garden tools. Her eyes adjusted to the dim light.

"Weirdest thing, Mrs. Lancaster." The young man Mallory had hired to remove the papers had cleared a semblance of a path through the stacks.

She yawned, parts of her mind still mired in the nap and wondering if no photos existed of Lydia's wedding because of the family's disapproval of the exotically handsome groom. She had a gut feeling that Lydia married him, with or without the benefit of her father's blessing. Had Lydia and Avram run away to Russia, perhaps found themselves on the scene during the days of the Russian Revolution? Were their descendants, in the present day, rejoicing at the death of Communism?

She told herself to stop day dreaming. It was speculation as silly as looking for Cunninghams in the Boston city directory.

She felt frustration. How to find out what actually became of Lydia? Too much time gone by, looking for Lydia was as quixotic a quest as spending hours searching for a manuscript that likely never existed in the first place.

His voice from the present recalled her from the past. "Wonder why anyone would block access to a door with a pile of out of date newspapers?" He pulled a random copy off the top of the stack. "This one is dated December 1938. They didn't recycle in those days, did they?" He tossed the single copy into a flat tired wheelbarrow.

"A door?" She crossed the dusty floor to join him.

His flashlight highlighted a sturdy lock protecting the sanctity of whatever lay behind an iron fire door. "Think that's just a closet, Mrs. Lancaster? Looks more like a vault or something. You'd need dynamite to pick a lock like that."

Or the keys to the past.

Carrie stared at the door, frowning. A sixth sense told her that the time was not right to confront whatever had rested sixty years and more behind that sealed entrance.

The present had to take precedence. A door slammed upstairs. The girls were home.

* * *

Late night, the lights out, Betsy startled at the sound of a dull thud in the attic. She put out a hand to reassure herself of the security of Dooley, coaxed into the room for protection. The old dog was out like a light. Betsy wrinkled her nose. Dooley was starting to smell his age, like sour wet wool.

"Bets, are you asleep?" The familiarity of Abby's voice was like a warm blanket on a cold night. After all of their growing up years complaining about sharing a bedroom, neither sister wanted to sleep in a room by herself in a house which was so obviously still another family's home.

"Nope. I was just lying here wishing I were back in my old bed in our old house."

"I'd settle for our old parents. Is Mom ever going to be normal again, Abby?"

"I don't know. In an odd sort of way she seems almost happy, if not her old solid self, again. She is madly in love with this house. It's Dad who worries me. He seemed like he was a million miles away at dinner tonight. Dad seems sad, almost lonely."

"How about his reaction when Mom suggested that we go Christmas caroling at Wyatt Wallace's house? I thought he went rather overly ballistic over a simple suggestion. Abby, who in the world is this Wyatt guy anyway?"

"In addition to being the brains behind at least half of your favorite movies, he is apparently Mom's new found closest friend. I met him one day. He was over here poking through closets in Hatton's old room. He's interesting. He has all sorts of Hollywood stories. Dad complains that he's polluted the whole house with his pipe smoke."

Betsy propped herself on an elbow and looked across the moon-lit room at her sister. "Abby, you're the one who's going to college just fifty miles from home in Tuscaloosa. Don't you ever make little inspection trips back to find out how they're doing?"

"I should do that, shouldn't I? Guess I prefer having my head in the sand. Whatever is going on between Mom and Dad is scaring me a lot more than anything in this house ever could."

"Well, I know one thing. This smelly dog has got to go back to their room." Betsy slipped out of bed and pulled Dooley's collar.

"I was just about to ask you if you had on a new perfume. I smell something kind of sweet and flowery." Abby frowned. Definitely missing in this house were the traditional spicy sweet smells of Mom's Christmas cooking.

Betsy tugged a groggy Dooley down the long dim hall, her parents ensconced in the master bedroom a whole length of house away. In the old small house of her whole life's experience, Nick and Carrie had always been so safely right next door. Close enough to hear them whispering before they slept, laughing together over some small joke. In the old house they had been happy, secure as only children whose parents are honest and open in their love for each other can be.

She pressed her ear to the door, reluctant to knock and possibly wake them. Each had complained at dinner of having bad dreams and sleeping poorly.

Easing the door wide enough to admit Dooley, she saw that they slept, backs to each other, as far apart in the bed as if there were things more interesting just over the outside edges. The sight made her uneasy.

Too many conversational references to Wyatt, little digs from Carrie to Nick about his never being at home, at dinner tonight. Was one of her parents fooling around? Both of them? What was happening to all of them?

Dooley stuck his nose under Carrie's outstretched hand. She turned in her sleep and mumbled a word, said it a second time more distinctly, as if she were calling out to someone in her sleep.

More confused than ever, Betsy closed the door and retraced her steps down the long, silent hall. Another element to add to the equation. She could not recall her mother having a friend named Lydia.

Lydia, sitting at the same place at the table reserved from her childhood, pushes her food around in silence. Violet has prepared old favorite morning dishes, as if serving plates of grits and memo-

ries, but she has no appetite. Home will be wherever Avram takes her.

Minnie joins her granddaughter and clears her throat, mentally composing opening remarks with a hesitancy that is uncharacteristic.

"Granny, I must live my life on my terms. Surely you have always sought and even fought to do the same."

"I have, and not always to my best advantage," Minnie answers, looking down and buttering a biscuit, avoiding the pain of having her brother's tormented green eyes confront her from her granddaughter's face. "Endeavor to learn from my mistakes instead of seeking to repeat them."

Minnie, rarely afraid to speak her mind, weighs her words before continuing. "Your Avram is, I fear, a man of the same dangerous breed as was my late brother, an idealistic dreamer, willing to sacrifice life, honor, or even ultimately love, made fatally stubborn by the courage of his convictions."

"But, Granny, hasn't Aunt Bess told us, more times than can be counted, that our great-uncle Alexander went to his death thanking heaven for being allowed to die for his belief in his country?"

"That he did, and that she has. More times than she should have. Truth be told, Lydia, there are elements of all of our stories which have been drastically altered or conveniently omitted." Minnie wants to scream out that all of their lives, past and present, have been predicated on falsehoods and fabrications. Her brother's last words ring in her mind, "The story must be told, Minnie. You will know the day and the hour, the messenger to whom to entrust the message."

Minnie squeezes her eyes shut, desperately entreating Alexander to break the bonds of the grave and speak to her.

Lydia puts a hand over her grandmother's. Granny both loves and understands her. She has no wish to bring grief to this old woman.

She places a book on the table between them. "Here, Granny, is a volume for your perusal. It has moved me to heights of great emotion."

Minnie examines the book, The Jungle by Upton Sinclair. She has heard talk of it, an expose of conditions in the American stockyards, penned by a Socialist reformer.

"Are you aware, Granny, of the cruel conditions that exist in *those mines that make my father a millionaire and me heiress to gains ill gotten? Innocent men and ignorant immigrants are swept up off the street on trumped up charges of vagrancy, afterwards subjected to involuntary and life threatening servitude. Men must subsist on salt pork, corn bread and syrup stirred together and served off of their shovels to allow us to dine here in luxury from silver platters. They sleep on hanging pallets because the floors and walls of their cells crawl with lice. Ten hour work days and whipped if they do not produce quota. Drinking filthy foul water and dying from dysentery. I know it is so. Avram has enlightened me. Violet has spoken to me of the sharecroppers, on plantations such as your beloved White Gardenias, who are told at the end of a bountiful harvest that the old boll weevil ate their share of the crop and any profits due them. Many of her people exist today as victims of a system as vicious as if Lincoln had never emancipated them."*

"There have been inequities throughout history, Lydia," Minnie, while agreeing with her granddaughter, argues feebly. "I am too intelligent to buy that insipid Willard's argument that the convict lease system is justified by saving the state tax money otherwise spent on maintaining felons and instilling in amoral foreigners the Puritan work ethic. Hogwash, as are most of Willard's opinions. If your young reformer is bent on exposing evil work conditions, send him instead to the cotton mills to interview little lint headed white trash children forced into labor to help feed their families. They are slaves to a system as well. If you have returned home bent on exposure, could you not have the filial decency to look to occupations other than those in which your father engages?"

There ensues a period of uncomfortable silence, finally broken by Minnie. "Did he take the morning train as directed?"

"If he had I would not be sitting here." Lydia rises from her untouched breakfast, looking for a moment so like Alexander Buford that the old woman feels for a frantic moment as if her entreaties have produced a specter.

"There is work to be done here, a compelling cause, and he, with my help as proof of my love for him, will see it to completion."

Head high, she sails from the room. Minnie, mind mulling over Lydia's cryptic final comment, hears the bang of the front door like a drum beat announcing a battle. She crumbles the remainder of her biscuit, tosses it out the window to the mockingbirds chattering in a gnarled and ancient oak tree.

Chapter Thirteen

Although customarily an early riser, Mallory Hudson groaned in disconcertion as she realized that the bedside clock read only four a.m. An empty morning yawned before her. No committee meetings to attend on Christmas morning.

Wishing for a cup of tea, she tucked her nightgown into the bathroom hamper and ran a hot bath. A lady, after all, never descended the stairs until ready to meet the public.

Her pearls in place, she hesitated in the hallway before the locked door. Better to spend Christmas morning alone than in the company of a ghost from Christmas past.

She wandered instead into Carrie's childhood room, frilly and feminine with twin tester beds with eyelet coverlets and canopies, dotted Swiss curtains still twice yearly bleached to a crisp perfection. From glass fronted cases the painted faces of the doll collection smiled at her. The pink and white skirted dressing table was topped with Mallory's mother's collection of crystal atomizers. The sweet scent of her mother's toilet water came back, a sensory feeling of safety, her mother such a lady, always in control and knowing just what to do, whatever the situation.

She had tried so hard to be just as strong for Carrie.

She opened a desk drawer. Cream colored note cards engraved "Miss Caroline Elizabeth Mallory Hudson." Standing on this very spot, looking over Carrie's shoulder, she had taught the child to compose a proper bread and butter thank you note.

The most recent acknowledgment of a wedding gift Mallory had received was on distressingly flimsy paper, stamped, not engraved, "Susan and Mike." What could she expect when her address on the invitation to the couple's wedding had been computer generated instead of properly penned and inked in calligraphy as Carrie and Nick's should have been? What was the world coming to?

Miss Caroline Elizabeth Mallory Hudson. A proud big brother's voice, "This is my baby sister, my very own Carrie Beth." How many years since anyone had called her daughter that? The childhood name packed away like a suitcase full of outgrown doll clothes. Such a nice southern custom it had always seemed to Mallory, double naming a daughter for women who had come before her, shown the way.

Jamie's voice rang in her ears like a gong sounding, its echo breaking her heart again and again and again. All the years passing had not lessened the pain of losing Jamie an ounce. The world turned upside down that Thanksgiving weekend and had never righted itself. Mallory told herself that she deserved an Academy Award for the performance of being functional she had put on day after day after day.

Jamie was gone, and thinking about him was not going to bring him back. It had to be Carrie who filled her mind this morning.

She thought back to the family's escape to Milan, to the three agonizing years she and David had spent pulling Carrie step by tiny step from the silent private world into which the child had retreated the day her brother died. Three long years later, she at last responded, but only when addressed as simply Carrie.

Mallory put more weight into worrying about Carrie's recent mental state than she was willing to admit to anyone other than herself. Seated at the desk of Carrie's childhood, she put her head on her arms. She could not survive losing Carrie too.

A wave of loneliness rippled through Mallory. The most poignant memories invoke all of the senses. The smell of Josie's Christmas day turkey browning. The taste of sweet potatoes smothered with marshmallows. The feel of an eager child's hand in hers as they prepared to descend the stairway to see what Santa had delivered. Hardest of all to bear, the sound of a little boy's voice singing "Merry Christmas, Mommy" from across the years. She struggled to hold back the years of accumulated tears that threatened to gush free like water from a frozen pipe finally bursting.

On the ruffle skirted table the phone jingled like Christmas bells. Only one person could be calling at this early hour of Christmas morning.

"Merry Christmas, Josie."

"Same to you, Mallory. It's a mighty strange feeling to wake up on Christmas morning without a turkey to baste. My granddaughter insists that she does not need one bit of help. Just six months married and taking on cooking the entire Christmas dinner! These young people today are something else. I don't mind telling you though that if she tries to roast that bird in the microwave the main thing I'll be biting into will be my tongue."

Mallory laughed. Like Josie, she was too old to change with the times.

"What are your plans for the day, Mallory?"

Mallory frowned. Without an organized scheme of activities there was too much danger of too much time to think. Holidays were hazardous. On a Wednesday in July she could so involve herself in something else that ghosts from the past had no chance of intruding. At Christmas they were the most prominent guests at the table.

"Josie, you know as well as I do that this is Ellen's year to hostess Christmas dinner. Heaven only knows what her idea of a traditional Christmas meal will entail. Do you remember the year she served lasagna like she was expecting the Pope to appear?"

"Now, Mallory, you hop off your high horse about Ellen Lancaster. You're dining Mexican tonight on a hot tamale casserole. Ran into Nick's mother in the market just yesterday. Grocery store lines were backed up a mile deep, and she said she always enjoyed last minute shopping because the crowds made the store so festive. That is one woman with a healthy attitude about life."

Mallory didn't reply. She did not believe in doing anything last minute, in allowing the potential for surprises in her life. The single overriding worst moment of her life had happened with too little warning.

"You know, Mallory, there's a certain bit of sadness to waking up on Christmas morning in a house where Santa Claus no longer stops," Josie continued. "Ellen has a right good idea for the day, and I was calling to suggest that you join us."

"Josie, if you're proposing that you and I attend Mass with Ellen, old age has addled your brain more than I thought."

"She and I are serving lunch to the ladies at the homeless shelter. Why don't you come too?"

"I've already sent a check to the shelter. I've done my part."

Josie took a deep breath. She had no inhibitions about telling Mallory Hudson something that needed saying. "Please, Mallory. Let me get you out of that big old empty house on Christmas morning. I hate to think of you all alone being eaten up by memories."

"Josephine Jones, you know perfectly well that I have never been a woman to dwell in the past."

"That I know. You can't dwell in a place you've never faced. Neither can Carrie. I am worried sick to death about Carrie, and it's past time to give Carrie the answers to some questions she's too afraid to ask."

"You're talking nonsense."

"I am talking the truth, and you and I both know it. Every time I try to bring up her childhood Carrie ducks for cover. You've got to do something, Mallory, or you'll force me to. Her childhood is like a blank slate in her mind. She doesn't remember her brother, Mallory, and it is past time someone told her the truth about him."

"You wouldn't dare."

"She's afraid that she's losing her mind, Mallory, losing her mind just like she lost her brother and her childhood."

"No, she is not! Not one person, ever, in this family, going back as far as records have been kept . . ."

"Stop it, Mallory! Stop hiding behind people who are dead and buried."

"You stop preaching to me, Josie. You have no right to interfere in Carrie's life. Old age is catching up with you."

"It is running just as hard after you. Who knows how much time either one of us has left? I have every right to 'interfere' in Carrie's life because I helped raise Carrie, and Jamie, and loved the both of them as much as I have loved my own children."

"So help me, if you bring up one mention of Jamie to Carrie, you will never again be welcome in this house."

"Fine with me. Past time I retired anyway. And now, if you will excuse me, I hear Ellen's car playing carols in the driveway."

Mallory heard it too. "God rest you, merry gentlemen. Let nothing you dismay."

She rose from the bed, smoothed the eyelet coverlet and went downstairs to meet the Christmas morning.

Mallory's tree was artificial, perfectly proportioned and professionally decorated by a floral designer, all white lights and crystal snowflakes. She hurried past the living room, in her mind's eye the bubble lights from her children's childhoods dancing on the branches of a pungently scented fresh fir.

In the study she took her place at David's desk, the desk that had before him belonged to his father and grandfather, the desk that should have been their son's. She opened the thick leather book in which she made her genealogical entries and began transcribing the names acquired from weathered barely legible stones in a Scottish graveyard.

A sea captain and his wife, parents of ten, three of them sons who entered the ministry and rose to prominence in the good bedrock church of the Presbyterians.

The stable sturdy stock from which she had come. Not a mention of madness in the bunch.

***

Wyatt Wallace had no Christmas tree. Even had he believed in a reason for observing Christmas, which he didn't, he was too busy to decorate a tree. He had a play to write.

It had been his practice for a number of years to avoid the hated holidays by taking a winter month of vacation in the south of Spain. He hadn't time for that this year. The play had to be completed. His time was running out.

Have to get started before you can finish, jeered the blank sheet of paper, as smoothly uninterrupted as a newly fallen blanket of snow. There cannot be an ending without a beginning.

He reached for the Scotch bottle in his desk drawer. Empty. Furious, he flung it into the fireplace.

The room was a shambles of empty bottles, ashtrays overflowing with spent pipe tobacco, and, littering every surface, the crumpled kernels of silent sheets of paper.

He rarely left the one room, a sanctuary no one else was allowed to enter. A maid service peopled by anonymous faces appeared like clockwork every Wednesday. He supposed that they changed the linens on a bed in which he rarely turned back the covers, his nightly self imposed stupors dropping him as often on the leather sofa of the downstairs study as the top of the upstairs bed.

On Christmas morning, Christmas was the farthest thing from his mind. What was it going to take to get him going, the words to budge from the back of his mind?

A missing manuscript and nothing less.

Across the room a single gift wrapped package caught his eye.

The temperature hovered just below freezing, too cold for taking even a short walk anywhere. He pocketed the keys to his grandmother's old Mercedes.

***

"But Mom, it just isn't Christmas morning without your cinnamon French toast casserole," Betsy wailed. "How can you serve cereal for Christmas breakfast?"

"Betsy, how many times do I have to tell you that being mired in the past does nothing but make you overlook opportunities for the future?" Carrie defended herself. "It doesn't stop being Christmas just because you change the menu."

"Mom hasn't thrown all the traditions out the window. We've still got presents to open," Abby offered as a peace proposal. "Come on, family, let's hit the living room."

Betsy sulking, Abby volunteered to act as Santa. "Here, Bets, first one for you."

Betsy untied the ribbon, pulled from the tissue paper an old fashioned locket on a thin gold chain. She turned it in her hand, frowning. "Whose initials are K.I.M.?"

"Katherine Isabel McShan. It was a gift from her father on her eighteenth birthday," Carrie explained with a look of satisfaction. Who could guess how much the locket, twenty four carat, would have cost in a vintage jewelry store? Nick should be proud of her. She had thought of a means of giving lovely gifts without spending a dime. You could recycle more than newspaper.

"This belonged to the old lady who lived here?" With a stricken look, Betsy dropped the necklace back into the tissue paper.

"Well, goodness, she wasn't always old. When she was eighteen, she lived in a house just down the street from your own great great-grandmother. I wouldn't be surprised at all if they were friends." As she spoke, Carrie questioned her supposition. In the dreams, friends seemed to be noticeably lacking in Isabel's life. She was a woman sheltered in the contained cove of family.

"Betsy, you know how your grandmother loves to waste her days down in the research room of the library. I asked her to look up the McShans' Victorian era address for me in one of the old city directories in the Archives. One day soon I'm going to check out whether their houses might still be standing."

"Carrie, don't you dare! The area where your father's grandparents lived is a dangerous part of town, and you know it." Nick flashed her a grim look of warning. Enough was becoming more than enough.

Carrie thought back to Willard Preston's words, even in his day so few of the fine old families left on that street. Sam and his new bride Adelaide had abandoned Kitty's dream house and built themselves a Greek Revival palace on Highland Avenue. That house was long since demolished, replaced by an ugly modern office building. She had already found that address and investigated. Between the building and the sidewalk was the most beautiful tree she had ever seen, blazing with brilliant scarlet leaves. Had Sam and Adelaide planted it? What if Kitty's house were still standing, now cut up into apartments and home to crack dealers and prostitutes? Could she knock on the door and have the nerve to ask admittance to the upstairs room where her dream had shown her Kitty's dying?

"For you, Dad." Abby passed a package, obviously a book. Nick looked miserably at the tattered leather cover stamped in gold. They had inherited a family, it seemed, who liked to put their initials on everything.

"*The Meditations of Marcus Aurelius*? In Latin? Is this supposed to be light bedtime reading?"

"It belonged to Isabel's great-uncle Alexander, the one who was a Confederate war hero, Nicky. It even has the notes he made in the margins. Look at the flyleaf. It's inscribed Heidelberg and December 25, 1859. Someone gave him that book for Christmas when he was a student in Germany before the war."

Abby hesitated before choosing a gift with her name on the tag. Had good old once so always dependable Mom totally flipped out? Had she given all of them gifts that had once been given to others, all now dead people? Goose bumps rose on her arms.

Sure enough it seemed. The package she unwrapped was a silver dresser set, "Lydia" etched into the backs of the brush and comb and mirror. There were cracks in the mirror's face, like a reflection of what was happening in their lives.

The rest of the gifts were more of the same. They were down to two packages under the tree. One was tagged "Wyatt." The other was a department store gift box, Nick's present to Carrie.

"I wonder what this could be?" Carrie asked, with a wink in the girls' direction. Nick always, year after year, gave her a new robe for Christmas. Good old practical Nick. He always said, "I figured you needed it." As if she didn't have enough robes stockpiled to do her service if she became an invalid for the rest of her life.

This year she was not the only member of the family who had broken with tradition. In the box was a bright yellow warm up suit, a new pair of tennis shoes, and a gift certificate for six tennis lessons. "To get you out of the house," Nick mumbled.

There was not a single one among them who had received anything for which they could or would have wished. The unhappy tableau of the family sharing Christmas morning was mercifully disrupted by the deep boom of the doorbell.

"It's always such a letdown when the last gift has been opened. Just what we needed, a Christmas visitor!" Carrie cried as she opened the door to Wyatt.

He pulled the brandy bottle, luckily found in his grandmother's sideboard, uncapped and tested on the short drive from his driveway to theirs, from the deep pocket of his overcoat. "Thought I would bring my neighbors a spot of Christmas cheer." Three members of the family looked from him to each other as if asking what else Santa could pull from a bag of bad mistakes.

Carrie went to the kitchen for glasses. Brandy was so festive. There was a carton of eggnog in the refrigerator. On impulse she stopped in the butler's pantry and took down recently polished silver Jefferson cups traced with Hatton's initials.

Nick was glaring at their guest and the girls regarding him with wary interest as she returned to the room. Wyatt was standing before the fireplace reciting from Dickens. Carrie paused in the doorway, feeling that a touch of magic had been added to her Christmas morning.

"A small token of thanks for your help with my play," he said, handing her a package.

She tore open the wrapping and held up the gift for the others to see. "How perfect! A book on old Alabama houses."

"According to the bookseller it is a fascinating account of antebellum homes which have either disappeared entirely or are in grave danger of going that way. It looked like the sort of thing you might enjoy."

"As I'm sure I will," Carrie responded, taking her gift to Wyatt from beneath the tree. It suddenly seemed something infinitely insignificant in comparison to what she imagined he must have this morning already unwrapped, tokens of how much they missed him from the rich and famous.

He riffled through the ribbon tied packet of letters, written from Vanderbilt by Hatton to his mother, found in the attic, and embraced Carrie. "The existence of these letters is proof, Carrie, that we cannot give up our quest to find that manuscript!"

"This is the weirdest Christmas we have ever had," Abby whispered to Betsy.

"I know. What's going to happen next?" she responded as she rose to answer the ringing doorbell.

"Goodness, who can that be? This is turning into a party!" Carrie was oblivious to the mixed bag of expressions as her family turned their collective faces toward the door.

"Josie! I thought you were going to be spending the day with your grandchildren."

"Microwaved turkey, dressing out of a box, store bought rolls. Whatever the world is coming to, I am too old to adjust to it."

Carrie frowned. Josie's usually cheerful face was grim. Carrie and Mallory teased her about being an overly indulgent grandmother. Something other than a new bride's attempts at modern meal making was obviously troubling her.

"I'm not sure whether I was fired or quit," she spoke to the faces turned to her. "But, whoever had the last word, the outcome is the same. Carrie, after all these years your mama and I have left each other."

"Betsy, run and call the cable news channels," hissed Abby. "I'm sure they will all want to compete to be first with the news that the world as we have always known it has just officially ended."

Chapter Fourteen

It was the first Christmas night of their married lives that Nick and Carrie prepared for sleep without calling the day just spent the best Christmas ever.

Stinging words passed. "Nick, I thought you'd be pleased that I had saved money. I thought that passing on some of the Prestons' prized possessions would make us feel more a part of their family."

His answer, cut and dried, was coldly delivered. "The whole point, Carrie, is that we are not, and never will be, and would not want to be if we could be, part of their family. You have a perfectly good family of your own, which you are throwing away in the process of playing whatever warped game this is, and I want it to stop."

She could not decide which hurt more, her family's negative reactions to her thoughtful selections, or Nick's insensitive suggestion through his gift that she get out of the house and throw herself into a sport that he enjoyed.

She had been a total failure at childhood tennis lessons. Before the memories of her youngest childhood efforts to learn the game could rear their ugly heads she shoved them into reverse.

From the attic above them came a crash, and Carrie's heart went out to the elderly cat, spending Christmas night cold and alone.

Nick turned his eyes upward. "First thing in the morning I am going to do something about that."

"Nick, I've told you. He's a poor old stray cat who has obviously had a hard life. Is it any wonder he's afraid of people? I have named him Willie because he's as difficult to just produce on demand as a will o' the wisp in an Indian graveyard."

"Carrie, ENOUGH!" Nick thundered. "There is no cat. The cat is all in your head. You know how Dooley hates cats. If there were a cat in this house don't you think that he would be at the bottom of those stairs barking his heart out? I don't want to hear that cat mentioned again, ever."

Unspoken between them lay Nick's angry reaction on finding out that Wyatt Wallace had arranged for and paid for the repairs to the attic stairs.

"It could be raccoons," Nick muttered. "Raccoons carry rabies.

I'm going to call Wildlife Rescue to bring some traps. Until they get out here, you stay out of that attic, Carrie."

And won't you be surprised when what they catch is one poor skinny raccoon wearing a cat costume, she thought to herself.

"How long do you think this little tiff between your mother and Josephine will last?" Nick asked, uncomfortable with argument, more so with the whole notion of Wyatt Wallace.

"Who knows? Neither of them will even admit what caused this rift in the first place. I suppose the biggest surprise of today was Josie agreeing to go to work for Wyatt."

"Carrie, you know what a teetotaler Josie is. She will last about one hour in his house."

"Too bad that Sears no longer sells the 'Famous Fifty Cent German Stop Drinking Cure.' It's funny, isn't it, all those good ladies of the Women's Christian Temperance Union slugging Nervine tonic down like lemonade and hiding the medicinal sherry in the pantry?"

"Carrie, what are you talking about? Listen to yourself! You're scaring the daylights out of me. Where do you come up with comments like that, or references to will o' the wisps in Indian graveyards? Never mind. I don't think I want to know."

"Just something I read somewhere. It's been a very long day, and I think it's past time to call it over."

Without a Merry Christmas he rolled away from her, marveling that she could put their disagreement so easily out of mind that she seemed to be asleep before her head made a dent in the pillow.

Minnie, victim of insomnia, pulls on her robe and creeps down the stairs and across the yard.

At the entrance to the carriage house she pauses, frowns. The door to the upper precincts, where are stored the things she brought from Selma, is ajar. There, deep in the hours between midnight and dawn, she often hides away, scanning page by page her letters from her brother and her father's coded daybook diary. She is certain that within its pages her father left the key to unlock the location of the hidden fortune in gold, her only hope for breaking the curse and setting the future of her family free.

She strains to hear voices coming from above. So it is here that Lydia has chosen to hide her illicit lover. She draws in her breath and listens.

"Lydia, I have reservations. Perhaps I should go as your father

commands, leave you to the life you knew before me and call what we have had together a brief and beautiful interlude in our lives. There are battles aplenty for fighting on other fields. I'll not have you hurt."

"Quiet your protesting, Avram, simply love me, love me," Lydia begs.

"Being with your family has not given you misgivings, second thoughts?"

"Have I not promised to be for the rest of my life at your side, to aid you in any and in all ways? I will not live long enough to ever have enough of you."

"We proceed then tomorrow as planned?"

"Absolutely and without hesitation, but only after you have loved me yet once more, fully and completely, enough to last for me a life-time."

***

Josephine Jones didn't really need to work. She had a house with the mortgage paid, a nice retirement nest egg, and an approach to life that craved few trappings.

She did not set much store in fate but had great faith in providence. From the proximity of Wyatt Wallace's house, she could keep a watchful eye on Carrie.

Josie didn't like that old drunk worming his way into Carrie's life, liked less the obvious tension between Carrie and Nick. Opportunity for intervention had presented itself, and she had grabbed it.

It just plain served Mallory right. Stubborn old woman refused to see the forest for the trees! Josie loved them both, Mallory and Carrie, too fiercely to stand any longer idly by letting the past grind up the present. David Hudson's death still hung heavy on her heart. Red meat was not as responsible for his heart attack as Mallory's refusal to let him unburden.

There was no reply to her knock at the door. Finding it unlocked, she found her new employer in his study. The balls of paper scattered around him reminded her of the aftermath of a summer storm with hail the size of baseballs. She had never, ever, in her life seen such a mess. A wonder he could work at all. His desk was the only uncluttered surface in the room. Absolutely clear except for an ancient typewriter from which protruded a blank sheet of paper.

He set the ground rules. "I must insist on absolute quiet for concentration. Should either the telephone or the doorbell ring, simply ignore it."

"Maybe I could begin with the grocery shopping," she responded. "There are few activities I enjoy so much as cooking."

"Splendid. There has not been a decent meal served in this house since my grandmother died."

"Anything special you like?"

Many days he spent so much time drinking that he forgot to eat. He opened his mouth to say "whatever's easiest," suddenly ached for his grandmother's cooking. "As a matter of fact, I would like pot roast, potatoes mashed with sour cream, and homemade rolls."

Mallory lately considering a salad composed of more than one variety of lettuce an over indulgence, Josie decided that she might be able to overlook a lot of things of which she didn't approve in Wyatt's room.

She closed the door and left him to his cluttered den of iniquity. There would be time for cleaning that room later. First she had to win his confidence.

***

"How could she? How could she? For forty years we have spent every day side by side as close as sisters."

Carrie could not decide whether to laugh or to cry. It was the closest she had ever seen her mother come to hysteria.

"Mother, I don't see how you can possibly expect us to help you if you won't tell us what brought on this impasse in the first place," Carrie argued.

Mallory gave her daughter a stricken look. She just could not let Josie go dredging up old hobgoblins. If only David were still around to reason with Josie!

"I think that you'd better bite the bullet and share the rest of the bad news, Mom," Abby said softly from the back seat. Mallory was really rattled, driving crazier than Ellen usually did. Fortunately it was only a few more miles to Saks, where they were going to shop for Betsy's debutante ball gown. Abby felt a twinge of guilt over directing her grandmother's focus onto something other than her own refusal to be presented. Betsy lapped that sort of thing up like a cat with a bowl of cream, which suited Abby, who found the process amusing and anachronistic, just fine.

"What could possibly be worse than what has already happened?" Mallory turned to look at Abby and almost ran off the road.

"Josie has gone to work for Wyatt Wallace," Carrie mumbled, trying to form a mental image of Josie marching into a bar.

"No!" Mallory almost missed the turn lane, swerved across traffic. "To think that I have been telling everyone in town that despite his years of exile in California the man has the soul of a true southern gentleman! I doubt very much that his grandmother would be proud of his actions, and I am going to tell him so. How dare he?"

"Maybe you could hire a cleaning service, Mallory," Betsy offered what she hoped was encouragement. She had made an advance reconnaissance mission and needed to stay on top of Mallory's good graces until that perfect pair of shoes, those shoes that penny pinching Mom would complain cost more than her first car, were safely hers and in the closet.

"Cleaning service? This has absolutely not one thing in the world to do with house cleaning, for heaven's sake!" Mallory roared. "Josephine is the best, the nearest, dearest friend I have got on this earth. How could she just abandon me?"

"Calm down, Mother," Carrie interrupted, "knowing both Josie and Wyatt, I am sure this new arrangement won't last long." Trying to be tactful, she had whispered to Josie that Wyatt had "a tiny bit of a drinking problem." She thought to herself that what he had was a great huge horrible habit and that it would not take much of Josie futilely trying to turn that around before they came to a mutual decision to part ways as precipitously as they had come together.

"And how are you today, Mrs. Hudson?" Mallory's usual sales lady was pleased to see her. She liked Mallory personally as much as she welcomed the commissions professionally. They had spoken on the phone earlier in the day. "I've pulled several dresses for Betsy. Can I get you coffee while she tries them?"

"I feel as though I've just lost my last friend," Mallory moaned. "Coffee would be wonderful, two creams and four sugars."

Carrie and the girls exchanged nervous glances. It was so out of character for Mallory to consume wasted calories.

"Look, Mother, if it will make you feel better I will go over to

Wyatt's right after we're through shopping and see if I can't talk some sense into Josie," Carrie consoled, squeezing her mother's hand.

The response came as thunderous and as unexpected as a bullet in a drive by shooting. "No! Absolutely not, under any circumstances! You listen to me, Carrie, and you listen well. You just stay away from Josie."

"Mother, you are talking like your mind left right along with Josie. Why in the world would you ask me to stay away from Josie? I'm as close to Josie as I am to you."

Betsy and Abby exchanged uneasy eye contact. Something simmering under the surface in all their lives was bubbling toward a boiling point.

***

He had told her to leave him alone, and she was complying. For the first morning in a long string of days of wordless beginnings, he had actually at last pressed tentative fingers against the keys. "Act One, Scene One" might not look like a great deal to the casual observer, but at least the page had been interrupted, did not look so much like a bright white reflection of failure.

Drifting down the long hall and sneaking under the crack of the closed study door, the scents from the kitchen sang like a siren.

He could have cried. The simple goodness of a baked from scratch breakfast changed the morning's whole complexion. He abandoned the typewriter.

"Josephine, you are an absolute treasure." Wyatt heaped his plate with grits, eggs, sausage and biscuits, poured orange juice and took from the refrigerator champagne to transform it into a mimosa. It was his house and none of her business. Her problem if drinking at breakfast offended her.

"Mr. Wallace, I was so pleased to see that you have a big old fig tree. Come summer, I'll make preserves to add to our biscuits."

She promised a taste straight from childhood. His mind traveled back to his grandmother and her garden. His grandmother kept a cat as a watchdog over her figs and tomatoes, an old tangerine tabby Isabel Preston had run off from next door. Grandmother had taken pity on the cat because Isabel had drowned her kittens.

Josie added half and half cream to her coffee, three heaping teaspoons of sugar, idly swirled a spoon around the cup. She wondered what Mallory was up to this morning. Her face creased into a frown. That house was so big and so empty, so quiet and so noisy with long silent voices. How in the world was Mallory going to get along without her?

Wyatt interrupted her reverie. "Josephine, perhaps we should have a discussion about what we expect each from the other." Wyatt, full stomach rendering him briefly a satisfied man, leaned back in his chair and lit his pipe. "Because the work is going exceedingly well, I must at all costs keep my concentration."

"I won't be bothering you," Josie replied, her mind still wandering the lonesome halls of Mallory's house. "But Mr. Wallace, I will warn you up front that I have always been a plain spoken woman. You would get a darn sight more work done in that room if you would let me have five minutes to straighten up in there, open the windows and air things out."

How he wished it were that simple. "Perhaps another day, Josie. I must admit that this morning's lines are the finest I have yet produced. Surely, fortified by such an excellent breakfast, even better efforts are about to unfold. I must get back to work."

Heart heavy with homesickness, she told herself sternly that she was there for a compelling reason. A short distance away, Carrie was in trouble.

Chapter Fifteen

Jack Lancaster studied the MRI. It was a severe sprain, not the ruptured disk initially feared.

"What she least needs at this point in her life, when what she most needs is to get out of that house, is a week to ten days of flat on her back bed rest," Nick said in agreement with his father's diagnosis. "She stubbornly refuses to tell me what stupid, house related, stunt she pulled to cause this."

The father placed a supportive hand on his son's shoulder. "Just be thankful she doesn't need surgery. Ellen can tear herself away from her computer long enough to pitch in and help. Take your wife home and put her to bed."

"Carrie is up to something, Dad. She could not wait for me to get out of the house this morning so that she could get started on it."

"Here's a little positive reinforcement to make her mind her manners as well as give her some relief from the pain." Jack tossed Nick a container of sample pills. "Two of these and she'll be out like a light."

Returning home, Nick carried Carrie into the house where her mother had already taken charge. The refrigerator was overstocked, freshly purchased linens were on the bed, and an insulated pitcher of ice water rested within convenient reach next to a vase of orchids.

"I had the lingerie shop send out a pretty new nightgown and bed jacket," Mallory said as Nick gently lowered a wincing Carrie onto the bed. "Might as well look your best for visitors."

She had not had so much as a passing telephone conversation with any of her friends in months, Nick thought despondently.

"Go on back to your surgery schedule, Nick," Mallory urged as she arranged a froth of lace around her daughter's shoulders. "I stopped by the bookstore and picked up all the current best sellers. Until the pain killers take hold, I'll just sit right here and read to Carrie, just as I did when she was a child."

Closing her eyes, Carrie gritted her teeth against the pain of a sudden flash of memory of a childhood illness, of voices reassuring that her mother would be back from a trip out of town just as soon as she could, of one voice in particular, reading aloud, "Christmas won't be Christmas without any presents," the opening lines of *Little Women*. Carrie suddenly felt, as if it were as fresh as the pain in her back, her nine year old heart's sadness at the death of Louisa May Alcott's character Beth.

"Go away!" Carrie cried, startling both her mother and her husband, neither aware that the words were not addressed to them.

The medicine worked effectively. Mallory turned off the light and tiptoed from the room, leaving Carrie to her dreams.

In a town where the sidewalks are rolled up before ten p.m., the midnight streets are deserted and silent, softly lit by a full June moon.

Behind the wisteria curtaining the porch, Minnie rocks and watches. Lydia receives a last lingering lover's kiss before slipping into the house through a side door. A troubled expression clouding a handsome face, he stands in the yard looking after her.

"Avram." His name, called from a disembodied voice, is spoken so softly that at first he thinks it imagined.

"Avram!" More insistent. He startles. They have been discovered.

She waves her cane, summoning him. "Sit. We must talk."

"If you mean to dissuade your granddaughter, perhaps you would be better served speaking with Lydia, Mrs. Hatton."

"I do not believe in wasting words, young man. I already know Lydia, far better than she knows herself. It is with you that I wish to reach a fuller understanding."

"You object to my background, to my religion."

"Stuff and nonsense! I could care less if you were an Eastern Indian mystic in a loincloth. I have no faith in organized religions of any persuasions. On the rare occasion that I see the need to appeal to any gods, I simply make entreaty to any who will choose to listen."

"I love your granddaughter, Mrs. Hatton."

"Anyone with eyes can see that. You're not the first poor young fool caught up in Lydia's whirlwind. She has for all of her life generated a dangerous charisma. Lydia, like my brother before her, is capable of engendering in another a fatal passion portending consequences lasting far into the future."

"You object to the paths on which life at my side may take her."

"Stop second guessing me!"

He takes a deep breath. "Mrs. Hatton, at the risk of sounding immodest, I believe that I have powerful gifts of self-expression meant to be used on behalf of those downtrodden, and I will not let anything, even my love for Lydia, distract me from that."

"I do not doubt you, Avram." She speaks softly, carefully formulating her own words. "Long ago, there was set in motion a chain of still unfolding events in which I have reason to suspect that you are to be a catalyst. In the moments before he died, my brother gave to me a message and told me that I must relay the same to the one who in the future would come to be the ultimate messenger. It is sometimes as if my brother still speaks to me, just this evening communicating in a voice as clear as if shouted through a trumpet."

The old woman is mad, he thinks to himself.

"If you would have my granddaughter, Avram, there are things of which you must be made aware. There was many years ago a curse placed on our family, a curse which can only be broken if the truth is made known to the one who is to be the last of the line that he, or she, might make an amending."

"I am a practical man, Mrs. Hatton, with no belief in curses."

"A practical man? I think not. All your talk of revolutions! You are as much an idealist and a dreamer as ever was my brother. My brother's idealism cost him his life, and the love of a singular woman, and the fire in your own belly may demand of you no less."

"I would gladly die to purchase the freedom of others."

"As did my brother."

"I have heard in the course of this day, Mrs. Hatton, many stories of your brother's bravery and sacrifice in the service of a cause predicated on slavery."

"You have heard a pack of lies! Those ninnies Bess and Adelaide and their compatriot Sisters of the Southern Cross prattle more mythology than Homer."

"Those who die young, such as your brother, often assume the mythic status of martyrs, Mrs. Hatton."

She nods in agreement. "How well the playwright Plautus spoke it, 'Quem di diligunt adulescens moritur, dum valet sentit sapit.'"

"I have no knowledge of the Latin language."

"More's the pity, a requisite component of the complete education. I will translate. 'He whom the gods love dies young, while he has strength and senses and wit.'"

Anxious to be away, Avram forces himself to settle back, to hear out the remainder of her recitation.

"To begin at beginnings, my father was prescient in naming me, as if he realized at birth my life long character. Lest you are equally illiterate in regard to the myths of the ancients, the Roman goddess Minerva was known to the Greeks as Athena. Never the patron of war, a course of action all women know to be the nonsense of grown men playing at little boys' games, she was nevertheless a warrior goddess, the essence of wisdom won from hard fought experience."

"My father and mother, George Washington and Charlotte Buford, were pioneer settlers of the Alabama Black Belt, journeying down the Federal Road from the Carolinas after the soldiers of Andy Jackson drove out the Red Indians. They bartered a crude cabin from an old Indian fighter and the Cherokee squaw with whom he cohabited for five from a set of six coin silver spoons. My father ever a shrewd negotiator, he knew that no Red Indian woman could resist any shiny trinket. In such rude surroundings my parents began their new life, and until the day of her death my mother rued the loss of all save one of a simple set of spoons as if the engraving of her mother's initials upon them represented something symbolic."

"The soil was fertile, and the slave markets of Selma, Montgomery, and New Orleans provided an abundant labor force. In a few short years my father amassed a fabled fortune. My mother had brought to Alabama cuttings of white gardenias from her mother's Charleston garden. From these was established a formal shrub bed so splendid that the magnificent mansion house they constructed, and all of the extensive plantation lands surrounding it, came to be known as White Gardenias. It was there that the story began and there, my brother prophesied, in a day yet to come it must have its ending."

"My father was fabled not only for his fortune but also for his hospitality. Down a dusty road, twice doubling across a meandering brook, through the great gates came many guests to be received at the double doors of White Gardenias."

"My mother was in those years often ill and confined to her bed, giving birth as annually as the crops coming to harvest in the fields of October. My mother bore thirteen children, and only my brother Alexander, born on the same fateful night in 1833 that the leg-

endary shower of stars fell on our state, and I, six years his junior, lived past infancy. My mother passed on to my brother through her Scottish heritage red hair, green eyes, a tendency to melancholia, and the terrible gift of the second sight, a gift in truth a curse, that power to see the future. She died in my twelfth year, never, truth be told, having been of much assistance to me in the process of growing up. Aided by Alex, I verily raised myself, learning to live by my wits and my own configuring."

"Isolated as we were as children, as prince and princess of the tiny kingdom of White Gardenias, my brother and I were inseparable companions. In the bitter days after war and death intruded, when our good name and memories were all I could claim as treasure, I often looked back to the happiest times of my life, the red-gold afternoons of autumns spent with Alex."

"It was our late afternoon custom to hitch our ponies and ride the short distance to the swamp where the Red Indians before us had buried their dead. Alex taught me there to face fear and conquer her, as the will o' the wisps, considered by the superstitious to be the glowing manifestations of the souls of the damned, danced around us. I have the tokens still, arrowheads, pottery shards, a human skull, tangible reminders of those sweet lost hours."

"My father recognized early in both of his surviving children intellects of uncommon strength and sought to provide us the finest in classical educations. He installed in residence at White Gardenias as my brother's tutor a young gentleman from New England, one Oliver Pennocott. It was a wily ruse the Abolitionists practiced, sending agents such as Pennocott south disguised as scholars. Thus was planted a sturdy seed in the sowing of my brother's eventual self destruction."

"War destroyed many men of your brother's generation," Avram interrupts.

"My brother would have been his own undoing with or without a war's facilitation! Just as our southern system would have collapsed in and on itself had the damn Yankees left us to our own devices. Mark you well the name of Pennocott, as the same will later figure prominently in my narrative."

"The year of turning twelve, the same age at which I lost my mother, had in my brother's own life also been a pivotal juncture twixt childhood and self-determination. Our father, grooming him for his future role as master of White Gardenias, took him off ostensibly to Mobile for the purpose of buying a score of field hands at auction. By pre-arrangement, along the way they met a man of my father's long acquaintance, a man in fact in my father's employment. Though trade with Africa had been for some years illegal, it was still possible for buccaneers to slip through to the secluded coves of Mobile Bay, where they offloaded cargos of freshly acquired Africans. My father financed such operations."

Avram feels his stomach turn. Surely such evil cannot pass down through the generations, tainting his Lydia's expansive heart, bruising with the sins of the fathers the children she is anxious to bear for him.

"On that day my father commanded my brother to employ the whip to speed the onward movement of a manacled coffle of human misery. Even years later, Alex could not talk of it without a convulsive shudder. It was on that day, I am sure of it, that my brother's soul was also struck, with the certain realization that destiny had misplaced him, that he would not, could not, ever assume command of my father's empire."

"My father was a great lover of the antique sagas of Greek mythology. All of our slaves bore the names of gods or heroes. My brother, like me never one to subscribe to the bugaboos of conventional Christian religion, at the end of his life chose to believe that it was the ancient Fates who on that dusty road that day set events in motion, events of import to you, Avram, as they are even now and yet to come unfolding."

"Something more powerful than a mere god of our human understanding had positioned at the end of that chain of suffering humanity a young girl of about the same age as my brother. Hecuba, as my father christened her, after the wife of Priam, king of Troy, was to have the greatest bearing on all of our lives. She was descendant of an ancient tribe of sorceress queens, possessor of the secrets of magic so potent that its effects will be felt strongest by the one who comes as last in the line of Buford. Her eyes locked on my brother that day, bewitching him into a love that would prove both blessing and bane."

"Given to me as a birthday token, she remained for all but the last months of her life my personal servant. Though I both trained, and trusted, and, yes, sincerely loved her, with her dying breath, in anger over an action of my undertaking, she would call down a curse on all who bore the name of Buford. Only to the last of the line will there be given the power and the opportunity to break the curse and pay the recompense, avenge the sins committed against her people. To the last of the line must the story be told."

Sensing that she has paused for full effect of what is coming, Avram raises his face from his hands and looks her squarely in the eyes.

"You, Avram, are to be the messenger."

Seeing Carrie's eyelids flutter, Wyatt leaned over the bed. "Sorry, Sleeping Beauty, waking to find an ugly old toad like me on duty."

"What are you doing here? You need to be working, not worrying about me." She stretched and winced at the discomfort the simple movement caused.

"You know that I never begin work past eight nor continue past noon. If I don't give my mind a rest after four intense hours, I become at creative risk of turning out gibberish."

He took a long pull on his pipe. Even gibberish would have been better than nothing at all. He was dried up, as bereft of words as an illiterate man in a library.

"Where do you get ideas, Wyatt?" She shifted in the bed, impossible to get comfortable, welcoming the diversion of conversation.

"Usually the most difficult stage is giving characters birth, defining them at their moment in time, something in telling Hatton's story fortunately already decided for me by the real historical facts of his life. Normally, I simply translate onto paper what characters say and do after they take on imaginary lives of their own. Again, in Hatton's case, I am bringing to the stage words actually spoken in life by the leading character, the reason it is so vitally important for me to access that last manuscript."

"Isn't it sort of spooky, finding yourself in someone else's head?"

"Actually it's more like being in a state of dreaming while awake, if that makes any sense."

Too much sense, she thought ruefully. She was becoming so wrapped up in other lives that all she had to do to find herself inside others' heads was to close her eyes.

"I cannot believe I did this to myself," Carrie gasped as she got out of bed and limped toward the bathroom. She complained not so much due to the pain as to her frustration that just before sustaining the injury she had almost succeeded in clearing enough of a path in the attic to allow her access to a roll top desk. Could it be so simple as the missing manuscript lying undisturbed all these years under the locked wooden canopy of the desk? She was beginning to feel like Minnie on a quest for a fabled cache of gold. She could not risk telling Wyatt how she had hurt herself, risk his going to the attic and finding it all on his own, leaving him no further use for her.

Back in bed, she asked him to search through one of the cardboard boxes of clothes for an old flannel bathrobe, a years ago Christmas gift from Nick. "Not only do I feel ridiculous in this 'bed jacket' I am about to freeze to death. My mother has very definite ideas about how ladies should dress for all occasions including ailing. I must look like the neurotic heroine from Ellen's novel, or a relic from Isabel's era."

He wondered if Ellen were at home as they spoke, feeling the joy of words tumbling from her imagination as her fingers danced across the computer keys. Ellen had the luxury of time and words to waste.

"Your mother has established a central command post downstairs, complete with charts outlining nursing shifts."

"She didn't call you to come and babysit!"

"I am officially on the nurses' registry." Truthfully, when Josie disobeyed orders and interrupted him with the telephone call, he had felt a mixture of irritation at being pulled away from his typewriter and relief that someone had provided him an excuse to abandon another morning of empty pages. Carrie drugged on pain pills gave him the perfect opportunity to poke through the house without her slowing the search by chattering and expecting responses.

"Mother undoubtedly sees this temporary incapacitation as a perfect opportunity to jump in here and tidy up the mess I've made of our lives," Carrie muttered as she eased herself back in bed. "The painting and papering and landscaping crews will probably be arriving shortly. My mother took my measure at a very young age and found me coming up short."

It was almost time to give her another knockout pill. He needed to shift the subject. "Want to share with your co-conspirator how you managed to do this to yourself? You haven't found something you're not telling me about, have you?"

Images of a door sturdy enough to protect a vault full of secrets and a locked desk rolled across her mind.

"Surely your husband makes more than enough to hire some yard help," Wyatt continued, thinking furiously that the last thing he needed was Nick and Mallory producing a cleaning service peopled by those who would not recognize a missing manuscript if they tripped over it. Time running out took on a feverish new meaning.

"Not all doctors are millionaires despite the popular perception," Carrie countered, not adding that her husband had put forth the very same suggestion of hiring assistance. Some of the things in the house were private matters, not some perfect stranger's business.

"Nick is very conservative," she continued, defensive. "I think it has something to do with all the talk he heard growing up about what a tough time financially his mother's family had. He insisted on paying for his own education, every nickel of it all the way through medical school. It took us years to pay back all those student loans. I wonder why it is that when you look back the hardest years always seem like the best ones."

He consulted his father's pocket watch. "I am going to follow your Mother's instructions and make sure that you, exactly on schedule, take two of these tiny wonder pill tickets to the restful state of oblivion."

Chapter Sixteen

Carrie had a nagging fear that if she discussed the dreams they would stop occurring, like losing an out of print book halfway through the reading.

She wanted the closing chapter, the resolution.

Obedient, minding her out of sight mother, she took a sip of water and washed down the pills.

"I was sent away to Philadelphia for schooling, and it was short-ly after the passage of my fifteenth birthday that Alex and I returned south for the summer. He had completed his matriculation at the Harvard College. It was time for him to assume his rightful respon-sibilities as Papa's heir to White Gardenias. Alex had other ideas entirely. He had fallen under the spell of the German philosophers and wished to continue his studies at one of the ancient Teutonic universities."

"My father saw in this scheme an advantage. Irascible over the usurious rates charged by the factors who marketed his cotton, untrusting in banks after the failures of 1837, he was determined to sell his crops directly for gold to the mill owners of the English Midlands. Amassing gold became an obsession. He agreed to my brother's acting as his overseas agent. Alex was even then pulling irreparably away from us, and Papa was either too blind or too self serving to admit it."

"Papa had, in that summer of my fifteenth year, other plans as well. Adjacent to White Gardenias was a large plantation, the annexation of which would have been most advantageous. I had completed more schooling than the average female offspring, even one as brilliant and precocious as I, could expect to receive. He would barter me as bride to the widowed owner of the land he craved with no more consideration of my desires than he practiced in selling off from their mothers at auction the light skinned slave children who were fruit of his own seed."

She relates it so matter of factly, marvels Avram. The sale of her own half sisters and brothers, Lydia's great aunts and uncles. He buries his head in his hands, not wishing to hear more.

"I overheard them, my papa and that rank old boar Octavius Allen, discussing the size of my dowry. I was the most desirable

belle in the county! I could have had the hand of any man!" She bangs the floor with her cane for emphasis. "I hitched a horse, rode hard into town, and threw myself at the feet of the most interesting man of my acquaintance."

"Cap Hatton was a roué of dubious breeding. The genesis of his nouveau riche family's fortune was rumored to have been the fortuitous turn of his river boat gambler father's marked cards. His mother was whispered to have been one of the more notorious courtesans of a New Orleans bordello, a pale skinned octoroon of dubious antecedents. All of Selma sneered and snickered at the gaudy opulence with which they surrounded themselves. When Cap's parents were killed in a fiery river boat explosion it seemed a dramatically fitting end."

"However murky their origins, whatever dark drops tainted the blood of the mother, they had produced a son of unparalleled physical features and fortitude. Indeed on the first occasion that he entered my awareness he wrestled a bear and bested the beast, at the annual Jackson's Day barbecue. I found it most thrilling. My father had refused him permission to court me. A reckless elopement made me his wife."

"I had made a mistake of the gravest proportion. He was crude and callow and barely literate, and during the years I was obliged to spend under his authority as husband I grew to feel a disgust which hardened into hatred. Just short of my sixteenth birthday, I was delivered of our daughter Bess."

"I endured by spending his money as if it were a freely flowing stream of water, holding my head high and closing my ears to the catty comments of more polite society. I had, after all, been born a Buford. I designed a Hatton family crest and created for my white trash husband a fantasy ancestry as illustrious as my own. I ordered that crest emblazoned on the doors of a fine vermillion carriage in which I was transported around the town by four perfectly matched Cleveland Bays imported from England."

"Cap became obsessed with the construction of a palatial home. He was as passionate about that hideous house as my father was about amassing a golden treasure trove. Over those last giddy rich years, before the war intruded, our home Hatton Hall grew ever more grandiose, an architectural Tower of Babel. Twenty four columns graced its facade, eight of the Ionic order, eight of the Doric, eight of the Corinthian. The central core was of the Grecian style, the left wing Italianate, the right Gothic. The whole was enough to cause agitation in any observer."

"When the war began, my reckless husband was among the first of the prosperous men of the county to raise a fighting force. Possessed of a violent temper, his nature was ideally suited to war. The prognosticators in Montgomery predicted a conflict of only ninety days duration. I hoped only that it would last long enough to claim him as a casualty. Cap Hatton would bluster his way through four years of war, emerging as a general."

"It was in the second year of the war that I determined to pack up the few things in my miserable mansion which mattered to me, a splendid set of Rose Medallion china, made for me in Europe and numbering 183 pieces, the handsome repousse epergne created for me by Kirk of Baltimore, other assorted articles, and to refugee to White Gardenias with my young daughter."

"I prepared to spend my last night alone within the walls of Hatton Hall. The child had been sent ahead to the country with the servants. I climbed the stairs to the third floor ballroom and lit the tapers in the branched candelabra set on demi-lune tables between the forty four pier mirrors."

"Suddenly, as quietly as a Red Indian arriving in a clearing in the woods, my long absent brother appeared in the room with me. Through gold and guile he had slipped through the blockade at Charleston, returning to fulfill what his heart determined to be his patriotic duty."

"My joy at the sight of him was boundless. You see, of all of those who have been a part of my life, none have I loved as completely, and without judgment or compromise, as I loved my brother Alexander."

"We talked until night turned into sunrise before journeying together the ten miles to White Gardenias. How I imagined Papa's joy on the prodigal's returning."

"My father and my brother adjourned into the library for a private conversation. Angry voices bridged the barrier of closed doors. My brother stood before our father and renounced his birthright."

"Hating that their parting words should be of conflict, wishing to use my charm to mediate, I entered the room just as my father's face contorted in a seizure of apoplectic arrest. Pointing at Alex, he screamed a strangled 'damn you' before crumpling to the ground unconscious. It was a cruel two months, his power of speech *stolen, before death had the decency to take him."*

"Settled back within the corridors of my childhood, I endeavored to make the best of a bad situation. I spooned soups between Papa's drooling lips. I read to him his favorite passages from the pens of Plutarch and Socrates. I tried diligently, desperately, to teach him some alternate means of communication lest he depart this earth with the gold's location his private secret. When at last he passed to the Stygian shores I was so angry that I instructed a servant to place him in that marble mausoleum without so much as the fanfare of a final prayer. The only mourner in attendance, shutting those iron doors on his mortal remains, was the faithful valet who had served him since boyhood."

"Interminable war was at last drawing toward its inevitable conclusion as the Christmas of 1864 came round on the calendar. We were by then fully feeling war's deprivation, coffee made from corn, newspapers printed on wallpaper, substitutes substituting for substitutes. Well I remember waking that nativity morning drooling from a dream of former years' feasts, of roast pork and calves foot jelly, the scent of exotic imported spices having become no more than a memory. I took Papa's old rifle, a relic of an earlier revolution and the only weapon left us, and went into the woods to forage. Three squirrels and a possum we turned into a stew and served in remembered splendor from the large silver tureen engraved with the Hatton crest."

"From the tureen's shining surface, the lines of Latin, lines of my devising, 'Fuimus qui sumusque futuri,' mocked me."

"The new year, the last year, turned over. It was a dreary season of interminable rain. I went occasionally into Selma hoping for news of Alex's brigade, praying to spot my husband's death notice. The posted lists of casualties, of prisoners, seemed to stretch as long as the road to eternity. The vast majority rotted where they yet remain to this late day. The once great, gay cities of the south, New Orleans, Memphis, Chattanooga, were held in the iron grip of enemy hands. Atlanta was burned, Savannah capitulated."

"It was in late March that war for me reached its penultimate conclusion. It was one of those stormy spring days when the distant thunder booms as though the gods are firing cannons. Late in the afternoon through the great gates rode our stalwart servant Hyperion, strapped behind him over a half lame mule the maimed and broken body of my beloved brother."

"We bore him into the house and laid him in the bed in which our mother had birthed him. My brother's life hung by a thread as slender as a spider's spinning. Infection rendered him incoherent, raving in the ancient tongues of the Teutons. The only utterance clear and understandable was Oliver. Oliver, Oliver, Oliver, Oliver. It was a name from our childhoods, that of our New England tutor, the man who had first planted in Alex's head the misguided notion of a northern education."

"I dreamt that night that my brother and I were hosting a ball at Hatton Hall. The ballroom's pier mirrors reflected the sparkle of candles glow, champagne bubbles bursting in crystal flutes on trays carried by liveried waiters. Soft music strummed by a string quartet wafted through the open windows. It was an evening in a summer time. As the musicians struck up the evening's final waltz, I begged my brother take me in his arms as partner. Suddenly the candles flickered, and all came crashing down about us. The guests leered the rictus grins of specters, the four and forty mirrors shattered, cobwebs draped the room, white gardenias in silver bowls withered, blackened, gave off the sour sickening stench of corpses rotting. A suffocating heat, as if produced by hell's own furnaces, enveloped the room. The soft strums of harp notes climaxed into a cacophony of crashing symbols. My brother, his fine features transformed into a hideous death's head, drew back from me, jeering."

"Through all those long days and nights of wretched despair, mere trial runs for greater misery yet to smite us, Hecuba, the sorceress servant who had cast a spell on him with their first encounter, never left him. She alone seemed to give him a sense of peace and consolation."

"Early on the morning of the first day of April, she brought to me breakfast and the joyous news that her magic had at last proved mightier than the fever's power."

"Larger crisis loomed, heralded by the appearance of three grey coated riders galloping up the drive, emissaries from my husband whose forces were camped to the north and west of us, lying in wait for the inevitable onslaught of the damned Yankee Wilson's pyromaniacal Raiders."

"The news from the northern counties of our state was bleak. The young university at Tuscaloosa smoldered. My husband held *out little hope that other than a similar fate lay in store for our little city."*

"General Forrest commanded every male of any age join in the defense of Selma, arsenal city of the Confederacy, or be drowned in the Alabama River for refusal. It was a futile call to arms. Selma's strong young manhood lay already dead in other trenches. Only old men and beardless boys remained to meet the challenge. A weak force of four thousand was mustered to meet General Wilson's, mightier by more than two times that number. In the game of war, Wilson held as well a trump card. A damn Yankee spy hidden in the Confederate ranks had supplied to him a sketch detailing the city's defenses."

"The end loomed within the span of hours. I was so very weary of war. Let defeat come and be done with it."

"The trio asked the whereabouts of my brother. Expressing gratitude for their interest, I told them that he mended within the walls of White Gardenias. This they promised to relay to my husband."

"Their return was on the subsequent Sunday morning. The paper they thrust into my hands bore the official seal of the Confederate Government at Richmond. They were under order to deliver to the commander in charge of the defense of Selma the person of Captain Alexander Washington Buford, branded as traitor, sentenced to be summarily and in the humiliation of public spectacle hanged by the neck until dead. The crime specific was the passing of information regarding the defense of the arsenal and city into the enemy hands of Union Commandant Oliver Pennocott. The scrawled signature on the execution order was all too familiar, General Henry Capshaw Hatton."

"I knew and understood them both too well, my brother and my husband."

"I begged of the men before me a few moments last communion with my brother, and, while arguing that time was of the essence, they gave deference to the obvious fact of my superior breeding, and this request was granted."

"It had come as no surprise. Deep within my heart I had long since grudgingly recognized that the cause that had called my beloved brother Alexander home to willingly sacrifice his life was the Truth as Mr. Lincoln saw it."

"I commanded Hecuba leave his side that my brother and I might have a private moment. Before so doing she leaned close for

a last lingering caress of his face, their eyes locking as if their souls were merging."

"He raised himself in the bed and gazed out the window, across the distant and now fallow fields of the lands called White Gardenias. His voice was as firm, his words as clear, as if of the old days. 'The gods were good to me, Minnie. I did in this life what they demanded.'"

"As do I now, my brother," I responded sadly. "It falls on me to me to protect for future generations the honor of the name of Buford, all that remains for any southern family to be able to claim as fortune."

"I would not have you do otherwise. I bear, as did our mother, the heavy burden of the gift of the second sight. I see it clearly, Minnie, far down through the unfolding of the future, as if forewritten by the Fates. Through me, and through you, will come the last in the line of Buford. To the last of the line the Truth must be delivered. You will know when comes the time, the place, and the messenger to whom it shall be entrusted. Promise me, on your word, that you too will carry out your duty."

"The sounds of heavy boots mounting the stairs grew closer. I made him my promise and quickly slipped from my pocket the small silver pistol duello with which my husband had more than once avenged what that scoundrel perceived to be his non-existent honor."

"I shot my brother."

"They stormed into the room. I maintained my dignity, commanding them, 'Return to my husband. Inform him that Captain Buford died this morning in the bed in which our mother bore him.' As they rode away, I took the rope and pulled the great bell which had pealed out the news of my brother's birth, on that night that a shower of stars fell over Alabama. The dirge tolled and was carried by the wind over the fields fabled far and wide as White Gardenias."

"Hyperion and I shrouded my brother's body in sheets and laid him in the black earth, in a grave metaphorically of his own digging."

Minnie unclasps a small gold locket hanging around her neck and passes it to Avram. "My brother commissioned this painted for me while he was a student in Germany. This, to remember him always, and a carved music box from Switzerland were the last Christmas gifts I received before the war began."

Avram opens the locket and holds the small likeness close to his face in the dim light. The resemblance between Alexander Buford and Lydia sends a chill of fear rippling through his heart.

"The sorceress slave woman Hecuba, on the same mule that had transported home my brother's broken body, took her leave of White Gardenias as we were disposing of the body. She was as free as the birds of the air to go wherever life would take her. She had always walked among us a queen, the only bonds that had truly ever held her were the golden chains of her abiding love for Alexander."

"I hitched a ride in the wagon of a passing stranger and rode into Selma to face the Yankees and my husband, too bone tired to examine which of the two I despised the more."

"It was a warm morning, that first Sunday in April 1865, the song of the birds and the softness of the air speaking so falsely of beginnings at that time of bitter ending."

"I arrived alone at Hatton Hall. In the ballroom I took the silver candelabra and broke the four and forty pier mirrors each and every one to slivers. I returned downstairs and shattered the ruby glass in the fanlights embracing the great entrance doors, as hell bent on destruction of all the representations of my husband's false pride as any torch bearing damn Yankee riding with Lucifer's legions at that very moment toward our town."

"The house had stood empty for two long years. All was dry and dusty. It took but a flicker of fire against the velvet draperies. In moments Hatton Hall was an inferno. The war, and the way of life that led to it, were for me at last over."

"I did not even once look back over my shoulder as I began to walk on the long ten miles toward home."

"Three days passed. Selma was in ashes. As a final retribution Wilson ordered, along with what pitiful few horses and mules remained to the citizens of Selma, eight hundred of his own battle worn beasts slaughtered, and the streets were littered with the carcasses of dead and dying animals. The only solution to the fearsome stench was to drag them into the river. The victorious invaders destroyed all food supplies, pouring together soap and syrup, leaving the innocent widows and orphans homeless and hungry."

"Montgomery gave up without a fight, with no more dignity than a cur with its tail between its legs in fear of a beating. Richmond fell on the same calamitous day that Selma went up in smoke."

"War was winding down, but an ultimate indignity still awaited us. Through the great gates he came, not welcomed, to a house once fabled for hospitality, a dirty ragtag straggler."

"Only one man, yet in his wanton ravishing he might as well have been a hundred, pillaging through the house, demanding liquor. In the dining room he shattered my precious Rose Medallion china service by flinging it piece by piece into the fireplace. I have left to me but a few teacups from a service of almost twice a hundred pieces. There is such a sadness to a cup without a saucer."

"He ripped apart my brother's books, looking for hidden money. Cursing, he struck a match and set the volumes, all except for a locket and a music box that I had left of my brother, blazing. A slim volume of the essays of Aurelius is all that today remains from Alexander's scholarly assembled library."

"I beat the flames out with the hearth rug, saved White Gardenias from a similar fate to Hatton Hall."

"Was there no method for bringing such a man to justice?" Avram interrupts, a man of words understanding, if little else in this dialogue, her deep offense at the destruction of books.

Minnie snorts. "Justice? The villain just described was my husband. Any court in the north or the south land would have called him justified. I was merely a woman. Any item in that household, worthless or of value, myself included, was his to do with to his liking."

"Cap planted a little patch of corn in the yard and within me a child we could ill afford to nurture, spent the remaining days of his life telling long winded stories of his battlefield heroics."

"He ranted of growing grapes and becoming a vintner, of importing Chinese coolies as replacement for the slaves fled off to freedom. He rode about the town in a tattered general's tunic, a comic figure. On his lucky days, foolish men provided him whiskey in gratitude for his sacrifice and service."

"Chiefly in those half dozen years between surrender and his ignoble death in a saloon shooting he dozed on the veranda and drank from my father's pre-war cellar absinthe, the green fairy wormwood that often rendered him delusional."

"I kept from him my knowledge of the cache of gold that my father had secreted and for which I conducted a ceaseless, futile searching. The gold, rightly my inheritance, lies to this day within the walls or under the dark earth of White Gardenias."

"We, who had once wanted for nothing, were destitute, our vast acres of land before the war worth more than one hundred dollars each now valued at no more than three to five dollars per acre. Had we had the hands to do it, there was no use in growing cotton for which we had neither railroad nor river steamer for getting it to market."

"The bonded debt of the Confederacy had been declared defunct, null and void. All I had on which to pin hope was the cursed gold. It was there, but where? I was as sure of it as I was of the fact that I had been born a Buford."

"Many a night I boiled a single squirrel for supper. Close to starving, I sent my darling Kitty off to the relative richness of relations in Birmingham. No one disputed that Bess would ever remain a spinster. Even unsuitable suitors were as scarce as hens' teeth. There were in Alabama as many or more widows as there were wives."

"But I must backtrack to bring my tale to its conclusion. It was shortly before the Christmas of 1865 when word came to us of the sorceress Hecuba. Through the shanty settlement housing the newly freed population of Selma swept a virulent epidemic of smallpox. The Union authorities, so verbally righteous in regard to those whom they had so recently released from bondage, turned their backs in fear on this loathsome pestilence. The charitable natives of Selma established a pest house for the afflicted. Retaining even in reduced circumstances our family's heritage of noblesse oblige, I dispatched Hyperion in delivery of a half dozen eggs for the nourishment of the sufferers."

"He returned in a fury of agitation, having found Hecuba, dying great with child. We bore her home to White Gardenias."

"Hyperion begged that they might be united in marriage, saving the child being born a bastard. I took my grandmother's old Episcopal Book of Sacraments and read the words of the rites of marriage."

"She was out of her head with the fever. I doubted that she was even aware of the proceedings. Her heart had already been pledged for eternity. It was only hours later, Hyperion downstairs, nailing her coffin, when she beckoned to me."

"Her voice was strong despite the grip of death upon her, saying, 'He saw down the days of the future, he told me of it, the ending of the line of Buford.' She struggled in a fit of coughing, for some moments unable to speak further."

"She suddenly rose up in the bed and screamed out words that I, though ignorant of her native tongue, knew instinctively to be the placing of an ancient curse on the future of the house of Buford."

"The child, a girl, came into the world with her mother's closing breath. Holding the orphaned infant in his arms, Hyperion made comment that she was as pretty as the first wild violet of spring-time, and after such we called her."

"The sun is rising," Avram says, running a trembling hand over his face.

Her lined face streaked with tears, Minnie lifts her chin and stares Avram fully, almost defiantly, in the face.

"Take care with the precious prize of my granddaughter, Avram. It is a bitter truth that in every life there comes those times when, however sincere our prayers may be, no gods choose to listen."

"All that I have spoken to you is documented in my diaries, in my brother's papers. They are secreted in a small trunk bearing Alexander's initials in the carriage house where you make love to my granddaughter. Take with you these words and mark them well. 'Fuimus qui sumusque futuri.' Who we were is who we are and are to be. Go with my blessing to share with your Lydia, if the gods choose to grant it, a long and a happy life together."

He plants a gentle kiss on her wrinkled cheek, and she clasps his hand.

From high in the glossy leaves of the old magnolia tree mocking-birds trumpet the morning.

Minnie dozes in the rocker, her task in a mission assigned years before accomplished. Her heart feels a small measure of relief tempered by a nagging sense of foreboding, the premonition that a fateful day is beginning.

Chapter Seventeen

Possessing the sixth sense that gives cats nine lives, the old yellow tom pricked his ears at approaching footsteps. He darted under the bed just as Ellen Lancaster shouldered open the door.

"I've brought you some breakfast. You must be famished. You slept right through dinner last night. Your mother volunteered for the five to seven a.m. shift. If I could make myself get up that early every morning I'd probably already be a published author. How are you?"

"Better, I think." Carrie wiggled gingerly under the covers. "Mother has got to stop acting like this is an intensive care ward."

"Don't be silly. You would be the first to do the same for any of us. Look at what a nice breakfast your mother has left for you."

"You know, Ellen, when that justice of the peace pronounced us man and wife, it ran through my mind that as a married woman I was never again obligated to force down Mother's requisite prunes with every breakfast."

"Shall I flush them?" Ellen gave Carrie a conspiratorial wink.

"Ellen, as long as you're on my side, why don't you help me up out of this bed and up the attic stairs. No one will ever be the wiser."

"Not a chance. I brought my new laptop, and I plan to help you pass the time by sharing portions of my novel. I'm fine tuning the last draft and trying to think how the readers can stay in touch with their favorite characters even after the book's conclusion. When I finish a good book I'm always left wondering what happened later."

"How many pages?"

"Two thousand, give or take a few. Some publisher will be astounded at how prolific I am for a first time novelist. The person who would have not been in the least surprised at what I've managed was my grandmother. When I was a child growing up poorer than a church mouse as a coal miner's daughter, my old Cornish granny always assured me that I could grow up to be anything. She was widowed, pregnant, at twenty, and picked up the pieces and kept on going, but that is another story with which I will not horrify you this morning. I'll begin on page 1743, where the action really gets going."

Ellen hoped that it was the tranquilizing effect of the pain pills rather than any boredom induced by the contents of her narrative as she realized that Carrie was out cold. She left the room and her daughter-in-law dreaming.

The pitch of night is punctuated by the eerie glow of oil lanterns. As dark as the night skies are the blackened faces of the men, grimly going about their work as a huddled group of women and children wail an ancient banshee keening. Fear always bubbles within the hearts of miners' women compelled to rise each morning wondering if the sunset will call them widows.

From far across the town a church bell chimes ten p.m. Six harrowing hours have passed since the malignant dust brushed lips with a flicker of flame and climaxed in explosion. In a Stygian underground tomb of fire and gas more than a hundred men waltz in a macabre dance with death. Those moving about above them wear the glazed expressions of earth bound men who have been permitted a preview of hell.

They move as in trance through this scene of temporal purgatory. A desperate and communal cry crescendos from the crowd each time the earth retches up another body bearing rescuer.

The corpses recovered, so far numbering half a hundred, are mangled and charred beyond recognition. A small black locomotive shudders to a stop on the railway siding, weeping soot as if mourning the burden its trailing cars must carry. A load of once warm flesh, now burned beyond humanity's comprehension, travels in a cortege past curious crowds of onlookers to a makeshift morgue a few miles distant.

There is not within the raw young city of Birmingham an adequate supply of caskets. Not since the cholera epidemic a quarter century before have so many been torn screaming from the land of the living in a single day. Telegraph operators race frantic fingers, tapping out orders to the coffin companies of other cities.

A man stumbles from the bruised opening in the earth. He carries what was on the day's more hopeful morning some soul's dinner pail.

The onlookers gasp, stunned beyond the power to scream, as a young woman, heavily pregnant, breaks free from the arms that seek to contain and console her, seizes the content of the pail like a bloody trophy.

She clutches it to her breast, howling, addressing the crowd in a voice brought with her across the wide Atlantic waters from her native Cornwall.

"It was the woman what caused it! It was the woman who tempted the fate of the ancients, calling down a curse upon our menfolks. May the same be upon her house and all who follow from it."

As if the archaic gods respond, a night breeze catches her apron, ballooning it over the distended belly. Lifeless eyes appraise the crowd as from the base of the severed head clutched tightly in the woman's arms the blood courses down, red staining the apron to the color of the mineral rich earth beneath her feet, covering the unborn child like a blanket.

Sam McShan and Willard Preston look on in stupefied horror. The younger man places a hand on his father-in-law's shoulder as Sam convulses in a spasm of weeping.

"It was inevitable that they place the blame on Lydia, sir. You know their superstitions. The Cornish are the very worst, for their primitive fears go back to the time before the Romans." Willard struggles to contain the small smug smile teasing his lips. She got what she deserved. For all the long years she has been away she has been constantly present as a throbbing ache in both his mind and body. How many times has he dreamed of a future in which some minor plague takes Isabel, allowing Lydia to fly to the waiting refuge of his arms?

Whore! Miserable foreign devil on whom she has turned such adoring eyes! If there were justice in this world, they would, both of them, have been blown away on this day into the very fires of hell.

"Who's to say, Willard? Who's to say? I never thought I would live to see such a day of destruction. Possibly a hundred of my best men dead, my daughter bringing down on my head a dishonor from which I shall never recover. Would that I had died among them."

"Take heart, sir," Willard soothes. "More than half of them were convicts, worthless vagrants whom the state in its wisdom saw fit to collect up off the street and put to some honest hard labor. No one will even mourn their passing. You know these for-eigners and coloreds breed so indiscriminately their own mothers would not recognize nor claim them. Take heart that we cull our labor force from a bottomless pit of humanity's well. There will be others to replace them. What we need worry ourselves with tonight is twofold, how quickly we can get this mine back in operation and

how this will impact on the unions' swelling numbers. They will doubtless double their efforts, squawking that unsafe conditions somehow caused this disaster. Better to let them hove to the old superstitions, think that Lydia's ill gotten actions somehow called down the wrath of the gods."

Sam shakes his head. Willard has become too caught up in the prevailing xenophobic ideology of the day. Sam has assembled his mongrel work force through a sense of practicality rather than through callous bigotry. His conscience stabs at his heart. He has let Willard have his way overmuch. Any humanity Willard ever possessed has been sublimated by greed's grasp.

He hangs his head, defeat humping his shoulders like the weight of old age. He is more than empathetic to the weeping women around him. On this day he too has lost a favorite child, in his case to the mortal wound of betrayal. Driven mad by love, she has placed another above the sacred bonds of family.

Across town the atmosphere of despair overwhelms other wailing women. "Lydia, how could you? How could you? Can you begin to comprehend the havoc you have wreaked? You have ruined us all!" Isabel shrills, tearing at her hair as her sister cringes, weeping.

"I love him!" Lydia screams. "I will go to my grave loving him."

"Consider the repercussions of your forbidden love! By your actions today a hundred husbands and fathers are now corpses. Because of your . . . your . . . lover families are shattered, and none more so than this one. I don't know how I shall cope if our fortune is now gone as well." Isabel spits her words like bullets.

"That is enough, Isabel!" Minnie says sharply. "Avram and Lydia no more caused today's tragedy than did you or I. Their intentions were to help not harm. You cannot lay at their feet the results of simple spontaneous combustion. Lydia, go and wash your face and remove that ridiculous clothing."

Lydia looks up miserably at her grandmother. How can their careful planning have gone so hopelessly awry? Her father is a sound sleeper. She has stolen into his room deep in the night after leaving her lover, pocketing the spare keys which have allowed them access to the locked drawers of his desk, to his records and later to the mine shop where they absconded with helmets and coveralls. Face blackened with soot from the fireplace, she has fearlessly accompanied Avram on an inspection of conditions about which he *will write an expose. Lydia and Avram neatly sidestepped death as they came into the sunlight mere moments before a gust of wind ignited a puff of dust and brought down the fire and flame of Armageddon. It was Sam himself, alerted by a foreman to their presence, who stripped the helmet from Lydia's head.*

In a state of shock, she numbly soaps herself. Touch me, Avram, there, and there, and there. Never again sings a sad voice in her head. Never, never, never.

He has fled in the night like a felon, returning under the cover of commotion to the family's home, retrieving from the sanctuary of the carriage house not only his satchel but a larger portmanteau as well, a cracked leather valise into which he has crammed a trunk's contents, diaries and letters, the message of which he is destined to be the messenger.

He is young and agile, jumping from the siding onto one of the slowly moving coal cars of the little train of the Mineral Railroad, on the first leg of a journey that will last his lifetime.

He has made a subsequent connection, on a northbound midnight express that whistles a blast of greeting to a passing freight coming south bearing a cargo of plain pine coffins.

From far off in the distance, the mournful voice of the locomotive carries on the summer breeze and through the open window of Lydia's bedroom, hanging on the air as plaintive as a sweet and sad goodbye.

What love he has given her must now be enough to last more than a lifetime and into eternity.

She has promised it.

The yellow cat's whiskers swept across Carrie's cheek, as gentle as a fairy's kiss. She stirred in her sleep and rolled over.

"What time is it, Willie?" she mumbled, squinting to read the face of the bedside clock. "Days and nights are running together."

Calling out for Nick and getting no response, Carrie put a tentative foot on the floor. Her back replied with only a dull thump of protest.

She resettled herself in bed with the wicker supper tray. Under the sandwich's lid of bread was lean smoked turkey with a smear of artificially sweetened cranberry sauce. Mayonnaise was, for her fat free mother, as much a part of the past as that rich roulage made of chocolate wafer cookies and whipped cream always served at bridge club luncheons. How many times had Carrie hung back in the kitchen with Josie, mouth watering, hoping that those chattering ladies would not eat every last bite of it? Her mouth watered in remembrance.

A sweet taste of memory. Bridge club chocolate roulage that followed the predictable preceding course of chicken salad, creamy with her grandmother's recipe homemade mayonnaise, a salad of a canned pear half or pineapple slice resting on a Bibb lettuce leaf and topped with another dollop of mayonnaise and a bright red maraschino cherry. Fat buttery yeast rolls.

A more dangerous memory squeezed through the tiny gap she had allowed to open and hovered just in the back of her consciousness like a snatch of song long unsung. Fifth grade. Nancy Drew. Feigning an upset stomach so that she could stay at home from school and learn the spine tingling secret behind a whispering statue.

Fifth grade was as gone from her, as lost to her, as if it had never happened. She had not the slightest recollection of the name or the face of her teacher of that year.

Little rusty chips of recall were too often lately floating to the surface when she least expected it.

She was frightened. Lying in bed left her too much time for thinking. Some of fifth grade had to still be there. All of it's there, Carrie Beth, mocked her mind. All of it! All of it! All of it! Red Rover, Red Rover. Ready or not, Carrie Beth, it's coming right over!

Shaking, she managed to bring the watered down glass of iced tea to her lips. The two pills slipped obediently down her throat, taking her safely away from that place in the past to which her mind was not yet strong enough to willingly return.

"Mama! Look! A letter to Lydia, bearing the postmark of Imperial Russia! Do you think she will care if I cut away the stamps for my album?"

"How should I know what she will or will not do?" Minnie snaps. "For how many months now has she refused to leave that room or to let anyone other than Violet enter it?"

"Maybe we worry needlessly, Mama. Mrs. Ashcraft said that she knew of a woman in Montgomery, just before the War of Northern Aggression began, who emerged from her room after forty six years absence from society and went that very same night to see the circus as if she had been but on a brief vacation." The widow Ashcraft has recently become the new Mrs. McShan, but

Bess cannot bring herself to vocalize the change in designation.

"I doubt very much that Lydia has any desire to see again the circus," Minnie grumbles. "She has left us for a private world."

"Well, perhaps the receipt of a communication from halfway round the world will cheer her. Perhaps it is from one of her northern school chums taking the grand tour or from young Mr. Cunningham declaring himself still smitten."

Violet delivers the missive along with the supper tray. "A letter for you, baby girl, but before you read it please take at least a few swallows of this chicken soup I made special for you." Violet begins to spoon feed Lydia as if she were an ailing child.

Protesting lack of appetite, Lydia unfolds the single sheet of paper. "My darling Lydia, as you will see from the mark of postage, I am returned to the land of my birth, assigned by Young's as foreign correspondent. The power of the proletariat rises! I have a strong sense of being a part of history's march toward all mankind's full freedom. As I am fluent in the language, my editors insist on my remaining until the triumphant day of revolution."

"I think of you often and hope that you are well. I will always regret the circumstances of our parting."

"While I cannot bear the thought of another knowing you in the intimacy that I did, I hope, I pray, that your future holds a loving husband and a tribe of beautiful children."

"As hard as you may find it to believe, I left you behind and without a final word of farewell because I did then and will forever deeply love you. Our love was doomed to be but an interlude, a few spring warm days in the depth of winter."

"Please give my best to your grandmother and thank her for me for the fascinating tale she shared. It is not a story I shall soon or, indeed ever, forget."

"Live a long and happy life, my lovely, lovely Lydia, and may your God go with you through it."

"Avram."

Chapter Eighteen

Mallory was perfectly happy for Nick to be on emergency room duty at the hospital. Who could argue that a child's passing forty meant that she no longer needed her mother?

It was easy enough to keep herself busy all day every day, but there was little palliative for long lonely nights in an echoing empty house.

Her routine of evening's end beauty rituals completed, Mallory turned back the quilt on the single bed, ran her hand over the smooth cherry spindles of the headboard. Very finely crafted, most likely a family heirloom.

The house had changed as little over a long time's passage as Carrie had changed so much in such a brief span. Always so like her father, so open, so honest as to be almost plain spoken, she had lately become furtive, self contained. It was troubling.

Taking to bed her copy of the book on which she had volunteered to report at her book discussion club, Mallory found it impossible to concentrate. Her eyes were stubbornly drawn around the room, to the college pennants on the wall, tennis racquet hanging from a peg, a framed master's degree diploma from Vanderbilt, an old bottle green shaded lamp casting shadows on doodlings on the desk blotter, a card table carrying a chess board, knights and pawns poised in a game that would never resume or conclude. It was a room frozen waiting in futile anticipation for a boy who would never again be returning home.

I understand, how I understand, she whispered as if commiserating with the spirit of Isabel Preston. In the back of her mind she heard the crack of a boy's voice in the process of changing, leaving childhood, moving toward manhood.

She turned out the light and wiped away a tear.

She was getting too old to continue to keep up a house spacious enough to be crowded with ghosts. A misnomer "garden home" without a yard, or an apartment in some nice retirement community was really the sensible alternative. Perhaps Carrie and Nicky could be persuaded to sell this gloomy old pile of stone and to move into her house, paint it pretty, bright, currently stylish colors, and update the kitchen.

Carrie used to be such a wonderful cook and so good at entertaining. Surely Carrie could go back again to being her old self, if given the right environment.

It was a natural solution. Carrie could do wonders to revitalize the big house in which Mallory had in the past thirty years changed little. She still left the porch light burning every night, went to sleep praying to wake up the following morning relieved that losing Jamie had all been just the very worst of nightmares.

Mallory served on the church board that administrated the retirement home. No waiting on a list for someone with as much influence as Mallory Hudson. Surely, through attrition of the aged, there was always an empty apartment ready and available.

A perfect plan. What a pity that it would not work. Mallory was not ready to give up a setting that still held so much of Jamie and doubted that she ever would be.

Refusing to move on was something that she and Isabel Preston shared in common. She turned her face into the pillow and as she had, every night, for the past thirty years, lost control and sobbed herself to sleep.

Down the hall her daughter dreamed.

"Can you believe it, Mama? A pilgrimage home again to Selma!" Bess adjusts her bonnet as they wait, bags packed and on the porch, for Sam and Adelaide.

"To think of the treasures of my ancestral home being brought to Birmingham to outfit that gauche and gaudy palace Adelaide is building on the Highland Avenue. Oh, bah humbug! Let her have it all and welcome to it. I dreamt last night of Papa. I believe I may at last have a most logical clue as to the location of the gold."

"Now, Mama, put your foolish thoughts away. You and I both know that there is no gold under the soil of White Gardenias."

Minnie stamps her feet and bangs her cane. "There is most certainly so! Oh, damn you both, Alex and Papa, for dying with your secrets!"

"Calm yourself, Mama." Bess takes a swig from the brown bottle and offers her mother a sip of the same, which she, as usual, refuses. Mrs. Ashcraft, as Bess continues to call her despite the widow's recent transition back to wife, complains that Nervine tonic makes her giddy. More likely that reintroduction to the marital state has made her head all spinny. Sam has announced his retirement. He seldom speaks of his younger daughter, and always in the past

tense, as if she were dead and departed. The portrait of Lydia as Queen of the Mardi Gras has been relegated to the attic.

"I wish that Violet could accompany us," Minnie frets. "She was always so strong of back when it came to the digging. Do you know that she and I have not been a day apart in more than forty years?"

"Now, Mama, with Willard so far away in Washington on official Congressional testimonial business regarding the Mary Lydia mine explosion, you very well know we could not leave Isabel and Lydia utterly defenseless. Besides, with none other allowed in her room, without Violet Lydia could starve right to death."

"Perhaps in Violet's absence she would at last choose to free herself from that self imposed solitary confinement."

"Do not give up hope, Mama! Did I not mention to you that Mrs. Ashcraft knew, in Montgomery, just before the Late Unpleasantness interrupted. . . ."

"Spare me the story, Bess," Minnie interrupts, adding emphasis to her words with a sharp rap of her cane. "I have heard it before. I do not have forty six years left on this earth to wait for Lydia to return like Lazarus from the dead and with a ticket to the circus. If I can find the gold, I will have means to affect her recovery. If I must finance a revolution to accomplish their reunion, so be it."

"Poor child, poor child," Bess clucks. "Is it any wonder she suffers from a broken heart, denied her father's love?"

"I agree that her heart is broken, but it is for her young reporter that she pines, not her father."

"Do not argue that I did not warn Mr. McShan. It was the northern education that led to her degradation," Bess huffs. "Mrs. Ashcraft says that all the town whispers about her. Oh, Mama, I fear that our Lydia is ruined beyond redemption. How could she have lowered her standards so?"

"Love is the most irrational of emotions, Bess."

"Well, regarding the Russian, I say good riddance to bad rubbish." She takes another hearty pull from her bottle of tonic.

"Actually, I quite liked young Avram. It is to what is left of Lydia to which we must turn our attentions. I only hope that White Gardenias has not deteriorated entirely beyond habitation. I am going to propose to Sam that we take Lydia home to Selma, where no one can deny that she through me was born a Buford. She is young and strong enough to assist me with the digging."

***

Missing Minnie, Violet draws the drapes against the evening.

"Oh, Violet, how the wind shrieks! The sound makes me quite fearful, us being all alone without any masculine protection." Isabel wrings her hands and paces the floor. She jumps as a bare winter branch slaps against the window.

"It's going to be the cyclone of 1901 all over again," she wails. "Oh, Violet, I just know it! Such devastation! Do you think we should seek safety in the cellar?"

"No, Ma'am, I don't. Who ever heard of a cyclone in January?"

"Death and destruction. I can just see it. Those little houses in the colored quarter will blow away like dust balls just as they did in 1901. The death toll will be worse than the Shiloh Stampede."

"Miss Isabel, please! The Shiloh Stampede had nothing at all to do with the weather. Someone yelled 'fight' which was heard as 'fire' in a crowded church."

"Over a hundred people trampled to death." Isabel clucks her tongue and shakes her head. "The National Negro Baptist Convention having as their speaker that trouble making Booker T. Washington, no wonder and serves them right it happened. Hardly a one in the lot with the resources for burial. Hard working tax pay-ers' good money wasted on burying them in that paupers' field."

"We just are not used to such an empty and a peaceful house," Violet soothes, having no desire to spend the balance of the night cowering in the cellar, or rehashing old crises. "I miss your granny something terrible. Imagine her, at her age, talking silly about us going back home to Selma. Why, if we had dug all those holes we made looking for that gold in one straight down direction we would have found ourselves slap dab in the middle of a crowd of Chinamen."

"Pay no attention to an old woman's dither dather about gold. Except for this temporary hiatus, Granny is not going anywhere. Although I would, I do not mind admitting, appreciate Lydia's exile from my household. My vain and selfish sister has always been spoiled by all of you, and look at where it has gotten her, lying up there locked away like Rapunzel in the tower, pouting because she did not for once get exactly and absolutely her own way. All those fine young men of good family who used to come around swooning at her feet. They would not have her now, would they? She is dam-

aged goods that can never be mended. It would suit me fine for Granny to take her home to Selma. If you ask me, the only place Miss Priss Lydia is headed is straight to hell."

"Lydia for sure ain't left nothing in Selma," Violet sighs. "All that Lydia wants from this life left on a northbound train."

"Such an evil man! Just look at the harm he left behind."

Left more than harm, Violet mutters to herself as she prepares Lydia's supper tray. She peers out the back door. The weather is unsettled and unsettling. Sleet by morning, sure enough. The chickens scuttle and squawk in their coop. She has heard the owl cry, one sharp warning. Through ponderous clouds the winter moon breaks a brittle bluish white.

Carrying the tray upstairs, she hears again the owl's hooting, a bad omen. She quickens her step and opens Lydia's door.

Wide eyed, Lydia jerks beneath the bed covers. Despite the cold wind rattling through the window frames, Lydia is flushed and bathed in perspiration. Hurrying to her, Violet makes a misstep. The contents of the supper tray lurch, toast coming to rest in a murky puddle of tea and broken bits of Isabel's buttercup patterned china like flowers strewn from an unbound bouquet.

"Hurts, oh, Violet, how it hurts," Lydia whimpers as Violet gently draws back the covers. At another spasm of pain, Lydia twists violently on the sodden sheets, jams a fist to her mouth and bites down hard on her knuckles, resisting the effort to cry out. A drop of blood spurts from her hand.

"Shush, baby, shush, baby," Violet croons as she cradles Lydia's head against her breast. "How long you been like this, all by yourself? Why didn't you call for me?"

Violet lifts the wet, clinging nightdress from Lydia's legs. "Won't be long, sweet Lydia, won't be long now."

The scream when it comes is higher than the wind's howl. Isabel's head swims as she braces herself in the door frame, certain that she is going to faint at the sight before her. She screams again.

"Isabel! Pull yourself together and be of some help to us!" Violet commands as Lydia convulses violently one last time, a small still form slivering in a rush of blood from between her legs. The room spins round and round in Isabel's brain, a dizzying kaleidoscope of the colors of Lydia's pale milky skin and bright blood.

"Isabel!" Violet slaps her hard, pulls her through the door, and

slams it closed behind them. Isabel sinks into a chair beside the bed and covers her face with her hands. Lydia rocks back and forth against the pillows, sounding a primal keening over the dead baby. Violet has had her supplies at hand for some weeks now. She takes a pair of sharp shears from the drawer of a bedside table and neatly severs the useless cord of life, separating mother from child.

The baby, making entry into the world eight weeks before its expectation, is little more than a pitiful, purple pound of flesh, dark against the pale blue veined breast at which Lydia futilely encourages her to suckle.

"It's no use, honey. Give her here to Violet." Violet gently disengages the lifeless form from Lydia's arms. Isabel retches once into a bedside basin, suddenly seems to come to her senses, and rises to her full height, towering over Lydia and Violet.

"Lydia, this is the ultimate degradation! A child conceived in sin and birthed in shame. May you and Avram burn in hell for what the two of you have brought upon on this family!"

"Hush that talk, Isabel!" Violet stands and meets Isabel eye to eye.

"Clean this filth up as best you can while I go and fetch your good for nothing husband. We will have to burn the bedding." Isabel turns and lurches in the queer sideways gait her twisted back produces from the room.

"What you want to get Cleotis involved for?" Violet asks, relieved in some measure that Lydia's secret has been shared, if only with Isabel, but reluctant to involve even her trusted husband in matters which must be kept close in the family. Carrying the burden of Lydia's condition all alone, she has refused to let her troubled mind think further into the future than the immediate problem of coping with the delivery. Lydia has been bound and determined to flee north to Avram's people as soon as possible after the baby's arrival. Unwavering in her love for Avram, she is convinced that their child will bring him back to her.

"The ground is frozen, Violet. The sounds of sleet are already on the roof. We will need his help to bury the baby before the sun comes up."

"No!" Lydia shrieks. "You cannot have my baby, Isabel, all that is left to me of Avram."

"Avram, like your baby, is dead and gone to you, Lydia," Isabel responds in a voice as icy as the precipitation ricocheting against

the window pane. "We must act before word can leak out and spread, or this whole family will be as shamed and ruined as you are. I will do whatever I have to do to hold up the good name which I am aware is my greatest treasure in life. Thank goodness Willard is away. He would have you on the street, in the gutter where you belong, by morning."

Lydia's body suddenly heaves in another convulsion. The second child springs free.

"What did you say to me, boy?" Isabel shrieks between chattering teeth as Cleotis, in his night shirt, shivers before her.

"I said 'No, Ma'am,' and I will say it again. I ain't burying no dead baby in no unhallowed ground under the light of no full moon. It will come back to haunt us for sure, little dead baby ghost."

"Cleotis Larson, you stop that sassing me! You will get some clothes on and get to work immediately, or I will hit you upside the head with this shovel and give you something to be bothered about!" Isabel raises the shovel above her head.

Isabel attacks the earth with a fury fueled by years of years of jealousy and hatred for her sister. Behind the barn, where household refuse is discarded, the hard winter ground is unresponsive. In the rose garden Cleotis has commingled a wagon load of country dirt from the soil of White Gardenias with the native clay. Disposing of the infant's body in the rose garden is Isabel's only option.

Afraid of Isabel, Cleotis reluctantly takes command of the digging. The wind whips the hair of Violet and Isabel as they stand as silent spectators, Violet holding tightly to the blanketed bundle. No suitable box being available, they have hastily appropriated for a coffin a small metal trunk that once belonged to Minnie's brother.

Upstairs, cradling her son, Lydia drags herself to the window, her unbound cloud of tangled red hair framing an otherworldly wraith thin face. Isabel looks up and catches her sister's eye. Even in her dishabille Lydia cannot escape a breathtaking beauty. She looks a fallen angel.

At last the little makeshift coffin is lowered into the earth and covered, earth tamped firm around a replanted rose bush just as the sting of sleet changes over to a softer spattering of snow. By morning the rudely interrupted ground will be covered, as silent as a secret. In the east the eyelashes of the rising sun blink open on the dark lid of the horizon.

***

"Please, baby, just a sip of broth, just a sip. We got to get your strength back," Violet cajoles. "You got to get strong for little Avram. You going to be the best mama in the world to this baby boy."

Lydia attempts to do as she is told, but coughs most of the nourishment back up, shakes her head when Violet raises the spoon.

"Herb tea with honey is what you need. You just rest a spell while Violet makes you a nice hot cup." From the clothes basket serving as cradle the baby whimpers. Violet gives it a gentle rocking. "Violet hasn't forgotten you, little Avram. I got a nice pan of cow's milk warming to fill that little tummy."

In the hall, Violet, clutching a foul smelling bundle of bloody rags, encounters Isabel. "Miss Isabel, we need to send for the doctor. That little girl is burning up, and I can't treat no childbirth fever."

"Violet, you know old Dr. Dalton's wife is this town's most vicious gossip. By nightfall the word will have spread like a wildfire and be on the train to Memphis and Montgomery. Lydia has made her bed, and now she must lie in it, soiled though it may be. It's a wonder I am not abed myself, suffering from pneumonia, burying babies in the middle of the night. And have I heard from her one word of thank you?"

"Miss Isabel, this is no time for you to go getting all self-righteous high and mighty with me. I am telling you that we need help. You going to risk your precious baby sister's life worrying about what people might say? They have already said it all and more where Lydia is concerned anyhow."

Isabel chews a fingernail and tries to rein in a racing mind. There has been no occasion in her life when decisions minor or major have not been made for her. Standing on her own two feet is a new and an unsettling experience.

"Miss Isabel, you go on in that room and see for yourself how sick your baby sister is."

Lydia's bright green eyes punctuate a face so pale that even the peppering of freckles has disappeared. Violet has tied the crimson mass of curls back from her face with a lavender ribbon, changed her into a pretty nightgown sprigged with flowers.

Isabel stares at her shattered sister, raises a handkerchief to her face. Lydia, lying crumpled in the bed, no longer smells of lilacs or patchouli. A fouler stench of blood and infection fills the room, and Isabel feels an unpleasant bubble of bile rising in her throat.

She puts a hand on Lydia's brow, confirming Violet's diagnosis of a raging fever. Lydia shivers, painfully readjusts herself in the bed as Isabel crumples into a bedside chair.

"Oh, Lydia, how has it all come to this? You had the world at your feet, and you threw it all away."

"Can you not understand, Isabel, that I would do it all again ten times over?"

"But why, why, why?"

"Not only did I love him, Isabel, I believed in what he stood for in seeking to make this world a better place. He is willing to risk his own life to improve the lots of others."

"And you have paid the price for him, Lydia. You had a good name, an adoring family, a fortune, the beautiful face and figure and brilliant mind that heaven denied me. Gone, all of it, for a man who was not fit to cross our threshold."

"You did not know him, Isabel, did not even attempt to know him, none of you did, save Granny. He has a mind and a spirit as broad as any ocean, such a vision of the future unlike this family so determined to perpetuate the past. Who wants a fortune if it is made on the backs of others, its origins in oppression?"

"Why, Lydia, you poor misguided fool, I expect that is how most fortunes are both made and kept. As for the past, I have always been taught that the past and the future are inextricably linked, as our family motto reminds us. I am content with the lot in life which I have been given."

"Are you, Isabel? Are you really? With a husband of Father's choosing, who will not even allow you access to a newspaper?"

"Mr. Preston is a decent and a faithful husband who sees to it that my every material need is met. How could I possibly wish for more?"

"But is there love there, Isabel? Is there a passion to be part of him, one with him in mind, in spirit, and in body?"

"Certainly not! Passion is not a lady's prerogative, and well we both were taught that. I endure the satisfaction of Mr. Preston's animal needs because that is my uxorial responsibility, but never ever would I lower my own more noble nature to pretend to enjoy *participation. It would be entirely against my upbringing."*

Out of breath from her diatribe, and painfully uncomfortable with the course of the conversation, Isabel blushes a deeper shade than her fever flushed sister. She has struggled to put aside shameful images of her sister pleasurably rutting like a cat in heat with the handsome stranger. She has even tried to convince herself that Lydia must have been a victim of an involuntary ravishment.

"Then I am sorrier for you than I am for myself," Lydia sighs. "If I have traded the rest of an otherwise long life for a short season of complete satisfaction then I go to my eternal rest with no regrets other than that I shall not know him again in that way in this life nor be so blessed as to see our son grow and develop into a decent and an honorable man, the image of his father."

Isabel's heart wrenches at life's unfairness. Why should she go for a doctor when she has since childhood wished her sister dead? The child wails from the basket, living symbol of Lydia's possession of one more treasure that a cruel life has denied her.

Lydia, too weak to stand, begs Isabel to bring the baby to her. "Isabel, I love you, sister, and the last thing I could have wished would have ever been to bring any sort of hurt upon you. Since childhood I have known that I must seek for something larger than myself. That I found in Avram. I meant to no one in this family any harm."

Isabel thinks back to evenings meeting the door to Lydia's legion of suitors, long envious hours spent assisting Bess in pasting up the clippings. Even then, even then when they teased her about being frivolous and flirtatious, some dangerous passion burned within Lydia.

Lydia drifts into a feverish sleep, and Isabel buries her face in the handkerchief, from its folds the scent of lilacs calling back a past which now can hold no future.

* * *

Not much longer now, Violet thinks to herself as she rocks the baby and keeps vigil at Lydia's side. She does not have her mama's witchcraft. Obvious her charm bag has done next to nothing. Violet reaches under the pillow to reassure herself it is there in place. She has prayed that her long dead mother will send her guidance from the supernatural and has taken one of the little scraps of rag she uses to piece her quilts and filled it with frog bones, a snake skin, horse hair and two spoonfuls of ashes. It is not working. She is missing the most important ingredient, the left hind foot of a rabbit. Country conjurer remedies. There are no rabbits to be had in the city. No doctors either as long as Isabel has locked the door of Lydia's room and pocketed the key. She is holding Lydia and Violet prisoners.

"Avram, where is Avram?" Lydia raves. "Oh, Avram, I need to feel your hands, your lips."

"Miss Isabel, you have got to go for the doctor. She is dying."

"Violet, hear for yourself the vile things she is saying. Whore's talk! She is out of her head. How can you presume to let an outsider be privy to such lewd meanderings?"

"That's enough! Isabel, I'm going for the doctor myself if I have to break that window and jump from the second story of this house! If I was not afraid you'd do harm to this precious baby while I was gone I would do just that."

"You but try, and you will never work another day in this house!"

"Fine with me! I'll gladly go back to Selma, I would gladly go back to slavery itself before I stand here and watch my baby girl bleed to death. She's been gushing like a river at flood stage for three days, Isabel."

"Perfectly normal and natural. You forget that I have been through the experience of childbirth, which you, I might add, have not."

Violet ignores Isabel's dig at a sore subject. "I grew up in the country, Isabel Preston. Just because the Good Lord has not seen fit to give me any children doesn't mean I haven't seen plenty of birthings. What is happening here is not natural."

"No, I don't suppose I can argue with that. My sister, raised under the same roof and by the same standards as was I, fornicating with a foreigner and giving birth to a pair of Jewish bastards is certainly entirely out of the realm of any natural occurrence I have ever known or hoped to imagine."

"There now. That's better," *Lydia says in a strangled whisper.* "Drink your fill and hush your crying." *She opens her nightgown and cradles the infant against a swollen nipple, begins to sing snatches of one of Kitty's childhood lullabies. She is oblivious to the presence of Isabel and Violet, beyond mere delirium and already on the journey to a world the bickering women at the foot of her bed cannot share with her.*

Chapter Nineteen

Dead tired from spending most of the night operating, Nick quietly entered the room where Carrie slept. She was smiling in her sleep, and it struck him that sleep was now the only state in which she resembled the Carrie who used to be. He slipped between the sheets, being careful not to wake her.

Willard Preston's shoulders sag under a mantle of fatigue. The journey from Washington has been arduous. A paralyzing snowstorm has swept from an unlikely nascence in the south up the eastern seaboard, making it impossible for him to cross the city of Washington on his last night there. He still aches with unfulfilled longing from a shortchanged final tryst in the best bed to be bought within the city. The bordellos of the nation's capital offer much sleeker and more sophisticated ladies than are available for sale in Birmingham.

He glares at his large and lumpy wife, the freakish hump of her back propped against the bed pillows as she cradles the baby. "You could have telegraphed me, Isabel. If I am to be master of my ship, I must be kept appraised of treacherous seas. I find it quite extraordinary to return from an absence of only a week to find your sister dead and buried and your having taken all matters into your own hands without seeking my wiser counsel. Who knows about the matter of this baby besides Violet?"

"Only Bess, Granny, Adelaide and Father. Bess has congratulated herself to Adelaide about what a good job she did in raising me to be such a modest woman that I kept the fact of my pregnancy private right up until the moment of delivery. Thanks to your spreading the rumor that Lydia was dying of consumption, outsiders have for some months avoided this household entirely. Thanks to my sister, I have been quite out of social circulation."

Not to mention that you have never had a friend to your name outside of the family, he thinks to himself. "And what say Mrs. Hatton, and your father and stepmother to such a pack of lies?"

"Why, Willard, I must admit that Adelaide, to whom I prefer that you not refer as if she has taken the place of my sainted mother, quite bruised my feelings commenting to Father that she had simply assumed me a victim of obesity."

"Fools the lot of them! Your Granny will see right through this situation as if it were a piece of flimsy netting."

"Poor dear Granny." Isabel sighs heavily, adjusts the blanket around the baby. "Granny went quite out of her head when she learned that the virulent fever had taken Lydia. Had one of her seizures. Her mind has snapped completely. I doubt very much that we will ever again be able to allow her to leave her room. I have ordered Violet to keep the door firmly locked and to serve all of her meals there."

Turning his back to Isabel, Willard's mind reels with the knowledge that Lydia is dead. Lydia, for whom since the first day he saw her, framed by a porch swing like a vision of an angel, he has felt such a longing that it has at times produced physical pain. He thinks of the way that Lydia looked at Avram, lustful loving looks passed one to the other, eyes undressing, minds caressing.

He thinks back to Isabel's stillbirth and subsequent surgery, the infection which very nearly claimed her life. Why, at one point the doctor told him that it was almost a certainty that she would not survive. He sat at Isabel's bedside, imagining himself the grieving widower comforting an inconsolable Lydia. Imagined himself taking the weeping sister in his arms, hearing her express for him a pent up longing equal to his own.

The silenced music of Lydia's laughter rings in his ears, and his heart twists in torment. She is now beyond his reach, finally, fully, forever denied him. He grinds his teeth in despair.

It all comes back to him like hammer blows to his heart, the missed opportunity, an afternoon of a rude interruption, but a few short months after meekly agreeing to open his home to another of Sam's cast off family characters.

It was a warm late summer Sunday. He watched the car fade off into the distance, Cleotis chauffeuring the women to their weekly Sunday communion picnic with Kitty in Oak Hill Cemetery.

Priding himself on his boldness, he quietly opened the door to her bedroom. Lydia, the one true love of his life, lay sleeping. Her nightgown was thin, almost transparent, and the sight of the long lean bones beneath it drove him mad with desire. Surely it was meant to be his right to take it.

Sleeping, she looked a virginal angel. She turned in her sleep, and he saw the bulge of her belly.

A guttural growl rose in his throat. Her purity and innocence had *been stolen, by a thief who ran away in the night on a northbound train.*

He stuffed the ripped away nightgown into her mouth to stifle her screams. Her nails were long and as sharp as cat claws. Fighting, in wounding his back she only compounded his pleasure.

Full, final conquest denied him, by the premature return of Cleotis. Bess had absentmindedly left on her dresser the bouquet of yellow roses she had picked for her dead sister, ordered Cleotis return for them.

Cleotis will keep his silence, of that Willard is certain. He has influential connections in the state and has left the servant in no doubt of it.

There is but one thing in life that Cleotis fears more than small haunts hovering over newly turned earth in a rose garden. Hooded men in the night carrying out lynchings are in these days quite common.

Isabel's voice interrupts his anguished recollecting. "Come, Willard, come and hold your son."

His son. His and Lydia's. Stiffly, he puts out his arms for the baby.

"I hope you don't mind that in your absence I chose the child a name, Willard. It was Bess's idea, actually. What better way, asked my aunt, to insure that he grows up to be a true son of the South than to give him hallowed family appellations? Just as soon as I am recovered from my delivery we will take him to church and have him christened. Hatton Alexander Buford Preston. I have vowed to devote the rest of my life to being his mama."

* * *

Wyatt was returned from an overnight trip to New York. An appointment at the venerable publishing house once literary home to Hatton Preston had whetted his appetite. He had the cab take him straight from the airport to Carrie's house.

"Why do airline seats, even in first class, feel more cramped with every flight? I'm afraid that in old age I am at risk of becoming a homebody. When I decided, with the work going too well to take a break from it, to forego my annual vacation in Spain, I was afraid that I would regret it."

"I've never been to Spain," Carrie answered. "We lived in Italy for a few years when I was a child. I really don't remember much about it."

She suddenly looked distracted. A taxi ride to an airport, leaving Rome on an August afternoon, a memory as sharp as the tingly taste of citron gelato on her tongue, a memory as a barrier behind which no farther past existed.

For some things she actually had a very good memory. She could still recite parts of the *Canterbury Tales*, memorized her senior year in high school. She could address letters to old college friends with whom she corresponded only once or twice a year without having to look up the zip codes. She could remember well enough being a teenager, being in college, being newly married.

The first dozen years of her life were a completely blank screen with a dark curtain drawn in front of it.

Wyatt frowned at her. He had seen that look on her face before. What the devil was it? It was as if something were chasing Carrie and clearly closing in.

She neatly sidestepped onto safer ground. "Look at where tearing my house inside out and upside down has gotten us. Me in the bed with a bad back and you reduced to playing nurse. Our digging through this house is about as productive as Mother chasing ancestors."

"I had an interesting conversation with your mother just before I left for New York. I ran into her in the library."

"Scouring the microfilm files, hoping to turn over that last little jigsaw piece she needs to complete the puzzle? You don't see Nicky's mother wasting her time going through old mining records trying to dig up her people. She's proud of the fact that they were blue collar immigrants. At least Ellen's trying to be productive, working on her book."

Wyatt, thinking of a manuscript that might, if stacked upright, be taller than its author by now, decided that Mallory pursued a safer hobby. "How she spends her time is your mother's business, Carrie."

"What a shame that Mother came along in a day when ladies of her social station had no option other than pursuing harmless hobbies. My mother would have made a brilliant lawyer, or doctor, or Indian chief. She simply accepted the role that her own mother planned for her as one of the last great southern belles."

"And, what may I ask, is so wrong with that?" If asked to

describe Mallory Hudson in a single word, he would pluck it from his grandmother's vocabulary. Gracious. That was one of the nicer designations he could think of to label any woman.

"She expected me to follow right along in her footsteps, to go to the most southern bastion on earth, Ole Miss. Mother was right in her element there where they think 'Dixie' is not only the football fight song but still the national anthem. Has my mother mentioned to you that she was Homecoming Queen at Ole Miss? Mother has been in training her whole life for the final act role of grande dame. When my time comes I won't be any good at that. It's for darn sure I won't have the right wardrobe."

"Carrie, I've never met a mother so obviously proud of a daughter as your mother is of you. Why can't you admit that to yourself?"

His own mother was ill during most of his early childhood, a frail and faint memory. His grandmother had been the defining force in his life. The thought prompted him to share something. "I was looking through those scrapbooks you find so fascinating while you were sleeping and ran across this." He passed Carrie a picture. "My great-grandmother playing simultaneous roles of aging matron and blushing new bride next to her second husband. Looks like a schooner in full sail, doesn't she?"

Carrie gasped. A face as familiar as if her own grandmother's stared back. From out of her dreams, Adelaide Ashcraft McShan. Eyes wide, she looked from the picture to Wyatt.

"Carrie, what in the world is wrong with you? You look as if you've seen a ghost."

"Oh, Wyatt. Why do I suddenly feel as though we are second cousins? Your grandmother was Adelaide Ashcraft's daughter Bitsy? She and Isabel were step sisters?"

"Of course. Have I not mentioned that? It's a minor importance reason for my consuming interest in a writer the rest of the world has long forgotten. If only by marriage, I am more or less related to Hatton Preston."

He left unsaid the other part of the equation. It appeared that he, like Hatton Preston, was to be doomed to die with his master work left unfinished.

"I think that it's time we admitted something, Wyatt. That novel isn't or wasn't any more substantial than a will o' the wisp in an Indian burial ground."

Where in the world, he wondered, not for the first time, did she come up with some of these expressions? He let it go. "It does exist! I know it does! I saw proof of it in New York. I've held in my hands the notes that Hatton's editor made after talking to him for the last time. 'Received call from Alabama. Hatton promises final pages no later than Tuesday next.' The memo is dated, November 10, 1938. Hatton died on November 26. I know because I went to the court house and looked up his death certificate. He had more than enough time to finish, was on that 'writer's roll' when the end is in sight and the words spilling out faster than you can type them. Damn it! Where is that manuscript?"

"What makes you think that Isabel didn't destroy it?"

"For one thing, the state of this crammed to the rafters house tells both of us that Isabel did not discard nor destroy so much as a grocery list. You know Isabel only from the material things she left behind, Carrie. You forget that I knew her as a living breathing human being."

"I know her better than you think, Wyatt."

It is a writer's stock in trade to listen carefully. Not for the first time he found it was curious that she referred to Isabel in the present tense. There was something that she wasn't telling him.

"Can you really think that a woman who devoted her whole adult life to doting on her son would have thrown away the greatest and the last accomplishment of his life?"

"No, of course she wouldn't," Carrie said slowly, thinking, trying to put herself in Isabel's place. Isabel wouldn't have carelessly discarded the last link to her son, but would she have hidden it, denied him the posthumous accolades of an adoring public?

"Wyatt, maybe there was a reason she didn't want that manuscript shared with the rest of the world. Isn't all writing at least a tiny bit autobiographical? Maybe she perceived Hatton as telling family secrets or something."

They are nothing but dreams, just stories my mind makes up, she reminded herself. Hatton in real life was Isabel's son, not Lydia's, no matter how much the romantic side of her nature loved a love story. The pills were making her woozy. She felt confused.

"Turning Hatton's room and half of your attic upside down is just scratching the surface, Carrie," Wyatt argued. "It's a big house. Haven't you any other idea where to continue searching? Have you explored the basement?"

"Not in my wildest dreams," she answered, with an almost hysterical giggle, her conscience reprimanding that she knew very well that something lay behind a locked door in her basement. One phone call to a locksmith, and Wyatt could have his manuscript. One phone call, and Wyatt would lose interest in her, leave her, all alone. She closed her eyes and pretended to sleep.

Wyatt took a long and thoughtful pull on his pipe. He continued musing aloud, not caring whether or not his monologue disturbed her rest.

"I would not put anything past Isabel Preston. She was as mean as a snake. I will never forget the time that I slipped through the woods to pick my grandmother a rose from Isabel's garden. She was obsessed with those roses that she had transplanted from her old house on Southside down to the dirt in which they grew. Selma dirt she called it."

Carrie's eyes flew open as widely as if he had thrown cold water in her face. "She moved the rose bushes from that house off Highland Avenue? And the dirt around them? Are you sure about that?" she shrieked.

"Absolutely. I can hear Grandmama now. 'Whoever heard of someone packing up dirt like a good set of china? Might as well have gone to Selma and transplanted the family graveyard.'"

Maybe a grain of truth in that observation, Carrie thought with a shudder of horror.

Lydia's baby, after all these years melted away to bone and dust, buried only a few steps away from her own back door?

Oh, surely not. Surely, surely not. She choked on the water as she swallowed her pills.

They were, after all, just dreams.

"Welcome, welcome to our first grand soiree." Adelaide *Ashcraft McShan beams with pride from the red tiled porch that she pompously terms her piazza.*

Squarely centering the mansion lined Highland Avenue, the house is a Greek Revival palace such as Alabama has not seen erected in almost a century. This house, so splendid that pictures of it have appeared in the Sunday newspaper rotogravure, is surely the sort of abode in which Adelaide, a minister's daughter raised in a modest parsonage, should have grown up, a belle with an unending queue of beaux. Better late than never.

"Oh, Mrs. Ashcraft, I feel as if I am about to be entertained by the Astors!" Bess squeals, causing Sam to shudder.

"Do you know I read just this morning, in an article entitled 'How the Other Half Live' that in Newport one must apportion $25,000 annually for good help alone." Adelaide, who pays her ninety year old maid Libby the munificent sum of three dollars per seven day work week, clucks her tongue.

"What would you know about the other half, preacher's daughter?" Minnie, mind returned by the stroke to the past, cuts in. "My husband just last week paid $5000 at the slave auction in New Orleans for a carpenter to build me a stairway. Trained craftsmen do not come cheaply. Double cantilevered, the marble from Carrara."

"Oh, my stars, what a parlor! Mama, have you ever seen anything like it?" Bess takes a seat, and hold of the conversation, and looks around her in wonder.

"The drawing room," Adelaide corrects.

"The ballroom of Hatton Hall will hold three hundred," Minnie mutters. "The glass prisms in my chandeliers were blown expressly for me in Venice. Cap is building the largest home ever seen in Alabama. The weirdest too, no doubt about it. Burned it to the ground myself," she cackles. "If the Yankees don't get lucky and kill Cap Hatton for me, when he gets back home he won't even find a pot to pee in!"

"Mama!" Bess hisses. "Quit that talking ugly like a man! You promised me that if we let you out of your room you would hold your tongue and mind your manners."

"I'm always nice in the presence of Adelaide. Didn't my mother, truth be told ended up mad as a March hare from constantly hatching children, teach me to always show a gracious condescension to those below me in social stature? I never go out without remembering to bring along my manners."

Ever since the stroke she suffered on learning of the death of her favorite granddaughter, Minnie has become like a parrot taught to curse, prone to outrageous statements at inopportune moments.

"I have in mind to plant a tree, Bess, at the curbside," Adelaide proposes. "I am chairwoman, as you know, of the Arbor Day Committee." It is a position which Bess coveted, and Adelaide knows it, out of pure meanness rubbing salt in the wound. "I thought perhaps a Tupelo gum tree. They display in the autumn such splendid red foliage."

"Each one of Hatton Hall's columns is constructed from a hundred foot tall oak," Minnie interjects to no one in particular. "Twenty four columns. Cap couldn't decide on the headers so he used them all, Doric, Corinthian, and Ionic. I designed the family crest. Told everyone that motto and herald go back three hundred years. Painted in gold on the doors of our fine new carriage. I shall take you for a ride some day, Adelaide, show you a thing or two about traveling in style. Cap's people were nothing, cracker white trash. His papa won his fortune as a river boat gambler. His mama was the highest priced whore in the whole Vieux Carre. Rumored that she had black as well as red blood in her. For a fact, she was not, like me, a blue blooded Buford."

Bess looks horrified. She must somehow silence Mama before she spills out every one of the family secrets. She crosses the room, tips her mother's head back, and pours down her throat a healthy measure of tonic.

Willard makes a move to change the subject. He has absolutely no interest in the chatter of women. "Sam, saw you in the morning paper the sorry state of the world in which we are living? Five persons bitten by a mad dog on the streets of Meridian, a Gadsden child burned so to death that her flesh was hanging in shreds, and worst of all a report that insane Negroes are on the increase."

"Oh, please, Mr. Preston, spare us the bad news!" Isabel seizes an opportunity to get a word in edgewise. "Did you not share with me from the very same edition that Mrs. Burton Smith plans to be in town giving a stimulating lecture on household economics?"

"I am an heiress to a fortune in gold. I need no knowledge of household economics," Minnie boasts.

"Gold, gold, gold, she is like a mockingbird mimicking itself," Willard complains.

"And when I grow up I shall dig up the ground at White Gardenias until I find it. It's going to be my gold! Mine, mine, mine, and only I can spend it!" Hatton shrieks, attempting to position himself in his customary place as the center of attention.

"If only that were true, my precious, precocious little soldier," Bess croons, running a hand through the child's red gold hair. "Hatton, dear, perhaps you would like to recite the lovely poem you wrote in honor of the birthday of our hallowed General Lee."

Hatton, dressed Sunday best in a miniature Confederate uniform that Bess has sewn for him, squares his small shoulders and begins a lengthy recitation.

"Spends too much time on that porch listening to old ladies spouting Confederate claptrap," Willard mutters under his breath as the group applauds. "Boy needs to play with other lads his age."

"Now, Mr. Preston, you know that I have a sacred duty to enforce the law of jus maternum," Isabel counters. "We cannot risk his exposure to young ruffians who might injure him at play or expose him to a host of infectious diseases."

"It is true! It is true! The only lie is in saying it isn't!" Minnie, mind still mining for gold, screams. "I have a letter from Papa's agent in Liverpool to prove it. Crocodile tears of sorrow at the outcome of the conflict! If the John Bull British had backed us with more than sympathy the outcome would have been entirely different." She waves an imaginary piece of paper in the air. "The gold was delivered to Papa. It's written quite plainly." She holds her pretend paper close to her face. "My papa hid that gold from Alex because my brother was a turncoat damn Yankee lover traitor."

Pointing a bony finger across the room, she continues at a fever pitch. "See! There! Soldiers with papers ordering his hanging! I will kill him myself for selling out our family's honor!" She points an imaginary gun. "Bang! How dare you dishonor the name of Buford?"

Bess becomes aware that Adelaide is suddenly listening to Minnie's ravings with interest. She feels overcome with consternation. Did she not argue with Isabel not two hours ago that it was a mistake to bring Mama? She flashes her niece a look of I told you so.

"Yes, what a sorrow that the British, and the French, disdained to come to our rescue," Bess hastily interjects.

"Dissolute frog foreigners quaffing red wine all day. What could you expect from the French?" Willard mutters.

"Doesn't the Savonnerie rug from White Gardenias fit nicely in our foyer?" Adelaide inquires of Isabel.

Isabel glowers. Adelaide has been greedy. Here on the Highland Avenue are all of the Bufords' fine possessions, treasures which should some day be Hatton's. Knowing Adelaide, it will all later be left to her own daughter Bitsy. Isabel has little desire to tour this showplace. In each room she knows she will walk on carpet even finer than in the one before it. She has pleaded with Willard until blue in the face. He thinks turkey rugs are an unnecessary extravagance. Her own floors are bare but for the rag rugs

Violet pieces from castoffs.

Mindless, Minnie seems to read Isabel's. "Until we can locate that gold, we are poor as Job's turkey. We must consider how ladies of breeding may make a living. Seances! There's the ticket! I must decode Papa's daybook to find the fortune. The clues in the daybook will explain the location. Someone has stolen Alexander's trunk! Did you do it, Isabel? Did you steal that trunk that hides the secret?"

Bess, Willard, and Isabel sigh collectively. They hear this litany many dozen times a day.

Adelaide has had enough. After pouting all afternoon over Sam's insistence that her first dinner party focus on his first wife's family, she is now relieved that the guest list was limited to these miserable misfit relations. How embarrassing it would be if others more socially prominent were on hand to hear them! She is on her way to becoming Birmingham's answer to Mrs. Astor. She picks up a small brass bell and rings for the maid. It is past time to feed and be done with them.

Imagine! Minnie calling her late heroic brother a Yankee loving traitor. She will speak privately to Bess as soon as dessert is cleared. Anyone in their right mind can see that the daughter is overdue in locking away her mother.

What a kindness they will proclaim it. Adelaide will offer the services of her own personal chauffeur and touring car to deliver Minnie, who loves to go on so about traveling in style, to her next change of address, the state asylum at Tuscaloosa.

* * *

Willard consults his watch. Perfect timing.

"Isabel, I think I will have Cleotis return me to the office. There are some pressing matters which require my attention. If you would wait up for me, I shall need a thorough irrigation before retiring after all that heavy food served tonight."

"As you wish, Mr. Preston," Isabel sighs.

Bess smiles at Willard as he walks out the door. How very hard he works to support them all! Why, at least three evenings a week he returns after supper to the office where he has slaved all day. Does not get to spend as much time as she is sure he would like with the boy, but then Hatton has been more than blessed being born into a house with so many ladies who love him.

A quarter hour later, as Isabel yawns over Hatton's prayers, Willard Preston licks his lips in anticipated pleasure.

He whines, strains at the ropes that bind him hand and foot. She will keep him waiting another five minutes. It is part of the ritual for which she is well compensated. She is but recently arrived in the city, a white trash sharecropper's daughter, oldest girl in a family with too many children. Her father drove her into town himself in the wagon, deposited her here to use her one asset, her beauty, to make her own fortune.

Her name is Rebecca, though Willard has rechristened her Dolores after a favorite poem by Swinburne. Having paid an extravagant sum to purchase her, body and soul, for his exclusive pleasure, he knows that he is an object of envy among the other patrons. Favored by fortune he considers himself, having been on hand the night the daddy delivered her. It was worth every penny it cost him for the pleasure of robbing her virginity. Wasn't that old crone Minnie always prattling on that the best of the servants were the ones you trained yourself? He has taught this little girl a thing or two.

Her voice and her laugh grate with the twang of the country. He forces his mind to sublimate the lyrical song of Lydia's laughter. Always with him. Always! Always! Always! The terrible burning itch for the great unobtainable desire of his life continues to torment without ceasing. He thrashes on the bed.

"You're late tonight, Willie." Rebecca looms over him. "Reckon you deserve to be punished." The scent of the lilac toilet water in which he demands she bathe herself reeks from her pores like over ripe blossoms.

He closes his eyes tightly and begins to mumble in anticipation. "Oh lips full of lush and of laughter, Curled snakes that are fed from my breast, Bite hard, lest remembrance come after and press with new lips where you pressed. For my heart too springs up at the pressure, Mine eyelids too moisten and burn; Ah, feed me and fill me with pleasure, Ere pain come in turn."

"My, my, my. You are one talented man at stringing words together. You trying to turn my head with poetry?" she responds.

His mind loses itself in an image of Lydia's face as Rebecca raises the whip.

Chapter Twenty

Wyatt slammed his fist against the typewriter keys in fury.

The sound of a conversation coming closer was unmistakable.

How dare Josie disobey his orders and allow someone into the house when he was working?

Working on what, asked the blank page before him? The words "Act One Scene One," his only progress, were reduced to ash in the fireplace.

Women were nervy. Josie, with Ellen in tow, burst into the sacred privacy of his study after barely knocking. Ellen struggled with a bulging cardboard box as the little Jack Russell flew around the room attacking wads of wasted paper. Wyatt ignored Zippy's insistent attempts to initiate a game of toss, instead growling at Josie to remove the animal.

"Here it is! Completed!" Ellen fell into a chair without being invited. "Two o'clock in the morning I felt as though I had drained myself dry of words. Have you ever had that feeling, Wyatt?"

He looked at her miserably and avoided responding.

"I hope that you can help me solve a spot of trouble with the ending."

He sighed in frustration. There were some things in life, like flu shots or paying taxes, that you might as well bite a bullet and be done with. "What seems to be the problem?"

Ellen began to dig through the box, dropping pages around her in apparently random order. He had a sinking feeling that this might be the type of work in which you could throw the whole thing in the air and have it matter little what landed where.

He did not have the time to spare, had wasted half of yesterday listening to Carrie's problems which were far down toward the bottom on his agenda. He only occasionally willingly listened to the lives of others for one reason. More than one successful story line had come his way in just that fashion.

"Here, Wyatt, have a look. Page 1995, right at the bottom."

Ellen passed him a typed page. "I have always felt cheated by books that do not, however happy the ending, leave the reader with all the loose ends knotted."

Endings. He would settle this morning for a middle, or a beginning.

He frowned down at the paper.

> Be the first on your block to receive Ambrodesia's Monthly Newsletter! Only $14.95 for 12 action packed updates on Ambrodesia, her friends and family!
>
> Send check or money order to:
> Mrs. John Nicholas Lancaster, Sr.
> 1400 Dryden Boulevard
> Birmingham, Alabama 35223

She did not plan to remain for long wordless. He groaned.

"I can tell that you love it! I stewed over that ending for longer than it took me to come up with Ambrodesia as the perfect name for my main character! I am still left with a couple of questions." She looked to Wyatt expectantly.

"Forgive me, Ellen, but it's still very early in the morning. Can you please be specific?"

"Two questions, actually. I do believe in equality for women. We've been an underdog minority for far too long. However, I am still a southern girl at heart. Do you think I should have readers send the check to Mrs. John Nicolas Lancaster or to Ms. Ellen Ames Lancaster?"

"Ask yourself, Ellen, how many books you have purchased with the author's name appearing on the dust jacket as Mrs. Sam Smith?"

"I just knew that you, being a professional, would know exactly what to do! By afternoon Ambrodesia can be on a plane winging her way to the publisher. I hope Jack isn't going to be tied up in surgery. I have no idea how to edit something that lives in a text box. Which brings me to my second question. Do you have any idea how one accepts Visa or Mastercard?"

"Don't look at me." He threw up his hands. "I have never even touched a computer, nor tried my hand at retail sales."

"Got to change with the times, Wyatt. Why, if you had a more up to date machine that play would be on the stage already."

There was no justice in the universe. Didn't this prove it? A woman with nothing worth saying being so profoundly prodigious on the printed page.

"Well, I won't waste any more of your time, Wyatt. I will be sure to give you well deserved credit in my acknowledgments."

He turned back to the typewriter with a deliberate expression of concentration. If rudely enough delivered, Ellen might get the message and get on her way.

As he reached for the Scotch bottle, a sobering thought came to him. What if he died that very morning, had a sudden fatal heart attack just like Hatton had, and years later someone came looking for his missing manuscript? He had, had he not, succeeded in convincing everyone around him that it was very nearly completed?

From across the room Josie frowned at him, only too aware of the game that he was playing.

"I'm going to go right home and write the date in red on my calendar. Jack and I will be looking so forward to it," Ellen called over her shoulder as she left the room.

"I beg your pardon?" With what new torture was heaven trying to torment him?

"Your dinner party. Josie let me take a peek at the menu. She is really planning to outdo herself this time."

Wyatt shot Josie a furious questioning glance.

Josie glared back defiantly. "We are having ourselves a little supper party, Mr. Wallace. I am highly experienced at organizing entertaining. I have already sent your tuxedo to the cleaners."

He wanted to cry, just put his head on the typewriter and bawl like a baby.

***

Carrie slipped quietly from bed, where she had been ordered to remain for at least three additional days, and made her way downstairs, her back making only grudging complaint.

The cat stole out of the shadows, looking left and right to verify that Carrie was alone before bounding across the kitchen, wrapping his long fluffy tail around her leg, sounding a meow like a question.

"I'm sorry, Willie," she said, wincing as she bent to take the cat in her arms. I know you can't help being shy, but as long as every-one else around here denies that you even exist, they can hardly be expected to keep your food bowl filled."

Nick insisted that the cat was a figment of her imagination. A picture would prove it. She took the camera from the still not yet unpacked box of household miscellaneous and snapped several shots of him gulping down his breakfast.

Sipping from a cup of coffee, she ran her finger down the table of contents of the book Wyatt had given her for Christmas. Hatton Hall had existed in more than her dreams. The book, *Lost Mansions of Alabama,* confirmed it.

According to the author, no drawing or photograph of Hatton Hall existed. The text described it as "a bewildering polyglot of incon-gruous architectural styles."

The chapter continued with eyewitness accounts excerpted from old diaries, graphic accounts describing Hatton Hall as the first structure to burn in Selma, Alabama on the fateful day when the Yankees came to town. Carrie wondered if she should set the record straight, call up the author and explain that she had more accurate documentation obtained from a dream.

Intrigued as she turned to the alphabetically organized book's concluding chapter and studied a black and white image of a house captioned White Gardenias, Carrie called information and obtained a number for M. C. Miller.

Photo credit told her that the author was also the photographer of the proof that White Gardenias remained standing, albeit as a shell into which a large portion of the roof appeared to have col-lapsed. Adelaide Ashcraft McShan had, like a bandit, stolen all the house's furnishings, but not even Adelaide could have made off with everything.

Could it be that the house still stood, ten miles from Selma, and held not only the memories, indelibly stamped like tea stains on tablecloths in its walls and woodwork, chairs and tables, beds and bookcases, but also and most importantly a coded daybook, all rot-ting away little more than an hour's drive from where she now sat?

It was possible. Didn't the author mention in the preface that many of the decaying antebellum mansions still scattered about the southern countryside improbably remained more or less fully fur-nished down to the teaspoons and the tester beds?

Not really so surprising. Poverty had forced many once proud members of the landed gentry to simply close the doors on the too hard to keep country home and go to town.

Carrie, despite the early hour, dialed the Miller residence. A friendly babysitting grandmother regretfully informed her that M.C. was off hiking in the hills of Scotland, "impossible to reach even if one of her children or her poorly house trained pets had some kind of emergency."

Agreeing sympathetically that M.C. was acting most irresponsibly, Carrie thanked the grandmother, left her phone number, and put White Gardenias away for another day.

The cat, suddenly struggling to free himself from Carrie's arms, scratched a gouge in her forearm. In a blur of yellow fur he was out of the room.

Someone was coming. Expecting Nick, and a lecture about being out of bed before her back was ready, she hastily swept the cat food into the trash can.

She was surprised to see her mother. The medicine was making her dopey. She couldn't keep track of who was watching over her when. More surprising that Mallory was disheveled, had descended the stairs looking as though she had just tumbled out of bed, without the benefit of makeup and pearls most evidently not in place.

"Mother, good morning. I didn't realize you'd stayed the night. That was sweet of you."

"Nicky had an emergency call. You were sleeping when I got here, and I hated to wake you. Carrie, what's wrong with your arm? You're bleeding." Mallory fumbled with the coffee pot, sloshed coffee on the counter and didn't bother to wipe it up. Carrie, running cold water over her injured arm, stared at her mother as if she were an apparition.

"You know, darling, as much traveling as I've done in my life you would think I could get a good night's sleep pretty much anywhere. I feel like I have been run over and left for dead."

Carrie was too polite to agree that was exactly how she looked.

"I had just dozed off last night, been asleep for maybe fifteen minutes, when I was awakened by the strangest sensation." Mallory shook her head, her hair matted on one side, tangled on the other, as if she had tossed and turned all night. "I thought I heard a train whistle, as loud as if it were running right through the yard."

"Happens every night. It's just the ghost of the old Mineral

Railway train hauling the last load of coal," Carrie mumbled. "You know the tracks are still there, our rear property line."

"I don't believe in ghosts," Mallory said automatically. "Must be the contour of the land carrying the sound from downtown. I thought of your father's people being so instrumental in bringing the railroads to early Birmingham." How she missed David. It was one of the reasons she'd had trouble sleeping. More than the train's whistle, it was the room's faint aroma of pipe tobacco that brought back past evenings, reading together in David's study, the good secure feeling that upstairs her children were tucked in bed, safe and sleeping.

Now I lay me down to sleep . . . If I should die before I wake. She was afraid of, dreaded, her own death. On some other side would there be a final confrontation?

"I believe I did hear that somewhere once before," Carrie said around a yawn, thinking here we go again, rocketing off on a ride down ancestor alley.

Her mother seemed to be full of morning surprises. Not only was she barefooted in the cold early morning kitchen, she let the subject drop right where she had left it. "Carrie, after I was awakened by that whistle I tried occupying my mind with my reading group's selection, but I find it confusing. There are too many characters. I came downstairs to look for an alternative choice in reading material."

"And?" Carrie could not for the life of her figure out where the conversation was going.

"There was a copy of the *Meditations of Marcus Aurelius* on the chest in the living room. I picked it up, thinking philosophy might be soothing on a night when sleep was elusive."

Nicky's Christmas present. Still in the same spot where he had dropped it that holiday morning. Carrie had left it there hoping to make him feel guilty about his reaction. He had hurt her feelings.

"Since that particular volume is in the original Latin I imagine you found it rather slow going, didn't you? Or do you still retain a perfect grasp of the language from the high school days when you won the medal?" Mentioned that as often as possible when I was in high school, didn't you, Mother? As a not so subtle reminder to me that I wasn't very much of a student.

"After all these years? Of course I can't still read in Latin. Agnus dei is about all I could still translate if some Roman held a gun to my head. I did look through the book. There were some interesting observations jotted in the margins."

"Mother, maybe I'm not fully awake yet, but I think you are trying to share some insight that was revealed to you last night. Go ahead and spit it right out."

Mallory put a hand in the pocket of her robe and pulled out a small object.

"I'm sure that you'll never figure out what it opens, but have you by chance been looking for a key? It's obviously an old one. It was tucked in the book."

Carrie choked on her coffee. It was the key to the lock on the door in the basement. Somehow she knew it as well as her name.

Like a warning, a sudden sharp pain ran up her back. The time wasn't right. The house wasn't ready to divulge its deepest secrets. She let her mother lead her back to bed.

"Oh, Violet, tell me what dreaded news there is from Belgium," Isabel begs. *"All the talk of the town is of the German menace, of fear of subversive, surreptitious actions by those of Teutonic persuasion perhaps even now transpiring. Why, Adelaide told me that someone on the street told her of a plot to unleash on the city bees infected with fatal germs."*

Isabel doesn't add that Adelaide also passed such off as nonsense. Isabel has firmly closed and shuttered every window despite the stifling summer heat and ordered Violet to begin the annual autumnal cleaning a few months early. One can never be too careful.

"Seeing as how Mr. Willard has gone out and won't be back until who knows what time of night I do believe you could read it for yourself," Violet counters, extending the newspaper in Isabel's direction.

Isabel shrinks back as if Violet offers a hot poker. Willard has already today given her what of the news he considers her fit to know. She is aware of the violent "Ludlow Massacre" mine strike in Colorado, just as she also knows that the New York Giants are squaring off against the Boston Braves for the National League pennant and that the sporty new Maxwell Roadster on which Willard has his heart set is capable of traveling at fifty miles per hour and available to anyone with $695 in his pocket. When she timidly begged him to give her any and all news of impending war he dismissed it as of little or no consequence, involving as it did an

Eastern Front ranging from the impossible to pronounce hamlets of Przmyslany to Brzozdovitza.

"You know Mr. Preston does not countenance my reading the newspaper and cluttering up my head."

"Are you forgetting that I was right there on that day that you tied a wedded knot? I could hear from the kitchen you promising to love, honor, and obey, but that minister didn't say one word about avoiding newspapers."

Violet mutters to herself before squinting to read aloud first the headlines, then the finer print from the newspaper. She pulls an old pair of Bess's castoff spectacles from her pocket.

"Before Declaration of War 100,000 of Kaiser's Forces Enter Luxembourg . . . Americans Panic, Try To Quit Europe. Thousands of dead and wounded German soldiers and a repulsed German army are the results tonight of an all-day battle near Liége, a Belgian city close to the German and Dutch frontiers . . . with the beginning of the German artillery attack women and children, weeping, were hurried away in every possible kind of vehicle and many on foot."

"Stop! No more! I have heard enough. Too much!" Isabel wrings her hands and tears her hair.

"Now, Miss Isabel, we must stay calm," Violet soothes as she continues reading to herself. The article is bylined Adam Livingston, and Violet is impressed by the war correspondent's way with words.

Losing patience, she puts the paper aside for later perusal and responds to Isabel's continued whimpering. "Just this morning I heard Mr. Willard say that this war will only last six weeks and that during its short duration it cannot help but be good for business with his mines turning out supplies for munitions, his mills cotton for uniforms. You and Mr. Willard are already rich and can't help but get richer over the next month and a half." She remembers how many times Miss Minnie remarked that those marching off to Civil War expected no more than ninety days duration. Never can tell when it comes to war.

"Oh, Violet, I am simply consumed by worry! Of all times in history for Bess and Hatton to have undertaken a tour of The Continent! They should have been well and enough content with viewing the old world safe right here in the parlor through their stereopticon. For my generous contribution of twenty cents to Mr. Sears and Mr. Roebuck last Christmas we have right here available views of the San Francisco earthquake, the Johnstown flood, the Great Wild West, and the slitty eyed peoples of the far eastern edge of the world. You don't hear me whining and pining and talking about making a return visit to the Lookout Mountain, now do you? Think of the perils facing an aging woman past sixty and an innocent lad of but fifteen tender years with war breaking out all about them!"

Violet suppresses a snicker. She has caught Hatton more than once salivating over Willard's cardboard stereopticon slides of nude women. Told Mr. Willard herself that he ought to keep his naughty pictures under lock and key.

Still echoing in Violet's ears are the screams so shrill that it's a wonder they hadn't brought Adelaide huffing and puffing all the way from the fashionable Highland Avenue when Isabel entered Hatton's room uninvited one night and found the boy carrying out a little experimentation. For the first and only time in the undisciplined child's life, a hysterical Isabel begged her husband to take a razor strop to the boy's already conveniently bare behind. Willard raised whelps while Isabel read aloud from a pamphlet entitled "A Young Man's Manual" outlining the fearsome damage of self-stimulation, shrinking of his private parts, sterility, blindness and epilepsy.

Violet shakes her head. With the notions put into that boy's head by the adults in this house, it will be a wonder if he ever turns out to be anything approaching normal.

She forces her mind's train off of that ill chosen track of thought. "Seems to me most of Miss Bess's life has been consumed with worrying about a war that was long ago lost and filling that boy's head with nonsense about battles, and generals, and good old days that weren't," she muses. "'Spect they might, the both of them, find it right thrilling to be caught up in the action. Don't forget that Miss Bess has already had herself some experience with war. How many times do you have to be told the story? How she had to hide out in the woods with my daddy Hyperion while her mama shot dead a Yankee? Despite the fact that she acts so flighty, if push met up with shove, she could be just as feisty as your granny."

"Do not even talk like that! I should die an early death if one hair of that precious baby boy's head were harmed." Isabel tears at her own hair in fear and frustration. "He is my whole life, Violet, *and all that makes the living worth it. He would never have left the safety of his dear mama's hearth and arms if Granny's meager inheritance hadn't financed such. It is all her fault. To think that she was able to squirrel away from her egg money more than five hundred dollars, and all of it in pennies and Indian head nickels and dimes!"*

Stole it, as many coins at a time as she could, first from Sam and then from Willard, good thing it was for the insomniac Minnie that both were such heavy sleepers, Violet chuckles to herself. Egg money!

Poor old Miss Minnie, still mumbling with her last breath about all that gold hidden in Selma. Violet squeezes her eyes closed over the threat of tears. She has given up hoping that anything will fill the huge empty hole in her heart left by Minnie's passing. Almost three years now since they took her home at last to White Gardenias, laid her in the family plot next to her big brother Alexander.

Violet mentally pictures the old slave cemetery at White Gardenias, feeling her fifty years, wondering where she herself will spend the ages. Won't be next to her papa, that's for a certainty.

"Violet! Your mind is a million miles away!" Isabel barks. "You seem unusually bent on trying my patience tonight. I have told you twice to make me a hot milk. I shall never be able to sleep tonight after hearing what you have just imparted. As good as I am to you, obviously spoiling you entirely rotten, I cannot understand for the life of me why you would choose to upset me so cruelly. What in heaven or on earth can be taking Willard so long at the telegraph office? You would think he was delivering the message to Belgium personally! I hope that he is right that Mr. Herbert Hoover, to whom the President has given the charge of refugee relief, can be of help and service to us. To think my sweet little innocent lad a refugee!"

She snatches another handful of hair before continuing. "Willard most likely stopped off at the office. Goodness me, that man is going to work himself into an early grave putting in evening hours to provide for us. Violet, please! Rouse your lazy bones from that chair and fetch my milk! My mind is whirling with your cruel sharing of knowledge that I would have been better off not knowing."

Maybe he's smarter than I've given him credit for being, denying her the newspaper, Violet thinks with a sigh as she forces her aching legs to an upright position. Maybe what Miss Isabel needs is a good dosing of Dr. Hammond's Nerve and Brain Pills. Are they not advertised as one hundred per cent effective, or money back, for curing a constant feeling of dread, as if something awful was going to happen?

Isabel, impossible to satisfy, has had her waxing and re-waxing the floors for the third day in a row, taking that old grey cake of Sapolio scouring soap and a bucket of hot water to every household surface including a few not meant to be washed in the first place. Complaining that Violet has left water marks on the mahogany. What does it matter to Isabel if Violet comes in contact with some of those nasty old German germs?

She longs for Cleotis to return from chauffeuring Mr. Willard to his assignation so that he can knead the knotted muscles in her neck. Cleotis is a good and a kind man. Cleotis for sure has never spent a single dime like that high and mighty Mr. Willard Preston, singing in the choir on Sunday morning and spending his nights buying love from some low repute woman.

She says a prayer that he really stopped, on the way to that whore house, by the telegraph office as he told Isabel he intended. If they don't find some way to get Hatton home soon, Isabel is going to drive Violet crazy enough to take herself to Nervine tonic.

***

Mallory Hudson was as much a fixture in the library's Southern History Department as the murals decorating the walls there. Anything to get out of that quiet house that was so noisy with loneliness. She was waiting for Josie to cry "uncle" first and getting tired of doing so.

Mallory twisted the heavy link of gold chain on her arm and pouted. Josie was too old to be trying to do heavy cleaning for a man who probably, true to his sex, discarded dirty socks and underwear and wet towels all over the place. How Josie used to get onto Jamie about that.

She forced the thought from her mind and got down to business.

The Civil War Records section was extensive. Mallory had pored through those shelves many times. She was pleased when Carrie asked her for the favor.

She found him almost immediately. "Buford, Captain Alexander Washington. Born 1833. Service Fifth Alabama Cavalry December 1862-April 1865. Wounded, reported disappeared from field hospital during Battle of Selma. Presumed dead."

That was all. A simple common soldier who had risen to a respectful but undistinguished ranking. Civil War hospitals were grim charnel houses in which the cure was as likely to kill as the wound. Nothing remarkable about going AWOL from such a place.

She had read accounts of the Battle of Selma. The city and its citizenry were left in shambles. Small wonder that the death record of a solitary soldier could be lost in the shuffle.

She inserted a second roll of microfilm. Now here was a hero. General Henry Capshaw Hatton. Multiply decorated for acts of battlefield bravery. Died 1874. Buried in Live Oak Cemetery, Selma. A notation that over his grave the United Daughters of the Confederacy had erected a monument.

She jotted down a few notes to take home to Carrie. Perhaps for the first and only time in her life she should take some good advice from Ellen, buy one of those little laptop computers to aid in her note taking. Pooh on that. She was too old for modern technology. Ellen was an idiot. Ellen could not write a grocery list interesting enough to be published.

She had run into Wyatt in this same room just days ago. He had proudly proclaimed the play almost written. Mallory wondered how long it would be before production. She already had in mind what she would wear to the premier. She had been for years a patron of local theater. Maybe, through her influence with Wyatt, the New York cast could be persuaded to put on a one night road show. She saw herself on stage at the curtain call, graciously receiving a bouquet of thank you roses.

Mallory slipped Carrie's notes into her satchel sized pocketbook, couldn't fathom why Carrie expressed so much interest in ancestors of the McShans and Prestons when she had a perfectly good set of her own in which to take pride.

Time to get on with more personally pertinent work. Moving across the research room, she took her seat at one of the tables and carefully smoothed the creases from an age faded letter.

The letter was dated April 1880. "Dearest Cousin Elizabeth, Everyone here is fine and dandy. I too am interested in the history of our family. Your grandfather, Henry Stainwright, resolutely refused to discuss his parentage. He would only describe himself as orphaned and left both brother and sisterless as the result of a tragic house fire from which only he and five silver spoons survived. To hear him tell it, it was as if his life began on the day when, under a kindly planter's patronage, he entered the University of Alabama. The War Between the States of course interrupted those studies, but praise heaven he survived unscathed but for the loss of his left arm and came back to complete his education. As you of course know, he was the Alabama Supreme Court Chief Justice. His tombstone gives his birth as '1830, Out From Selma.' I believe that any more details of our family record are now lost to history. Your ever affectionate cousin, Eloise Casswell."

Mallory tapped her pencil in frustration. She had found the scrap of letter, written to her grandmother, deep within the pages of an old family Bible. She imagined a beautiful columned mansion full of heirlooms and family records blazing against a dark night sky. Was she supposed to search every birth record for the year 1830 for every bump in the road community in the vicinity of Selma?

She took down a thick book of baptismal records, Dallas County, Alabama, 1825-30. Her illustrious ancestor Henry Stainwright had not emerged fully formed, like Athena from the head of Zeus, on the antebellum campus of the University of Alabama.

Patiently she traced a perfect peach fingernail down each column of records. What did it matter if it took all day, the rest of her life for that matter?

She was in no hurry to go home to a house to which three of the four people who had mattered most in her life would never again be returning. David and Jamie were dead and buried. Josie was simply stubborn.

Chapter Twenty One

A sneak preview of spring was playing in January.

Carrie stooped to pick a daffodil. It came to her, another prematurely warm late winter morning. Her mother had scolded her about picking flowers from a neighbor's yard without permission. She woke the next morning to find herself under a blanket of daffodils, picked just for her and without anyone's blessing.

She threw the blossom to the ground and ran the remaining distance to Wyatt's.

Carrie slumped in a chair, disappointed. Josie had gone to the market. She had spent the morning working up the nerve to ask Josie some questions.

"Talk to me, Wyatt."

"About what?"

"Anything, just preoccupy my mind."

He frowned at her. Carrie's sudden early morning appearance came as a surprise. She had never received an invitation to his house. She very well knew that the hours between eight and noon were sacred.

It came to him, a sudden burst of what seemed most lacking in his life, inspiration.

"I have an idea, Carrie. There's fried chicken, potato salad, and peach cobbler in the refrigerator. Josie cooks like she's expecting an army for dinner every night. Be a good girl and pack us up a picnic."

"Josie's peach cobbler. Makes my mouth water to think about it. I remember Josie putting up peaches every summer like a squirrel storing nuts for the winter."

I remember, I remember. Somebody help me, it's all coming back. Dizzy, she grabbed the edge of the counter for support.

"Carrie, are you all right?"

"Who knows? I guess I'm just weak from spending so much time in bed. I'm not supposed to be up yet, but I escaped. I had to get out of the house. Those pills were giving me funny dreams."

It was neither far to their destination nor a location that Carrie would have suggested for a picnic. "Grand old southern tradition, is it not," Wyatt, pleased with himself, said with a grin, "holding a family picnic among the departed?"

As Wyatt spread the quilt, Carrie studied the marble markers.

Gooseflesh prickled her skin. It seemed a bizarre irreverence, spreading food squarely on top of the remains of Hatton Preston.

"Carrie, serve the chicken. If Hatton sits up and expresses a preference for dark meat it's past time I had a word with him anyway."

Nibbling a drumstick, Carrie wondered who had cared enough to order the simple headstone that marked the final resting place of Katherine Isabel McShan Preston. She pictured a bored secretary in the office of some estate attorney.

A cold wind suddenly whipped in from the north, pushing a cloud bank over the sun and eclipsing momentarily the out of season sense of springtime.

"Do you ever, Wyatt, wish you could go back in life? Do some things differently?"

"Doesn't everyone?"

She took a sip of wine, leaned back against Hatton's headstone, and closed her eyes. "When we were first married, and Nicky was in medical school in New Orleans, on the weekends we'd get up very early in the morning and put the babies in their strollers, go down to the French Quarter and eat beignets and drink strong chicory coffee in the Café du Monde. Those old French Quarter houses are such pretty pastel colors. I loved the peeling stucco and iron balconies and closed tight shutters as if all those old buildings were hiding secrets."

She was quiet for a few moments, savoring a memory. "There was one house in particular that always fascinated me. It had partially burned, probably years before. The shutters were hanging off of it, and, even with half the rooms gutted, you could see that it had been in its day incredibly beautiful, a house that some woman had loved and been proud of. I always wished that it could tell me the stories of all the people who had been born and made love and argued and died there. I wanted to buy what was left of that burned house and save it. I loved living in New Orleans. I cried for days when Nick graduated and said we had to come back here, right back under my mother's thumb."

"Carrie, are you by chance afraid of your mother?"

"What a silly question. Of course not." She paused in self analysis. "I'm afraid of disappointing my mother, which is not very

201

difficult to do. In some ways I've always felt closer to Ellen. Ellen gets herself into so many predicaments that she finds it easy to give the benefit of the doubt to others."

"They are two very different women entirely."

"You can sum up the difference in one simple word."

"Which is?"

"Baseboards. My mother is such a fanatic about nice people not having dusty baseboards that before she has a party she'll be on her knees inspecting the upstairs bathrooms. Ellen, on the other hand, simply dims the lights, puts out a few candles, and has a great time."

Concentrating on catching any whisper from Hatton Preston, Wyatt was only half listening to Carrie and didn't interrupt her. She refilled her wine glass.

"My mother sets her clocks fifteen minutes fast and her scales four pounds below zero to protect her from the two things she fears most in the world, being late or overweight."

"Your mother means well."

Carrie let out a little sigh that dangerously approached a burp. So peaceful in the cemetery. Her mind was becoming pleasantly cloudy.

With her finger she traced the motto carved beneath the family crest on Hatton's tombstone. Fuimus qui sumusque futuri. Who we were is who we are and are to be.

∗∗∗

Nick paced the empty house. For years it had been a given, taken for granted, coming home at the end of a long hard day and finding Carrie waiting.

He had purposely come home early. It was past time to get some issues out in the open. She and Dooley were both missing. Unlikely they were taking a walk, Dooley's arthritis had become crippling.

It was hard to accept Dooley's aging. Good old Dooley, day in and day out utterly dependable, wagging his tail and wearing what looked like a punch drunk grin. He could count on Dooley, who, unlike Carrie lately, never demanded to carry out his own agenda.

Who knew any more what Carrie was capable of doing? He switched on lights, glowing a dim yellow through the sallow silk of old shades. An uneasy feeling rippled through him.

He took a beer from the refrigerator and went to the living room, fell in a chair and put his head in his hands. The damnable house was eating him alive. It had nothing to do with money. They could afford not only to live there but to put the place in an at least presentable condition. He knew that he was resisting making improvements that implied that they would be staying.

It was so quiet he could hear the grandfather clock in the hall ticking like the house's heavy erratic heartbeat. Sometimes the clock's hands ran an hour early, at other times an hour late, as if during the deep dark of the night different pairs of hands reset it. What did it matter what time it was? They were stuck in a stalemate, going nowhere.

Emptiness echoed through the house. Where in the world was Carrie?

Maybe Carrie had gone somewhere with his mother. He felt a twinge of pain, imagining comments of derision when his mother's five pound manuscript arrived in the office of some publisher. In the manner of sensible sons born to feckless mothers, he felt as protective of Ellen as he did of Carrie and the children. As father, son, and husband, he felt it his duty to take care of all of them.

A car door slammed. He parted the drapes and frowned out the window. What was Carrie doing with Wallace, and why was she stumbling?

"What are you doing home?" She squinted at her watch and hiccoughed.

"What a way to greet me. Good grief, Carrie, have you been drinking?"

"Just a little wine. Wyatt took me to Oak Hill Cemetery on a picnic."

"Since when did you start having dates with other men in the middle of the afternoon?"

"With no one here but me and the ghosts of Isabel and Hatton this old house gets lonely. You're never around."

He looked at her miserably. "Carrie, life used to be so simple."

"Who wants to live a simple life? I have decided to make some changes and start living what's left of my life with abandon."

He went to the coat closet and jerked a jacket off a hanger.

"Are you leaving?"

"I need some cold fresh air to clear my head. I think I'll take

Dooley for a walk. Exercise will do him good."

"Why don't you teach him to play tennis, or maybe you need to find the old boy some pretty little bitch dog to be his companion."

What in the world was she saying? He had to get out, straighten out his head with the comfort of his dog's companionship, before he said things later regretted.

"Where is Dooley anyway?"

"How should I know? I just told you I've been away all day. Probably out in the woods being mean to my cat. Oops, sorry, I completely forgot that I'm not supposed to mention my fictitious feline and remind you that I'm crazy."

"You didn't leave Dooley outside in the cold all day?"

"I did, and I didn't. I left him outside, but it wasn't cold. It was in fact just like springtime. Wyatt and I had a lovely picnic in the cemetery."

She used to be so sympathetic to Dooley's stiff joints and failing hearing. If Dooley was spoiled, it was Carrie who had done it, Carrie who had slipped him scraps at the table and made the poor old dog feel like a fool wearing a special Christmas collar.

Nick slammed the door as he went outside in search of the animal.

Carrie yawned, wishing it were later than seven o'clock, closer to bedtime. She fell back on the sofa, her eyes traveling upward on the fireplace wall where two niches held urns. They reminded her of containers for dead loved ones' ashes. She thought of Isabel's family rowed out in the cemetery. All but one. What in the world had become of Lydia? She'd dreamed it, hadn't she, just a few days ago? Lydia dying with everyone out of town, and Isabel slapping her in Oak Hill as hastily as if she'd carried the cholera.

On the other hand, maybe she had married Rad Cunningham after all, rested peacefully in some pompous plot in one of Boston's better Beacon Hill cemeteries.

Stop acting like you are engrossed in some nonfiction novel, she muttered to herself. They are only dreams, manufactured by your own psyche. She felt strangely comforted by the thought. She didn't want Lydia to have met a tragic ending.

"Carrrrrie!" The shout caught on a current of cold night air and penetrated the living room. Carrie ran outside.

"Carrie, I need some help here. Come on old fellow. You can

do it. Dooley, you're too heavy to carry. He's freezing, Carrie. Help me get him inside."

She put her hands to her face to shut out the horror. Nick sat, rocking back and forth, on a bed of wet leaves in the old rose garden. Tears streamed down his face as he cradled the dog's head in his lap. Dooley's big liquid brown eyes stared blankly. His lips didn't quite meet over his teeth. In death he looked, as he always had in life, as if he were smiling. It struck Carrie like a whip across the heart that in all the years they'd had him it was the first time she had ever seen Dooley with his always frantically wagging tail hanging limp, like a death announcement.

"Oh, Nicky, I'm so sorry, I'm so terribly sorry." Carrie knelt down and took her husband's head in her arms.

Pushing his wife away, Nick buried his face in Dooley's golden coat and sobbed uncontrollably.

She looked up at the stars winking on the dark screen of the January sky. Catch a falling star and put it in your pocket, save it for a rainy day. Not now! You go away and stay put there. I have to now, at this moment, deal with a problem more pressing.

"Come in the house, Nick," she whispered softly, her own tears falling freely. "Come in the house and let me take care of you."

"I can't leave him out here all by himself in the cold, Carrie. He's just really crippled up by the arthritis and having trouble getting his legs under him. Come on, old buddy. Come on, Dooley."

"Nick! Listen to me!" She turned his face to hers, eye to eye. "You need to come inside."

"Carrie, how could you possibly understand? How many times have I heard you complain that your mother never let you have a dog?"

She looked at him miserably. What did you do on a rainy day when you reached in your pocket and found it with a hole in it, empty of stars?

Past due in coming, a memory flashed as bright as a comet. A Christmas morning, a fat honey colored puppy with a huge red bow on his collar, growing into a big dog, chasing a bicycle. The pain raged through her.

"We most certainly did have a dog, Nick. A big golden retriever a lot like Dooley. His name was Winkie for Wee Willie Winkie of the nursery rhyme because he was so little and cuddly when we got him. He grew into this great hulking hundred pound dog that drove

Mother crazy knocking her trinkets off the tables by wagging his tail. He did a lot of tail wagging. Winkie was a happy dog, a laughing dog just like Dooley. One day he left us, and I don't know what happened to him. I don't remember, Nick. I'm so afraid to remember."

Heaving sobs convulsed her. Why had Dooley chosen to die on the one day she'd drug him outdoors by the collar and left him alone at the edge of the woods, telling him "stay" as she walked to Wyatt's? She'd gone off on that picnic and forgotten all about him. She felt as consumed with guilt as if she had murdered him.

If she had been home as she should have, could she have stopped his dying? Could have stopped, could have stopped, could have stopped . . . NO!

She struggled to stop her mind's spinning and take the risk of letting out just one memory. What had happened to Winkie? Couldn't ask her mother, not about a dog so much a part of Jamie. She needed to know. She was going to have to ask Josie.

***

Ten o'clock passed. The grandfather clock in the hall bonged eleven times. Carrie lay in bed trying to will herself to remain awake until Nick gave up trying to convince himself that Dooley wasn't dead and came in from the cold.

She had never, ever, not once in all the time she'd known him, seen him cry over anything. He hadn't cried when she lost her father, when the two of them had lost their baby.

She rolled on her side, turning her back on the place in the bed where she supposed he would eventually join her.

The streets of Brussels remain as lovely as if war is no more than a distant, rather than a growing daily nearer, rumble. The late summer flowers bloom in the window boxes, bright red geraniums and pink and purple petunias oblivious to the goose stepping soldiers of the Kaiser, wearing iron spiked helmets and bathing in blood the surrounding countryside from which refugees stream in by wagon and on foot, clutching their bundles of clothing and terrified children.

Vacationing American tourists, taken as much by surprise as the rest of the world at the results of a wrong turn on a street in Saravejo, make panicked purchases of return tickets to a safer new world.

No where in the city is there to be purchased at any price a comforting tincture of Nervine tonic. Bess is beside herself, huddled wailing on the hotel bed. She lets out an ear piercing scream at the knock on the hotel room door. Can it be an emissary of the evil Hun come to carry them away as hostages?

Hatton, possessing a teenager's surety of invincibility, answers the door.

The man at the door, on seeing the boy, feels his heart constrict. Never has he encountered one who looks so much like a long lost other. The present is too fraught with peril to let the past intrude. He summons his composure. "I am Adam Livingston, correspondent for the International Herald Tribune. I have been sent by Mr. Herbert Hoover, who has been charged by President Wilson with the safe removal of American citizens, to be of personal assistance to you and your great-aunt."

"Hatton! Into the bathroom! Close the door and lock it tightly! Quickly!" Bess screeches from beneath the bedspread where she unsuccessfully attempts, covers over her head, to hide.

"Please, Miss Hatton, I can understand your reluctance to participate in any scheme of my devising," the visitor argues, shouldering his way past Hatton and into the room. Hatton, a little less cocksure than he was moments before, does as his aunt directs. Clearly visible is the lump of a pistol in the stranger's pocket. "I assure you that I am your best and only hope in this moment of crisis. I do not share the world's naive view that this is to be but a brief and easily patched up spat between bickering neighbors. It will be as protracted, bloody and brutal as that long ago conflict that your father predicted would rage but ninety days."

"Avram?" The word, but a whisper, catches in her throat. She peeps from beneath the covers like a child playing peek-a-boo. The passage of years has etched lines of wear and tear but left the handsome face still recognizable. He is as a ghost returned from a round trip ride on a midnight train.

"Based in London, I now call myself by an Anglicized name," he explains, his own voice trembling as the sight of the aunt brings Lydia back full force, the terrible yearning that never leaves him intensifying. "I mean only to help you and the boy. I do not mean now, as I did not mean then, any harm to anyone."

"You will rot in hell for the harm you caused."

"Perhaps and justifiably so." He runs a hand across a tired

face. "The past is beside the point. You must pack quickly. I have, courtesy of my newspaper and Mr. Hoover's intervention, train tickets out of the country. I will accompany you as far as Paris, from which return passage to America has been booked."

Bess chews her lip. She has for her beloved great-nephew sole responsibility. This means of escape is the only option before her. Frantic cables from Willard and Isabel, imploring her to do whatever, whenever, however, Mr. Herbert Hoover commands, litter the desk.

She rises from the bed and squares her shoulders, glaring at Avram who now claims to be Adam. Treacherous traitor who put their lovely Lydia into the melancholia from which she never recovered, making her weak in body and spirit and thus susceptible to the fast acting fever that claimed her.

Hesitantly, he asks the one question which has tormented him every waking and sleeping moment of every day and night for the previous dozen plus years.

"Well, how kind of you to inquire," Bess replies in an icy voice that Hatton, overhearing, didn't know she had in her. Thinks to himself, why, she sounds as mean as Great Granny.

"Lydia is fine and dandy, thank you very much for expressing interest. She and Mama are residing in Selma, enjoying a very tranquil life at our beloved White Gardenias. Indeed, Lydia has so put the past behind her that she doesn't ever even call your name in passing."

Chapter Twenty Two

Carrie peered out the window. Under the moon's light Dooley's body was covered with a blanket.

Nick was no where to be seen. Called to the hospital, or seeking comfort elsewhere? She crawled back in bed and resumed her dreaming.

"Thank you for coming, Doctor." Isabel closes the front door behind the family physician. "Isn't it a wonder, a man the age of Willard coming down with a childhood ailment like measles?"

"What I cannot figure is why, if he did not have the malady as a child, he did not contract it from Hatton, whom I recall having a mild but unmistakable case," the doctor answers.

"Oh, I beg to differ on that score!" Isabel retorts. "Your memory must be failing. I didn't get one wink of sleep during those two weeks that the virulent virus attacked his little body. We were sure, Willard and I, that we were going to lose our baby, the only child that heaven chose to grant us. Perilous times!"

The doctor shakes his head, thanking heaven that Hatton has at last passed through not only measles but chicken pox and mumps and whooping cough as well. He is not sure he would have the stamina to go through another two week long bout of anything else afflicting Hatton with Isabel.

Alone with Willard, examination completed, he pulls a chair up next to the feverish patient and questions him about other, seemingly unrelated symptoms.

"About six months ago you say?" the doctor asks, scribbling on a small note pad.

"Have you ever heard of a case of measles taking six months to germinate?" Willard asks hesitantly.

"Your symptoms in sum lead me to unhappy diagnosis, Willard, and it always saddens me to have to give a man such news."

"What do you mean?" Willard demands.

"It's not measles, Willard, but something far more serious for which the few remedies available are not always effective at the stage of the disease to which your case has advanced."

"Speak up, and give it a name." Willard, visibly shaken, grabs the doctor's arm.

"The French pox," the doctor says, blushing despite himself.

"Syphilis?" Willard mouths the word so quietly that Isabel, straining to hear on the other side of the keyhole, misses it entirely. She is struggling with the euphemism, mind racing with the horror of the fact that she has just last night had Willard cable Bess and Hatton that they are to seek any means of removing themselves from Belgium to the safety of France. Now will Hatton be in even more danger, at risk of contacting some heretofore unknown Gallic disease? Why, oh why, oh why, did she ever agree to let Hatton out of her sight?

"We must start mercury treatments at once," the doctor says. "They are painful and protracted and not always successful but the only medicinal weapon available. At best you may have ten years or so before the full effects are manifest."

"The full effects?" Willard strangles.

"Not a pretty picture, Willard, but I believe in being truthful. Blindness, deafness, insanity, paralysis."

Isabel, disgusted at Willard's loud sobs and wishing she could remember more of Bess's geography lessons from the years of her limited education, tears at her hair. Germany. They should have told Bess and Hatton to go to Germany. No! Her tortured mind screams. Germany is the country that is causing all this trouble. She puts her ear back to the keyhole.

"You must not blame yourself, Willard. It is a condition seen all too often among men who only had their delicate wives' best interests at heart in seeking an outside outlet for masculine energies, but she must be told. She too is most likely infected."

"Not my angel Dolores," Willard sobs.

"Fully ninety percent of them harbor one or more of the social diseases. It is for the angel of this house that I fear. Do you still impose carnal relations on Mrs. Preston?"

"Only on Thursday evenings," Willard mumbles.

"More than often enough to infect her," the doctor sighs. "She will have to be examined."

On the other side of the door, Isabel's scream is so piercing that the chickens outside the back door dart for cover in the coop, ignoring the handful of corn dropped by a startled Violet. "What now, what now?" she mutters in their direction before gathering her skirts and running back inside the house.

"Now, Miss Isabel, you got to calm yourself," Violet protests *over Isabel's wails of misery. "You heard that doctor. He said this is a four part condition, and you are just under the influence of part one. He can fix you up just as good as new. Mr. Willard is not so lucky, but then he brought it on himself consorting with that harlot. You can't say Cleotis didn't warn him to repent before it was too late. We got to look on the bright side. This means Mr. Willard won't ever again bother you on a Thursday night. You and I both heard that doctor tell him it is forbidden ever again with anyone. Mr. Willard's days of fancying himself a bull with all the cows in the field in season are over and done."*

"Violet! Please! I am, whatever shameful malady has befallen me, still a lady of breeding, and I will not have such common talk in my house."

"If you ask my opinion, if so many things that were intended to be a natural part of life were not so hushed up and treated as shameful and secret in this house we would not find ourselves in quite so sour a pickle jar so often."

"What will Hatton do with me dead and gone? Oh, Violet, however will the poor babe manage to go on without me? You know I am the sun and moon around which his life like a little planet revolves."

"Hush that silly talk! You are not fixing to die. I got an old country remedy that will fix you right up right as rain and better than anything that doctor ever thought of. You are forgetting that my mother was a witch doctor. I just got to get my hands on a few ingredients that may be hard to come by here in the big city, swamp roots and such like." Out in the country they used to swear by a pinch of arsenic in just such a situation. Easy enough to come by some rat poison. "Don't you worry yourself, Miss Isabel. Violet will take care of you."

"Oh, Violet, what would this family do without you?"

"That I'd hate to contemplate."

"Perhaps you should check on Willard now. The doctor was quite clear, wasn't he, that Hatton cannot contract this by casual contact?"

"Clear as day, Miss Isabel. Isn't but one way to get it. You get some sleep now. One day this will all be behind us like it was no more than an old bad dream."

"Please, Mr. Willard, please, you too upset to go confronting anyone right now," Cleotis begs as Willard hunches down in the

back seat of the car, snarling snatches of poetry.

"I compensated her well to remain pure for me. She has been soiled by others. She must pay the wages of the fallen angel," Willard shrieks. Cleotis wonders if the fever is making his employer delirious, or if Willard has lost his mind entirely. "I must teach her a lesson. 'In yesterday's reach and tomorrow's, out of sight though they lie of today, There have been and there yet shall be sorrows that smite not and bite not in play. The life and the love thou despisest, These hurt us indeed and in vain, O wise among women and wisest, Our Lady of Pain.'"

Cleotis creases his brow in confusion. If that kind of fancy gibberish talk is what you learn in college he himself is just as happy to be uneducated.

The house is full of customers, all preoccupied. The parlor, where the available women customarily wait, is empty. Willard stumbles up the stairs unnoticed. Before the fever took hold of him, he had planned this night to be away on business. Rebecca, unsuspecting his arrival, thanks the gentleman and pockets his money. He tips his hat to Willard in passing in the hallway, mutters "Best women this house has to offer. Shame she's so rarely free."

Startled, a half dressed Rebecca stares open mouthed at the sight of a fevered and disheveled Willard lunging through the doorway.

"Of languors rekindled and rallied, Of barren delights and unclean, Things monstrous and fruitless, a pallid and poisonous queen," he hisses. "'Dolores' by Algernon Charles Swinburne."

Her last thought is of betrayal. All these months of spouting fancy words. To think that he told her he had written those poems himself.

***

"No! No! No! No!" Violet screams over and over and over, a primal litany of denial. This time the tables are turned. It is Isabel who implores Violet to pull herself together.

"Violet, please! Hysteria will get us nowhere." Violet continues screaming. Isabel slaps her.

"He didn't do it. You and I both know that he didn't do it."

"We do not know anything of the sort, Violet," Isabel says in a

voice so calm it borders on coldness. "If he was innocent, why did he run?"

"They shot him in the back like he was a dog," Violet weeps.

"Routine police procedure in the case of a fleeing felon," Isabel responds.

"Now, Isabel Preston, I ask you, why in the world would my Cleotis, who wouldn't hurt a flea, have beaten to death some prostitute?"

"The motive mentioned was robbery compounded into murder," Isabel replies. "That woman, despicable though she might have been, was brutally bludgeoned. Cleotis was reported high tailing it out of town alone after stealing Willard's motor car."

"You and I both know that is not the truth."

"I know only what I have been told by officers of the law. It is a tragedy to be sure, but thankfully one on which the final curtain has been drawn. Tried and convicted, if you will, Cleotis is dead, Violet, and no amount of caterwauling and second guessing can bring him back from that eternal condition. We must get on with our lives." Isabel arranges her face in the same expression of prim beatitude she did on the night that Lydia died.

Violet, patient and long suffering, reaches the end of a very long tether.

"Mrs. Preston," she begins, rising to her full height and glaring down at Isabel. "I will be out of here on the first train tomorrow morning."

"You stupid goose! And just where do you propose to go?"

"Like Miss Minnie said we should have done years ago, I am going home to Selma."

"To Selma? To Selma?" Isabel's laugh is high pitched and hysterical. "Don't be ridiculous! Whatever do you plan to do there? How will you support yourself? You'll never even get day work without a reference from me."

"Don't forget that Miss Minnie didn't leave all of that egg money to Bess. I got enough to get by on I reckon. I can always take in laundry."

"You don't even have a place to stay in Selma. Stop talking like a child!" Isabel struggles to restrain her consternation. Violet cannot add fuel to the fire of gossip by leaving. Scandal enough that the crime was committed by someone in the Prestons' employ, but then didn't Isabel herself tell the police that for years she had

feared to terminate him due to the fact that he was dangerous and unpredictable when angered? As with any lie, the more times the telling the softer blurs the distinction between the truth and false-hood. Isabel shudders at the thought of what harm he could have done to any member of her family.

"I have faithfully kept this family's secrets, every dark and dirty one of them, Isabel McShan Preston, but no more, no more." Violet's voice is clear and firm, all traces of grief and emotion pushed back, saved for the luxury of a later day. "You have crossed the line tonight. I heard you calling the police and telling them that poor Cleotis was not only drunk but also armed and dangerous and had stolen Mr. Willard's car. You know Cleotis never took a drink in his life. You were the one urging them to shoot him dead and ask questions later. You made my husband a scapegoat to protect your own just as surely as if you had pulled the trigger."

"Violet Larson, you and I both know that in our separate com-munities murder does not carry the same social stigma. Your peo-ple kill each other at the drop of a hat. You will still be able to hold your head high among your contemporaries. Didn't Granny warn you all those years ago that no good could come of marrying a no count like Cleotis?"

"An innocent man died tonight, Isabel. You are going to answer for it in the next life if not in this one."

"Well, you let me worry about the state of my soul. How can you be talking nonsense about running off from here when the police haven't even released the body for burial? You're not think-ing straight."

"I've never thought straighter in my life, Isabel, and for once it's me whose going to do the telling in this house about how things are going to be and you who's going to follow the orders instead of giv-ing them."

"I've a good mind to fire you sassing me like that! I would have done just that, and years ago, at Willard's urging, if you hadn't been family. That's what I always said when he complained about your impertinence. 'Why, Willard,' I always said, 'Despite her deplorable lapses of manners, Violet is just like family.'"

"I am family, Isabel. No getting around that, and you and I both know it. I'm family, and I'm leaving home, and I reckon it is about time I came into my rightful inheritance. First thing tomorrow I am

getting on a train, going home to White Gardenias, back to my peo-
ple, back to where I belong."

"I never heard such a crazy notion in all my days! You've never
been on a train by yourself in your life. You saw how ill Willard felt
when Cleotis brought him home. Just you wait until my husband
feels perkier. He'll put a quick stop to all of this nonsense."

"Mr. Willard can't stop me. Nothing stopping me from going
clothesline to clothesline up and down this street sharing with 'my
contemporaries' about a little virus going round this house, or a
baby's bones fertilizing the rose bushes, or who somebody's right-
ful parents are, or . . . . ."

"Stop it right this minute! You wouldn't dare!"

"You sign over the deed to White Gardenias to me tonight, and
I will be out of here in the morning and back where I came from,
where I belong."

"That is blackmail."

"Maybe so, but come that final day of judgment, blackmail is a
far sight farther down the list of sins than murder."

The two tall women face each other down, eye to eye, until
Violet breaks the stalemate. "Take your choice, Mrs. Preston. A
crumbling old house in the country that doesn't mean anything to
you anyway, or the continuation of that good name you hold so high
and mighty. It's all up to you. The cards are in your hand, and the
deck is stacked against you."

The sun was rising, a cantaloupe ball of color in the east. Carrie
got out of bed, stumbled to the bathroom and threw cold water in
her face. She stared hard at herself in the mirror, feeling guilt over
her abandonment of Nick the previous night. Was living in this
house doing something evil to her, making her as hard and cold and
mean as Isabel?

She snapped up the shade and looked out the bathroom window.

She gasped, cried out "No!" and, grabbing her robe from the
hook on the back of the door, flew down the stairs as fast as her
legs would take her.

Right out the window she had seen the impossible.

Nick had a shovel. He was going to bury Dooley. In the rose
garden. Right next to one last stubbornly still blooming yellow rose
bush. Right there in that good river bottom Selma dirt brought from

Isabel's old house on the Southside right along with . . . No!

Calm down, calm down she reassured herself. You are losing your mind here. It was only a dream. There are no remains of a baby's bones rotting in the rose garden.

"Nick," she yelled across the driveway. "What in the world are you doing?"

"What does it look like? I'm not planting rose bushes."

"But you might want to later," she stammered. "You can't put Dooley in Isabel's rose garden."

"It is no longer 'Isabel's' rose garden, Carrie. Or Isabel's house. Or Isabel's china. I am sick and tired of sharing a house with a woman who has been dead for more than twenty years. Like it or not, it's my house now, my yard, and my dog that needs burying. I will bury him anywhere on this property that I damn well please."

Carrie thought hard. Surely there was some simple and reasonable solution. She put a restraining hand on the arm that held the shovel. "Dooley never liked it here very much either, Nick. I know what we should do. We'll take Dooley home, bury him in the backyard of our old house, right in the shade of that big sweet gum tree where the squirrels used to tease him."

"Dooley would have been happier if he could have spent the remaining months of his life there. So would I. That, however, is beside the point. Can you imagine the reaction of the new owners if we knocked on their door and said 'Don't mind us while we bury our dead dog.' They'd think we were crazy."

Half of this duo is exactly that, thought Carrie helplessly. She had to get control of herself. It was just a crazy dream, probably something her mind had twisted out of the death of her own baby. The sun rose a little higher, putting a more reasonable face on the morning.

Nick turned back to the task at hand. Furious digging.

Carrie let out a screech when she heard it. A sound too distinct to be but one thing.

Only a foot or so down. Without Cleotis around to help her it must have been only as deep as Isabel on her own had been capable of digging. Only a foot below the surface of the garden.

The shovel had made contact with something metal.

Chapter Twenty Three

"Josie, about this dinner party to which you have invited guests without consulting me . . . ."

"You want pancakes with or without blueberries, Mr. Wallace?"

"With." In a few short weeks he had gained five pounds on her cooking. "Josie, I hardly consider myself an overly demanding employer . . . ."

"Bacon or sausage?"

"Both, and to save your further interrupting me, I'd like orange juice halved with champagne."

"I do not serve liquor at breakfast."

She was driving him to utter distraction.

She set the plate of pancakes in front of him, took her seat across from him and stared him squarely in the face. He thought to himself that she would have made a lousy poker player.

"Mr. Wallace, I know I probably should have consulted you regarding the guest list in case you have friends I forgot to invite. A dinner party seemed like a good idea to me at the time and with passing time has seemed even more so."

"Josie, Josie, Josie! I know you perceive of yourself as trying to take care of me. I have, however, been quite self sufficient and as set in my ways as a fence post in concrete for years. As I have so patiently tried on numerous occasions to explain to you, I am living as a man whose days are numbered. I cannot and will not abide interruptions when I am working."

"Did I ask you to cook the food, or wash the plates, or sweep the porch steps for the company coming?"

"Josie, I am not going to back down. Ask for a rain check, or tell them I'm terminally ill, or something."

"If you would stop living your life all in a snit about dying, you might actually get something done. I'm not calling and canceling anyone, Mr. Wallace, because nice people don't behave like that."

She changed the subject in an attempt to make amends. "What's in that big old box sitting in the hallway?"

"You can read the label on the carton as well as I can."

"Took Ellen's good advice I see. Got yourself a fancy computer."

"I doubt very much that I'll ever even use it. You know, Josie, you can no longer buy ribbons for my father's old typewriter. I am now down to the very last one. I can afford to waste neither time nor words, precious commodities both of them."

"Well, you get to work then while I do the last minute shopping."

He breathed a sigh of relief. As long as Josie was not around, she could not answer the door and/or the telephone and assure the callers that he had spent the morning waiting with bated breath for the intrusion.

"I'm going to get a sympathy card for us to send Nicky," she called over her shoulder. "Dooley always put me in mind of a dog that Carrie and Jamie had as kids. Goodness me, I've never seen a boy and a dog that were closer than Jamie and Winkie."

"I've never had time for an animal."

She scowled. Maybe a dog was what he needed. "Winkie was a sweet tempered dog, and he was getting awfully old and was nearly blind, but neither of those things was good reason for him dying."

"What happened to him?" Wyatt asked with little interest as he pushed back from the table. He had better things to do than expend sympathy over a dog's demise.

"A terrible thing, if you ask me." She pursed her lips in deep disapproval. "Mallory had Winkie put to sleep. Took him to the vet herself not more than an hour after Jamie's funeral. She said that she couldn't bear to think of Jamie in heaven without his dog."

Enormous tears suddenly ran like rivers down Josie's cheeks.

He shooed her out of the house. He had no time this morning for weeping women. Even less interest in either dead dogs or brothers.

With a shudder of revulsion at the depth of his desperation, he ripped open the box containing the computer.

***

Carrie stared out the window at the freshly turned dirt in the rose garden, the single defiantly surviving yellow rose bush blooming like a cemetery arrangement. She had the shivery sensation that past and present had that morning come very close to colliding.

She fingered the key in her hand. It was time.

Outside the locked door, like a New York Public Library guardian lion, the cat sat licking his whiskers and waiting.

Her hand trembling slightly, she inserted the key and twisted. The hinges were rusty from the damp and decades untested, protesting in creaks like the groans of the dying.

Carrie aimed the flashlight. It was not a simple closet but a lead lined vault, the interior swathed in a gossamer netting of cobwebs and pale layers of dust. Carrie pushed aside the translucent curtains spun by long still spiders.

It lay on the floor at her feet, a small metal trunk identical to the one in her dream. She took her shirttail and wiped away the dust. The initials AWB. A coffin containing a baby dead even longer than this house had been standing?

The trunk was not heavy. Baby's bones long disintegrated to dust would not be. She carried it upstairs.

The latch was loose, fell off in her hand. She felt the briefest moment of doubt before lifting the lid.

The box was empty.

Feeling a curious mixture of relief and disappointment, Carrie abandoned her finding and, a hand to her back for support, half walked, half crawled back to bed where she belonged.

"Hatton Alexander Buford Preston, you put that head back on your shoulders instead of up in the clouds where it has no business being!" Isabel snaps. She is short on patience after a morning spent trying to make her household account balance so that Willard will not be obliged to berate her for arithmetical incompetency.

Dratted numbers. Dadgum that Violet for running off and leaving her! For years Violet, who has a mind like an abacus, has done the sums for her, a fact of which Willard has been ignorant. Efficient bookkeeping is one of the few things on which Willard has ever complimented her.

"Mother, please, I've been offered a scholarship to one of the most prestigious universities in this country."

"I have spoken, Hatton. The subject is not open to discussion. Howard College, right here in Birmingham, will suffice nicely for your continuing education. How many times in your childhood did you hear your Great Granny bemoan that her brother, your namesake, died from the effects of a northern education?" Isabel does not need to peer that far back in the past. Just look at the degradation a northern experience brought down on Lydia.

"Great Granny's brother Alexander matriculated at Harvard. You

can see for yourself, Mother. This letter bears the official seal of Princeton."

"They are all alike, every last one of them. I'll not have your head filled with Yankee isms."

"Walker Wallace is going. His mother is proud of him."

Isabel suppresses a sniffle. How can her baby boy even consider leaving her? Bitsy Ashcraft Wallace will live to rue the day she gave Walker her blessing, of that Isabel is not only certain but expectant. I told you so is one of Isabel's favorite expressions.

"One more word said on this subject will be treated as impertinence to your mama, Hatton. You may be eighteen years old, but to my mind you are still a child and not too old for a good whipping."

Angry, Hatton strides from the room. In his life he has only received one whipping. His father acted as if he enjoyed the process. His mother does not even consider his body his own. His mind is another matter.

His mother has left him only one option.

***

Isabel clutches the sheet of paper and lets out a blood curdling scream. Her maid, Harriet, takes the stairs two at a time.

Harriet, hands still dripping soapy water, and Bess, called from the bed in which she has remained uncharacteristically late this morning, complaining of a vague feeling of ague, descend upon the wailing Isabel.

"Harriet, send Henry for Willard! At once! None of your usual dawdling. A terrible tragedy has befallen us. How could he have taken such leave of his senses and done such a thing after I have devoted every waking moment since his most difficult birth to his every need and nurture? How could he?" She screams again.

"Merciful heavens, Isabel, you are frightening the very wits from me," Bess interrupts, breathless. "You cannot be saying that some tragic event has taken the baby boy from us?" The two women cling to each other, swaying back and forth.

Isabel crumples the paper in her hand and sobs. "How could such a minor confrontation have resulted in such an unthinkable tragedy? Howard College, right here in Birmingham, so close to his mama, is a fine institution."

"No one can argue that. It was the alma mater of my late husband Arthur, back in the days when the academy was located in Marion." No one thinks to comment on the sudden appearance of Adelaide. It is her practice to walk in unannounced, as if she owns the place.

"Oh, never again on this earth to know a happy hour or moment! Hatton, our precious baby boy, how could you have done this to us?" Isabel and Bess resume the piteous wailing.

"Goodness, gracious, what in the world is all this fuss and folderol?" Adelaide interjects. "You talk as if the boy has done himself in. He hasn't, has he?"

"For all intents and purposes. He has run away to join the Royal Canadian Air Force. The cause of world peace is not worth the harming of one hair on his fair head. I can see it clearly, can you not too, Bess, our beloved boy broken and bleeding, the lifeblood and promise draining out of him, soaking the fields of France."

"Oh, Isabel, I can! I can! Just as clearly as if I had my old Scots grandmother's cursed gift of the second sight! Mama having selfishly taken the very last space remaining in the old family plot behind the Selma home place, we will not even enjoy the solace of planting him where he, as both a Hatton and a Buford, rightly belongs, at White Gardenias."

Bess sniffles into her sleeve, worrying that burned hair will be brittle and next to impossible to fashion into any piece worth wearing. "Oh, I do hope it is not a fiery crash! Charred remains are always so unattractive, and there is just something so incomplete about a closed casket service."

"Quiet up, the both of you!" Adelaide shouts above the ruckus. "Stop burying the boy before the dust has settled on his fleeing footsteps. Harriet, get Mr. Preston on the telephone. Surely he can find a way to return Hatton, all in one unburnt piece, from our near neighbor to the north with a war winding down."

"The perfect solution! Oh, Mrs. Ashcraft, I always told Mama you are just a whiz when it comes to thinking." Bess disengages herself from Isabel and throws her arms around Adelaide. "The rainbow is rising in the sky before the rainstorm even got good going. If you will excuse me, I am feeling quite peaked. I believe I'll take myself back to bed."

Adelaide is doubly irritated, that Bess stubbornly refuses to address her by the proper surname and that she has chosen this morning to be ill. She has a few particularly juicy items of gossip *that she planned to drop on her plate this morning. Of course Howard College is good enough for Hatton Preston. Everybody knows her own grandson Walker Wallace, on his way to Princeton, is smarter by half.*

"Get hold of yourself, Isabel, you ninny. You are causing enough of a commotion to wake snakes over nothing!" Adelaide snaps.

"You wouldn't understand, Adelaide, having never had a son. Why, you could not get Bitsy out from under your skirts if you tried. Haven't I often remarked to Mr. Preston that my very favorite war tune is 'I Didn't Raise My Boy to Be a Soldier'? It's the idea that he could wish to leave me which has left my heart shattered into irreparable pieces."

"All children are ungrateful," sighs Adelaide. "They hardly give you the credit due for having labored to birth them."

Chapter Twenty Four

Josie felt fairly out of practice whipping cream, but making roulage was like riding a bicycle, something you pick right back up again easily.

The recipe had bided its time in her mind all these years, a sweet memory of Jamie and Carrie waiting in the kitchen for the bridge ladies' leftovers.

Josie admitted that the world was changing. If there were still ladies who played bridge today, they probably lunched on yogurt and granola. She wouldn't know. Mallory gave up bridge when she ran off to Milan. To this day, she avoided small group activities that might lead to personal discussion in favor of the solitary game of genealogy.

She had to face Mallory in less than an hour. Without asking Josie's opinion, Wyatt had invited her. It was his house, wasn't it, where he could do just exactly whatever he wanted to, and didn't he tell her just that on a daily basis?

Josie opened Wyatt's grandmother's silver chest. A variety of silver patterns monogrammed with an alphabet soup of initials. She picked up a bent spoon and studied its handle. Old coin silver, engraved with exactly the same initials as those spoons that Mallory took such pride in. This had to be the missing sixth spoon from the set.

She shook her head, puzzled. Mallory had sent her spoons off to a shop in New Orleans for appraisal. Josie remembered Mallory crowing triumphantly, "I told you these belonged to one of my early ancestors, definitely vintage early 1800s."

Josie, entering the hall on her way to the dining room, still mulling over the enigma of Wyatt possessing a spoon matching Mallory's, paused in her tracks and pitched what her mama would have called a fit of conniptions.

"Mr. Wallace!" she screamed. "Just what is going on here?"

The antiques furnishing the hall looked like dark hulled ships anchored on foamy waves of packing peanuts, such a scene of confusion that the study was tidy tranquility in comparison.

"I wasted all morning trying to make heads or tails of that bloody blasted computer. Wrote a letter to my publisher to test drive it. When it was completed I realized that I had no way to print it."

"So you went back to the store and bought yourself a printer." Hands on her hips, she stared down at him, sitting on the floor like a storm survivor in a field of debris.

"Yes, I did, and, to be on the safe side, and to save myself further excursions to the office supply center, I also have as you see, not one printer but two, should I decide to write a play in color. I have a scanner, a fax machine, and a copier."

"You don't understand, Josie. I have got to complete this play! I cannot end my life with what I was put here to do unfinished." There was a pleading note in his voice, like a little boy caught at mischief saying I didn't mean to do it.

"I will say it again, Mr. Wallace, you're going at life all backwards."

Simultaneously, the doorbell rang, and his grandmother's grandfather clock chimed, booming the chords of the Westminster Cadence.

"What a lovely home you have, Wyatt." Mallory nodded curtly at Josie, who held out her hands to receive the fur coat.

To Josie's relief, the arrival of the other guests was just as timely. It was not the time, nor the place, for a verbal sparring match with Mallory.

"I have always felt that large numbers were not necessary for an evening to be elegant," Mallory, admiring Wyatt's freshly pressed dinner jacket, commented. "The world is losing too many of the old formal social graces."

"Mother, remind me to, at the end of this evening, before even thinking about sleeping, write Wyatt a proper little bread and butter thank you," Carrie teased.

"Why ever should I have to remind you of something I well taught you as a child, my darling?"

Carrie smiled at her mother. Refrained from adding, screaming, because I have no childhood, Mother. I lost it. I cannot remember.

Josie opened the door to the dining room and led them directly in to dinner. A compromise between Wyatt and Josie, the pairing of saint and sinner, wine with dinner if they dispensed with the cocktail hour. That didn't bother Wyatt in the least. He'd had three drinks already, all by himself, a private cocktail hour.

"I am glad to see, Wyatt, that you have decided to join the

parade of progress toward the future," Ellen commented. "That play is as good as on the stage now that you possess the most cutting edge technology. That scanner will be really handy to transfer the pages you've already typed into the computer. Who would want to dwell in the dark ages?" She cut her eyes in Mallory's direction. No one had to remind Ellen that the young girls of Mallory's so very smart set had seen no need to develop marketable skills like typing. Having mastered boxing paragraphs on the computer, Ellen had spent the afternoon adding graphics to her newsletter. Mallory was so old fashioned she probably still took notes with a pencil.

"Wyatt, something about this house puts me in mind of my mother's home in Montgomery," Mallory commented, her eyes appraising the room's furnishings.

"Must be nice to have such pleasant upper crust memories. My grandmother lived in a shack with a tar paper roof in a mining community," Ellen muttered. "Of course I must give Mama credit for always looking on the bright side. I can hear her now, telling me, any time something happened that seemed like the worst that could be, the story of how her own daddy was born on the same night that his daddy was decapitated in the Mary Lydia mine explosion."

She paused a moment, wondering at the sudden stricken expression on Carrie's face. Her daughter-in-law looked as if she had just seen a ghost. It was a grisly story that Ellen had kept to herself since childhood. She could not have said what prompted her to continue talking about it.

"It was a terrible tragedy, more than a hundred men killed and less than half the bodies even recovered. The Mary Lydia held one of the richest veins of iron ore ever struck in Alabama. The owner, out of respect for the men whose bodies they couldn't recover, just ordered it sealed off and shut down tight. Grandma blamed it on an old superstition. Said a woman had been seen in the mine that day. The Cornish believed that a shrouded woman, a premonitory spirit, appeared on a mine site just before a disaster."

Carrie paled. Mallory yawned. If they were going to tell ancestor stories it was fine with her, but who at this table wanted to hear the story of the coal and iron industry?

"Go on, Ellen," Carrie said with a shudder.

"My daddy was such a devout United Mine Workers member. He said the younger men discounted the concept of a curse and saw it as the turning point for the acceptance of the union in

Alabama. Of course it was just a few years after the Mary Lydia blew that U.S. Steel came to town, and Birmingham became an absentee owner operation run by Pittsburgh."

"Growing up in Montgomery, we always socially dismissed Birmingham as just a big old blue collar Yankee type town," Mallory sniffed, grateful that she had not been born, like Ellen, or the singer of the country music song, a coal miner's daughter.

"My daddy must have told that Mary Lydia mine story a million times as if he had been there," Ellen continued, undeterred by Mallory's interruption. "A head brought up in a bucket."

Nick knocked over his wine glass. Carrie choked.

"Really, Ellen, can't you think of more suitable dinner table conversation?" Mallory interrupted, determined to redirect the conversation. "Wyatt, I can't help noticing that you have some very fine old antiques. Inherited family pieces?"

Wyatt took a sip of wine and lit his pipe. He had taken his requisite one polite bite of dessert just as his grandmother had taught him and found it too rich for his liking. Carrie was spooning hers like a condemned woman with seconds left to enjoy her last meal before facing the gallows.

"Actually, both yes and no. Most of the furnishings in this house, such as that sideboard and those small mahogany card tables, some sterling and coin silver flatware, originally came from an antebellum home near Selma. My grandmother, you see, made a second marriage to a gentleman who had inherited his late wife's family home. The house was rotting away in the country fully furnished, and my grandmother rescued these and other pieces to furnish a house she built on Highland Avenue."

Carrie swayed a little in her chair. She studied the sideboard, an Empire piece with a confusion of decorative detailing, acanthus leaves, cornucopias, and gadrooning. Had this very sideboard once served as a repository for groaning silver salvers in the dining room of White Gardenias? She had felt it in antique stores, looking up at a partially burned house on a street in New Orleans, eating on special occasions with her mother's cherished coin silver spoons, a sense that houses and objects could hold on, like eavesdroppers to secrets, to memories of people and events they had witnessed.

She felt dizzy and disoriented, past and present merging. The room spun, the faces blurring. She was on Highland Avenue, listening to the demented ravings of a stroke maddened Minnie. "The clues to the gold's location are contained in the daybook. Did you steal that trunk, Isabel?" Why had Isabel felt compelled to put a Fort Knox lock on a storage vault hiding an empty trunk? There had to be something else of value in that dark, dank little cubbyhole.

"Carrie, are you all right?" Nick put an arm around her, glared at Wyatt Wallace as if to say only I am allowed to touch her. "You look a little green around the gills, honey."

Carrie's mind snapped back to the present. "Wyatt, I hate to be the one to break up the party, but I think I'm a little weak from a week in bed. Would you mind terribly if Nick and I ended the evening a little early?"

"I expect we had better call it a night too, Wyatt," Jack Lancaster added. "The roads are icy, and I don't trust some of the fools in the late night traffic. Thank you for a very pleasant evening."

Wyatt saw them out the door, only Mallory remaining. Pride would prevent his admitting it to Josie, but he had thoroughly enjoyed the whole undertaking.

"A nightcap before heading out into the cold, Mallory?"

She smiled at him. "I think a brandy would be just lovely, and I would especially enjoy it accompanied by more of your wonderful old family stories. We'd all be better off if we had paid more attention to the things our grandmothers tried to pass on to us, just like heirlooms those precious and priceless old family legends."

The clock chimed, marking a final countdown of hours like a warning.

* * *

The January thaw had come and gone like a magician's illusion. The rain quickly glazed over on the hard frozen ground.

"Carrie, I'm so concerned about you," Nick began as he pulled off his shoes.

"Don't worry about me. I'm fine. A backache's a piece of cake for a woman who once gave birth to twins." She winced despite her words.

"You looked at the dinner table like you were going to faint."

"Too much roulage." She shrugged. "Just like when I was a little girl." She had decided to allow herself the memory of roulage.

A person had to have at least a few childhood memories, didn't she?

"Carrie . . . ," his voice was tentative. The dull ache of wanting to touch her was turning into something of more intensity.

She paused in her hair brushing and turned to face him.

"Carrie, I don't say it enough, or display it enough, but I do really with all of my heart love you."

"Oh, Nick, do you?" She put down the brush and got in bed beside him, her heart constricting as she waited for him to finish the sentence by adding "but . . . ."

Stalling for time, she turned her face to be kissed, hadn't done that in such a too long time.

The phone interrupted.

"Don't tell me you're on call tonight," Carrie groaned as she heard him respond that he would be right over. She was ready to get what he had to tell her over and done with.

He got out of bed and dug through a box, looking for insulated underwear. Peppercorns of sleet popped in the fireplace.

"Bad wreck," he called over his shoulder as he closed the bedroom door behind him.

The old nagging voice of doubt grew louder in her head. The hospital, or someone else?

Alone in the big bed, Carrie tossed and turned. Sleep and its sanctuary eluded her. Had the dreams wound to conclusion and deserted her? Like an interesting book with the final page turned, was the story over? Maybe it was time to admit that the house was a mistake and hope that he would be willing to say the same about the other woman, to try to start over.

Carrie's stomach, grown accustomed to being empty after months of little appetite, churned as if unsure what to do with an overload of whipped cream and chocolate. Her mother always said that a glass of milk was a sure cure for an unsettled stomach.

She was at the top of the staircase with her hand fumbling for the light switch when she heard it.

Footsteps downstairs were followed by a crash from the kitchen. Someone had stumbled over the trunk.

She stood at the top of the stairway trying to calculate if she could be down it and out the front door before the intruder in the kitchen could get there first and be waiting to grab her.

An icy gust of wind rattled the glass in the leaded glass window on the landing. She was in a thin flannel nightgown without even a pair of slippers. Her car keys were in the kitchen. She'd freeze to death stumbling barefooted through the woods to Wyatt's.

Go back in the bedroom, lock the door, call the police, you idiot, self preservation screamed at her.

She flipped the lock and dove for the phone. Felt her heart skip a beat.

No sound of a dial tone.

She could hear her heart pounding so loudly it almost drowned out the sound in her ears.

The person in the kitchen was talking on the telephone, making herself right at home.

And the person in the kitchen had every right to be so doing. Of course she did. It was perfectly natural.

How many times had Carrie said it?

It was her home too.

* * *

Nick sat in the doctors' lounge sipping a cup of coffee. The emergency room nurse had been profuse in her apologies over calling him out on such a nasty night. The accident had resulted in a head injury. What they needed instead of Nick was a neurosurgeon.

He was seized by a sudden memory of Carrie, in labor with the twins all those years ago, so young and so determined not to be frightened. The babies were arriving prematurely, and the obstetrician was concerned about giving Carrie too much medication. Nick had never been so afraid in his life. He was filled with self condemnation. Poor sweet Carrie. Look at what he had done to her. He wanted to take off through the door and just keep running.

He and Carrie had made such a good life together, or at least he thought they had. Funny how things in life had a way of turning out for the best. Walking down the hall of the hospital a year before, he had run into the woman he would have married had Carrie's unplanned pregnancy not changed the course of things. He had taken her to a restaurant near the hospital, bought her lunch, and tried to offer comfort over her just received knowledge that her mother was dying. Halfway through the meal she had looked at him and said, "You know we would have been absolutely wrong for each other!" He agreed, and they clasped hands and laughed, a light moment in an otherwise somber conversation.

He had been looking for another partner to join the practice and pick up the slack caused by his father's easing into retirement, allowing him to take some time off for traveling with Carrie, when she made the surprise announcement that she was pregnant and this time had carefully planned it.

Guilt chewed on him like a dog with a fresh bloody bone. He had been working too hard. Carrie had gotten pregnant because she was lonely and at loose ends in her life.

He had agreed to take on the extra evening emergency room shifts as a favor to an old friend from medical school whose wife was dying. He found that he enjoyed the frenetic pace, so different from the grown boring routine of office hours.

Who was he fooling? He was offering to take other doctors calls, sleeping too often in the doctor's lounge, to avoid that house and dealing with the stranger who had taken the place of Carrie.

***

"Abby, oh honey, you don't know how good it is to see you!" Carrie threw her arms around her daughter.

"I didn't mean to wake you, Mom. Trying to study for exams in the dorm is a complete impossibility. I thought I'd come here for peace and quiet."

"I'll bet I scared you half to death, making all that noise. I tripped over that box."

What, Carrie wondered, would her daughter say if she were to correct her? Can't you see, isn't it obvious, my level headed daughter, that's a baby's little coffin. Baby's not in there, but I know that she once was because I dreamed it.

"What is that stuff in that trunk, Mom?"

"What are you talking about?" Carrie almost screamed it. When opened, the trunk had been empty.

"This old junk." Abby walked across the kitchen and returned with the false bottom of the trunk. "This came loose when I fell over it. Very strange. Letters, some kind of ledger, written in code."

Carrie almost crumpled to the floor as the realization hit her. From the dream, Minnie's words tumbled around in her head. "Did you steal my brother's trunk, Isabel? The location of the gold is in the daybook."

She had not been taking information from her own mind and weaving it into dreams. She was dreaming of tangible items before she found them. She hunched over the sink, her stomach heaving.

"Are you all right, Mom?" Abby looked at her with concern. Something far past odd was going on in this house. "Let me make you a cup of tea."

Trying to recover her composure, Carrie joined Abby at the old enamel kitchen table, and together they began turning pages of Washington Buford's quotidian record.

"How did you know what this was, Mom?" Abby asked, eyes skimming up and down each page despite the fact that, written in code, it might as well have been Greek. Part of it was in fact Greek, the code composed of Greek letters and Roman numerals.

"I've been on a history reading kick lately," Carrie stammered. "Most planters kept a kind of diary and general idea book."

"Most of this just looks like junk to me," Abby said, as she thumbed through loose leaves. "Old newspaper clippings, advertisements for archaic farm equipment."

Carrie continued staring at the fading sepia ink as if the symbols could translate themselves and speak to her.

"Mom, listen to this. 'Curatives. For worms: Jerusalem weed. For gonorrhea or other clap: opium, sulphur nitrate, oil of turpentine, to be taken morning, noon, and night.' A sure bet for making sure that you didn't die from venereal disease. The cure would have killed you first!"

"The location of the gold is in the daybook." The words drummed through Carrie's mind so loudly that she only heard her daughter with half an ear until Abby screeched and dropped a paper as if it had burned her.

"Maybe garbage like this is why I like math and science more than history. How could civilized people have allowed this?"

"What, honey? Let me see it." She reached across the table for the paper.

A handbill, an ancient advertising flier, a notice of a sale of slaves to be conducted in the auction house in Selma. Her eyes reached the last item on the page. She gasped in horror, sharing Abby's reaction.

"Fine light babies from White Gardenias Plantation. To be sold by the pound."

Her eyes met her daughter's.

"This isn't some dry fact presented in a history book, is it, Mom? This is real. This is grotesque. This has been held in the hand of someone who bought and sold children as if they were meat, someone who was the essence of evil."

Carrie's stomach lurched again. Minnie explaining to Avram that the sight of a coffle of chained humanity had turned her brother into a Yankee, that her father's light skinned offspring brought higher prices at market. She said a silent prayer of thanks to Alexander Buford for turning traitor to the South.

"How badly do you want to decipher that code, Mom? I can probably figure it out pretty easily by running permutations on the computer, no more difficult than a math problem."

"Would you do it, Abby? It really is sort of important to me."

"Sure. It will take me a while to type in a sample page because I'm not familiar with the Greek letters."

"What if you had a scanner, Abby? Would that make it easier?"

"That would be great! I didn't know you had one."

"I don't, but Wyatt does. Get your coat on. Let's go."

"Mom, it's almost midnight. If we go waking up the neighbor he'll think we're crazy!"

Carrie smiled at Abby and said, "I think this book holds the answer to the location of something he's seeking. He'll be only too glad to see us."

As the scanner hummed, Wyatt and Carrie looked over Abby's shoulder.

"The child is a genius," Wyatt whispered.

"I agree. She inherited the exceptional mind of her father," Carrie concurred.

"Let's go in the kitchen and have a drink, Carrie. We'll leave Abby to play Einstein in peace. I know something myself about interrupted concentration."

"Oh, Wyatt, you were working. I'm sorry we barged in on you."

"Not a problem. I was just at the point of taking a break in the action. How about a midnight snack? You looked at dessert as if you hadn't eaten in months."

"Three servings! I embarrassed myself as well as my mother."

He looked at the packed shelves of the refrigerator. "Banana pudding?"

"My heart says yes and my stomach no. There is nothing on

earth like Josie's banana pudding. She uses an old recipe of my grandmother's."

"So I was told. I casually mentioned how delicious it was, and your mother went off like a rocket, telling Josie that baking her mother's banana pudding in someone else's kitchen was tantamount to treason."

He chuckled. "I hope that I'm not facing soon again being left to my own wicked devices. Josie's car battery was dead, and your mother insisted on giving her a lift home."

"Oh, that's wonderful! I cannot stand this much longer, Mother and Josie being on the outs. You know, Wyatt, for all that my mother is so socially savvy, for all her committees and heading up organizations, my mother doesn't really have another friend who understands and loves her as much as Josie."

"Do you think that a dead battery can be a tool of divine intervention?" Wyatt asked, chuckling, as he speared a bite of banana.

"What?"

"Something Josie said. She tried to get that car to crank until she flooded the engine. Your mother practically shoved her right into the passenger seat of her car. Would not take no for an answer. That's what Josie said, 'This feels like divine intervention.'"

"Everything in Josie's life is based on faith. Don't ask me why, Wyatt, but I have the oddest feeling that the answer to your search lies in that daybook."

"Now that would be interesting, wouldn't it? The key to the location of Hatton's manuscript, buried in pages written by his great-grandfather more than a hundred years earlier? Isn't that somewhat asking the past to appear before the present?" He puffed on his pipe and studied her.

Carrie blushed. If he only knew.

"Here you go, Mom, the whole story, all in understandable English." Abby passed her mother a sheaf of printed pages. "The author of this story wasn't half as smart as he thought he was. The computer broke his code in less than a minute."

Carrie thought of the picture of White Gardenias in the book Wyatt had given her for Christmas and of the man who had built it, enjoying the rewards of an evil system. She could imagine him, late of an evening, sitting by flickering candle flame, bent over these pages, scratching with a quill pen those Greek letters and Roman numerals, never dreaming that the far distant future would expose him.

It had all begun with Washington Buford. It was time for the Bufords' story to reach an ending.

"Don't keep me in suspense, Carrie," Wyatt demanded. "Please, begin reading."

Carrie frowned down at the page before her. What was she looking for in this whole proposition? Pots of gold were found only by leprechauns. "Most of this is of no interest to anyone. Records of buying and selling, horses and twine and cotton and . . . and a bunch of other things related to the management of a plantation. Not a word about gold. Let me skim over a few pages."

Wyatt puffed his pipe impatiently. Gold was the last item on his agenda.

"I hate to interrupt finishing what the two of you seem to find so fascinating, but I have got a huge exam tomorrow," Abby interrupted. Willing to humor her mother, she did not find one thing worth knowing about the life of George Washington Buford.

"Go on home, child," Wyatt muttered. "Your mother and I are on a quest for the one tangible thing that will allow me to complete my life's work. I'll be sure that you receive complimentary tickets to the opening night's performance."

Abby hung back for a moment, reluctant to leave her mother alone in the middle of the night with this disturbing man. She had not heard him utter a sentence that didn't begin with "I" or end with "me." He was probably old enough to be her grandfather, but something about him was oddly alluring. She went out the back door and off to do her studies.

The doorbell chimed. Wyatt waved a dismissive hand. "Let it ring. Probably just a magazine salesman."

"In the middle of the night? It's bound to be important."

She went to the door and quickly returned.

"Wyatt, get your coat. It's a policeman."

"A policeman? Am I being arrested?"

"They've been trying to contact us. I must have left the telephone off the hook."

Wyatt frowned. She was as pale as if she'd seen a ghost.

She tugged at his sleeve like a child begging for candy. "Please, Wyatt. We have to leave. We've got to get going, immediately. To the hospital. Mother and Josie. There's been a terrible accident."

Chapter Twenty Five

Dawn broke, stretching like a waking sleeper over the horizon of the city skyline. Through the hospital waiting room windows, the sky recharged a hopeful pink and gold.

Wyatt stared moodily out the window. He consulted his father's old gold pocket watch, forty seven minutes until he and Carrie could see Josie in the intensive care unit. Mallory, only bruised but hysterical, had been ordered sedated.

Forty seven minutes. According to Nick, as long as forty eight long hours until they could pronounce her out of the woods. Josie's life hung by a raveling thread.

"Do you know what I'd do if I had unlimited money to waste?" Carrie cut into his mental wanderings. "I would redecorate every intensive care hospital waiting room with nice cheery chintz upholstery and provide soft classical background music. I'd have Jamaican Blue Mountain coffee, and real cream instead of this packaged chalk, and a nice silver service for dispensing it into porcelain tea cups instead of plastic."

For the first time in hours, he laughed. "Carrie, you are, after all, your mother's daughter. Do you really think that life's little elegant amenities would make it any easier for poor slobs like us sitting watching the hands of the clock drag around?"

"Could anything make it any worse?"

He looked at her miserably, ignored the no smoking signs and lit up.

"I'm so scared, Wyatt. I'm so scared of losing someone else I love. My mother taught me all the right manners, but she failed miserably in teaching me how to handle loss." She looked so small and vulnerable, like a child, that he put the pipe down, crossed the room, and put his arms around her.

Over her head, in the doorway, his eyes met her husband's.

"I hope you know, Wallace, that you deserve more than a small share of the blame for this, putting Mallory on the spot about staying at your house for after dinner drinks."

Carrie interrupted. "Shut up, Nicky. You heard that policeman. Black ice caused the accident, and you very well know it."

He gave them a cold stare, turned on his heel and left them to each other.

Her back hurting, Carrie stretched out on the hard vinyl sofa of the waiting room. Wyatt offered to go to the hospital cafeteria, seeking more palatable coffee. If up to him, every hospital would offer a bar.

Nick came back to the waiting room, ready to give Wallace a piece of his mind. He refrained from waking Carrie. He was too emotionally tangled up in a knot to talk to her. Sleeping on that sofa wasn't going to do her back any favors, but he knew there was no point in waking her. She had been up all night, but she would never agree to leave her mother and Josie, despite the fact that there was not one thing that she could do for either of them. The old Carrie, his Carrie, who always relegated her own needs to doing something for another, could not be completely gone. He could not accept that.

He cursed Wallace's absence. Probably gone back home to get drunk and pass out to a good night's sleep in the comfort of his bed. The most self centered man he had ever met in his life.

Carrie twisted, her body instinctively seeking a more comfortable contortion on the hard sofa. Nick put a hand on her hair, let it remain there a moment.

Carrie mumbled in her sleep, unaware of her husband's presence.

The First World War has claimed almost forty million soldiers, tragically supplemented by the loss of ten million civilians. The influenza pandemic of this, the war's final fatal year, rages around the world, locking twenty million in death's cold embrace.

It is eleven a.m. on the eleventh day of the eleventh month of the year 1918, and across the land church bells chime out the news that the peace has been accomplished in the affixing of signatures to a document of Armistice, for too many too late, this ending that had its beginnings in a wrong turn on a street in Sarajevo.

The church bells chorusing hallelujahs strike Isabel's ears as jarring notes. She thinks of her grandmother, too many times repeating the tales of Alexander Buford's birth and of his dying, of ringing the gong of the old plantation bell in commemoration. Isabel supposes that it would be fitting for someone to do the same on this day. There is no one at White Gardenias she could ask to pull the rope. The old retainers who did not run away have died away, only a few of their children and grandchildren still straggling on as sharecroppers.

She supposes that Violet, who proved to be a traitor, lives on in the old house. Isabel has had no contact with her since she fled on a southbound train, clutching Minnie's old portmanteau and Lydia's yellow cat, that cat that Cleotis was too good for nothing to catch and drown as she had ordered. Willard was generous enough to offer funds for the burial of Cleotis, but Isabel overruled him and let the city put him in a pauper's plot.

She supposes it would have been the decent thing to do, to have let Violet know of this, the family's latest loss. She was for all those years, after all, treated like part of the family. Just goes to show that you cannot in this life trust anyone, even and maybe especially family. Violet's betrayal was as self serving as Lydia's.

They are gone from her life now, all the faces and figures from her childhood. She feels little sense of loss or longing as she stands here at Oak Hill Cemetery on a bitter chill day, facing a newly dug grave.

A cold November wind whips through the trees, and the minister steps up the pace of his prayers. Time to get this over and done.

Bad luck to look on an open grave Isabel reminds herself, turning her gaze to the distant perimeter of trees. Startled, she clutches Willard's arm. Surely just her eyes playing tricks on her.

Surely it was just an illusion, thinking she sighted Violet moving through the trees in their direction. She pulls her lips in over the porcelain plates, steeling herself to give the woman a good piece of her mind should she seek to intrude, as unwanted as an ant at a picnic.

There, moving closer and ever closer. It is she! And she is not alone. There, as clearly as Isabel's myopic eyes can see she comes, moving steadily closer, the spectral form of dead Minnie at her side. Isabel lets out a wild shriek of panic, collapses at Willard's feet and very nearly into the yawning grave.

"Forgive us. Excuse us. Overcome by emotion," Willard mumbles as he half drags, half carries his wife from the little knot of mourners. The preacher says a hasty amen.

"Leave it to Isabel to make a spectacle of herself!" Adelaide

harrumphs to her daughter Bitsy loudly enough for the crowd's concern to turn to titters. That idiot will find a way to make a fool of herself at her own funeral."

Fearful of taking a chill in the cold November air, of also succumbing themselves to the deadly influenza that called Bess's life to conclusion, the little group quickly disperses.

Remaining behind is one last lone straggler. He scoops up a handful of fresh turned earth, crumbles it, and lets it drift to rest on the gun metal grey of the coffin lid, saying a final farewell to a gentle old lady who loved him.

The wind riffling through his red gold hair, he walks away, feeling in a heart as hard packed as the red clay that stains his shoes not a trace of sorrow.

The death of his great-aunt and the intervention of a few of his father's associates influential in the government have ended his military career before it began. He had no choice but to accept the dictates of his parents, to return to their home and enter college as a day student.

Aunt Bess has left him a legacy that he has already claimed. Only moments after the doctor signed the death certificate, Hatton slipped into her room and removed the pasteboard boxes from under the bed. Discarding the lovingly labeled packets of hair, late in the night he began his reading, supplementing all the stories she has told him over all the years with the written records she kept locked away.

All the stories of warriors and heroes, of battles bold, of an Old South that refused to admit defeat or to die. He will remember through her memories lives lived by others.

He will write of it.

Chapter Twenty Six

Josie was holding her own.

Nick had Wyatt evicted from the hospital for lighting his pipe outside the intensive care unit.

Wyatt pounded on Carrie's front door and received no response. He felt as abandoned as a puppy left out in a rainstorm, needed to talk to someone to settle his head down. They were all otherwise engaged, sleeping, tranquilized, or dying.

He was exactly where he had been proclaiming so loudly for so long that he wanted to be.

Utterly alone.

Upstairs Carrie, asleep, lost in someone else's memory, unconsciously ignored him.

Isabel carefully, methodically, folds the previous day's newspaper, perused while sipping coffee from a buttercup patterned teacup received as a wedding gift.

Having been enticed by an advertisement, she makes a mental note to call Loveman's Department Store and order a complete set, from plates in breakfast, luncheon, and dinner sizes, down to a gravy boat and a dozen demitasses, in that lovely Persian Rose pattern by Minton that she has so admired for so long in the china department. Never mind the expense, no one any longer has the right to question the extravagance.

One particular and pleasing item of yesterday's news has been read and reread this morning so many times that it is committed to memory, like a favorite poem.

She carefully clipped it from the paper. It was not a front page story, that leading edge being taken this 1923 October morning by other items deemed by the editor to be of greater import, the governor of Oklahoma placing that state under martial law to subdue the rising terrorism of the Ku Klux Klan, labor unions cheering the institution of the eight hour day by United States Steel under pressure from President Harding, and a report from Paris that French women use an average of two pounds of face powder a year.

Willard has been relegated to page ten, but he has received the recognition of a photograph and a two column header, black bordered, according him more prominence than any of the other local residents memorialized by obituaries.

The words refrain in her mind like lyrics from the chorus of a long loved song. "Local attorney and industrialist Willard Horace Preston passed away yesterday of an apparent heart attack at his residence on the city's Southside. Mr. Preston had suffered ill health for the several years preceding. Ever vigilant of myriad business interests, including coal mines and cotton mills, he despite ill health daily continued to labor in his office in the Massey Building accompanied by his faithful manservant Henry."

"Mr. Preston came to this city a quarter century ago as a graduate of the University of Pennsylvania and took a position as executive assistant to the late Colonel Samuel A. McShan, whose daughter Katherine Isabel Mr. Preston shortly thereafter took as his wife. Theirs having been a long and blissfully happy union, the sympathy of the entire community goes out on this doleful day to the bereaved widow."

"Mr. Preston was active in a number of civic organizations as well as holding an honorary membership in the Sons of Confederate Veterans. His passionate avocations included the study of the Victorian poets, in particular Mr. Algernon Charles Swinburne."

"He leaves, in addition to the widow, one son, Hatton Alexander Buford Preston, presently pursuing graduate studies at Vanderbilt University in Nashville, Tennessee. Interment of Mr. Preston will take place in Oak Hill Cemetery, where are buried other family members prominent in the founding of this city."

She has woken this drizzly, bleak October day for the first time in her life in charge of her life, a novel experience.

She has telephoned the newspaper and ordered that henceforth every edition of every paper printed, both morning and evening, be delivered to her door. She has taken, in fact, a lifetime subscription. In the next election she will be the first in line to vote. The women of America received the right and privilege of the ballot in 1919, Isabel only the day before yesterday.

She gave him the word just after administering his medicine. "Open wide for your arsenic, dear Mr. Preston. To put us both out of our misery I have doubled the dosage. Pity your blindness precludes your watching yourself writhe in agony like a dying rat as the poison surges through you. I hope the pain is merciless, my devoted husband. Excuse me, sir, but I must leave you to suffer while I read the news from cover to cover."

The doctor has been discreet. Willard has gone to the everlasting silence of the grave with the dirty secret of his fatal malady unspoken outside of the family. The syphilis took nine years sweet time in decimating Willard's mind and body. Isabel merely aided it in speeding to claiming a grim victory.

The mercury treatments proved, as the doctor promised, painful and ineffective.

Modern medicine for all its claims cannot be half as effective as some of the old country remedies Violet brought to the city as heritage of her witch doctor mother. Had not small doses of arsenic cured Isabel as completely as if she had never been tainted by Willard in the first place?

Isabel adjusts the veil of her widows' weeds black hat one final time and calls for her driver Henry.

He tips his cap in deference as she slides into the back seat of the big black Packard touring car delivered just after this morning's paper. Despite the fact that Willard worked himself to the bone, evenings as well as mornings, he could never overcome his meager beginnings. Appearances being everything, Isabel feels justified in at last traveling in a conveyance suitably proclaiming her social station. They pull smoothly away from the curb and head in the direction of downtown, where Isabel has two morning appointments. The future is now firmly in her hands, and she is prepared. The rest of their lives, her own and Hatton's, for which she bears the overriding responsibility, begin this very day.

"My son has made it abundantly clear that he has no interest whatsoever in continuing any of his father's business pursuits," Isabel says firmly. *"He is convinced that the future of our Southland rests in turning aside from progress and commerce and returning to our agrarian beginnings, ideas that are much in vogue at Vanderbilt."*

"But, my dear Mrs. Preston, I beg you not to act so precipitously, being as you are in the throes of overwhelming grief," the banker argues. *"Our trust department is committed to assisting you in totally managing your late husband's assets. You must have faith in our wiser heads. We are the trust department and trust is after all our raison d'etre."* *This is all quite outside the realm of the banker's experience. Most women in her situation sob and plead for any man to take over responsibilities for which they are by the nature of their femininity incapable of dealing. Isabel presents her-*

self determined, demanding, and entirely devoid of any emotion.

"Please, Mrs. Preston, let the dust settle," he stammers. She didn't shed a tear at the cemetery either, he reminds himself. Stood there as composed and straight as her crooked back would allow while the son looked as bored as an atheist at a revival meeting. Hatton took himself right on back to Nashville not an hour after they got his daddy in the ground, or so the banker's wife has clucked at breakfast. Gossip travels quickly.

Isabel makes a great production of checking her watch, pulling on her gloves. "I must not be late to my next appointment. If you will be so good as to follow my instructions and sell off every stock, bond, and business interest in the more than reasonable period of the week to follow I shall be most grateful. I will again present myself here at your office precisely one week hence."

"Mrs. Preston, surely we must carefully monitor market conditions . . . ."

"One week, sir. You can find someone to buy it all. Yankees are always in the acquisition market regarding successful southern companies. Shall I return at that time with suitable satchels, or is such a service of your institution?"

"Suitable satchels?" He gives her a dumbstruck expression.

"For the conveyance away of my assets. I would, by the way, appreciate bills to be of one hundred dollar denominations."

"Mrs. Preston, dear by grief stricken Mrs. Preston, surely, surely I am misunderstanding. You are not proposing to withdraw from this bank what, even if we act so, forgive me for saying it, ill advisedly and impetuously, and liquidate in the time so specified, will no doubt amount to several millions of dollars in cash?" He takes a handkerchief from his pocket and mops his dripping face.

"Precisely, sir, my intention." She rises to leave.

"But your son? His future?"

"As I have stated, my son has not one whit of desire to follow in his father's footsteps. My son, you see, is of a poetical nature. He bears no resemblance at all to his paternity. He has always considered himself more of a Buford than a Preston."

Leaving the dejected banker with his head in his hands, she calls to Henry, waiting patiently outside the office. "To the office of the architect, Henry. We go to plan for the construction of our future."

"I have in mind a residence in the new Redmont Park area of

the city, a stately demesne in which my son and I can comfortably reside while he pursues his literary career through the rest of our lives together. I wish to build, you see, a house for Hatton."

The young architect suppresses a too eager smile. The fledgling suburb, with its pretensions to English gentility, is a fertile field for every local home designer. Without a husband to restrain her, Isabel Preston offers him free rein in carrying out the commission which will forever establish his reputation. His fingers itch to take up his drafting pencil.

"I have taken notice of the medieval manor house that you designed for Bitsy Ashcraft Wallace after she so thoughtlessly sold my father's home on the Highland Avenue. I should like a home in a similar style but at least two times larger. I have in my mind a dwelling not unlike the one here pictured." She pulls from her handbag a cracked picture postcard, signed on back "All of our love from Merrie Olde England, Bess and Hatton."

He gasps. It was the talk of the town when old Sam McShan passed on, leaving full title to the most grandiose home on the prestigious Highland Avenue to his widow Adelaide, who immediately deeded the property to her daughter Bitsy and returned to live out her twilight years near her roots in Montgomery. Bitsy and her husband wasted no time in delivering to Isabel the ultimate indignity by selling the mansion off for use as a funeral parlor, where just day before yesterday Willard Preston experienced the embalmer's artistry.

"Replicating Chatsworth, the ancestral home of the Dukes of Devonshire, will be a formidable undertaking," he whispers as the full implication of her intentions begins to register.

"A challenge which I have been assured you are capable of meeting," she says. "I understand that a sizeable piece of property abutting my dear stepsister Bitsy Wallace's home is available for purchase. Please arrange this for me. Money is no object. Nothing is too good for my boy Hatton."

"My son will be completing his graduate degree studies in the period of one year, at which time I expect the prodigal's permanent return to me from the north in Tennessee. It was a compromise you see. Our family has not in the past had favorable outcomes from northern educations. See to it please that by that time all is in readiness for our reunion," she concludes.

The door clicks closed behind her.

It occurs to him that she may be out of her mind.
He picks up a pencil and quickly begins his sketching.

* * *

"Carrie, what in the world are you doing in that nasty basement?"

"Stay put, Nicky, I'll be right up." She almost screamed it. The basement vault was her secret, as private as something personal.

"What's the latest news on Josie?" She held her breath.

"The best I could bring you. She's begun to turn a corner. She'll be laid up for a while, but she's definitely on the mend."

"Carrie, what is this junk?" He had the typed pages of the daybook in his hand, was reading.

"Nothing important." She snatched them from him.

He was as tired as he ever remembered feeling, having trouble thinking straight. What was she trying to hide?

"Carrie, it is past time we got some things out in the open. Whatever little game you're playing in this house has got to stop."

"You don't understand, Nicky. I would hate to think that you just don't care."

His voice was flat. "What we need to discuss are this house and Wallace."

"And while we're at it, and speaking of games, you can tell me where you've really been going all those nights you said you were on call. You can tell me the truth, Nicky, even if I'm obviously not strong enough to take it. Tell me where you were, and, more importantly, with whom." She felt a rush of relief, a blister on her heart breaking.

"Carrie, what in the world are you implying?"

"Spit it out in plain English, Nicky."

"I hate this house, Carrie. I hate what it's doing to us. It's as though this house exerts some malignant influence that's changing us."

"That's ridiculous. I could not be happier with where I'm living."

"You've got your priorities all out of kilter."

"Because I no longer always put you and the kids before what I want to do, what interests me? It's suddenly very clear to me that I have spent the last twenty plus years prioritizing around everyone else. The kids are for all intents and purposes gone, and there are not going to be any more kids to fill their places. All you care about is work, or whatever you're doing when you say that you're working. It's about time I woke up and smelled the coffee and got a life of my own, or one day I'll wake up and find myself Mother, desperately signing on for one more project, one more committee, any group that expresses some need, to fill my empty hours. I can understand that you don't know who I am because I don't know who I am either."

"Carrie, I agreed to take on the extra hours in the emergency room as a favor to a friend with a problem, a man who understandably wants to spend as much time as he can with a terminally sick wife in whatever short time she has remaining. I'm finding that I get a satisfaction from the challenge that is missing in regular office hours. When it comes to the day to day practice, I'm burned out, Carrie, plain and simple."

"And I don't have a right to be? Wyatt at least has given me a sense of purpose, made me feel I'm doing something that counts. When that play hits the stage, I will have been part of it. Besides which, he's always around, good company, interested in me, which is more than I can say about you."

"Carrie, I told myself that I was going to ignore that little scene between the two of you this morning, but I think I have just changed my mind about doing so."

"He was simply offering me comfort, more than you are willing or capable of doing. You're the one who set the pattern, Nick. You're emotionally never around when I need you. You were as gone the night our baby died as if you had been on a medical mission to China. Remember when my father died? Of course not. You weren't around. You were tied up in surgery."

"Your father dropped dead on the golf course, Carrie. It was not like he called me the day before and asked if I could fit his death into my schedule."

"Maybe, this morning, when I was afraid that I was going to lose Josie, I did the most logical thing in my life and turned for comfort to someone I could trust not to run right out and leave me."

Nick slumped in a chair, put his head in his hands and tried to get all of the issues boiling in his head to focus. It was make or break time. He loved her, but the ball was in her court.

"Give this house, and Wallace, up, Carrie."

"I can't."

"Are you sleeping with him?"

"Are you crazy?" Her words came out a screech.

He wanted so to believe her.

He walked out the door without a goodbye.

* * *

Wyatt strode through the hospital lobby bearing two dozen long stemmed red roses.

He marched right past the sign warning that the hospital observed the strictest of visiting hours, a period not set to begin for fifteen minutes.

Mallory was propped up in bed wearing a froth of lace bed jacket. She kept a few such items of lingerie as insurance against unplanned emergency hospital visits, like a boy scout, prepared.

"Oh, Wyatt! For me? How long has it been since anyone brought me roses?"

"The florist had a disturbingly large selection of colors, but somehow I knew you were a classic red rose lady." He pictured her in the past, an American beauty waving from an open Cadillac convertible, a homecoming queen.

"As I am and always have been."

"They tell me that Josie is being moved out of that dreadful little nest of intensive care boxes tomorrow. What color should I send her?"

"Choose something for her yard, an azalea perhaps. Josie is too practical for cut flowers. Get anything but an altar arrangement for her church to display in thanksgiving. I have already arranged that."

"You know, Mallory, you are really a very thoughtful woman."

"If I might correct your semantics, I have always thought of myself as a lady. There is a difference you know."

He laughed. "I suppose you're right, in this part of the country at least."

"Tell me, Wyatt, how is the work progressing?"

He considered a moment before answering her question. Lying, whether to himself or to others, was becoming enervating.

"Actually, Mallory, I have been caught in something of a rut lately. Sometimes something intervening, like an accident, can lead to self assessment. It occurred to me this morning that what I need to do is face up to a writer's hardest moment of truth, say that while the idea has merit, the characters value, the work to date is fit only for the waste pile. The story, you see, was heading down a road of wrong direction. Instead of simply synthesizing a single man's life story, I need to expand the play's perspective. Hatton Preston was the product of an entire family."

Mallory consulted her watch. "Oh, dear, visiting hours are almost upon us. I suppose I must steel myself for Ellen's inevitable appearance, bearing no doubt some of her peanut butter white chocolate macadamia nut fudge that she insists will cure anything which ails you. So rich just the thought of it makes my teeth ache." Mallory shuddered under the lace.

"Ellen is a good sort, a big hearted woman."

Her response surprised him. "You know, Wyatt, when Carrie and Nicky came to us with the news that they had run away and married precipitously, for the worst of reasons, I was absolutely mortified to the marrow of my bones."

"What a wonderful southern term! I can't imagine anyone in California admitting to being mortified. A word for my play. Remind me to spend more time around you, Mallory. You're a positive inspiration."

"Why, thank you, but as I was saying, if Nick had come to David on bended knee with a diamond ring as big as a grapefruit and begged for his blessing and the hand of our Carrie I would have insisted that we withhold it, largely because of Ellen of course. She has absolutely no background, is an avowed liberal, a Democrat, and a Catholic. Of course Jack comes from a good family. We have never been able to imagine how he puts up with her."

"Mallory, being a Democrat, or a liberal, or a Catholic simply represents holding some perspective different from your own. None of those things are contagious, you know. I find Ellen like a breath of fresh air on a stifling day. That car for example. When she arrives in the driveway and announces her arrival by blowing that horn, tune changing with the seasons, I get the same little thrill of dread that I do when the meteorologist appears on television warning of a coming tornado."

"I would hate for her to know it, but over the years of life tossing us together like ships in the same channel, I have modified my opinion. When I look at Ellen, many times I am envious."

Wyatt could have fallen out of his chair.

"My mother was so rigid. I was raised with rules for everything from how to properly fold and hang the linen towel after washing my hands to the number of bridesmaids in my wedding. I had to leave out one of my favorite sorority sisters because Mother considered more than eight attendants common. Ellen has tossed convention to the wind and given people cause to talk about her, but she has also always lived her life with abandon. There are things that I have missed."

"Such as?"

"You might find this surprising, Wyatt, but when I was in college I majored in education not because it was the choice for all girls who were in school only as a way station along the road to marriage but because inside of me there was a tiny hope that Mother would actually let me get a job for a few years. I really wanted to teach mathematics. Mother was horrified at the very idea! Teaching in those days was for those doomed to be spinsters. I did things just as my mother expected. David's fraternity pin the fall semester of my senior year, a ring at Easter, married two weeks after graduation. Betsy has already promised that when some young gentleman slips an engagement on her finger she will let me know in advance that I might be on hand in the chapter house to hear her sisters serenade her just as I was the night she was initiated with the pearl and diamond pin from my days in the same sorority."

Carrie's right, he thought. I am only a visitor. I am not part and parcel of this part of the country. They are too full of mysteries and little rituals passed down like the family silver for me to ever fully understand them.

"Ellen has a quality my father always admired in men. Ellen Lancaster has gumption."

Gumption. A word coming from the southern speech dictionary on a page coming before mortified and after common.

"Wyatt, this accident has started me thinking, about lost opportunities, missed adventures. Instead of doing as society and my mother demanded, I had in the back of my mind a very well constructed dream. I wanted to, the day after graduation, pack up my convertible and drive all the way across the country to California, where I would spend an entire year lying in the sun, baking the magnolia paleness right out of my skin, reading William Faulkner, considered at the time too racy for nice young ladies, and living on wine and avocados."

"What's stopping you now, Mallory, from doing any or all of those things?"

"The sun is treacherous, Wyatt. I can tell by looking at you that you have never suffered the pain of a facelift." She paused a moment. "And besides, if I left here, who would keep an eye on Carrie?"

"Yoo hoo, anyone home in this room? As soon as I heard, I got out my fudge baking pan. Along with the foil wrapped pan of candy Ellen thrust in Mallory's direction a ribbon tied bunch of early blooming wild flowers.

"Now, Mallory, before you go wasting your breath saying 'you shouldn't have,' thinking that I plunked down a fortune at the florist, I will tell you both a little secret. I pulled those flowers right out of the highway median and looked both ways before doing it so that I would not get arrested by some highway patrolman. As I can vouch from my last two tickets, those guys are not hired based on a sense of either humor or compassion."

Chapter Twenty Seven

Carrie weighed whether the ache was greater in her heart or her back. She downed her last two remaining pain pills without water, buried her face in the pillow that retained the scent of Nick.

Her words ring clearly in his mind from more than three decades before. "White Gardenias still stands, down the long and dusty road, twice doubling across the meandering brook."

The car has bumped and sputtered and finally successfully forded for the second time the small muddy creek. Plagued by memories, he is seized by a hesitation uncharacteristic for one who has always met life boldly. He has but one task remaining to accomplish before facing death in a similarly forthright manner. Paying a final debt to two women from the past, he comes, this day, to this place, the messenger.

In this flat riverbed landscape, eons ago the floor of a vanished sea, the house sits on a gently rising slope of ground. It is November, and in all directions the flat fields stretch in brown desolation toward the edge of the horizon, barren stiff stalks of cotton stubbornly retaining a few wisps of white, like the morning stubble on an old man's chin. To his left he hears the churning of the river, sees the swamp cypresses and the willows, bending ballerinas in the wind, along its banks.

He looks ahead, through the broken gates hanging by a whisper on rusted hinges, down a long allee of oak trees. There is a surreal sense of coming home, to a remembered scene he has visited only in an old woman's ramblings and through the stories spun out on the yellowing pages on the seat beside him.

Only scattered souvenir flakes of white paint cling here and there against bare boards. And yet, there remains a haughty confidence about the house, the faded arrogance of a past her prime grande dame whose bone structure remembers younger beauty despite the ravaging wrinkles of time.

A dog barks halfhearted warning as he shuts the car door. The dog is emaciated, black and brown with a sharp pointed muzzle, the product of years of mongrel miscegenation but still heir to drops of the blood of the fine hunting hounds that once greeted their masters on frosty autumn mornings in these fields. Having done his duty, too stunted in spirit to follow up bark with bite, the dog slinks back under the house.

He startles as a shadow pauses, then passes across the great blue black slate squares of the veranda. He shudders, sharply reminds himself who and what he is, a journalist of world repute, a seasoned war correspondent, a realist. He does not believe in ghosts.

Oh, no? Why are you here then, mocks a voice in the back of his mind.

It is unseasonably warm for November, gathering clouds to the west hinting of storms waiting in the wings of the day. The tall double doors are open, and through them a woman, desultorily sweeping bare pine floorboards in the shadowy recesses of the wide hall, startles at the sight of him. Tall and stooped, wearing a faded house dress, she recovers her composure and makes her way to greet him as if an uninvited stranger's appearance is the most natural thing in the world here in this isolated setting. In his head rings Minnie's description of the home's fabled hospitality from another porch, another lifetime ago.

"Hope you're just looking for directions. We got no money to buy anything this morning," the woman announces, resigned but not unkindly, assuming he is but yet another straggler in the march of desperate Depression ravaged men going door to door, hoping for a handout. She does not, initially, even bother to make eye contact. It is hard, hurts her loving and generous heart, to turn such men away, but the man of the house has demanded it. He has wealth but no interest in hard luck stories.

Squinting in the bright shaft of sunlight that breaks through the cloud cover, she looks him full in the face and gasps.

"No! Not you! Not after all these years. Not here." She takes a backward step, raising her arms as if to defend herself.

"Miss Violet. It is good to see you again."

"Can't say the same for yourself."

"May I come in?"

"Don't see why you should. What in the world can you want from us after all this time? You took enough from us the first go around."

"Violet, who in the world are you talking to?" The deep voice is slurred. The man stumbles, catches himself against a marble topped hall table.

"Just a ghost from the past," she mutters. "I'll leave you to deal with it if you can stay on your feet that long. You always were fascinated with stories of haunts in your mama's rose garden."

"Adam? Adam Livingston?" Hatton runs a hand across his bloodshot eyes.

In the older man's memory frozen forever as a lad of fifteen, trying to appear braver than he felt as he and his aunt made their way across war shadowed Belgium to Paris, Hatton is now, at almost forty, showing the early vestiges of an adult life wasted in dissipation. There are shadows of grey in the red gold hair, fine spider webs of wrinkles fanning out from the bright green eyes. The nose, traced with broken veins, is still long and aristocratic, gold dusted with a peppering of freckles. Adam's heart catches. There is no doubt in his mind who was mother to this man, or who fathered him.

"Your family first knew me as Avram Livinsky. I have in my life gone through several metamorphoses."

"Have to give you credit for having the sense that a Jew name would get you no where except maybe into one of Herr Hitler's barbed wire villages." Hatton wrenches open the weather warped door frame from which all vestiges of screen have long since vanished. "Come in, have a drink with me. I hate drinking alone, especially in the morning."

"Perhaps coffee, if it's not too much trouble?"

"Sure, sure, whatever you like. Violet! Get off your lazy rear and put a pot of coffee on. I believe I'll stay with the hair of the dog that bit me."

Bare wooden floorboards from which Adelaide years before removed the rugs echoing their footfalls, visitor follows host down the shadowed hall, past firmly closed doors to dusty chambers echoing with silence and into a room with enough books left on its shelves to remember that it was once a well stocked library. The room in its present state is as self-sufficient as a monk's cell, furnished simply with a bed, a small table bearing a typewriter and the remains of an uneaten breakfast, and a cracked porcelain chamber pot.

At a second thundered summons, Violet reappears carrying a tray with a tarnished silver teapot, two gold rimmed cups minus saucers. Minnie's words come back to the older man like a haunting, "There is such a sadness to a cup without a saucer."

"I would apologize for Violet's seeming to be missing her man-

ners this morning," Hatton snorts. "But it's hard to misplace something you never had in the first place. Blame it on Great Granny treating her like she was white folks. As my dear mother is so fond of saying, Violet's whole problem is that she never learned her place, much less to stay in it. Guess a sassy maid is about all that Great Granny left to us."

Violet breaks her silence. "Don't you be bad mouthing Miss Minnie, boy! I don't care if you are on the short side of forty years old. I won't put up with you disrespecting your great granny." She glares for a long moment at Hatton before striding from the room and struggling to maneuver the great pocket door closed on its track.

"How far the noble house of Buford has fallen," Hatton says with a shrug, uncapping a bottle and sweetening his coffee.

"I have followed your career with interest," Adam begins.

"As I have yours," Hatton interrupts. "Damned fine book you turned out on the Russian Revolution. I used it in my classes when I taught at Vanderbilt."

"I can only imagine your Aunt Bess's dismay at the demise of the Romanovs. Is she . . . ?"

"Dead? Of course. All of the Bufords are resting, not necessarily in peace, but quietly now at least. All of them but Mother and Violet and me, just us dregs and leavings. The last of the line as my Great Granny would say."

A shudder passes through him at Hatton's choice of words. He looks down at the cracked leather satchel at his feet, the purpose for his coming.

"I've been away so many years," Adam sighs, running a hand over his face. "I've lived a peripatetic life, chasing wars and civil strife, never really had a home in all the years since I took that midnight train from Birmingham. I suppose it was too much to hope that after all this time I could come back, simply see her once more before dying. My dreams have always found her living the charmed life for which she was intended. Did she marry, has she children?"

Hatton narrows his eyes and studies the haggard face of the man seated next to him. Death has already teasingly left its calling card with a promise of soon returning. Hatton suddenly sloshes the brandy laced coffee into the fireplace and pours himself a more sobering cup. It has been months since he has had, in his self imposed isolation, any conversation other than caustic comments *hurled back and forth with Violet. His frantic mother has no idea of his whereabouts, taking little reassurance in his publisher's assurances to her that he is both well and working. He realizes how intellectually unchallenging his carefully chosen exile finds him.*

"My aunt Lydia died less than a year after you ran away. I never even met her. Heard one too many stories of how she died of a broken heart after you abandoned her."

The older man feels his own heart constrict, puts a hand to his chest, silently praying to Minnie's "whatever god may choose to listen" that he be allowed to hold on just a little longer, to finish that which he has promised. He is the only man on earth who possesses the possible power to save the soul of Hatton Preston.

Hatton, as a misanthropic favor to his hated mother, plunges the knife without pity. "You ask about children. Violet has told me the whole story. The 'haunt in the rose garden' to which she made reference goes back to the night that she and my mother buried your bastard daughter in the yard. Lydia died of postpartum sepsis two days later. In a very literal sense you killed her."

"Is she here?" Adam asks as his heart begins the wild familiar dance that steals his breath.

"As a matter of fact she is," Hatton says. "Great Granny and Bess were away when she died, and Mother got her in Oak Hill Cemetery before her corpse had a chance to cool, but, years later, my grandfather's second wife Adelaide wanted herself a spot in the plot in Birmingham and had Aunt Lydia dug up and reburied in the Buford family graveyard here at White Gardenias, right up there inside that wrought iron fence where Great Granny can keep a watchful eye on her for eternity." He jerks a thumb over his shoulder in the direction of an open window. Rotted strips of yellowed lace move in the breeze as if nodding confirmation.

"Come on, Adam, and let's go say hello to her. Maybe some fresh air will help clear my head. This bootleg rotgut is tap dancing on my brain. Can't seem to drink without writing or write without drinking." Hatton shrugs in the direction of a towering pile of neatly stacked typed pages.

***

The storm bears down from the west like an out of control train, its engine a cold mass of furious air cloaked in dark thunderclouds.

By late afternoon it is as dark as midnight. Violet lights oil lamps in a house that has never known electricity.

"I don't care what you choose to call yourself, Mr. Avram Livinsky," Violet snaps. "You can't run away from consequences just by pretending to be someone different. I expect you're going to have to spend the night with us. Tree just blew down across the driveway. You still avoiding ham?"

"No, I gave up my father's religion along with his name. I will very soon go to my grave a poorer man for abandoning both."

"You figuring on making some kind of peace with this family before you go?"

"Peace with myself I suppose. I am here to tell Hatton things that he must know."

"Hatton is not going to hear one word he doesn't want to."

"You don't have support his biases to agree that he is brilliant, Violet."

"So the newspaper says. And all those folks who buy that clap-trap he writes. Listened to too many of Bess's stories if you ask me."

"Who we were is who we are and are to be."

"You don't have to quote Miss Minnie to me."

"I saw from her gravestone that she did at last get her wish to return to Selma."

"She's right here in the spot she chose for herself, next to her brother and my mama, close enough to hold hands with Lydia. My Miss Minnie just plain and simple, all of her life, hated for anyone, even those 'gods who chose to listen' to tell her what to do. All my Miss Minnie wanted out of life was a chance to live it on her own terms."

Violet's heart begins to soften. Holding a grudge against a dying man will not change the past one iota. "That was a mighty fine article you wrote about the convict miners, Mr. Livingston. I'm sorry Lydia had to die before knowing she had made a difference, even caught the attention of the United States Congress. Mr. Willard was called to Washington to testify about the explosion in the Mary Lydia, was there the night that . . . well, let us let dead dogs lie sleeping."

"May I ask you a personal question, Violet?"

"I may not choose to answer."

"Is it not a little out of custom that your mother is the only per-

son of color buried in that family plot?"

"My mother, Mr. Livingston, was born with a queen's birthright and died a free woman. Hyperion played the role of the best and most loving kind father any daughter could have hoped to have. A more decent man never walked this earth."

"I know that I am the only child of Alexander Buford," she continues. "Why should I care if the polite society of the world chooses not to acknowledge who fathered me? The line ends with us, Mr. Livingston, with Hatton and with me. The curse on this family is their inability to break the bonds of prejudice. The choice of whether or not to deal with that is up to Hatton. You've heard his ranting and raving, championing that Mr. Hitler. Hatton's learning tolerance is not something I expect to happen. We have come to the time of the closing of the circle."

Just the two of them, living out here all alone, in a crumbling house at the end of a long and winding, a lonely road. It occurs to Adam that the situation is somehow poignantly appropriate.

She seems to read his thoughts. "I own this house, and I have a legal paper to prove it. It was the least Isabel could do under the circumstances. Hatton is here as my guest, not vice versa. I was living myself a peaceful old age, tending my little garden, visiting with the sharecropper children of slaves who remain here. They're good to this old woman, my people, always bringing me a fresh chicken or a mess of greens. They respect me. I was happy here, perfectly contented, and then, out of the blue and uninvited, all the way from New York City, where he had been trying to escape from his mama, about six months ago here came Hatton. Sleeping off whiskey all day, clickety clacking on that typewriter all night." She consults her watch and sighs. "Five o'clock. He'll be up from his passed out nap pretty soon, dealing us both fits."

"Does he know?"

"The truth about me, or that you and Lydia are his natural parents? I have told Hatton only half the story, the story of the baby girl who died. I will leave it up to you to paint the rest of the picture, if you think it will make a difference. I take some blame for Hatton. I helped raise him after all. He irritates the living daylights out of me, but I'd defend him with my dying breath. He's the closest thing I have to a child of my own, and, if nothing else, I'm responsible for having stood by while Bess and Isabel filled his head with nonsense and convinced him that he could do no wrong.

Between them and that prissy little daddy of his, the boy didn't have half a chance to turn out normal."

"There is talk in the publishing houses of New York and London that he is close to completion of a masterpiece."

"That I would not know. I don't go into that room except to empty the ashtrays and the chamber pot and to put his meals in front of him to be ignored. He has for sure spit a mess of papers about four feet tall out of that typewriter."

"He's a genius you know, a genius with a talent too great to waste on the drivel he's been producing."

"Miss Minnie used to say that the fine line between genius and madness was no thicker than a strand of that red hair."

"I heard that he married."

"Marriage lasted about half an hour. That little spoiled rotten thing got enough of trying to live with Isabel, packed her bags and headed back up north to her daddy. Had a baby girl Hatton's never even seen. Isabel mails them a check every month all the way to Paris, France. They are nothing to do with us. Like I said, Hatton and I are the last of the line, counting out our days back here where it all began."

"But the child?"

"Isn't Hatton's. Girl he married was the daughter of his book publisher. It was a marriage of convenience for both parties, a tidy way of preserving the good name of a rich young tramp in trouble, of stopping some nasty rumors that Hatton had some peculiar pro-clivities that were not acceptable in polite society. Hatton's never had the least urge to be in love with anyone, male or female, except himself."

"Put that nasty flapping tongue of yours back in your mouth and fix us some supper, Violet," Hatton growls from the hall.

Hatton takes the chair Violet vacates, shivers as a gust of wind driven rain lashes the windows. Outside the storm howls, and the old house creaks in protest. A shutter bangs once, clatters to the ground, defeated.

"So, Adam, tell me about the situation in Europe. I know from the newspaper stories you've filed that you have collected first hand reactions."

"I dread what is to come," Adam sighs. "The war to end all wars was but an unfinished prelude to the holocaust the world now faces. There have been great advances in modern weaponry. Europe is

likely to lie in ruins in our lifetime."

"Perhaps Germany will triumph this time. You know my great-uncle Alexander, for whom I was named, was quite an admirer of all things Teutonic. He was in school in Heidelberg when the War started, used some of his father's fabled gold to run the blockade and come home to die for the Confederacy. I have to say that I do admire this fellow Adolph Hitler. Has some damned fine ideas about the importance of racial purity. We'd do well to follow his ethnic cleansing practices in this country."

Avram doesn't bother to argue, consumed with sorrow that Hatton, of the hard head and harder heart, is beyond salvation.

"Soon as this storm passes, it'll be cold as a witch," Hatton mumbles. "This is the last fireplace in the house with any decent mortar left between the bricks, only room in the house that's a few degrees warmer than the grave. As you may have noticed, my grandfather gave that old cow Adelaide all of the fine furniture. Violet and I are living with what we could dredge up from those old cabins in the slave quarters. Wouldn't the world be astounded to see it?"

"Hatton, you're a huge commercial success. Surely you can do better for yourself than living here in a crumbling old mansion."

"I got a pot to pee in and a servant to empty it after me," Hatton says with a bitter laugh as Violet silently deposits a tray with two steaming bowls of soup. "I write about the South, Adam. Haven't you read the reviews? 'Gently nostalgic glances back at a society long vanished but never really vanquished.'"

"I've read both the reviews and the books, Hatton. Your style is a tribute to the English language. Your content is so much clap-trap."

"I was named the United Daughters of the Confederacy's Man of the Year. Wouldn't Aunt Bess have been proud?"

"Why, yes, I suppose she would. To see her little stories turned into literature. You're taking it, all of it, from Bess's notebooks. Bess was doing more in the dark of the night than staging private romantic seances. She was scribbling a romanticized and sanitized version of the family history that she hoped to some day see published, a genteel way of making her own living."

"You've been messing in my papers, you and Violet." Rising to his full height, the two day stubble on his chin giving the appearance of a full red beard in the backlighting of the fireplace, arro-

gance and anger twisting a handsome face, Hatton's appearance gives Adam such a turn that he instinctively clutches at his racing heart. Here, in this room, before the very fireplace where Alexander Buford once stood down his father, resigned his birthright and all that went with it, it is as if the other man, long dead, has returned. Read and reread from the pages of Minnie Buford Hatton's journals, the story is engraved on Adam's heart like a crest.

"My great-grandmother never loved me," Hatton has earlier in the day complained like a peevish child. Too strong was the resemblance Adam thinks to himself. He must have been, even as a toddler, like a ghost returned from the grave.

"You were not yet born when I spent that short span of days in Birmingham," Adam says. "It was as if in every conversation they were desperate to convey not so much who they were as who they thought or wished they had been. Enough of Bess's stories were aimed at my ears for me to recognize the source on the first page of your first book."

"So I used her characters, her anecdotes, her reminiscences? The words are mine, as is the family."

"And what a way with words you have, far too much of a way to waste so many."

"You didn't come here just to lay a rose on Lydia's grave, did you?"

"No, my primary motivation for making this trip, against my physician's strongest protestations, was to entrust to you a legacy of pages that I have carried with me, all of these years, across all of those fields of battle. It is the story of your family, in its truth and its entirety. It is your heritage, your inheritance."

Hatton throws back his head and laughs. "So that's where they've been. I've torn this house apart searching. My Great Granny's journals, the real true story, better than anything Bess could have invented. All along you had them. Great Granny used to scream and squawk that Mother had stolen them."

Hatton's chuckle is bitter. "You know, I figured life would hand me the ultimate irony, that eventually I'd stumble on the daybook, and that cache of gold Great Granny used to rant about, and pass right by those papers. I need those papers a lot more than anything a pile of gold would buy. You're a writer so you should understand. What I want most is for history to remember me."

Adam makes a halting progress across the room, opens a

cracked leather valise in which string tied packets of papers lie as neatly stacked as ransom money.

"I leave this with you, Hatton, in hopes that through these pages you will find not only your real power as a writer but your humanity as well, what your great-uncle Alexander sought and ultimately gave his life for, the truth with a capital T."

In the dim light of the basement Carrie picked up the random newspaper tossed in the wheelbarrow, out of curiosity skimmed down the headlines for December 3, 1938. Her eye caught on a tiny wire service story, tucked between the news articles chronicling John L. Lewis's election as the first president of the Congress of Industrial Organizations, the recall of the German ambassador to the United States, and the New York Yankees' besting of Chicago in the World Series.

"New York. Socialist journalist and war correspondent Adam Livingston collapsed and died of heart failure outside the offices of his publisher yesterday evening. Livingston, a native of Russia born Avram Livinsky, was one of the pioneer muckrakers, beginning his journalistic career with *Young's Weekly*. His dispatches from the 1905 Russian uprisings were followed by coverage of World War I from the front lines and a first hand account of the Russian Revolution of 1917, which he compiled into an internationally acclaimed treatise on that upheaval. He was most recently returned from observing the Civil War in Spain and the growing Nationalist Socialist movement in Germany."

"Never married, Livingston, 58, leaves no survivors."

Chapter Twenty Eight

A concession to modern technology in a time warp trapped house, the caller ID box on the persistently ringing telephone displayed the name Miller and an unfamiliar, out of state, number. Carrie scowled at it. Telephone solicitors. Let it ring.

She carefully blotted a tear from the faded ink of the letter, found in a far corner of the basement vault as if flung there, returning from signature to opening lines for a second reading.

For Carrie, through her dreams privy to the unhappy ending of their love story, Avram's unanswered plea to Lydia held a special poignancy. "Find it in your heart if you can to put your family's objections behind you. If you write me back acceptance I will hurry by boat, by train, by foot if I must walk, to find you. The revolution is coming, and I want you by my side to share it. I have found in my travels that there is nowhere on this earth that I can go that my love for you will be less than the uppermost and most consuming thing about me. I cannot comprehend a life without you. Write me, Lydia, please, to say that you feel the same. The magazine's editors will know where to find me. From wherever I am I will run to you with the sincere promise that never ever again, for any reason, will I leave you."

Perhaps, Carrie hoped, as he drew a last breath before dying, he felt an overdue sense of peace in knowing that all those long lonely years before she had not simply ignored him, that she had been dead before the letter reached her.

It was Carrie who had slit the envelope's seal. Isabel had not bothered to open it.

"Miller" nagged a little voice in the back of her mind.

She grabbed the phone, hit call review. The Miller who wrote of lost mansions. "Answer the phone, M. C. Miller," Carrie muttered into the phone. "I can tell you a thing or two you don't know about both Hatton Hall and White Gardenias. So much, you may have to publish a supplement to your book."

What would M.C. Miller think if she spit out the whole story, and backed up her facts by adding, "I know it's all true because I dreamed it?"

* * *

Carrie pulled into the rutted gravel drive of the country store. A rusted sign advertised grape soda. Only a few dilapidated buildings remained on the main street of the abandoned cotton country hamlet. A small frame church, with cardboard instead of stained glass in its windows, and a roofless brick building that once housed a post office represented the modern day despair of the Alabama Black Belt. It was such a ghost town that it had no zip code.

Venturing inside, she took a soft drink from an ancient metal cooler. Cold sweat dripped from the old fashioned green bottle, and she laid a dollar on the counter, having no plans to either drink it or return it for deposit, small price to pay for needed information.

"I wonder if I might ask some directions," she addressed a teenager, whose sullen face betrayed little hope for the future, as he slowly turned coins in a cigar box on the counter as if unsure how to make change. "Do you know White Gardenias Plantation? I was told it was on the road from Selma to Cahaba, about midway between the two."

"Ain't nothing left of Cahaba 'cept a sign marking where it used to be," he mumbled as he handed her a quarter and some pennies. "Cahaba used to be the capital of Alabama. Not even a ghost town nowadays. Don't know nothing about no White Gardenias."

"The old Buford place," Carrie continued, resisting the urge to correct his grammar. That was his mother's business. Carrie bit her lip in frustration. She wasn't about to give up after driving half the morning, and this little store seemed the only outpost approximating civilization along the country road. What she had seen of houses consisted of a couple of kudzu covered chimneys rising from ruined foundations.

"Surely you must know of a big white house around here somewhere," she begged. "I promised to meet someone there this morning." She knew that she would probably get a good deal more of his attention if she added, "He's a dead man you see. His name is Hatton."

"Down the road a piece, dirt road off to the left, ain't a mailbox," volunteered a young woman who appeared from a back room, apparently a sister or a girl friend.

Carrie twisted the large blackened silver key in her pocket, the key retrieved from the vault in her basement where Isabel had hidden away all the ball gowns, the Mardi Gras Queen's crown and scepter, the letters, even the spell bag of charms that had held too little too late magic to save the life of Lydia.

Something told Carrie that this key was the one Minnie had brought with her to Birmingham after being forced to abandon White Gardenias. Even if the locks had been changed, she might be able to force a window open. Ascertaining current ownership could be time consuming and complicated, involve researching court records. She hadn't had time for that this morning. Miller's assurance that the house was vacant, certainly not habitable, seemed a good omen.

Less than half a mile away, a dirt track intersected an unplowed field. She turned down it, shifting into four wheel drive, suddenly sure she was heading exactly in the right direction, and bounced along for another quarter mile through the fields, passing twice over a small trickle of stream.

What was left of the house was as pitiful as M. C. Miller had described it, or possibly even worse.

She felt a stirring of sadness as she drove past the rusted wrought iron gates, centered with the curlicue initials GWB, fallen from the brick pillars that had once supported them, lying on the ground like open arms bidding any enter.

She thought of Minnie's words to Avram, to him at the time so cryptic in meaning. You will go some day to White Gardenias. Where it began and where it will end, just as my brother spoke it.

The land was clearly posted, "no trespassing, no hunting." She was hunting, but not for the kind of game the poster of the signs had in mind.

After talking with Miller she had briefly contemplated phoning Wyatt and asking him to accompany her. She had put the thought aside, preferred to walk the halls on her own, alone. In many ways she felt much as if she were coming home. Like Violet, she felt like family.

The porch steps were rotten, fallen away from the house entirely, but the veranda was not but a few feet off the ground. Carrie grabbed a column, a firm column, constructed she knew from Washington's daybook notes from a single massive tree trunk covered with creek bed gravel, sand, and molasses stirred together to form a plaster, and pulled herself up. A few flakes of white paint clung forlornly to the facade.

The key was a useless accessory. The massive front doors pushed in easily, the quality of the original craftsmanship outlasting the warping waste of time.

It was cold and of course dark inside, this house which had never known electricity, shaded by the massive branches of the surrounding trees, trees planted more than a century before by the slave laborers of a young George Washington Buford. She pulled a flashlight from her pocket, hoping but unsure that the treads of the massive curving staircase would hold even her light weight.

The rooms on the first floor were, thanks to the greed of Adelaide, mostly unfurnished, huge and hollow and lonely. The double parlors, the music room, the library. She would have known them all, these dream familiar rooms, with or without the clues provided by furniture. Vandals had made a sloppy attempt to pry the marble mantles from the walls. Chunks of gray veined stone lay scattered on the buckled oak floors, filmed with plaster dust. The lathing of the ceiling and walls was visible in places where the plaster had cracked and crumbled.

Shards of glass from a broken whiskey bottle were littered like a dead fire's embers in the parlor fireplace. A delicate lady's desk, one leg missing, lay toppled on its side. Carrie ran a hand over it. Queen Marie's little writing table that served as such a prominent prop in Bess and Minnie's seances?

Carrie felt a twinge of amusement, thinking of Minnie's elaborate tale of her mother's fine French ancestry told to the seance participants. Leave it to the Bufords to lie any time so doing gave them an advantage. How many times had Carrie dreamed it? Charlotte Buford was as Scottish as a tartan, passing on to her descendants the grandfather clock, the green eyes, the gift of the second sight, and probably more than a measure of madness.

Tendrils of the ubiquitous kudzu vine had stolen through the windows. It was just a matter of time before the encroaching green vegetation covered this old house entirely.

In the hall Carrie pulled the cord of an annunciator and heard a distinctive ring from the long silent system by which the masters and mistresses of the house had once demanded a slave's attention. In this quiet house no one had called for anyone in a very, very long time. In the dining room she set the punkah swinging, disturbing swirls of ghost white motes, dusting the spot where the table would have been laid for Christmas feasts, roast pork and calves foot jelly served on silver, during the golden years of plenty.

Feeling not at all an intruder, she made her way from room to room, leaving a trail of footprints. Stopping before a pair of closed doors, she knew without a doubt that she had arrived at her destination. The heavy mahogany door groaned along its tracks and slid into the wall pocket. The library, just as Carrie had dreamed it. Hatton's typewriter still sat on its table, the tall pile of pages seen in her dream blown around the room by many winters of winds whistling through the broken glass of the windows. Beside the typewriter rested an empty, dust rimed whiskey bottle.

As if respecting Hatton's privacy, Carrie pulled the door closed on leaving. Time seemed suspended, of little essence. She wanted to see the rest of the house before gathering up those papers. Why had Isabel not taken them?

In the great drawing room leaks had mottled a marbleized design on the walls. Pieces of a gilt frame were tossed into the fireplace like kindling.

A breeze through one of the broken windows blew a torn square of canvas across the floor. Carrie stooped and retrieved it. The painted face of a young Minnie Buford, supremely confident as the most beautiful belle in the county, stared back at her as if issuing a challenge. Carrie looked around the room, thinking of Minnie's life long obsession with hidden gold, her description of her Papa's house having many cryptic nooks and crannies. Like a child playing blindman's bluff, hotter and colder, getting warmer, she knew she was close to something. They were here, some answers.

A gut instinct had told her that the papers in the library were likely not the elusive missing manuscript. Hatton's last words were in the house, but she knew they were not abandoned where one might most expect to find them.

A scrap of dream came back to her. Crossing the room, she pressed a square of paneling in the same place Minnie had the night she secreted her money box before facing the sheriff.

The door in the false paneling swung open easily. The compartment was deep, dark, dusty and almost empty. Carrie gently lifted the carved wooden music box, along with the locket Minnie's last Christmas gift from her brother, and turned the key. The notes issuing from it sounded poignant. She replaced the box and closed the panel, leaving Minnie's memories to repose in silence.

Carrie cautiously tested each step as she ascended to the second floor. She pushed open the doors to the balcony, saw in the distance the river, imagined its mud brown water churned by a steamboat, bearing a distinctive white gardenia painted between its smokestacks, making landing to pick up a load of cotton, to welcome the Bufords as passengers floating down the river to Mobile to indulge their whims for silks and satins, sideboards and silver.

The allee of oak trees still stood, not as sturdy or as strong or as complete as it once had, more than a few of the trees having fallen victims to storms over the years, leaving the whole parade like the gap toothed grin of a Halloween pumpkin. Down the drive and through the great gates, through the mists of time a veil parted, and she could see it as clearly as if happening in the present, the tall proud figure of Alexander Buford, son and heir to this house and all the fields surrounding it, riding away to school in the north, coming home from a war on the back of a mule, broken in body but never in spirit, the trio of grey coated horsemen bearing a death warrant.

Two of the bedrooms were more or less furnished, pieces of mahogany passed over because their massive dimensions rendered them impractical to move to even a house as large as Adelaide's gaudy Greek Revival palace on the Highland Avenue. Strips of faded wallpaper hung at random, stained bed covers huddled in the heap into which they had been flung on some last morning. Hadn't her mother always told her that if you left the house with the bed unmade you were asking to meet up with some dire catastrophe, giving those gathered at your funeral the chance to whisper about your sorry housekeeping? Carrie reached down and gently smoothed the covers, whispered, "It's all right, Violet. I won't tell a soul, especially not my mother."

She could imagine Adelaide Ashcraft McShan, an aging new bride, making her inspection of these rooms, pointing a greedy finger and saying "I'll take this and this and this as well." She thought of the furniture in Wyatt's house, of coin silver spoons, so much of it passed down from his grandmother, transferred legacies from White Gardenias.

On a table next to the bed the remains of a candle guttered down to a pool of wax filled the base of a silver stand. Carrie lifted it. It was heavy, solid, would bring a fortune in any antique shop. She replaced it, picked up a book lying next to it, a dog eared Bible. The flyleaf was inscribed, "To our beloved Violet on the occasion of her twelfth birthday. Well done good and faithful servant." Bess's handwriting.

Carrie thumbed through the book, seeking something more down to earth than divine inspiration. There it was, slipped between the Psalms, crude in its rendering but architecturally accurate down to the three differently capped columns, the picture Minnie had drawn for Violet, the only existing representation of the garish facade of Hatton Hall.

Whatever the silver candle stand was worth in the sophisticated shops of New Orleans, she was sure M. C. Miller would happily part with twice that amount for the possession of this small scrap of paper. She tucked it securely back in the Bible, put the book right back, exactly where she had found it, aligning it in the little rectangle on the table it had left in the dust of all the years since Violet, for all of her life to all those she loved good and faithful, had read the final passage.

Carrie stared up the attic stairs in frustration. The cupola in the roof had collapsed, making any farther upward progress a complete impossibility. No one would, ever again, enter the attic of this house, a space that had ceased to exist like a secret does when told to another.

She gazed dreamily out the window centering the rear wall of the wide central hall. Behind the house the smokehouse was in ruins, the brick kitchen boarded up, nailed shut. Outlined in vines, still visible was the foundation of the little schoolhouse where a New England tutor put into Alexander Buford's young mind the seeds of ideas, dangerous northern isms. In an area once a manicured garden, perennial descendants of daffodils and hyacinths, quince and bridal wreath spirea, golden forsythia, and Confederate jasmine were all blooming early, as if stubbornly confident that nothing in life is devastating enough to stop the spring from coming. The family graveyard in the grove of cedars and weeping willows, crowded with graves and overgrown gardenia bushes, was clearly visible in the distance.

Before she could make her way back downstairs to make a pilgrimage to the place where so many of those she felt she had come to know lay sleeping she was interrupted by a summons from the hall below her, a voice too firm and deep to be ghostly, a voice very clearly a part of the present.

***

"Now let me see if I have all the facts straight," Nick said angrily, sounding more like a television police detective than a frustrated husband. "You decided, because we own a house that once belonged to Isabel Preston, that you had every right in the world to lie to me about where you were going, to steal my hunting truck to get there, and to get yourself arrested for trespassing and breaking and entering an abandoned house that once belonged to Isabel's grandmother. All in the course of a morning's time? Carrie, how could you?"

"Some of your facts are correct, some less so," Carrie snapped back. She had gotten herself out of it as well as into it, and it was really none of his business. "Incorrect fact number one, I entered but was very careful not to break anything. The house was as wide open as if it were the number one attraction on the Selma Pilgrimage Tour of Homes."

"Carrie, I am seriously worried about you. Seriously worried! Normal, rational people do not do the kind of things you are doing. Suburban housewives play tennis, and get their nails done, and most of all pay proper attention to their own husbands and children without feeling the need to take on problem plagued neighbors and dead people whom they regard as relations. Suburban housewives do not get themselves arrested." He was almost screaming.

"Nicky, calm down! Incorrect fact number two. I was not literally arrested. I was just detained by the sheriff for a couple of hours. It wasn't like they took a mug shot and fingerprints, for goodness sake. The sheriff was actually very nice, and he makes a great pot of coffee. Someone ought to hire him to service the machine in the intensive care waiting room at your hospital."

He was not letting Carrie off the hook that easily. "If you weren't arrested, why did you feel the need to call your mother and ask her to involve the governor?"

"Because when you have friends in high places you might as well use them. It simplifies things by half, let me tell you, when the sheriff gets a call not just from the governor's office but from the main man himself."

"Carrie, you don't sound as if you're the least bit remorseful."

"Maybe because I'm not! I'm sorry that you were inconvenienced by not being able to have the oil in the truck changed today, but if you hadn't so generously offered my car to my mother to use until she can replace hers I'd have taken my own. I am not going to continue to sit around and have you tell me every move to make, to get on my knees and beg you to let me live my life as I want to live it, like you're Willard H. Preston, II or something."

"Carrie, listen to yourself. What in the hell are you talking about?"

"I'm talking about Isabel. If she had just once, just once, stood up for herself maybe she would not have ended up the way she did. She spent her whole life being pushed around by other people. I am capable of calling my own shots in life."

"Carrie, I can't understand why you are persisting in living in some kind of a bad dream world, a world populated with people who are dead, for crying out loud."

Carrie screamed, "They're as real to me as you are sitting here. Dead people make safer friends than live ones anyway. There's no risk of them running off and leaving you. You think I need some constructive activity? Maybe I'll go into the seance business like Minnie and Bess did. From now on, I think maybe I'll be exclusively friends with dead people."

"Carrie, I am beyond my limit. I'm not spending another night under this roof."

"Fine. You go right ahead and leave. I'm not going with you. I'm not done here."

Frightened out of his wits, he slumped in the chair, face in his hands, as the woman who used to be his wife ran sobbing from the room.

They slept, that night, in separate beds, Nick so troubled that he stayed at his parents' house. His wife and his life were falling apart. Somehow, some way, he had to get them out of that house.

At home in Isabel's house, Carrie also wrestled with sleep. Now really, she asked herself, exactly what harm had been done to anyone? The governor, a good humored sort of man grateful during both of his two terms in office for the support of the influential Mallory Hudson, had acted as if he thought the situation was hilarious.

It wasn't like she made a practice of riding in the back of police cars. She had never even had a speeding ticket. How could she have known that abandoned houses out from dried up little country cotton towns were becoming hot beds of illegal drug activity, that the dumb sounding kids in the store were actually college educated narcotic detectives working undercover?

Often lately she had been acting on pure gut feeling, and somehow visiting the house had just felt right. Hadn't the expert on such things, M. C. Miller, said it both plainly and plaintively? That old house's days were numbered. One more summer of rain on the kudzu crop or a good spring storm and it would likely be no more than a memory.

The cat had deserted her, was acting as if he had been posted as guard in the basement. Tired from an eventful day, she turned her back on Nick's empty side of the bed and slept, alone and lonely, not even a cat to keep her company.

"So, Howard, what do you think of the latest?" Hatton cradles the phone against his shoulder and lights a cigarette. Outside the phone booth, a middle aged matron, handsomely turned out in fox fur wrap and a pillbox hat, impatiently taps an umbrella and glances at her watch. Hatton blows her a smoke ring like a kiss.

"Nothing short of masterful, Hatton." The reply snakes around static through the miles of wires connecting Manhattan to Selma, Alabama. "They should start polishing the Pulitzer based on what I have read so far. I sense a definite power up to now merely lurking behind your words, as though you are letting loose something deep within yourself."

The words are not merely an editor's stroking of without argument his most egocentric author. He glances down at the pages on the desk before him. Of such are the careers, of editors and authors alike, made into legends. Let Maxwell Perkins have Hemingway, a dozen Scott Fitzgeralds. After the world gets a look at this book there will not be a writer alive worth mentioning in the same breath with Hatton Preston.

"Hell, I'm not even drinking some days, Howard. The words are flying onto the page faster than I can type them."

Howard holds his breath, refrains from commenting "perhaps it's because you aren't drinking." He's got to somehow hold Hatton together long enough to see this book to completion without the usual interruption of weeks long binges which render a genius as impotent with the written word as if he were illiterate.

"Hatton, how soon can you have a complete outline to me?" With Hatton an outline is essential. The editor has had to finish

several of the Red Camellias books himself after the author appar-
ently lost interest.   A Depression dulled reading public does not
even notice where author leaves off and editor takes over.   Hatton's
stories provide his audience with a little sorely needed distraction,
an escape from hard times to good times gone.

"I'm not writing this one by outline, Howard."   Hatton grinds the
cigarette out with his toe while the woman outside fidgets.   "This
story has a mind of its own.   I never know myself what's going to
appear on the next page."   He laughs, thinks of the tantalization of
Minnie's yet unread pages, a plot twisting and turning with bends in
the road which surprise him.

Funny how Bess, who was so proud of her daddy lying under that
big old monument right down the street in the Selma cemetery, for-
got to mention that Cap had a twin brother, at an early age escap-
ing one step ahead of the local sheriff, never again to show up to
claim his half of the lost inheritance.   Probably long lost relatives he
wouldn't even recognize passing him every day on the streets of
Selma.   Interesting technique, Great Granny writing her husband's
story backwards, beginning with his death.   Hatton has almost read
his way back to Cap Hatton's beginnings.   Tonight's chapter will
introduce Hatton to his paternal great-great grandparents.

"Hatton, are you there?   We seem to have a very bad connec-
tion."   The words jerk him back to the present on a Selma, Alabama
street corner.   They have acknowledged it for generations, now
haven't they, the fact that the Bufords are several cuts above all
others?   Can't that woman tapping her parasol so impatiently rec-
ognize a genuine member of the southern aristocracy?

"I'm here, Howard."

"Do me a favor, Hatton, while you're at a telephone, please call
your mother.   She is driving me crazy, deviling me with questions
about your whereabouts."

"Now, Howard, you know we can't have her showing up at White
Gardenias, totally disrupting my creativity, souring the mood of Old
South ambiance that my faithful retainer Violet and I share in our
peaceful solitude.   White Gardenias is the last place on earth the
old hag would think to look for me.   I've got to go, Howard.   I put
four more chapters in the mail to you this morning.   I'm going to go
back and drive on to conclusion."

He chuckles to himself as he lights another cigarette.   Imagine
the nerve of that pompous Violet telling him that she has a few

words to add to Minnie's narrative, a true life love story with a bittersweet ending. He might write romantic rubbish, but he certainly doesn't believe in it.

The connection is broken. Hatton leaves the phone booth, whistling, winking a green eye and tipping his hat to the weary woman in waiting.

Chapter Twenty Nine

Ellen slammed a box of cereal on the table, slapped the milk down next to it so hard that it sloshed from the carton, pooled in a puddle.

"I get the impression that you are unhappy with me this morning, Mom."

"Unhappy? Whatever gave you that idea, Nicky? I am way, way past unhappy. I am disappointed in you, and that feeling puts unhappy in the shade of a tree on a summer afternoon. I didn't raise you to be a coward, to run away from problems."

"Look, Mom, I'm sorry if I didn't explain things last night. I was too upset to talk about it. I came here because I had to get out of that house, and I couldn't think where else to go. Maybe I should have gotten a motel room."

"Oh, Nick, you know that your father and I would rather die than have you feel that you had any problem you couldn't bring to us. I am just sick over your having these problems with Carrie. It's a difficult stage to go through, son, your forties. Hot flashes and cold sweats come over you when you think about where you're going in the future."

"Mom, I am at the end of that proverbial rope you have been telling me to tie a knot in and hang onto. I can't take another minute of it. My wife seems to be obsessed with dead people."

Ellen felt a queasy pang of dread, both at what he was saying and at what she was about to tell him. They had all been living a lie for long enough. To hell with Mallory Hudson.

"Nick, there's something you need to know. All of those years ago, the day that Carrie lost her brother, your father was the doctor on duty in the emergency room."

***

Three hospital volunteers wheeled the carts, azaleas in every blooming color, a riotous flower garden trucked in on trolleys.

"Couldn't make up my mind, so I told them two of every color," Wyatt explained. "Now I'm not sure that all of these various shades go well together."

"The Good Lord did not put any colors in nature that don't compliment each other. Thank you, Mr. Wallace. I will get my grandsons to help me plant them. Having all of my children and grandchildren here in one place at one time is a miracle that hasn't happened in years."

"Speaking of miracles, you're looking awfully fit already. Scared the pants off of me, thinking that we might lose you."

"Mr. Wallace, I know where I am going and I look forward to getting there. I expect that I am going to be around a while in part because I've still got some unfinished business and have been given a very clear signal to get about doing it. When is Carrie coming to visit me, and, by the way, have you been eating right instead of just drinking?"

"You'll be pleased to know that I have invited Carrie to go out to breakfast. She has found some old family papers in her house that may be of value in my work and is going to share them with me. I don't mind telling you though that my mouth veritably waters at the thought of getting you home to me." He was not yet at the point at admitting out right that the house was lonely without her.

"Mr. Wallace, like I said, I have some unfinished business. As soon as I get out of here I'll be getting myself back where I belong at Mallory's, where we are going to tie up some old loose ends, whether she likes it or not."

There was something in the background of the past niggling and nagging at all of them. It had nothing to do with him.

"Pull your chair closer, Mr. Wallace, and indulge me for a few minutes, and put away that pipe, or I will ring for a nurse to take it from you."

Why did people have to feel they could turn their hearts inside out to him? Maybe he should warn her that he had been known to turn true confessions into dialogue, put them on the movie screen for viewing by anyone with the price of a ticket.

"There was something that happened a long time ago when Carrie was just a little thing, something so horrible that it took her childhood from her. She has shut it out. A person can't deal with, or be done with, something they cannot remember. You're important in Carrie's life, and I think that you need to know what she is running from."

He fingered the pipe in his pocket, wasn't sure he wanted to hear it.

"It came to me, **Mr. Wallace**, as I lay here teetering on that fine line between life and death. You and I working together can give Carrie back her childhood and allow her to save her marriage. She and that man love each other."

"I married three times for varying reasons, love never being one of them."

"You should try it for the right reason sometime, but I'm not going to let you be your usual selfish self and turn the conversation right back to you. We're talking about Carrie. Nick is a good man, Mr. Wallace, as good as they come. His biggest fault is that he loves Carrie so much that he has trouble dealing with it when something hurts her. He's like a scared little boy taking off down the street with the bogeyman after him when anything threatens her. No, sir, it's up to me and to you. There are some demons chasing Carrie, and we have to help her defeat them."

She pinched a fading blossom off of one of the azaleas. "Life doesn't happen just by random chance, Mr. Wallace. I think you were sent to us for a reason."

Their eyes met.

"With or without Mallory's approval, you and I, Mr. Wallace, have got to help Carrie get back her childhood if she's going to have a future."

$$* * *$$

"It's open, come on in," Carrie responded to his knock on her back door.

"Ready for breakfast?" After the conversation with Josie, he looked at her in a whole new light. "You're still in your robe. Did I arrive too early?"

"No, I've been up for hours, trying to decide whether or not my husband has left me on a permanent basis or just until he can come to his senses that he is making a mighty mountain out of a molehill."

"I can no more imagine Nick leaving you than the Sphinx, like London Bridge, deciding to start a new life in the Arizona desert. He's a good man, Carrie, a good solid husband who loves you."

"Too good for the likes of me it would appear. I think that Nick, for the past year or so, has been having an affair with the woman he would have married had I not come along and thrown a monkey wrench in his plans. I got pregnant last year on purpose, because I didn't know what to do with my life other than being a mother. We can't continue on like we're going, so I suppose the great burning issue becomes where we go from here. Nick is adamant that he doesn't intend to spend one more night in this house."

"Carrie, has anyone ever told you that you have a very active imagination? I would bet my bottom dollar that having an affair with an old girlfriend, or anyone else, has never, ever, even remotely crossed Nick's mind. Male wisdom assures me that you're barking up the wrong tree with that one. What does he have to say about it?"

"We've never discussed it. I saw him with her one day, holding hands with her. What more do I need? I tell you, Wyatt, I have spent my whole life majoring in doing just the right thing, just what I was supposed to do, and when I weave the least little bit out of the straight and narrow Nick and my mother make a federal case of it. I was always one of those children who colored exactly within the lines. I always put the little plastic clip on the bag of chips that someone else has thoughtlessly left open, obligingly pour for myself the flat diet soda from the can from which they took one sip and discarded instead of being wasteful. I am a good girl, and I dare anyone, most especially Mallory Hudson or Nick Lancaster, to dispute that."

"My goodness, what brought all that on?"

"I made a little pilgrimage yesterday to a place where the sheriff of Dallas County did not think I had any right, when I had every right, to be."

"Carrie, I am having the greatest of difficulty following this narrative."

"I am so torn, Wyatt, by what is happening to me. I'm afraid. I don't know if I want to go on with this." She was shaking.

"Give me an example, Carrie."

"This 'daybook.' She held the little book up by two fingers as though it might burn her. "I'm almost afraid to be in the same house with it. It's evil."

"It merely chronicles odious things which ended well over a hundred years ago, Carrie. It has no potential to harm you in the here and now. You said last night that you think that daybook holds the key to the location of the missing manuscript. We've got to get around political correctness and keep on searching."

"I'm not so sure about that. I'm beginning to feel as though I'm part of someone else's grand design or something."

He thought of Josie's words, why you were sent to us. He no more believed in grand designs than he did in ghosts or divine intervention.

Carrie's fingers scrambled through the computer print out, finally coming to a page with the corner turned down. "I have found Mother's elusive missing link ancestor, Wyatt, and it's not a pretty sight."

He took the pages from her and frowned as he read a highlighted diary entry. "Sent the half breed injun boy, Little 8 now calling himself Henry, off to Tuscaloosa to get himself an education. A wise move on my part. Child displays a mind as fine as my own son Alexander's with none of my own boy's high mindedness. Little 8 is practical and totally lacking in conscience, just like his daddy. Let Alexander rant and rave and preach to me idealism. He will not manumit what he will now not inherit. I have changed my will and left my only son out of it. Minnie's Cap will someday inherit my lands and my chattels. My son is as a dead man to me. May he burn in hell for his delusions."

Wyatt cocked his head at Carrie. "I have not got a clue as to whom any of these people are, Carrie."

"'Little 8' was the ancestor Mother knows as Henry Stainwright, son of the gap in the lineage chain who claimed to know nothing of his parentage but who started the family's Anne Boleyn legend. Mother was on the right track all right. If you can believe Washington Buford, we really are related to some fine old English gentry."

"And how do you come to that conclusion?"

"Last night, after Nick stormed out of here, I had trouble sleeping. I read that daybook from start to finish. The father of that boy that George Washington Buford sent to the University of Alabama runs through the narrative almost from page one. When Washington and Charlotte Buford came to Alabama in the early 1820s to take up a grant of land, they found squatters on their property living in a crude log cabin, which the Bufords promptly confiscated. There is a description that would turn Mother's perfect head of hair white. The Stainwrights were living on bear meat and berries and cradling their infants in hollowed out logs. The man, Mose Stainwright, was one of Andrew Jackson's Indian fighters who had recognized good rich dirt when he saw it and come back from Tennessee to claim some. He also claimed that he was the son of a fine British lady who got herself into a spot of trouble with a handsome stranger. Her family disowned her. She died when he was a child, and he grew up pretty much living off his wiles."

"Shades of Ellen's heroine."

"No joke. I hadn't even thought of that. To continue my story, Washington Buford must have been spouting off about his own superiority, and Mose Stainwright decided to add a little background of his own, telling Washington how his mother's people had come from England, were in fact cousins to Henry VIII's Anne Boleyn. Mose had a common law Creek Indian wife and a brood of about nine or ten children, one of whom he called Henry, VIII. These were backwoods people, Wyatt. They simply referred to the boy and taught him to sign his name not with the illiterate's usual x but with instead the number 8."

"You're right. Your mother is not going to like one bit an ancestor who was thought of as just a number." He was trying hard not to laugh over how seriously Carrie seemed to be taking all of this.

"Washington Buford was the sorriest sort of scum. Even though the importing of slaves was no longer legal, he had money enough to finance private dealings with a renegade boat captain. He was still bringing in Africans as late as the 1850s, into hidden coves in Mobile Bay. He recognized a shrewd horse trader when he saw one, and so he set Mose Stainwright up in business as sort of a middle man. Now this business was flourishing, making a fine profit, but Mose had a problem. He would occasionally, let us hope eaten by conscience, do a little drinking and decide to go back to his woman."

"Understandable. As you may have noticed, I like a drink every now and then myself. I fear I may have at last outgrown my need for a woman."

"Wyatt, please stop interrupting! Washington Buford finally had enough of that. He went to the woods one night and burned the cabin to the ground while they slept, Mose's woman and all of those children. The only one who escaped was Little 8, clutching Charlotte Buford's coin silver spoons, now safe in Mother's sideboard." Big tears rolled out of Carrie's eyes. "I hope it was guilt so strong he was having visions of hell opening up to get him when

Washington Buford took that child on, and called him Henry, and paid for his education."

She was silent for a long few minutes. Wyatt told himself that the plot was about to thicken.

Instead she seemed to change the subject. "Wyatt, that manuscript is simply not here. Not in this house, not in the dreams I've been having, a secret I have decided this morning to share with you. I know, from those dreams, that we are all somehow interconnected, and I'm afraid. A curse was placed on the Buford family, the curse that ultimately killed Hatton."

Wyatt spoke softly, "Once again, your imagination is getting out of hand, Carrie. I've seen his death certificate. Hatton Preston died of a heart attack. Century old curses do not bring on a coronary."

She looked up at him miserably. "I think we may be playing with fire here, Wyatt."

"Like Shakespeare and Henry James, I have not yet made up my mind about ghosts. I do, however, very strongly disbelieve in curses," he argued. "What are you not telling me?"

"I figured out yesterday exactly where that manuscript is. The sheriff just didn't allow me time to retrieve it. Everything that belonged to Isabel, including her memories, belongs to me now."

"You know where Hatton's manuscript is?" The words, coming out, almost choked him. He felt his heart racing. Time could not run out, not yet, not for him like it had for Hatton. He felt it like the voicing of a prayer.

"Should have been obvious to us from the beginning," she answered as if telling him something as plain as the nose on his face. "You've read all of Hatton's books, haven't you?"

"Most of them more than once."

"Well, there it is." To his minor annoyance she turned her attention to the tiny television on the kitchen counter as she talked. On the screen a cooking show hostess frosted a multi-tiered birthday cake. The backdrop of the morning show featured clusters of red balloons and streamers.

"Stop and ask yourself the setting of every single one of those books. Hatton wrote about the antebellum South. Hatton never wrote a word about Birmingham, a city that of course didn't even exist before the Civil War. Didn't you just tell me that you looked at

Hatton's death certificate? Where did he die, Wyatt?"

"Selma," he whispered, an obvious truth dawning.

"It came back to me yesterday, something my mother said the first time she entered this house. She told me that Hatton's mother had suffered the ultimate heartbreak of not knowing her son's whereabouts at the time of his death, that they never got to have a final conversation. He did not die in this house, Wyatt. From a heart attack, or a curse, or whatever killed him, Hatton Preston died at White Gardenias. I am absolutely certain that Hatton's manuscript remains there. Isabel wasn't overly intelligent and also lacked some key background information necessary to put her hands on it."

"Hatton's last words and Minnie's pot of gold, are right there still, after all these years, and I know exactly where to find them."

Stunned, he nodded agreement. To the readers of the 1930s, the fictional home of Red Camellias would have been as real as Margaret Mitchell's Tara. Hatton had literally gone back to his family's roots and died there.

"Wyatt, what was the best birthday you ever had?" Carrie asked, her face still locked on the television screen.

"Same as every other red blooded American boy's, the year I got a brand new bicycle." His mind was whirling with the certainty that Carrie had indeed reached an obvious conclusion. He was not about to get distracted by birthdays.

"My best birthday was the year I was ten. I woke up and jumped out of bed, and when I opened the door I could not get out of my room. My brother had built a wall on the other side of the door, a wall of red balloons."

So close to remembering, sobbing, she collapsed against him. From the shadows, the yellow cat licked his whiskers and purred.

***

Wyatt's grandmother's old Mercedes, recently tuned, still possessed a powerful engine, and Wyatt ignored the posted speed limits as the two of them sped south and west, retracing Carrie's route of the day before. Wyatt felt like a crusading knight in sight of Jerusalem.

He looked at Carrie sitting next to him, hunched down in the seat, spent from crying, exhausted and escaped into what appeared to be a troubled sleep.

On the run away from and toward a pair of dead men, he felt a sense that a circle was closing. For all of them, a long awaited resolution was coming.

He pressed harder on the gas. Beside him Carrie cried out, the single word "no" in her sleep.

It was the last dream. It was almost over.

It was Violet who found him, Violet's the ancient and anguished screams of a rendered childless mother that traveled across the winter fields, whipping through the leafless trees, catching the attention of an old sharecropper chopping wood for his fireplace.

"Three days and three nights he's been locked up in that room banging on that typewriter, never surfacing for food or even drink, typing like he was running from the hounds from hell. Then last night, long about midnight I heard him, out in that old graveyard, crying and shrieking like a banshee," she sobs. "I just took him for drunk again, out there yelling and screaming at them like they could talk back to him. He'd often go out and prowl around that old graveyard like a cat on Halloween, talking to them, jabbering at them, asking them questions. Last night was different. He was screaming their names, over and over, Alexander Buford and his mama. He beat on his mother's headstone so hard he knocked it down."

"Miss Violet, you so upset you're talking out of your head. His mama's in Birmingham. We got to call her, but first I reckon we had best call the sheriff," the old man says softly, gently stroking her bent back, remembering her father Hyperion, likewise old and stooped, passing on a long lifetime's worth of advice about planting and sowing. He has lived all of his life within the long shadow of this great rotting house. He is, like Violet, offspring of the slaves who raised these walls. They share a common heritage that makes them kinfolks in times, like this, of trouble.

"No!" Violet's voice is suddenly strong. "For all that Isabel did to me and to mine, I cannot do that to Miss Minnie's memory. I may not owe Isabel Preston much more than a by your leave, but for all the water that's passed under the dam we are family still. I cannot, and I will not, betray Miss Minnie and what she meant to me by having scandal sully the last to bear the good name of this family. The day that he was born, I promised his sweet mother that I would always protect him."

"What you propose we do then?"

"His mama can't help him, so I've got to do it for her. We going to get him in his bed, call Isabel Preston in Birmingham, and inform her. She's got money and influence. She'll figure out how to handle it, how to hush things up and keep folks from talking. We'll tell her that the baby boy she raised and ruined has had a heart attack, died in his sleep in his bed."

"He be a big man, Miss Violet, and both you and me on the far side of seventy. How you figure we going to handle that?" He gestures without looking in Hatton's direction, seeks to look anywhere other than on the face of a man who died in torment.

"His great-grandmother was a little old bitty slip of a thing never did weigh more than ninety five pounds soaking wet. If she could shoot a Yankee, I reckon the two of us can handle one poor broken body. Like she always told me, somehow, some way, a Buford will find the strength sufficient."

Violet looks up at the grotesque, purpling face, all traces of the handsome Hatton having passed with the last breath, the green eyes, staring dim and dull in death. A gust of wind passes under the eaves, the body sways on the rope hanging from the attic rafters.

Violet heaves herself to a standing position. "I've been taking care of him since the day he was born. He was like a son to me. I told him the truth about himself because somebody had to." She wipes away her streaming tears, stares up at Hatton's lifeless face.

"The story has reached its conclusion. He was all the best and all the worst of all of us. He was the last of the line to bear the name of Buford."

Chapter Thirty

"Should we hide the car inside this old barn in case the sheriff decides to reappear? I've probably used up all of my good favor with the governor," Carrie asked Wyatt.

"Looks like it still contains one of the Bufords' vehicles," he answered, yanking open the door.

Carrie gasped and pushed past him. "Minnie's carriage! It's still here!"

"How do you know it was Minnie's?" he asked.

"The Hatton coat of arms," she whispered, rubbing her shirt tail against a coat of dust and revealing traces of flaking gold paint. "Poor outspoken, arrogant Minnie. So much of her life was either out of her control or based on outright lies. As she would say, truth be told, deep down I think she enjoyed all the conflict more than she would have things running a smoother or a more predictable course. She was born a rascal and a renegade."

"Come on, Carrie. Let's get moving. I doubt that the sheriff would expect to see you back here any time soon, but nevertheless this may be our only shot at it. By the way, on whose property are we trespassing?"

"Some northern syndicate of investors. I very much doubt that a one of them has ever set foot on the place. Too much trouble to even tear the house down. I called a lawyer friend who traced the title to the plantation. Interestingly, she told me that even when property changes hands legal rights to a family cemetery always remain with the family. Just like Violet, I am family."

Wyatt took a crow bar from the trunk of the car, and together they set off to retrieve the last pieces of the puzzle.

Inside the little iron ringed quarter acre, blooming with the early spring Confederate jasmine, Carrie paused a moment and said a silent prayer that lovers found reunion in a next and more just world before kneeling to place a bouquet of daffodils next to a crude stone scratched with the single word Lydia.

It only took one attempt to pry the iron door open. It swung out on rusty hinges, and Carrie and Wyatt stepped into the dark, dank sanctity of Washington Buford's mausoleum.

***

Along the interstate the trees were budding, tinged with the lemon lime green of new growth. From the car radio a disembodied voice warned that a change was blowing in from the north and west. Carrie had her window cracked. She could feel it in the wind, the change that was coming.

It was seventy five degrees. The anonymous forecaster predicted that by morning Alabama could expect to record the coldest temperatures of the season, possibly even snow. The state had not been subject to such a bizarre convergence of weather patterns in more than a century. Carrie snapped off the radio and murmured, "I wonder if the weather man knows that on a night in the 1830s the stars fell on Alabama."

Resurrecting literally from the grave where they had rested for decades the concluding pages of Hatton Preston's final novel made Wyatt feel, like Lazarus, a man reborn. In his head the dialogue took shape, the words tumbling like rocks from a mountain after a rain storm.

Beside him Carrie fingered a small leather bag containing a handful of gold coins, lost in her own thoughts. She had no idea what Minnie's inheritance was worth, was more than sure it was not legally hers, but, like Robin Hood, she found justification in stealing from the rich to give to the poor. Whatever Washington Buford's ill gotten gains represented was going to be donated to helping others. It was past time that the curse was broken.

It amazed Carrie that a woman as intelligent as Minnie had not seen a clue as plainly in view as the nose on her face. "Here my earthly treasure lies." The inscription was carved in stone on the marble face of the Buford mausoleum.

"Wyatt, what do you think drove him over the edge? What was the final straw that pushed Hatton to suicide? Was Minnie right that the line between genius and madness is sometimes a fine as a single red hair?"

"Maybe we should chalk it up to a curse finally coming to conclusion. In a curious reversal of light and dark, Hatton was the worst of them, Violet the best, and both of them the last of the line of Buford."

Carrie stared out the car window, watching weather fronts battling each other for precedence. "Why is southern society so bent on keeping secrets to keep up appearances?"

"You've been awfully busy the past few months pealing the petals of the past back to get to the essence of someone else's family. I think that it's time that you had a heart to heart talk with your mother, Carrie Beth."

She shot him a stricken look. "Why did you call me that, Wyatt?"

"It's past time to take your brother down from his pedestal and put him where he rightfully belongs, in perspective."

"You know, Wyatt, I don't even remember the day of his death. In the past year, since Daddy died, it's like Jamie has been trying to come back to me in bits and pieces. If I can suddenly have a little snatch of memory of an insignificant event, balloons on my birthday, why in the world do I have absolutely no recall of the most important day in Jamie's life, the day that he died? My brother is no more real to me than if I simply dreamed him."

"I had a conversation with Josie about this subject just this morning. You've got to get a realistic mental image of Jamie to live your own life on a more productive basis than you have lately been doing. You've wasted a lot of time coming up short comparing yourself to someone who wasn't what you think he was, a perfect person. Based purely on gut instinct, I think you may have misjudged your husband because your brother years ago left you coming up short in the trust department."

He took her hand and squeezed it. "It's time make peace with it, Carrie."

She nodded in agreement. It was time to stop focusing on sleepy images of the past and not too late to formulate dreams for the future. She asked Wyatt to drop her not at her house, Isabel's home, but at her mother's.

It came to her as clearly as a rainbow after a thunderstorm as he turned the car into her mother's driveway, the first day of school, the fifth grade. She was uncomfortably warm because her mother insisted that she wear an appropriate fall outfit even though it was ninety degrees in the shade outside. A dark cotton plaid dress, with a cardigan sweater, knee socks and new penny loafers. Her father pressed the bright copper coins into the shoes just before she left for school, pennies for good luck in the year upcoming. She wore on the collar of the dress a gold circle pin, a birthday gift from Jamie. She was hot, but, as her mother reminded her, little ladies did not wear white after Labor Day or a minute before Easter. It was a rule, one of those definitions of what nice people did and did not do, invented years before, most likely by a cluster of old ladies sitting around drinking tea in Montgomery.

Her mother welcomed her, as she always did, with open arms. "Call Nick, Wyatt too, if you like. You can all have supper with me. I can't think what possessed me to have the club cook a whole leg of lamb when I am the only one here. It's left over from last night, not nearly as good and juicy as the lambs Josie used to cook back in the days before she and I watched our diets, but acceptable. Remember when you were a child, and how we laughed about Sunday night suppers of cold leftover lamb and mint jelly, about eating lamb-jam sandwiches?"

"No, Mother, I don't remember, but I'd like to."

"Don't be silly, Carrie, you have a much better memory than I do."

"Until thirty minutes ago, I could not remember the name of my fifth grade teacher."

"I'm not sure why you would want to. She was terrible, young thing right out of school and could not control the classroom at all. I'd have been better off keeping you home and teaching you myself."

"I don't remember much of anything at all about being a child, Mother. That is something that, until just recently, I have been embarrassed to admit. The earliest memory I have readily available is of leaving Italy."

"We had such a good time that last summer in Italy, didn't we?" Mallory smiled nervously at Carrie, not comfortable with the direction the conversation seemed to be going. "That last summer, your father took a three week vacation from his work, and we just toured and traveled. Do you remember that wonderful little hotel in Venice? The Flora, wasn't it? Just a few steps from St. Mark's Square. You and your father and the fun you had feeding those nasty pigeons! And the apartment in Rome. Goodness that was a hot month!"

Mallory puttered around, mixed herself a drink, trying to think of another subject on which to turn the talk. "Speaking of hot, it has been extremely unseasonable today. Look out the window. You can see the storm coming. I never heard such a forecast, possible tornadoes followed by snow."

"I remember leaving Rome, Mother, hating to leave Rome, afraid to come back here. It is past time that you talked to me, Mother, talked to me about what I've run away from all these years, about what chewed Daddy up for the rest of his life and spit him out in little miserable pieces. It was if every time Daddy laughed he almost felt guilty to be happy. We have got to face some things, Mother. Now. Today."

"I don't know what you're talking about," Mallory stammered, jumping, spilling her drink, as the full fury of the storm roared in from the west. The sky blackened, and, with the crack of a falling tree pulling down the power lines, the house went just as dark.

"Sit down, Mother, and look at me face to face and talk to me about what dark horrible memory I have hidden from myself all these years. I have to have it, the whole story."

"Have you been talking to Josie?"

"I don't have to have a bulletin from Josie, Mother, to know that there is something on your conscience. All these years you've been running too, maybe even harder than Daddy and me. Let's get it out in the open and deal with it, Mother. We can start with your truthfully answering a question for me. How did my brother die?"

Mallory swallowed more than a sip of her drink. Carrie noticed her mother's hand tremble as she lit a candle and placed it on the table between them.

"You've got to tell me the truth, Mother, before I completely lose my mind."

Mallory took a deep breath, struggling, forcing herself back thirty painful years. "He was having difficulties at school. I told myself that it was simply routine college adjustment. We had been so proud of him, being the only one in his high school graduating class accepted at an Ivy League school. He was caught cheating on a test. The day before he came home for Thanksgiving a college counselor called and told us that he was being expelled, suggested strongly that we consult a psychiatrist. We were so bewildered. It was as if his whole personality had changed. Jamie was rebellious and irrational when we tried to talk to him, obviously in the midst of some sort of breakdown, and I thought we could talk our way out of it. Nice people didn't need psychiatrists in those days. There was too much chance of the word getting out, of people talking."

"It was actually then, not after his death, that your father applied for a transfer overseas. We thought that if we got him out of the country we could straighten out his problems on our own. Obviously he had greater problems than even we, his parents, realized."

"Your father took him hunting that day, figuring some time in the woods alone together would be good for them. They fussed and fought all day. Despite his killing an eight point deer, it was simply a disaster from the moment they pulled out of the driveway. He slammed into the house ranting and raving about how we were trying to control his life, expecting perfection from him, putting him under more pressure than he could bear. He stormed into the library, didn't even notice you sitting in there absorbed in one of those Nancy Drew books. I heard the shot, then your screams, screams so terrible they have echoed in my dreams every night for the past thirty years."

"It was not an accident, Carrie. Jamie very deliberately, right in front of you, put the gun in his mouth and blew his brains out."

"Oh, Mother, poor mother," Carrie wept, taking her mother into her arms. Mallory's eyes remained dry, staring out at the fury of the storm.

"I can't cry any more, Carrie. I haven't any tears left in me. I had to learn to control my tears or otherwise I would have simply cried until I was crazy."

"I have blamed myself all of these years," she continued. "Someone had to be responsible. Jamie was gone, and I blamed myself for holding him all the years of his life to some impossible standard. He and I were so very much alike, and yet, because he was a boy, the future could hold for him things it never could have offered me. My options in life were so limited, only the one option really of being a well bred and well behaved southern lady. Jamie could have been president of the United States or even a fireman for goodness sake. Do you remember . . . no, I suppose you don't . . . when you were five and announced that you were going to grow up to be a fireman? You can't imagine how heavy it made my heart to tell you that was not an option for little ladies."

Carrie laughed through her streaming tears. "There are female fire fighters today, Mother. The world has moved on without you being a part of the parade."

"Well, yes, so there are. Female fire persons I suppose they call themselves, but I would hardly refer to females doing that sort of work as ladies."

"Since we've begun this story, I suppose I must finish it. You were left, Carrie, like a little wounded bird, almost catatonic. For months you simply sat mutely and stared into space. We were frantic for you. We took you to Italy, and bit by bit, piece by piece, you started to come back together again. It was clear to us that you didn't remember, that some physic defense mechanism had closed the memory down."

"Mother, is this somehow related to what all the years of chasing ancestors has been about?"

"I suppose so. All the times that I reiterated to myself that there had never been a shred of madness perhaps what I wanted, what I was looking for, was one stark raving mad ancestor on whom I could place genetic blame for what had happened to my precious Jamie. Anyone I could blame other than myself."

"We've got to let him go, Mother. We have got to finally, and forever, set Jamie free."

"How do we do that, Carrie?"

"I'm going to get myself some counseling, put the house on the market and try to put my life back together. I love Nick and my kids, I love myself, and you, too much to lose any one of us. All families have problems, Mother, even the very best of families, the very nicest of the nice people. There's no shame in having problems, only in looking the other way instead of trying to right them."

"Look outside, Mother. It's starting to snow. Do you remember the Christmas Eve that it snowed, and Jamie and I went Christmas caroling?"

"Do you remember it?"

"It's one of the few memories I have allowed myself to have. I want them all back. I need to both bury my brother and at the same time get him back and hold him tight, and to do that I'll need your help. For now, let's walk outside and watch the snow fall."

Hand and hand, they went through the French doors onto the terrace. A cold wind blew in from the north and west. Their breath made little puffs of fog in the night air. Above them the sky was a curious mixture of stars and snow clouds.

Carrie turned her face up to the snowflakes, tumbling down in exuberant showers, clouds raining stars, falling once again on Alabama.

Epilogue

Driving home from the airport, Carrie and Nick yawned in unison, happily tired from a long flight back from a second honeymoon, Nick's first trip to Italy.

Jack Lancaster retiring, Nick was joining a new sports medicine clinic on the cutting edge of orthopedic medicine. He predicted that retirement would not mean taking it easy for his father. Ellen had plans for a whole new career for her husband, as business manager running the Ambrodesia spinoff enterprises, from newsletters to dolls in period costumes.

Ellen was as calm about making her television debut on the most popular weekday afternoon interview show as if it were the most natural thing in the world to be the guest of honor, discussing the runaway success of a best selling first novel.

On the New York stage, *Hatton and the Bufords* was drawing rave reviews. When not in New York supervising production, Wyatt invited himself to dinner with a reunited Josie and Mallory on a regular basis. Wyatt teased Mallory that she had used her southern charm and accent to sweet talk the New York cast into coming to Birmingham for a hometown performance at the historic Virginia Samford Theater.

Carrie and Nick celebrated the first anniversary of being comfortably settled in a new house, chosen together. Mallory was also making plans for relocation, not to a small apartment in a retirement community, but instead to a large penthouse condominium with spectacular views of the city.

Isabel's house no longer stood. A year earlier, a few days after Carrie and Nick said a grateful goodbye to it, an early morning fire reduced it to rubble. Arson was more than strongly suspected, but Carrie and Nick, negotiating a contract with a developer interested in subdividing the property, no longer carried insurance on the house or its contents. They assured the fire marshal that the cause was not worthy of investigation.

Carrie did not even have a photo of it for remembering. It was behind her.

She had, in packing her camera to go to Italy, removed a forgotten roll of film and had it developed.

In one photo, clearly visible on the kitchen table were the routine early morning commodities of a coffee cup and saucer, Minton's pattern Persian Rose, a newspaper, a pair of reading glasses. Focal point in the photo was a half eaten bowl of cat food.

The image of the yellow cat was as nowhere to be seen in the photo as if on that morning he had already run away into the woods, making a last look back and flicking his tail in a gesture of farewell, as he did just before Carrie left the house for a last time, on the morning of the fire.

The scar left on her arm from that morning that he scratched her, just after she took his picture, the morning her mother presented a key to her, had faded, was almost invisible.

It was all behind them, as put away as a bad dream after waking.

As they unlocked the front door, the phone was ringing.

Carrie answered, confusion crossing her face for a moment before she said goodbye and burst out laughing.

"Nicky, you will never believe what I'm about to tell you. History repeats itself over and over, and don't let anyone ever tell you otherwise."

Putting her arms around him, she kissed him before explaining.

"My mother has just eloped with Wyatt Wallace."